A PARCEL OF ROGUES

Pamela Belle

Pamela Belle Books

The characters and events portrayed in this book are fictitious. Any similarity to real persons, living or dead, is coincidental and not intended by the author.

978-1-0686784-1-7

This book is dedicated to the memory of three inspirational women:-
My mother, Sylvia Belle (1915-2005), nitpicker extraordinaire, who loved and championed all my books
Dorothy Dunnett (1923-2001), a guiding star to all historical novelists
And last but never least, Barbara Tollinton (1951-2003), a true and supportive friend, quick to listen, slow to judge, and ALWAYS ready for coffee and cake!

CONTENTS

PART ONE

London, Bristol & Bath
Autumn, 1715

CHAPTER ONE

'Clothed in Black you tread the busy Town'

"They say you are an honest man, sir! I beg of you, please help me!"

The person to whom these frantic words had been addressed seemed oddly diverted by this statement. He paused and turned, looking down with interest at the short man in the brown wig, who had accosted him amid the bustle and scurry of Long Acre. "You cannot have any knowledge of this town," he observed caustically. "Or you would not even consider uttering such a transparent untruth."

"My apologies, sir." The other man was small and well-furnished, with plump round features and a blunt, jutting nose. Ever in the oil light of the lamp above them, his desperation was painfully apparent. "But they said you would help me find my daughter."

"Your *daughter?*" Incredulity was plain on the taller man's lean face. "Don't be absurd. As well find a blade of grass in the field, or a grain of dust in the street. London is full of daughters, and every last one of them urgent not to be found. You are wasting your time, and mine. Good day to you, sir." He began to move on, and found his way obstructed.

"But they said in that coffee house that you would help me." His inquisitor had boldly laid thick stubby fingers on the other man's coat sleeve. "They *assured* me that you would help, and when they pointed you out to me as you passed by, it seemed like a gift from Heaven. I beg you, sir, you are my last hope of finding my sweet little Mary, and I will pay you handsomely if you do!"

Several Mohocks, loud, swaggering, violent, were surging down the street towards them, pushing passers-by aside, offering assault to anyone who blocked their path. "Quick, stand back!" He pulled the little man close in to the side of the street as the gang swept past, already bully-drunk, hands on swords, boasting loudly of the whores they were going to debauch, the heroic quantities of spirits they planned to consume that evening, and the men they would kill if thwarted. "This is no place to talk. I know somewhere close by that's quiet, and private, and safe." A sudden, quizzical glance caught Mary's father by surprise. "And if this is to progress beyond idle words, I had better know your name."

"It's Jessop. Samuel Jessop of Oxford, humbly at your service, sir."

"*Au contraire*, Mr. Jessop – shouldn't that be the reverse? My name is André Dark, and *I*, sir, am surely at *your* service." A quick lift of his dark eyebrows and a quirk of the long mouth lent warmth and humour to the tall man's rather severe features. "But enough of this idle chit-chat – let us be gone. And for God's sake keep close, or you'll be lost."

Although darkness was already dropping over the rooftops of Covent Garden, light poured from the windows of the taverns, shops and coffee houses which gave this part of London its life, and its reputation. The teeming throngs of people clogged the pavements while carriages, carts and sedans jostled past each other in the street. Sam Jessop followed Dark as nearly as he could, afraid of becoming separated in the crush. Ahead of them the Mohocks, braying with malevolent enthusiasm, were getting their evening's entertainment off to a good start by taking it in turns to kick a beggar, while decent men and women hurried by, averting their eyes.

"This way – down here."

Somewhat to his confusion, Jessop's companion

ushered him through what at first appeared to be the doorway to a tavern called The Bird In Hand. Instead, it led into a narrow alley, almost entirely dark save for one or two lamps lit by public-spirited citizens. Above them, roofs, chimneys and gables all but crowded out the dim blue of the evening sky. Things stirred and rustled in the shadows. Suddenly beset by fears of robbery or worse, Jessop said sharply, "Where is this?"

"Conduit Court. I was on my way here when you stopped me – it's as good a place as any for our talk. Have you got four shillings on you?"

"Yes," said Jessop, wondering in bewilderment what it might be needed for: ale, wine, spirits, a meal, a woman? All sorts of lurid imaginings coursed through his mind, heightened by the days he had already spent in London on his vain search. He opened his mouth to ask, and found that they had stopped in front of an anonymous door. The tall man rapped the knocker, and it was opened almost immediately by a very thin, elderly person whose face seemed to consist entirely of nose and chin. Between the two, his mouth split into a wide smile. *"Ah, Monsieur Dark! Bon soir, mon ami, bon soir!"*

Jessop stared at the two men with deep suspicion. Was this a nest of perfidious Frenchies, spying for the wicked Papist King Louis? He began to wish that he had never accosted the black-clad man called Dark, who had seemed as English as himself, but who was now jabbering away in that filthy incomprehensible tongue as if he were a subject of England's greatest enemy. He took a step backwards, but the movement returned Dark's attention to him. "Don't go away, Mr. Jessop," he said, with a smile. "Fear not, Jean Chaboner is a Huguenot refugee, as indeed am I, and although we were both born in France, we are loyal and Protestant servants of King George. You'll look after us, won't you, Jean?"

"Indeed I will, sir, indeed I will," said Chaboner, in good

but accented English, and with a respectful bow. "Would you both come this way, sirs? We are not busy this evening, and there is a bath waiting. Will you have the sweat first?"

With alarm, Jessop realised that they must be in a bagnio. He had heard of such places, ostensibly establishments where you could sweat away your ill-humours and diseases in hot rooms and hotter baths. He had also heard that very often these places were not as respectable as they pretended, being little better than brothels. However, there seemed to be no stray women lurking in the entrance hall in which they stood. It was well-lit, with a fine gilt-framed mirror above the marble mantelpiece, and although this autumn had so far been comparatively mild, there was a fire glowing hot in the grate. He felt perspiration beginning to prickle at the back of his neck, under his wig.

"Are you game for this, Mr. Jessop?" Dark asked him, a glint in his eyes that made Sam even more uneasy. "It's five shillings for one, but with two of us sharing it'll be four apiece. Do you want to be cupped as well?"

"Eh? No, no thank you," said Jessop, rather more emphatically than was proper. At the best of times, the prospect of having blood let was unpleasant. Now, in these strange, disturbing surroundings, in company with a man quite unlike anyone he had met before, he wanted all his wits about him.

The old Frenchman conducted them along a passage and into a small, even hotter room with rows of pegs around the walls, from some of which hung discarded clothes. Another servant appeared, much younger, and with a round, pleasant face, full of eagerness to please. He helped Jessop to undress, while Chaboner assisted his companion. To Sam's relief, the two men were now conversing amicably in English, about the recent trial of a notorious pickpocket.

Sam had long ago come to terms with the defects and

limitations of his own body, but even so, this disrobing in front of strangers made him feel uncomfortable. He was acutely aware of his scrawny legs and prominent paunch, the results of a life spent eating too much and exercising too little, and the fact that most men of his age and station were in the same boat did not help now. He glanced covertly at Dark, noting with envious regret the tall man's lean physique and the absence of any flabby signs of idle living. Without his plain campaign wig, his face beneath the nap of cut brown hair looked surprisingly young.

The servant handed him a brief linen clout, which barely encircled his generous waist, and left him feeling almost naked. Dark, being constructed more sparely, was also more comprehensively covered. "Do you wish to be cupped, sir?" the young man asked eagerly. "We use the easiest method, with a special scarifier, so that you'd hardly know it had been done. If you've any old injury, or aches and pains that poultices or plasters won't cure, you'll find that a good sweat, and a cupping to draw out all the bad blood, will make you good as new."

Dark's dry amused voice intervened. "Don't listen to Will – I think he must be a secret blood-drinker, he's so eager to take it. For my part, I mean to hoard all mine to myself. A sweat, a boiling hot bath and a rub will do just as well. Are you ready, Jessop? Then let us go and be baked."

"You will need these, sir, don't forget," said Chaboner, and gave Sam a curious pair of shoes with thick wooden soles, a little like the pattens which country women wore to lift their feet out of the mud.

"The floor's hot," Dark told him, taking pity on his bewilderment. "So hot the soles of your feet will be burnt if you don't wear them. Even if they are a little on the large side."

Feeling more than a touch ridiculous, his clumsily shod feet clacking like a loom, Jessop shuffled towards the doorway where the young servant waited, his hand on the knob. Then the boy opened the door with a flourish, and a scorching blast struck them like a wall. Sam gasped, and wavered.

"You'll be all right, sir," Chaboner advised him kindly. "It will feel cooler after a few minutes. *Soi vite*, young Will, don't stand there with the door open letting all the heat out, show the gentlemen in!"

His lungs labouring to suck in any breath of usable air, his pores flooding sweat, Sam stumbled past the servant, and into the next room. There were, he was glad to see, two wooden benches against the further wall, with a neat stack of folded linen on one of them. Gratefully, he staggered over, sank down and put his streaming head in his hands, wondering if he were about to die.

Beside him, the wood creaked and settled under someone else's weight, and Dark's voice, still carrying that unholy thread of amusement, sounded in Sam's ear. "Jean's right, you know – in a moment or two you'll be used to it."

His head was swimming, and he seemed to have lost all sense of who and where he was. Dark added conversationally, "And if you think this is tropical, wait until Will stokes up the furnace. Infernal, I believe, is the only word for it. Then once we've worked up a good sweat, and relaxed in the bath, Jean will rub us down. Feeling better yet?"

"No," Sam gasped. "What have you got against me, that you put me to the torture like this?" He found, to his astonishment, that some powers of thought were returning to him, and that he could breathe a little easier.

"I have a grave dislike of any man who comes from Oxford," said Dark solemnly. "Those I meet are instantly subjected to the sweat, so that their ill-humours may be washed out of them."

Relieved that he did not appear to be about to die after all, Sam mustered a contemptuous snort. He looked up with some care, and saw his companion at close quarters. Dark's eyes, he noticed, were a flecked greenish brown, surprisingly light in his tanned face, and Sam was vengefully pleased to observe that his skin was also running with perspiration. "You see?" the other man said. "Better already."

"Don't patronise me," Sam said, still too uncomfortable to employ any courtesies. His own eyes, an undistinguished blue, were stinging as the salty sweat washed into them, and he wiped one of the squares of linen across his forehead. "In your view I may only be an insignificant and ignorant little squab from the country, but I am as good a man as you or any other, and I would be grateful if you would remember it."

There was a small, taut silence. Then suddenly Dark smiled. It was a remarkably attractive smile, curling his mouth and crinkling around his eyes, and it made him look years younger, and much more human. He held out his hand. "I stand rebuked, and deservedly so. My apologies, Mr. Jessop, I have treated you very shabbily. Will you forgive my boorish behaviour, and let me make amends?"

It was handsomely done, and despite his annoyance, Sam could not help but feel a growing liking for this mysterious and rather intimidating man. He put out his own hand, and their hot, wet palms clasped in friendship.

"I'm glad," Dark said, mopping his face and the back of his neck with another piece of linen. "It would have been damnably difficult to find your missing daughter otherwise. They will be back shortly, to take us to the bath – can you tell me a little about her now, while we are still alone?"

Mary. His beloved, precious girl. How to begin to describe her, who had been both the light and the bane of his life? Sam swallowed, feeling a curious mixture of grief and anger. If he ever did find her, he would embrace her with tears of joy and thankfulness. And afterwards, he would try to implant some sense into her.

"She is seventeen come December," he said, "and my only living child. She is very pretty, though I say so myself. Indeed, everyone says it. Lively, lovely, she dances like a nymph and sings like an angel. I am a wealthy man now, but I was born poor, and I wanted to give her everything that I had never had when I was young." He glanced at Dark, and smiled wryly. "Yes, I know what you must be thinking, and it's true, she has been much indulged. My poor wife, while she lived, could never deny her anything she wanted. I do my best to provide some discipline and authority, but I am often away from home on business, and so I must leave her in the care of the servants. And last month, before I set off for northern parts, I instructed Mrs. Langton, my housekeeper, to find a dancing master for her. Mary wanted to go to assemblies with her friends, and naturally she must shine her brightest to attract a husband." He could not help a tinge of bitterness in his voice. "Of course, I thought that she was too young to be married. I couldn't help remembering my sweet little girl, all curls and smiles, playing with her kitten and her dolls. So I saw no danger until it was too late."

He swallowed, remembering. The return from York, with gifts for his beloved daughter. The dreadful news, given by Mary's maid with a smirk of satisfaction that had earned her nothing save instant dismissal, for she must have been complicit. And the housekeeper, full of terrified apologies that had done nothing to mitigate his horror.

There were tears in his eyes, but fortunately they were indistinguishable from sweat. Sam wiped the cloth over his face and added baldly, "As you may have guessed, she had run off with the dancing master. A plausible rogue with a handsome face and a charming tongue on him, by all accounts. And French, a people I have no love for, begging your pardon, sir, and this one must be one of the worst of them. A sly, scheming, wicked rogue. I just pray that he has treated my Mary well, and not discarded her in the gutter as so many seducers do, once they have tired of their prey. Sometimes at night I lie awake and wonder ..." He broke off, and hastily mopped his face again.

"What was his name?" Dark's voice was surprisingly sympathetic.

"St. Clair. That is all I know, as to his Christian name I have no idea, Mrs. Langton never asked for it, and the servants disliked him – he gave himself airs, considered himself a gentleman, dressed finely and wore a sword. A man of good height and slender build, they said, quite young and very handsome. He must have been, to catch Mary's eye. She likes beautiful things." Sam's tone hardened. "But by God, if I ever come face to face with him, I'll make sure he never seduces any other young and innocent girl."

"So – when did you discover this?"

"On my return home, ten days ago. I remember it particularly because there was trouble again in the town, windows broken and so forth. Nothing so bad, though, as the riots we had at the King's birthday and then at Restoration Day. That was a disgraceful business, and the Jacobites at the bottom of it as usual, plying the mob with strong drink and encouraging them to rampage through the streets. It's a miracle no-one was killed."

"And you yourself are not a lover of James Stuart, Mr. Jessop?"

Sam snorted again. Curiously, he had become so accustomed to the intolerable heat that the air he breathed seemed almost comfortable. "No, sir, I am not. My father was a Dissenter, and though I now go to church, rather than to a meeting house, I have no love for Papists or Non-Jurors or indeed anyone who refuses to recognise that King George is the rightful ruler of England. People have very short memories, they all seem to have forgotten why the Pretender's father was kicked off the throne nearly thirty years ago, when I was a young man. If the Jacks had their way, we'd be a province of the King of France inside a year, and all our freedoms taken away from us. And then there would be a civil war."

"I can't disagree with you," Dark said. "I fought in Marlborough's wars, in the Low Countries, and saw the horrors of religious conflict with my own eyes. But you haven't finished your story. Tell me what you have done, up until now."

Sam said bitterly, "I have been doing a great deal, sir, but my search has been hampered by the fact that I did not discover that Mary was missing until I returned from York, and by then they had been gone for five days. I was able to enlist the help of my brother and my nephews, though, and we asked at all the inns in Oxford. The only definite news was that a man and a girl of their appearance had boarded the London coach in Henley, the day she vanished. So I followed."

"Unfortunately, so much time has passed that your Mary could now be anywhere – perhaps even in France." As Sam flinched in dismay, Dark added more kindly, "But it may be that you are worrying unnecessarily. St. Clair's intentions might be entirely honourable. There are several places in London where you can marry whom you choose without hindrance. She may have a wedding ring on her finger, and a devoted and attentive husband. If you discovered her in such circumstances, would you still order her home?"

"Of course not," Sam said. "But even so, I would like to find her, and congratulate her on her good fortune. And also to tell her that no matter what she has done and what has happened, that her father still loves and cherishes her. Do you have children, sir?"

He was not surprised when Dark answered, after a moment, "Not to my knowledge, Mr. Jessop." Somehow, the possession of a wife and the production of offspring seemed entirely foreign to this alarmingly self-assured man. Although he must be close on twenty years the elder, Sam, buffeted by his desperate emotions, knew himself a little afraid of Dark, despite the glimpses of humour, and the sense that beneath the forbidding exterior lurked someone rather more human than had at first appeared. But he must swallow his feelings. He had been told that Dark could help him. And since ten days of exhaustive and exhausting enquiry had been almost entirely in vain, he must now clutch at any straw that passed, even one as unpromising as this. Dark's words had been meant to reassure him, but they could not. Nothing he had heard of the plausible Frenchman could persuade him that St. Clair had encouraged his daughter to elope with him because he wanted to marry her. If he ever did find Mary, it would be in some squalid garret, or an even more sordid brothel.

Or walking the streets, selling herself for a few pennies to buy food, or gin, or a lodging. The thought of his pretty, foolish child, with all her life glowing before her, reduced to such desperation was almost enough to break his composure entirely. He said, "I will pay you any sum you wish, sir, if you will help me find her."

Dark said softly, "I can't promise to find her – no man could do that. But I will do my best. I have many friends in this town. Someone may recognise her, may even know her."

"How can they recognise her?" Sam asked wearily. "I have no picture of her, nothing save a few words that might be said of a hundred girls."

"But I can give you one," Dark said. "You can describe her to me, and I can draw her. I paint portraits, Mr. Jessop, and I imagine that is why you were told I could help you."

Some time later, duly sweated but not cupped, Sam lay like a boiled pink pig in the steaming waters of the hot bath, his eyes resting with indulgent idleness on the artful depiction of a simpering milkmaid and her persuasive swain, done in Delft blue on the tile immediately in front of him. He did not want to move, and doubted whether he could, although his toes and fingers had become white and crinkly from long immersion, and the water, which had at first been unbearably, scaldingly hot, was now beginning to cool slightly.

"So, you will draw Mary's likeness for me, Mr. Dark?" he enquired, after a long and languid interval.

"I will," said the other man, gently stirring the soft, fragrant water so that a renewed aroma of sweetly pungent herbs tickled Sam's nostrils. "But not here and now."

His tone was perfectly serious, but Sam was already becoming attuned to the subtle nuances of Dark's voice. Matching it, he said, "For sure it would make the ink sadly liable to run."

"Indeed it would. Although I can use plumbago, which is something like a soft grey chalk, but much less easy to smudge. Would that suffice? I have some in the pocket of my coat, I always carry it with me." He turned his head to look at Sam, and the corners of his mouth tucked suddenly inwards. "In case I am accosted by men with missing daughters."

"An everyday occurrence, of course," Sam said drily.

Chaboner and the young servant now returned to help them out of the bath. His head swimming as wildly as though he had sunk several pints of wine, Sam was guided back into the room where they had been undressed, an age ago. To his relief, one of the tall sash windows had now been opened just a few inches, to let in a cool night breeze. Obediently he lay down upon one of the low couches against the wall, and submitted himself to being massaged and rubbed as if he were a high-class racehorse, a ministration which induced such a feeling of drowsiness and well-being that he almost fell asleep.

"Wake up, Jessop, unless you want to spend the night here," Dark said, sounding amused. "Although you can if you wish, for a few extra shillings, and very comfortable it is too. This is the place where Lord Mohun and his second stayed, the night before his fatal duel with the Duke of Hamilton."

Sam sat up, yawning, and allowed the servant to put his shirt over his head. "I have a room at the Black Swan in Holborn, and I would like to return there."

"That might not be wise, unless you have a companion. At night, the courts and alleys – even main thoroughfares like Drury Lane – are not safe for a solitary walker. You could be set upon from behind as you pass a dark alley, knocked on the head and robbed of everything save your shirt before you've a chance to draw breath – unless, of course, they've hit you so hard you never draw another. I will walk with you," said Dark, in the kind of voice which brooked no argument. "But will you take a dish of coffee with me before we make our way to Holborn? It'll clear our heads and dispel all these noxious fumes."

Chaboner, helping him on with his coat, was heard to sniff. Dark laughed. "Are you ready, Jessop? Then let us go. I'll see you in a few days, Jean, if your sins have not caught up with you."

"Or yours with you," said the old man, a cheerful gleam in his rheumy eye, and ushered them out.

In the narrow nooks and corners of Conduit Court, the shadows congregated threateningly, with whispers. One of them detached itself from the walls and approached, a torch slung over its shoulder and illuminating the pinched face and ragged hair of a London street urchin. "Carry a light for you, Mr. Dark?"

"I'll consider it," said Dark, with a sudden death's head grin in the sullen yellow light. "This, Jessop, is Gin the link-boy, who's studying to be the most unrepentant rogue in all the town. Take note of him now, and if you should find him picking your pocket on another occasion, don't bother with the magistrate, send word to me and I'll deal with him. So watch your step, Gin, or it'll be the worse for you."

"If you says so, sir," said the boy, in a surly whine. As the two men crossed the court, he fell in behind them, so that their shadows, monstrously vast, traversed the cobbles in front and wavered up the walls, briefly obscuring a whore and her customer, who were conducting their business in a doorway with urgent efficiency. Sam gave the woman a sliding, desperate glance, but her dirty hair was light brown, and the thin arms sticking out of the cheap gaudy sleeves were covered in sores. No, this was not his Mary, so pretty and plump and cherished, but a terrible portent of what she might become, if he did not find her.

They came another way out of the court, not into the broad busy thoroughfare of Long Acre, full of shops and substantial houses, but into a narrower, meaner street lined with humbler dwellings, and at this hour all but empty. Dark had a long stride, and Sam hurried to keep up, glancing every so often at the unlit corners and alleys where danger might be lying in wait. The boy Gin was trotting beside them, his torch bobbing up and down so wildly that if there had been any hazard in front of them, it would have been nearly impossible to detect it amidst the oscillating shadows. But they arrived without incident at the Piazza, the glowing, vibrant heart of Covent Garden.

By day, it was a packed and busy market, thronged with men and women selling all kinds of fruit, herbs, vegetables, flowers and plants, and those who came to buy them, or to gawp at the puppet show, the prize fighters, the impromptu games of football and all the other activities, harmless and otherwise, that took place within the wide confines of the square. At night, there were still many people about, but of a very different kind. There were, certainly, those who were purely in search of a congenial tavern or coffee house where they could spend the evening with their friends, but the women here, Sam knew, were not so respectable, and they sought their customers with a boldness he still found disconcerting.

"You're a handsome cully," said a wheedling voice, and Sam felt his arm being grasped. With an angry exclamation, he shook her off, and earned a torrent of abuse which impugned, amongst sundry other things, his parents, his potency, and the size of his manhood.

"He's out of your class, Peggy," Dark said to the whore. "I should try someone less choosy. How about that lad over there, the one with the withered leg and the pockmarks?"

"You wasn't so high and mighty last time I saw yer!" screeched the whore, with venom. "I hope yer prick rots off, yer stinking molly!"

"Such a delightful turn of phrase," Dark commented as they hurried on under the arches of the Piazza, illuminated in fits and starts by the lighted windows. "Here we are. Not the best-known coffee-house, but the brew is excellent and the owner's a friend of mine. You'll hear livelier talk at other places, meet more interesting people, but it's quiet and private, and I take it that's what you want." He opened the door, and they walked into the welcoming, aromatic warmth of the Seven Stars.

CHAPTER TWO

'The Ballad-Singer's shrilling Strain'

In the course of his search, Sam had set foot in numberless coffee-houses, but he was not sure if this had been one of them, for at first glance they all looked so alike. A booth in the corner, where a handsome young woman dispensed punches or spirits, according to the speciality of the house: an open fire with hobs on which the coffee pots sat, watched by the waiters in case they boiled and ruined the taste: tables and benches for the customers: and a very varied array of cheap engravings, quacks' posters, and advertisements for auctions and plays, hung or pasted on the walls.

There were only two customers within, sitting at separate tables, one of them glumly perusing a copy of *The Flying Post*, the other apparently asleep, his head on his arms and his wig askew. A scrawny youth with a wicked, snub-nosed face was sweeping the floor: as Dark and Jessop entered, he put on a show of brightness, propped the broom against the counter and went to greet them. "Good evening to you, Mr. Dark. You're very welcome, sir, what will be your pleasure?"

Dark ordered two dishes of coffee and, at a nod of assent from Sam, a couple of pipes of tobacco as well. They made their way to the furthest table from the counter and waited while the youth busied himself with pots and cups by the fire. Sam, facing the wall and one of the windows, read the tattered notice just to the side of Dark's head, advertising something called 'The Electuary of the Balm of Gilead', guaranteed to cure all ills including gout, rheumatic aches and pains, and the afflictions of Venus.

As their coffee arrived, his companion leaned back,

partially obscuring the crude portrait of the purveyor of the Balm of Gilead. "Thank you, Kit – and three or four sheets of paper, if you please, good quality and none of your rags."

"Planning a likeness of me, Mr. Dark?" asked the youth cheekily, and skipped nimbly off into the dim recesses behind the counter, from whence he returned a few moments later with the requested sheets, plus a pot of cut quills of various sizes, and an inkwell. "That'll be sixpence for the paper and sixpence for the coffee and tobacco. Shall I put it all on your slate, Mr. Dark?" He set everything down on the table next to the candle, and added to Sam, "If you're thinking of letting him take your picture, sir, I should think again – believe me, you won't like the result, he sees far too much for anyone's liking."

"You mean for your liking, Kit," said Dark without rancour. "Be off with you, before I show you for what you really are." When the boy had strolled off, with a studied walk just short of insolence, he took a sip of the steaming coffee and put the dish down. "So, now to business. Your daughter Mary – describe her to me."

Sam waited until he too had drunk some coffee before he answered. It seemed impossible to him that any artist, however skilled, could produce a recognisable image of someone he had never seen – and if Dark could capture a likeness so well, why was he here, rather than holding court in some silken stateroom with a herd of lackeys to wipe his brushes and powder his wig? Carefully, he gathered his thoughts and his memories, conjuring up the semblance of Mary until she stood before his mind's eye, glowing, vivid, laughing.

"She has dark brown hair," he said at last. "She wears it swept back from her face, and knotted up under a little lace cap. It has a curl in it, so that she has no need to put it in papers. A few stray wisps around her forehead – yes, that's exactly so."

Dark was sketching swiftly as he spoke, using a stick of soft smoke-coloured material instead of the pens, and Sam saw his daughter's coiffure take miraculous shape on the paper. "With a lock of hair on her shoulder," he said, not troubling to hide his wonderment. "How do you know, sir? How do you *know*? When you have not even met her?"

"I use my eyes," Dark said. "Look about you – every young lady with any pretence to fashion wears her hair just like that. I doubt your Mary is any different, and so you have confirmed. Now for her face." He stroked a faint curved line below the hair. "An oval? Longer? Heart-shaped?"

"Her cheeks are a little plumper than that, perhaps," said Sam, fascinated, craning his neck. "And her chin much more pointed. She has a look of great determination."

"Reflecting her character, no doubt," said Dark dryly. He turned the paper round so that the ghost of a face, featureless under the thick dark hair and lace-edged cap, stared blindly up at Sam. "Is it like her thus far?"

"I think so," Mary's father said honestly. "But there is hardly enough there to tell yet."

"Patience is a virtue, so they say," Dark commented, taking the paper back. "Eyes? Blue, brown, round, narrow, wide-set?"

"I have never properly looked at them," Sam confessed. "At least, not at their shape. They are blue, though, a strong bright blue. Round ... yes, I suppose they are round, and her lashes are very long and dark. She is so pretty, often I would look at her and marvel that she was mine. But there is no doubt of it," he added, glancing sharply at the artist. "Although she favours my poor late wife in looks and colouring, she has my nose and mouth."

"That is helpful," Dark observed. His hand was working so swiftly that Sam could hardly follow it. "I will sketch this out and then you can tell me what I should change. Eyebrows?"

"Eh?" Sam, bemused, needed time to think. "She plucks them to a better shape, of course – a little peaked, I think – no, not so much as that. I am sorry, sir, not to be of more help. It is extraordinarily difficult to remember all the little details of someone's face, even one so familiar to me as my own daughter."

"I must admit, I would not care to be in your position," said Dark. Again, he turned the drawing so that Sam could see it. "How is that?"

"It does have a certain look of her," he said slowly. "But Mary's mouth is not so wide, and hers turns up a little at the corners. And the nose, perhaps, a little more curved. Yes, yes, now you have it! And that expression, that look of mischief, that's hers exactly!"

"I'll do a fair copy," Dark told him, taking another piece of paper and a long draught of coffee, by now somewhat cooler. Appreciating these moments of respite after the hectic and unforeseen events of the evening, Sam lit his pipe and sucked in the hot, restorative smoke. Already his own coffee was glowing comfortably behind his breastbone, banishing the drowsiness that had afflicted him in the bagnio. He felt refreshed, reassured, and much more hopeful. Dark really did seem to have contacts everywhere. If Mary had gone to ground here in Covent Garden, indeed anywhere in London, Sam was confident that sooner or later, the artist would hear of it. All he had to do now was to wait for the word, and his daughter would be restored to him.

Wreathed in tobacco smoke, he imagined the scene. With tears of repentance, she would admit that she had longed for this moment. He would not lose his temper and scold her, as she so richly deserved, for her selfishness and her folly. He would fold her in his arms and tell her how much she was loved, and missed. Afterwards, he would take her home.

No, said the little voice of reality, unwelcome at the back of his mind. *You fool, you know it won't be like that. She'll argue and shout and refuse to be parted from her lover – anything, rather than admit she was in the wrong. It will be everyone's fault but her own, you know it will.*

Sam sighed. Much as he loved his daughter, he knew in his heart that despite the loveliness of her face, she was far from perfect. However much he might pretend to himself that St. Clair's seductive, plausible lies had led the girl astray, he was well aware that Mary was quite capable of embarking on such an escapade with a reckless disregard for sense or propriety.

He became aware that Dark was saying something, and that a sheet of paper was being passed across to him. With an effort, he concentrated his mind on it.

And there she was, looking up at him, with just that playful, infuriating glance that presaged all manner of trouble. Sam drew in his breath sharply, and felt tears spring to his eyes. He said, stammering, "It – it is her, sir, to the life! You must know her, you *must*, I don't believe that you have never seen her before!"

"I can assure you, Jessop, that I have not. I have a knack for capturing a likeness, that is all. So, if you were to show this to someone who knew your daughter, they would recognise her?"

"Of course they would," said Sam, still shaken. "Oh, thank you sir, how can I thank you enough? Would twenty guineas be sufficient?"

"Save your thanks, and your coin, for when we've found her," Dark said. "But if she is in London, then sooner or later we'll track her down. I warn you, though, you may not like what we find. Are you prepared for that?"

"I only want to know that she is safe," Sam said stubbornly, and meant it with all his heart.

He gathered up the precious paper, folded it with great care, and stowed it in the pocket of his coat, while Dark made another swift copy for his own use. The temporary effects of the coffee were now sadly beginning to wear off, and he yawned almost as widely as the waiter Jack, who was obviously anxious for them to leave. Dark glanced at the clock, ticking solemnly on the mantelpiece, and rose to his feet. "Nearly half after ten, we should be gone. I'll walk with you back to Holborn."

"Really," Sam protested, "you've done more than enough for me, sir, I can assure you there is no need – "

"There's every need, and it won't take long. And we have Gin to light our way, if he hasn't sloped off somewhere – ah, there you are, brat!"

The ragamuffin child struggled upright, the torch still beside him, though it had expired. "I thought you was never coming," he complained, in the nasal whine that was so jarring to Sam's provincial ears. "Ain't you got no beds to go to?"

"Indeed we have, so look lively there," said Dark briskly. "For a start, we could do with some illumination."

"Uh? Oh, it went out. You couldn't get me a spill, could you, Mr. Dark? If you please," the urchin added, very much as an afterthought.

"Kit might give you one, if you asked him very nicely," said Dark, jerking his head at the lighted doorway of the coffee house. With a dramatically heavy sigh, Gin parked his light against one of the columns of the Piazza and trudged inside.

"He has a peculiar name," Sam commented, his own curiosity sharpened by the child, and the unconventional relationship he evidently had with Dark. "Surely he wasn't baptised with it?"

"I doubt he was christened at all. His is a sordid tale, but all too common, alas. His mother was a harlot who took to drink and died, leaving him orphaned and living on the streets. He told me she called him Gin because that was her favourite tipple. For some reason, he seems to have attached himself to me – though not because of any especial kindness on my part, I can assure you."

Sam was not assured, but kept silent. In any case, the boy now darted out again, a lighted taper in his hand, and soon they were walking down Russell Street towards Drury Lane. The famous coffee houses, Button's on one side and Will's on the other, were still open, their windows pouring light and laughter and talk, while those who had had enough staggered homewards, and the whores touted for business with considerable success. If Sam, a prudent and moderate man, had ever felt tempted by them, the thought of his daughter's possible fate had now made any such idea utterly abhorrent. Full of pity and revulsion, he quickened his stride and ignored their brazen invitations. They went safely past the Rose, a most notorious tavern and the scene of several murders, though all seemed comparatively quiet tonight, and came to Holborn without incident, much to Sam's secret relief. At the door of his inn, he paused. "When shall we next meet, sir?"

"Perhaps in two or three days' time, once I have had the opportunity to hawk my picture round the places where your daughter may most likely be found, and you can continue your enquiries with the other copy. If I have any firm news of her, I will send a message to you here. And you, likewise, can find me in Half Moon Street. I lodge at Madame Rousselle's house, ask about and you will be directed to it."

"I am grateful beyond words, Mr. Dark," said Sam, trying to keep his voice steady. "I really cannot thank you enough for your help and your kindness – you have been a remarkably good friend, and yet we were strangers until this evening."

"Pray think nothing of it," said the other man carelessly. "It serves to keep boredom at bay. So, good fortune go with us both, and I will see you at the end of the week, if not before."

*

"Who's the mort what you drew in the Stars?"

The tall artist glanced briefly at the child walking beside him, the flambeau slung over his bony shoulder, and said, "How do you know what I did in the coffee house?"

"Looked through the window, didn't I," said Gin, unabashed. "So – who is she?"

"Why do you ask?"

"Cos I seen her before."

"You've seen her?" Dark stopped so suddenly that the boy's chin grazed the arm of his coat. They were in Drury Lane, where it was unwise to linger too long late at night, but he showed no inclination to move on. "Where have you seen her?"

"At the theatre. Lincoln's Inn Fields. The new girl they're calling her. Looks like that piece you did." Gin habitually spoke in a kind of nasal shorthand, which needed familiarity to interpret, both for his pronunciation of the words, and the sense of them.

"How do you know?"

"Told you. Cos I seen her, coming out after her practice earlier. Lit her home in her chair, didn't I, and she gave me *sixpence*," said Gin pointedly. "Kind lady, she was, and free with her tack."

"If I made a habit of giving you three times the usual rate, I'd be beggared rather than generous," Dark commented.

"Tell me what she looks like – and be quick about it, before those coves over there decide to rob us."

"They won't touch us," said the boy, with insolent confidence. "That's Three Finger Jed, ain't it? And Moses Johnson. Oi!" he yelled. "I got Dark here, so leave us be, you slabberguts!"

With some muttering and a further exchange of insults, the pads dissolved into the shadows of the nearest alley. His hand on his sword, Dark began to walk again, and the child, in his ludicrously oversized coat and flapping shoes, had to gallop to catch up. "You'd have liked her," he said gleefully. "She's a bang-up piece of stuff."

"I don't doubt it," said Dark. "Rich wouldn't have anything else on his stage. But what does she look like?"

"Dark hair, under one of them little white caps, and a curl on her shoulder. And blue eyes," Gin told him, with unwonted lyricism. "Blue as a summer's evening. Nice little dimple, just here." He touched his left cheek. "Poll, I heard 'em call her."

"Poll." Dark paused. "Are you sure?"

"I ain't deaf yet," said Gin, aggrieved. "Course I'm sure." His voice became deceptively casual. "Short for Mary, ain't it?"

"I believe so," Dark said, in a careless tone which did not deceive his companion in the least.

"And Mary's the name of the piece you're looking for, ain't it?"

"You ask altogether too many questions," said Dark forbiddingly. "Have a care with that torch, you nearly set fire to my wig just now."

The only reply was a scornful sneer of denial from the boy, though he did take care to move sideways a little, out of reach of a long and possibly chastising arm. A drunken couple passed them, arms round each other, both singing with surprising tunefulness, and the strains of *Over the Hills and Far Away* bounced off the high walls and windows of Drury Lane and echoed into the soft September night. Under his breath, Dark began to sing along.

"'O'er the hills and o'er the main
To Flanders, Portugal and Spain,
Queen Anne commands, and we obey,
Over the hills and far away.'"

"Where you been?" demanded Gin caustically. "We've had King George for more'n a year now." And perhaps in a spirit of dangerous mischief, the boy turned down Playhouse Yard, a narrow alley hazardous even in daylight. Beside them, the slumbering bulk of the theatre was unlit, not only because of the lateness of the hour but because it was closed at present for redecoration, leaving the ground clear, for a few weeks, for Rich's company at Lincoln's Inn Fields: the company which, at present, seemed to include a young woman named Poll, who might or might not be Sam Jessop's missing daughter.

He only had Gin's word for the resemblance, of course, and he placed no reliance on the link-boy's words. Gin lied as habitually as everyone else breathed, and was particularly skilled at telling you what you wanted to hear. It took the perspicacity of long acquaintance to discern whether he was speaking the truth: it also needed broad daylight, to look penetratingly into those bright shifty eyes.

"Is there a play tomorrow?" he enquired. Gin would know. Gin knew everyone and everything, surviving on his wits and very little else. Dark had no idea how old he was, and Gin did not seem to know either: he could be any age between eight and eighteen, but inside his head, he was older than Methuselah.

"First of the season," Gin said. *"Hamlet Prince of*

Denmark. Runs mad, don't he, the Prince?"

"So I believe," said Dark gravely. "Then I take it this Poll creature is an actress?"

"Nah. Sings. Like a nightingale. She sang *As I Walked Out* and even Rich was wiping the tears away. I sneaked into the gallery to listen. You could do a lot worse than her," said Gin, considering. "You ain't had a regular piece in a while."

"Confine yourself to lighting my way, brat. How do I know you aren't her bully?"

"Cos I ain't," said Gin succinctly. "But you ain't come home to a warm bed since I don't know when. Like I said, you could do a lot worse."

He was right, of course. Gin was often right. Sometimes Dark was amused by the way the scrawny undersized boy took it on himself to be the artist's protector. Their relationship was complex, as Sam had perceived, because, unlikely as it seemed, each in some sense had need of the other. With a wry smile in the gloom, Dark acknowledged the fact to himself. If it had not been for Gin, his own life might have come to a premature end. And without him, the boy would long ago have succumbed to malnourishment, or winter cold, or been taken up for thieving. So he tolerated Gin's outspoken comments, and his attempts to run his life for him. Of course, there was talk about them, in the coffee houses and taverns clustered so thickly around the Piazza. Some people said Gin was his bastard son, others, in the teeth of considerable evidence to the contrary, that Dark was a molly and the child his bum-boy. The people who mattered to him all knew that neither was true, and that was the limit of his concern.

They crossed the Piazza in a watchful silence, and arrived at his lodgings in Half Moon Street. At this hour his landlady would be abed, and in any case she knew what sort of hours he kept. He found a couple of pennies in his pocket and gave them, with an air of flippancy, to the link-boy. "Here you are, brat, and don't spend it on women and strong liquor."

"'S if I would," said Gin, with a quick flash of sharp, gappy teeth. "Going to the play tomorrow, then, are we? Light your way, your honour?" he added, in the wheedling tone adopted by most link-boys and shoe-blacks.

"If you have nothing better to do." Dark paused as the boy took a step back, the flickering light illuminating the tightness of his fist, clenched around the precious coins. He added, "It's late. There's a spare bed here if you want it. Madame won't mind – she likes you, believe it or not."

"Nah," said Gin cheerfully. "I'm at the Hole-in-the-Wall tonight. See you whenever." And he turned, the torch still slung over his shoulder like a musket, and trotted off into the night.

* * *

The playhouse at Lincoln's Inn Fields had only been open under its new manager, John Rich, for nine months, and the paint was hardly sooty at all, the gilding still gleamed, and the curtains were clean and as yet unmolested by moths. Dark had arrived in good time, paid over his three shillings to the doorkeeper, and now sat on one of the benches in the second row of the pit. Normally he preferred the gallery, from whence he could survey the audience below him, and make quick sketches without being noticed, but tonight he wanted a close view of the woman called Poll. He had slipped one of his little leather-bound notebooks into the pocket of his coat, along with several sticks of chalk, plumbago and charcoal, so that he could draw her from the life as she sang. And beneath his assumed air of unruffled calm, his mind was filled with a pleasurable sense of anticipation.

It was the opening night of the season, so the theatre was packed, despite the familiarity of the play. Before it started, he had leisure to study the new painting of Apollo and the Muses, which hung above the stage. The god, fondling his lyre and surrounded by nine beautiful women, appeared intolerably smug. Not for the first time, Dark wondered why the ancients had considered astronomy to be worthy of a muse. Surely the people who had revered Praxiteles could at least envision a goddess devoted to sculpture, if not to drawing and painting? And Terpsichore, coyly simpering amidst a clutter of drapery, was definitely too earthbound ever to dance with any grace. He began to view the picture with a professional eye, a certain sign that the artist had failed. Urania had a telescope, an artefact surely unknown to the ancient Greeks, and in real life Clio's book would have slid off her improbably sloping lap and clouted the plump, wistful Erato on the head. In his mind's eye, Dark compared his own recent embellishment to the ceiling at Drury Lane, a scene from *Macbeth*. He had used some of the denizens of Covent Garden as his models, deriving much amusement from the fact that the three witches were represented respectively by a well-known market vendor, the ancient and malevolent proprietor of a notorious brothel in Bow Street, and Peg Morris who did his washing, while Macbeth himself, looking haunted, was a lifelike portrait of John Mills, who had triumphed in the part last season. And the ghostly child, pale and staring, his hair in muddy ringlets around his pinched face, bore a remarkable resemblance to Gin at his most obnoxious.

The curtain went up to reveal the castle of Elsinore, most splendidly painted (though the perspective was more than a little awry). The people around him shifted and murmured in eager anticipation of bloody deaths, delicious madness and a ghastly phantom, but Dark paid scant attention. If the 'new girl' that Gin had described was indeed Mary Jessop, then perhaps her lover St. Clair was in the audience. There were several overdressed beaux in the pit, corresponding to the popular stereotype of the foppish Frenchman, but he knew all of them by sight. He could, of course, be lurking in one of the side-boxes, where those who fancied themselves as wits or men of fashion liked to sit, or even in the gallery, but short of standing up in the middle of the play and peering round, there was no way of knowing. And in any case, Jessop had been unable to give him any detailed description of the dancing master, beyond the fact that he was tall, handsome and arrogant.

He knew the play so well that he could almost have taken one of the parts, and it seemed a very long time before the first interval. Dark brought out his notebook and plumbago, but to no avail: a Spanish dance was announced, and he had to sit and watch de la Garde and Mrs. Bullock shake the boards with much emphasis and drama as they performed what they fondly imagined to be a parody of Iberian haughtiness. As they finished, the man on Dark's right, a soberly clad youth with an eager expression, wondered aloud if the newest ornament of the stage were to appear that night.

"The newest ornament? Who do you mean by that?" enquired Dark encouragingly.

The young man, who had the look of a student at one of the Inns of Court, sighed gustily. "Why, have you not heard, sir, of the delectable Mrs. Paradice? I had the greatest good fortune to behold her yesterday, in this very theatre, as she sang at the rehearsal – such an angelic voice, such exquisite beauty, such a lovely and modest demeanour – I am sure England, no, the world itself entire, cannot hold such another!"

"I am sure it cannot," said Dark, his voice lowered because the play was about to recommence. "Do you know if she is to perform tonight?"

"I understood that she was – perhaps she is indisposed – or perhaps her sudden fame has caused in her a surfeit of that sweet feminine modesty which she seems to possess in such glorious abundance – oh, I do hope she does!" cried the young man, in an excess of passion that caused everyone in the pit to turn their heads and stare at him.

To Dark's relief, the actors at that moment came out to continue the play, and the youth was forced to silence. But as the second interval approached, he began to rustle and shuffle in his seat, and to suck at his orange with great fervour, as if he imagined himself ravishing the lips of the delicious Mrs. Paradice.

"If you do not leave off doing that directly," Dark said very softly into his neighbour's ear, "I will take the greatest pleasure in pushing it down your throat."

The young man gave him a startled and terrified glance, and instantly threw the remains of the orange down on the floor. On the stage, the play came to its temporary conclusion, and the actors withdrew, accompanied by enthusiastic applause. Then a low hum of anticipation began to rise above the pit, and murmur along the galleries. William Bullock, the theatre's senior actor, appeared before the curtain, and lifted his hand. There was a last scrape of sound from a dilatory fiddle player, and then silence.

"My lords, gentlemen and ladies, I have the greatest pleasure in presenting for your auditory enjoyment, a youthful nightingale, a songbird of such beauty, I have never heard or seen the like – for the very first time upon the public stage, I give you ... the glorious Mrs. Paradice!"

A wild eruption of applause from the youth next to Dark almost drowned out his last words. As Bullock stepped aside, a young woman walked out onto the boards and stood facing them all, her head tilted slightly to one side, her eyes bright and her lips slightly parted. Was this Samuel Jessop's daughter?

At first sight, the likeness to the drawing still in his pocket was considerable. As Gin had said, she was very handsome: a fine-looking girl with a trim figure and a sparkle in her eye that spoke of mischief and laughter. Under her lacy cap, her dark hair curled and gleamed, catching the light from the myriad candles around the stage, and her slim pale fingers grasped an exquisite ivory French fan, extravagantly beribboned and feathered. A present from her lover? As the musicians played the opening bars, she held it teasingly, fluttered it in front of her face and down. Then, with an enchanting smile, she opened her mouth, and song poured forth in a torrent of sound.

There was no doubt that she had a wonderful voice. Sweet, swooping, absolutely pure, it compassed all the notes of the song with effortless power. The audience sat enthralled, in utter silence. Afterwards, Dark could remember nothing of the tune, nor even the words, save that it was a lyric in praise of love, so long as the lovers could be faithful: and almost every man in pit and box and gallery swore in his heart to be faithful to Mrs. Paradice, if only he could have her.

Almost every man: for André Dark, who was no longer susceptible to a lovely face if he did not know what lay behind it, had no intention of laying siege to her virtue in her dressing room afterwards. His eyes fixed on her, he was committing her likeness to a page of his notebook with swift, unerring accuracy. There was a very great resemblance to the sketch he had made for Sam: the fashionably styled hair was the same, of course, the tilt of the dark eyebrows and the merry set of the mouth. Perhaps this young woman's nose was a little straighter, her chin more rounded, but the divergence was not so great as to make it certain either way. There were vast numbers of pretty girls in the world, and many had lightness of heart, dark brown hair and blue eyes, though fewer also sang so beautifully. But Sam had said that his daughter possessed the voice of an angel, and 'Poll Paradice' was surely too whimsical to be her true name, so perhaps this really was Mary Jessop, hiding behind an unlikely alias.

She finished the song to a roaring storm of applause, and dipped a graceful curtsey in acknowledgement. Dark, observing her closely, wondered if she might be too knowing, too experienced, to be Sam's spoilt and sheltered daughter. He remembered, though, that Mary Jessop had run away nearly two weeks previously. With St. Clair to tutor her in the ways of the world, even in so short a time she might indeed now possess the demeanour of a seasoned performer.

She spoke, and the audience clung to her words like the lovers they wished to be. "I thank you all, kind ladies and gentlemen. Would you like to hear another?"

Their response left her in no doubt that they did. She smiled brilliantly, her whole face incandescent with delight. "So you will, sirs. And since I have already sung of love fulfilled and happy, I will now sing you a tale of love in all its woe, of betrayal and sorrow, that I learnt when I was a child at my mother's knee. I bid you, be silent."

And so, now, were the musicians: she sang unaccompanied, as tuneful as when the violins and flutes and hautboys had played with her, and more than one masculine eye filled with tears at the tale, so familiar and yet made wonderfully new, of love lost and faith denied.

"'I never thought that my love would leave me
Until one evening when he came in.
He sat him down and I sat beside him,
And then our troubles did begin.

Oh, love is teasing and love is pleasing
And love's a pleasure when first it's new.
But as it grows older it waxes colder,
And fades away like the morning dew.'"

Dark found that he was remembering things that he had long thought safely forgotten, things that belonged in the past. Beside him, the youth was sitting rapt, tears sliding unashamed down his smooth cheeks.

"'There is a blackbird sits on yon tree,
Some say he's blind and cannot see.
How I wish it had been the same by me,
Before my false love I did see.'"

Nor was Mrs. Paradice unaffected by what she sang: with the clear gaze of the habitual observer, Dark saw the tears glitter and tremble in her own eyes as she gave them the final verse.

"'Oh, I wish my father had never whistled,
And I wish my mother had never sung,
I wish the cradle had never rocked me,
And I had died low, when I was young.'"

The last note lingered sadly in the air around them, and even the terracotta busts of Shakespeare and Jonson, poised above the stage, seemed to sigh a little, and settle back into their poses. For an instant, there was absolute silence, before the cheering exploded. Dark kept his gaze on Mrs. Paradice, who looked suddenly as if their applause had struck her with the force of a physical blow. Then she smiled again, even more dazzlingly than before, blew a kiss at the pit and another at the gallery, picked up her skirts and ran.

CHAPTER THREE

'A fraudful Nymph'

It was a long time before the theatre was sufficiently quiet for the actors to begin the final part of the play: and by then, Dark had extracted himself from the exultant denizens of the pit. He made his way back to the front entrance, and addressed the doorkeeper sitting there, on guard against latecomers who might wish to sneak in without paying. "Good evening to you, Mr Gallant. Has Mrs Paradice gone? I have urgent business with her."

"Indeed she has, sir – called for her chair and her light, and left for home. She's singing tomorrow, though, as the afterpiece of *The Busy Body*. I hope you ain't thinking of troubling her – Rich is very tender of his new girl, he won't want her upset, and if you do, there'll be hell to pay."

"Don't worry," Dark said: Gallant knew very well that he was closely connected with the rival establishment in Drury Lane. "I have no intention of poaching her from you. Good evening to you, and many thanks for your help."

Outside the playhouse, night now covered the city, and a wet, soft drizzle was falling, making the paving as lustrous and slimy as a snail's track. Despite the weather, Portugal Street was full of importunate whores, eagerly awaiting the exodus after the play was ended. They called to him, and one or two, the boldest and most desperate, even approached, but he ignored them. Near the theatre door, a huddle of talk and torches indicated where the link-boys also waited for custom. Dark walked over, and amidst the rabble of voices begging him to let them light him home, said sharply, "Where's Gin?"

"He ain't here, your honour," said a lanky youth, his

breath whistling through a lamentable absence of front teeth. "Ain't seen him today."

"Saw him yesterday, though," said another, much younger child, who bore the unlikely name of Dumplin. "Lit the Paradice home in her chair."

"Lucky cove," said another boy. "I'd *pay* to light her to her bed any time." He sniggered, and there was a subdued cackle of raucous laughter in support.

"So he didn't light her home tonight," Dark said patiently. The boys were a law unto themselves, a shifting population who made ends meet by lighting the way, sweeping roads, blacking shoes and picking pockets, amongst the more or less respectable means of earning a few pennies. Like Gin, they were children who had been reared on the streets, whose parents were inadequate, destitute, dead or, just as useless, sodden with drink. Because they knew that he himself had secured Gin's somewhat grudging respect, they were prepared to talk to him, even when there might not be any monetary reward in the offing.

"Nah," said the toothless boy enviously. "Pocky Tom got that job. Dunno why, he's as clod-skulled as the King of Spain's trumpeter. He's probably lit her past the Strand and into the river."

"She lives near the Strand, then?" Dark enquired casually.

"Might do," said the youth. "What's it worth, yer honour?"

"A penny or two?"

"Nah. She don't want no followers. Got a bully, ain't she."

"That ain't so no more, Ben – he's scampered, I heard," said Dumplin, obviously delighted at being able to put his senior right.

Another snigger ran round the group as the boys assimilated the implications of Mrs. Paradice's single, unprotected status.

"Some cove's paying her rent," said the toothless one, Ben. "Must be her bully. You don't live in a prime sleeping-house and not have a bully. Rum blowen like her, must have a bully."

Since the conversation seemed to have strayed off course, Dark said, "There's a pig for any of you who can give me her direction."

As he had expected, the offer of sixpence brought a flood of replies, from which he deduced that Mrs. Paradice, with or without her lover, or her pimp, lived in Flying Horse Court, on the south side of the Strand. "The ken that's furthest in," said Dumplin. "Sign of a prancer with wings above the door."

"Just what I wanted to hear," Dark said, pleased. He tossed a handful of coins to the boys and walked off down the street, whistling the tune that Poll Paradice had sung with such heart-rending beauty, such a short time ago.

The Strand, when at last he came to it, was still busy, with coaches going up and down, chairs in plenty, and many people making their way home, more or less steadily, after an evening spent in coffee house or tavern. The lights shone from the windows and lamps and torches, and gleamed brilliant in reflection on the wet street. Dark knew Flying Horse Court: it was one of the alleys tangled between the Strand and the wharves and warehouses by the river, not far from the old Savoy Palace. The houses, he seemed to recall, were well built and comparatively new, with a view of the Thames from their attic windows. If Mrs. Paradice did indeed live in one of them, her protector was certainly a wealthy man.

He crossed the Strand just by the Exeter Exchange, a handsome two-storey building full of shops and booths, now closed and shuttered for the night. The alley he wanted was thirty yards away on his left, and even as he identified the opening, one of the chairs jolting along the street ahead of him turned down it. He had walked briskly, and taken a very hazardous short cut through Clare Market, so it was quite possible that he had caught up with Mrs. Paradice's much slower sedan. With quiet care, he followed it.

Some of the houses, though not all, had lanterns lit beside their doors, so the gloom was not entirely impenetrable. Dark lingered, watching, as the chair was carried up the steps of the house at the end, immediately opposite the court's entrance. The door opened immediately, the light from within illuminating the railings on either side of the damp steps, the neat cobbled paving in the alley, and the sign of a flying horse, swinging from an iron bracket above the lintel. The link-boy, much taller and less ragged than Gin, raised his light high, and a cloaked and hooded figure emerged from the sedan. The bearers and the boy were paid off, handsomely to judge by their respectful bows and the appreciative sound of thanks, and their customer ran inside.

He withdrew discreetly into the shadows as the chairmen and the link-boy passed him, deep in an animated discussion about Mistress Paradice's pretty face and her kind and generous heart. The object of their approval had vanished inside the house, but a well-dressed black maidservant emerged and, standing on tiptoe, set a spill to the lantern hanging beside the porch. She paused, looking around, and then she, too, went back in. The door shut behind her, and Flying Horse Court was once more quiet and deserted. After a while, Dark emerged from his hiding place, and moved softly down the alley.

It was far too late to knock on the door and ask for

admittance. He would have to come back tomorrow. But at least he knew where she lived, and that her circumstances were comfortable: in fact, probably a good deal more comfortable than his own lodgings in Half Moon Street, not far away on the other side of the Strand. He stood for some time in the shadows where a branch of the alley bent round to the left, gazing at the house with an observant and thoughtful eye. If – *if* – this was Sam Jessop's runaway daughter, she had certainly done very well for herself: so well, indeed, that she was most unlikely to want to return home. And with her face, and her voice, surely a splendid future beckoned. A young woman who succeeded on the stage, in any capacity, would have no shortage of wealthy gentlemen, or even noblemen, eager to become her latest protector. If she were prudent and sensible – although not many of them were – she could pick and choose her lovers, milk them dry, and store up sufficient funds and property to see her into a contented retirement.

So where did the mysterious St. Clair fit into the puzzle? Surely an impecunious French dancing master would not be able to afford to set up his mistress in such expensive style? If he had, in the link-boy's words, 'scampered', who was now paying for Mrs. Paradice's fine house and fashionable black maid? And above all why, if she had a lover, would she court his displeasure by disporting herself on the public stage, and therefore implying that she might be available? Very few men of any stamp would tolerate such behaviour from a woman for whom, essentially, they had paid to possess body and soul.

He was so intent on these questions that his ears, customarily sharpened for any unusual sound, missed the unmistakeable signs until it was almost too late. Only the sudden scrape of boot-leather on stone, as someone stumbled on an unevenly set cobble, alerted him to the danger creeping up behind him. He whipped round, but before he could draw his sword, his arms were grabbed, some kind of hood was forced over his head, and a voice hissed in his ear, "Come quietly, sir, or it'll be the worse for you!"

There were two of them, and they had him pinioned so effectively that there was absolutely no point in trying to break free. He was marched a short distance, pushed stumbling up a flight of steps, and inside a house.

It was obvious, of course, whose house, and his guess was confirmed when his captors flung him down, so violently that his knees crashed painfully on bare floorboards. He swore, and a woman said, "Don't be too gentle, Dick. He deserves all he gets." There was no mistaking the firm young voice, with its faintly rustic intonation.

"Shall we stay here, ma'am?"

"You can wait outside the door. I will call you if you are needed."

The two men left, their feet tramping loudly. Dark fumbled for the hood and pulled it off. As he had expected, it was the mysterious Mistress Paradice standing before him. In the theatre, her beauty had been a wonder, partly created by the adoration of her audience. Here and now, in this ordinary room with its painted panelling, shuttered windows and handsome hearth, she was still an uncommonly pretty girl. She had changed from silver satin into a wrapping gown of printed Indian cotton, and the sapphire necklace she had worn in the theatre no longer circled the slender beauty of her throat. By the kind candlelight, her skin glowed golden and flawless, her hair was a rich glossy brown, and her eyes intensely blue. The effect was considerably spoilt by the deep frown between the elegantly shaped brows, and by her mouth, which was set in a thin line more severe than any judge's.

"What were you doing, watching my house?" she demanded, meeting his stare with a rank hostility that he, surely, had done little to earn. "And who are you?"

"I might ask the same of you," he said, feeling that

attack was the best form of defence. "And enquire also, why your two bully boys assaulted me and dragged me in here."

"Don't be a fool," said the singer sharply. "You know very well who I am – I saw you in the pit this evening. And you were drawing me, were you not?"

"I plead guilty," Dark said. "I was merely wondering if the name you go by is your own."

There was a snort of contempt from the black maid, who had been standing by the fireplace. She advanced on him, her gaze even more hostile than that of her mistress. "Madam asked you a civil question. Will you answer it?"

"Do I have a choice?"

"No, you do not," said Mrs. Paradice. "And if you cause any more trouble, Dick and Will are just outside the door."

"Men who attacked me just now, without the least shred of warning or provocation. I am well acquainted with several lawyers," Dark said. "Perhaps I should consider bringing a charge of assault against them."

The young woman laughed. "Believe me, sir, if they had really wanted to hurt you, they would have done so. My maid saw you from the window, so I asked them to bring you in here to answer my questions, which I will put to you again. Why did you follow me, and why were you watching my house?"

As Gin had said, her eyes really were an extraordinary colour, the deep and unfathomable blue of the evening sky. Dark said quietly, "Let me be plain with you. I am seeking a young girl by the name of Mary Jessop. Not long ago, she eloped from her home in Oxford with a French dancing master called St. Clair. She has dark hair and blue eyes, and sings and dances like an angel. Your appearance fits that description, and the name you go by is so fanciful that it is surely false –"

"It is not – it is the name I was born with!" The girl

was not tall, but the power of her indignation and the strength of her character made her seem to tower over Dark. "I was born Mary Paradice in the town of Bradford in Wiltshire, I have never been to Oxford, and I have *certainly* never heard of this Mary Jessop."

"It's all a tarradiddle of lies," said the maid, glaring at him. "I think he must be turned in his wits, madam. Shall I call for Dick and Will to throw him out?"

"Yes, pray summon them, Hannah," Mistress Paradice said coldly. "And in the future, if you are ever seen skulking around my house without my leave, sir, I do not think my footmen will be so gentle with you."

Dark spoke quickly, while he still had the chance. "I must explain myself before I go. My name is André Dark, I am a portrait painter living in Half Moon Street, and I have been asked to find Mary Jessop by her father. If you are indeed not Miss Jessop, then I have made an honest mistake, and I humbly beg your pardon for it."

"You don't seem very humble to me," said the girl caustically, looking him up and down. "You look like an arrant rogue, Mr. Dark – if that is *your* real name – and you will be treated as such. Will! Dick! In here at once!"

The men entered, extremely large and intimidating in their moss green livery, their faces grim with purpose. "Do you wish this person removed, madam?" the stouter one enquired.

Dark said courteously, "There will be no difficulty. I can remove myself without assistance. I apologise most humbly for troubling you, Mistress Paradice."

"And so you should, sir. Will, Dick, pray escort Mr. Dark from the house. Immediately, if you please, it grows very late and I am passing weary of this encounter."

"I likewise, madam," Dark said. He rose rather stiffly

from his enforced kneeling position, and bowed. "I regret the circumstances, Mistress Paradice – perhaps at another time, in another place, we might have parted friends."

"I doubt it," said the lady, with a cold glare. She watched impatiently as he walked with deliberate dignity to the door. The hall beyond was long and narrow, with a round, gilt-framed mirror hanging just where a woman careful of her looks would check her appearance before going out. Dark glanced at his reflection as he passed, and could not wonder that this grim, black-browed man had been taken for an arrant rogue. The footmen ushered him out into the chilly wet air, which smelt of washed streets and the smoke of thousands of coal fires, lit against the September night. He walked down the steps and paused, looking back. Mistress Paradice had come into the hall, presumably to ensure that he had indeed left the house. At once he smiled, and sketched a brief salute. "Thank you for your hospitality, ma'am. And although you will doubtless spurn the compliment, I must tell you that your name is most appropriate for one who sings as if from heaven."

Fleetingly, her expression changed. Then she walked forward, past the maid and the footmen, to shut the door. The crash reverberated all round Flying Horse Court, and Dark was left alone in the rainy night, to make his way home to Half Moon Street.

* * *

"You ain't got the sense you was born with," observed Gin caustically. "You should'er known better than to go creeping about in dark alleys at that time of night." He cackled delightedly at his own jest, and added, grinning, "*Dark* alleys, eh? That's a good 'un!"

"Only if you've the wits of a hare-brained tortoise," Dark said. He glared at his tormentor. "How have you contrived to live so long, boy?"

"I don't go down *dark* alleys on my own," said Gin, with considerable satisfaction. "So they were the Paradice's men, eh? But why drag you off? You was only on watch."

"That's just what I was wondering. If she's not Mary Jessop – and she was absolutely adamant on that score – then why have her footmen grab me? But if she is, then she may have thought I was going to snatch her and take her back to her father."

"He wouldn't do that, he ain't that sort of cove," said Gin wisely. "He's a tomdoodle with that girl, you can see it."

"Yes, but St. Clair might not know that," Dark pointed out. "If he's only left her temporarily, he could well have told off the footmen to keep an eye out for suspicious strangers. But why bring me indoors? Why not just hit me over the head and leave me there in the rain?"

"To find out what you was there for?" Gin suggested. "Here, have some more bingo." Without waiting for an answer, he upended the brandy bottle, and the dregs splashed into the glass on the table by the fire.

"Well, I told her that, and it was plain she didn't believe me. She let me go peacefully, though – but I suspect those footmen of hers would have liked to have hurled me down the steps, at the very least of it."

"A good thing they didn't, or you'd have likely broke your head," Gin told him. "And she's a peach, ain't she, that Poll Paradice," he added slyly. "You could try your luck with her – with her bully gone, well, while the cat's away ..."

"I'm not entirely soft in the head. I'll tell you this, insolent brat, if I ever go back to Flying Horse Court, it'll be in a full suit of armour. No matter how peach-like Mistress Paradice may be. *If* Paradice is her real name, which I very much doubt, despite her protestations. Think you can find out any more about her? Sniffing round *dark* alleys being your speciality ..."

"I ain't your slave," Gin said, adopting his habitual whine. "I got other things to do, you know."

"I'm sure you have. All manner of thieving, diving, moon-cursing –"

"Oi!" said Gin, stung. "I ain't *never* done none of that!"

"Haven't you?"

"No," said the child savagely. "But if you wants to think it, Mr. High-and-Bleeding-Mighty André Dark, then I can't stop you, can I? Good *night*."

Dark, left abruptly to his own devices, listened as Gin's feet clattered loudly down the two flights of stairs to the front door. The ensuing slam rattled the windows and brought an indignant screech from Madame Rousselle, the tempestuous old harridan who owned the house. But at least he was alone now, and he could think.

He drained the glass of brandy, and then leaned back against his chair, staring at his familiar chamber as if he had never seen it before. The floor, its wide elm boards stained and smoothed with the passage of more than fifty years, was bare, with a worn turkey carpet in hues of dull reds and browns before the hearth its only concession to comfort. His bed had seen its best days when Madame Rousselle herself was likewise new and freshly upholstered, and on it, so she was wont to boast after a glass or two of brandy, King Charles, Old Rowley himself, had seduced her.

It was possible that her acquaintance with the king, if no-one else, had been imaginary. But she had certainly been one of the first actresses on the English stage, a famous toast of the town and the quarry of every beau in London. Now, with at least seventy years to her discredit, only the ravaged husk of her past beauties remained under the thick white paint, and the gorgeous chestnut hair had been exchanged for a supremely unconvincing scarlet wig which reminded Dark irresistibly of Good Queen Bess at her most grotesque. From some past alliance, though, if not from King Charles, she had obtained the freehold of this house in Half Moon Street. Liking the company, so she said, she only charged him five shillings a week for his bedchamber, as well as a reception room which he had had decorated in some style and in which he hung his best pictures for the edification of his customers, and the long bare attic with its dormer windows, in which he painted. With his income fitful at best, and sometimes vanishing away into nothing, at least he had a roof over his head. It was security of a sort: and it was more, so much more, than the likes of Gin possessed.

Gin. He would have to do something about Gin. The brat was becoming a pest. He had encountered him on the way back to Half Moon Street, and even though Dark had neither wanted nor needed his assistance, he had been unable to dissuade the boy from escorting him home. An unwilling smile twitched the artist's mouth. *Dark* alleys, indeed. He needed some stern words, the next time they met.

His knees ached savagely, reminding him of his earlier humiliation at the hands of Mrs. Paradice and her footmen. He closed his eyes, and at once her image, clad in silver satin, her dark hair coiled on her bare shoulder, and singing more sweetly than any nightingale, rose up in his mind. Was she really Mary Paradice of Bradford in Wiltshire? Or Mary Jessop, beloved and wayward daughter, of Oxford?

There was only one way to find out, but it could wait until morning. Everything – sending a message to Sam Jessop, the problem of Gin, and Mrs. Paradice, whoever she was – could wait until morning. For now, all he wanted was to sink his bruised body into blissful oblivion, and to sleep until daylight.

CHAPTER FOUR

'The Crowded Play'

After yet another day of fruitless enquiry, Sam returned to the Black Swan in Holborn, and was eating a plate of mutton chops and a mug of warm spiced ale in his chamber when a potboy brought him a message. He almost ran downstairs, and found Dark at the window of one of the private parlours, idly sketching a pair of gossiping maidservants in the yard outside.

"Are you ready?" was the artist's instant welcome, without any other word of greeting. "We might be in time, if we hurry."

Weariness, and the ale, had dulled Sam's wits considerably. "In time for what?"

"In time to see the girl who may be your daughter, of course," said Dark over his shoulder, and all the exhaustion and petty torments of a long and trying day dropped away from Sam as if by magic, leaving him restored and invigorated.

"To see her? My Mary? Is she well? Have you spoken to her?" The questions came tumbling out of him as if he were an eager schoolboy, instead of a respectable merchant of close on fifty.

Dark paused in the doorway, and the look on his face was surprisingly sympathetic. "I did not say she was certainly your daughter – I said that she *may* be. I have asked her directly if she is Mary Jessop, and she has strongly denied it. But she is very like your description, and in her character too. When she was on the stage I made a quick sketch of her – take a look." He passed his notebook to Sam, opened at a previous page. "I had to work very fast, and the light was not good, but I think I have caught her essence. Is that her?"

There was a pair of candles fluttering in a wall-sconce in the passageway just outside the parlour. Sam held the drawing at arm's length beneath their flames, frowning because his ageing eyes would not now permit him to inspect it closely.

It was Mary, and yet not Mary. He had never seen her so finely dressed, there were more ribbons and lace on her bodice than was proper for a merchant's daughter, and it was cut much too low and without any kind of a modesty piece or even a wisp of lace. Once more, dreadful doubts assailed him. He knew his daughter, he knew how headstrong and self-willed she was, and he could imagine, only too clearly, what she might say, and do, if he were to present himself at the theatre and demand that she abandon fame and the illusion of fortune and return to her humdrum, ordinary life in Oxford. The perils that awaited her seemed so obvious to him: but at sixteen, with the beaux of London at her feet, she would surely be blind to everything save her present glory.

"It is certainly very like," he said, fighting to control the apprehension in his voice. "And yet she denies who she is?"

"She has run away from her father," Dark pointed out. "Of course she will not admit to being Mary Jessop, if she fears that by doing so she will be hauled off home in disgrace." His glance at Sam was surprisingly full of sympathy. "I can draw you a thousand pictures, all of which might be very like, but nothing can compare with a sight of the girl herself. She is singing at the theatre tonight, so you can see her from a distance – that way, if she is not your daughter, you may withdraw without making your presence known to her. And if she is ..."

"I only want to know that she is safe, and happy," said Sam stubbornly.

"Then let us go at once," said Dark, throwing on an air of brisk resolution like a cloak. "Already the first act of the play must be all but over – we may miss her. It's not far, are you fit enough to walk?"

"I may be of advancing years," said Sam severely, "but I am not yet in my dotage, Mr. Dark. Lead on, then, as quickly as you can."

They were lit through the rainy streets by Gin, his dank hair plastered to his head under a greasy hat that was, like his other garments, far too big for him. Desperate to see if this mysterious singer was indeed his daughter, Sam hurried beside the artist, dodging puddles and carriages and spouting gutters with as much agility as if he, too, had been London born and bred. At the theatre, Dark tossed Gin a couple of coins and told him to wait for them. A doorkeeper charged them the reduced price for latecomers, and they were allowed inside.

"The gallery," Dark said softly. "It's less obvious than the pit, and easier to see without being seen. Have you been in a theatre before, Mr. Jessop?"

"I regret to say I have not, sir," Sam muttered, puffing up the steep, narrow wooden stairs in his wake. They arrived at the top, and a couple of serving men in livery, frowning at their entrance, shuffled along the front bench to make room for them. Sam leaned forward, his elbows on the rail, and looked down at the stage with a thumping heart: but he knew already, from the sound of speech, that the play was still in progress. A mixture of sweat and rain was running down his forehead, and he pulled out a handkerchief and wiped his streaming face.

"I pray you, do not die before the lady comes on stage," Dark murmured in his ear, surely in a spirit of mischief. "We are in time – this is only the second act, and she is due to perform during the next interval. Up here, she should not see us if we take care to skulk convincingly."

"And if it is Mary?" Sam demanded, in a hoarse whisper. "Then what do we do? Rush the stage?"

"No need – I know where she lives, we can call on her at

our leisure. This play is still very popular, I see, and deservedly so. It's called *The Busy Body*. Did you know that it was written by a woman? Mrs. Centlivre, to be precise."

"No, I did not," said Sam, who had no interest in anything except the imminent appearance of the girl who might be his daughter. The atmosphere in the gallery was hot and stuffy, permeated with the thick aroma of smoky candles and unwashed bodies, and the sweat was still pouring off him. His head itched like the devil, and he pulled off his hat and his wig and mopped at his glowing, slippery scalp with the kerchief. As he replaced them, there was a rattle of applause and the curtains were dragged across, announcing the interval.

A man came out in front of the curtains, and began to speak. At once his voice was drowned out by a wave of stamping and cheering from the pit and from the upper gallery where Sam and Dark were sitting. As the applause intensified, a girl in blue ran onto the stage and made a deep, graceful curtsey of acknowledgement.

She had dark hair, and she was beautiful, and she sang as if she were the human spirit of the nightingale, which has the power to enchant all lovers. But after the first, frantic glance Sam could not prevent the tears from welling up in his eyes: for despite all his hopes, the young woman below them was not his daughter.

* * *

A letter arrived the following morning at the house in Half Moon Street, addressed to André Dark. Madame Rousselle's footman brought it to him with eyebrows raised so high that they almost met his immaculately powdered wig, and retreated with an expression that on anyone less professionally urbane would have been considered a smirk.

Billets doux had not been received at this house for many a day, and from the sweet scent of lavender that rose from the fine creamy paper, this was surely a letter from a lady.

Even before he had opened it, Dark was certain of her identity. The superscription was carefully written, in a neat round hand with lively loops to the y's and g's that spoke of a mischievous, even reckless character, and he was not at all surprised by the signature.

Sir,

I am reliably informed that you are indeed what you claimed to be, and in consequence I beg that you will wait upon me at your earliest convenience, so that I may present my apologies in person, and also pass on to you some information concerning your quest, which you may find of interest.

M. Paradice

With a wry smile, Dark wondered what this meant. Certainly, the tone of the letter did not exactly convey the kind of grovelling regret which might have been thought customary under the circumstances. There was no 'humble servant', no expression of ladylike desolation at her unpardonable error. Whatever else she was, Mrs. Paradice was no milk-and-water miss.

But young women in her situation were usually creatures of spirit and determination: those less well endowed with such qualities remained in cottage or hovel or poorhouse. Polly Paradice, for so she must really be, must have employed all her courage and resourcefulness to survive in a perilous world. And from the little he had seen of her, so far she had succeeded.

Well, he would certainly take her up on her offer, and as soon as might be, though he doubted she had any news of value about Mary Jessop. But he had no intention of going to Flying Horse Court alone, even in broad daylight. So within the hour, in obedience to his summons, Sam Jessop arrived at the house in Half Moon Street, and was shown upstairs by the supercilious footman.

Despite his attempt at a cheerful greeting, Sam looked as deflated as a pricked bladder this morning, and Dark felt a renewed surge of sympathy for the hopes so definitively shattered.

"Look," he said, passing the letter over. "It's from Mistress Paradice. She wishes to apologise for the ill-treatment I suffered in her house." He had told Sam about it the previous night, on the way back from the theatre. "And she claims to have information that might help us."

Sam gave it a cursory glance, hardly long enough to assimilate the first line, let alone the rest. "But how can she? London is so vast, and so full of people, she cannot have any knowledge of a complete stranger who has only been in town less than a fortnight."

"I have no idea. Nevertheless, she may be speaking the truth." Dark paused, seeing again the girl who had ordered him from her house with angry contempt. What had persuaded her to change her view of him? And why had she invited him to see her, when a slightly more fulsome note than the one in Sam's hand would have sufficed as an apology? Did she really have knowledge of his daughter's whereabouts, or was it some elaborate ruse? More than ever, she intrigued him. Who was she? And who was her lover?

"It will be another vain hope. I do not think we will ever find her." Sam's voice, the drooping set of his shoulders, the lines on his face, which seemed to have aged many years since Dark had first met him only a few days previously, all spoke of the cruel disappointments he had suffered. "Dark, she could be anywhere. Quite probably you are right and they have gone to France, so I must resign myself to the fact that I will never see her again. But how can I return to Oxford without her? I have failed, and now I cannot forgive myself for it."

"Then you are a fool, sir," Dark said, giving him a sharp glance. "And a faint-heart, to give up so easily, after just one reverse. She has not been translated to heaven or swallowed up by the earth, and we will find her. If you give up the search now, you are abandoning her, just as her lover will surely abandon her eventually. Can you live with that, for the rest of your days?"

Sam's eyes, raised to his face, were haunted. "No," he said at last. "No, I can't. You are right, I know. It is just that – that I was so certain that it would be her. At first I couldn't believe it was not, I could hardly credit the evidence of my own eyes." He gave Dark a sad smile. "It isn't surprising that we were mistaken. She is very like Mary. The same colouring, the same way she wears her hair, even the same look of mischief. But I'm sure that if they stood side by side we would wonder why the confusion had ever occurred."

"An opportunity unlikely ever to arise," Dark commented dryly. "Well? Do you wish to meet with Mrs Paradice, and discover what information, if any, she claims to possess? Or do you have other lines of enquiry you wish to pursue?"

"No, alas, I do not," Sam said. "So I must muster the courage to clutch at this one straw, hopeless though it seems."

"Then we will go together," said Dark, suddenly waxing lyrical with an ironic gleam in his eyes. "Come with me, Mr. Jessop, on this morning of serendipitous delight, to behold our Paradice."

* * *

Flying Horse Court looked quite different in daylight. The houses were new and neat in red brick, with cornices and quoins of dressed stone, and gleaming front doors embellished with a variety of brass ornaments. One of them housed an apothecary well-known for his restorative waters, a print shop which had taken some of Dark's engravings occupied the corner by the Strand, and an upholsterer presumably plied his trade at the sign of the tasselled cushion. This alley with its respectable businesses seemed an improbable place for a famous, or notorious, *chanteuse*, but London was full of such unlikely neighbours. Dark climbed the three stone steps to the front door of Mistress Paradice's house, and rapped the knocker smartly.

After a brief moment, it was opened by one of her footmen, resplendent in his livery and powdered wig. "Yes, sir?"

Dark surveyed him. "Is Mrs. Paradice at home?" he demanded.

"Your name, sir?" The footman's voice had the accent of Wales, its lilt in contrast to his intimidating expression.

"I think you are well aware of it," Dark said. "We shall wait within – it looks very like rain." Before the footman could make any move to prevent him, he walked calmly over the threshold and stood in the hall. "Come on – Will, is it not? I do not intend to be kept waiting."

Reluctantly, the footman stood aside to let Sam enter too, then shut the door and vanished up the stairs. There was the urgent sound of voices, and Dark smiled. "That's rattled him! I'm looking forward to Mrs. Paradice's apologies."

"I can't understand why she felt it necessary to order them to attack you," Sam whispered, obviously conscious of the fact that unfriendly ears might be listening. "Unless –"

"Unless she has something to hide?" Dark said.

"And why should I have?"

Both men turned abruptly. The woman calling herself Mary, or Polly, Paradice stood above them, at the turn in the stairs. Sudden sunlight thrust through a window high-set behind her, illuminating her neat, slender figure with a shaft of autumn gold. Today she wore a simple dress of harebell blue, its low neckline filled by a gossamer wisp of white linen, and the generous petals of the skirt flowering over a narrow hoop. The black maid, attired in a yellow gown hardly less fine than that of her mistress, hovered a few steps behind her.

"Good morning, Mistress Paradice," said Dark, ignoring her pointed question. He bowed with courtly elegance. "I trust I find you well?"

"I thank you, yes," said the young woman on the stairs. She descended with deliberate grace, pointing each toe, her skirts swaying around her. Two steps from the foot, she paused and surveyed them coolly, with an air of polite enquiry. "I can recall my invitation to you, sir, with great clarity, but who is your companion?"

"Samuel Jessop, humbly at your service, ma'am," said Sam, making a leg without any of Dark's arrogant assurance.

"Ah," said Mrs. Paradice. "So you are the father of the runaway? In that case, sir, I am very glad that you have come, for I may have news of her."

Dark was unimpressed. "So you said in your note, madam. I beg you, tell us more."

"Indeed I will. Hannah? Pray bring chocolate and refreshments to the parlour. Please come this way, sirs."

They followed her into the room to which Dark had been brought two nights previously. Then, he had paid it little mind, but now, with the leisure to look about him, he glanced curiously around. It was well-proportioned, the walls lined with panelled wainscot, painted an airy light blue – not the cheapest colour, as he well knew – and the plasterwork on the high ceiling picked out in what appeared to be gold leaf. There was a large gilt-framed mirror above the marble fireplace, with many-branched sconces on either side. A coal fire, well banked, glowed beneath it, a welcome sight on a chilly autumn morning, and the air of domestic comfort was completed by the tabby cat curled asleep on the thick turkey rug before the hearth.

There was only one picture, hanging on the wall beside him, fully lit by the window opposite. He looked at it with professional attention, and found his interest immediately engaged, for it was a flower painting, undoubtedly of Dutch origin, and executed with remarkable skill. If Mrs. Paradice had chosen this herself, it displayed a fine taste in art rare in any female, let alone one of presumably humble birth. But of course it was probably part of the furnishings of the house, and therefore not of her choosing.

"A pretty picture, is it not?" said Mistress Paradice, smiling beside him. Her head, neatly capped, only just passed the level of his shoulder, but the self-contained strength of her personality was ample compensation for any disadvantage of height. "Dutch, of course, but no less beautiful for that."

"Indeed not," said Dark, choosing not to inform her that his mother had been Dutch, he had been born in Amsterdam, and that he knew that country, and its artists, tolerably well. "The *Rosa Centifolia* is remarkably finely painted," he added.

If he had thought to confuse her with his knowledge, she refused to rise to the bait. "So I observe," said Polly Paradice serenely. "But I find the Latin somewhat cumbersome for everyday speech – a plain cabbage rose is what my father would have called it, Mr. Dark, and so do I. Pray be seated, sirs, and Hannah will be back soon with your chocolate."

With a glance at Sam, who was also looking round with interest, Dark took the chair furthest from the fire. "Do you have any other pictures of such quality, Mistress Paradice?"

"That is by far my best," said his hostess, sliding gracefully onto the chair next to him. For the first time, her voice became animated by something other than mere civility. "But I hope to add more to my collection. I find I do not care so much for these old Italian Masters that are all the rage, they show such an excess of sensibility that I grow weary just to look at them – whereas a vase of flowers in the drear days of winter can lighten my spirits as nothing else. And when all is said and done, a vase of flowers is just that – a vase of flowers, and carries no other meaning." She glanced at him, as if gauging his reaction, and then smiled. "But of course, sir, being an artist yourself, you may beg to disagree."

"Indeed I do, madam," said Dark, inclining his head in acknowledgement. "But courtesy forbids me to do so at this moment."

The maid entered the room, bearing a laden tray which she put down on the table, and proceeded to set out the Delftware cups, plates of light, wafery biscuits, and a tall silver pot rich with the aroma of chocolate, well laced with eggs, milk and cinnamon. She waited as her mistress dispensed steaming cups between herself and her guests, then curtseyed, took the tray and withdrew.

"And now, Mr. Dark, let me come straight to the point," said Mrs Paradice, turning to him with a charming smile, lightly dimpled. "I must present my humblest and most sincere apologies for the indignities you suffered in this house the other night. It was a very great error of judgement on my part, and I do pray most earnestly that you will allow me to make amends."

"This excellent dish of chocolate is recompense enough, madam," said Dark generously, though his eyes betrayed amusement.

"Then you are very easily satisfied, sir," Mistress Paradice remarked, not without a hint of the tartness that the rich sweet chocolate entirely lacked. "But I hope you will be better pleased with the information I have for you." She sipped delicately from the cup. In daylight, at close quarters, it was obvious that she was perhaps ten years older than Mary: though her complexion was pale, fresh and fine, lines were lightly traced on either side of her pretty mouth, and at the corners of the wide blue eyes. But her age sat very lightly on her. Girls with the glowing bloom of youth were commonplace, less so the woman who managed to keep such looks well into her twenties.

"Information concerning my daughter?" Sam asked, putting down his own cup.

"I believe so," said Mistress Paradice, turning her attention to him. "If the name of your daughter is Mary Jessop, then, yes, I do have word of her."

"May I ask how?" Dark interposed, sounding sceptical in the extreme. "After all, it does not seem very likely that you and she would move in the same circles –"

"I have news of her," said their hostess firmly. "You may believe it or not as you choose, sir, but I will lay the truth before you as it has been related to me. She is in Bristol."

"Bristol!" Sam's voice squeaked upwards in astonishment. "*Bristol?* But I was certain she would be here in London – "

"I believe she may have been, briefly, but now she is in Bristol. With her lover, St. Clair. If you make haste, you may find them there before they move on."

Sam stared at her, desperate hope struggling with the inevitability of failure. In the end, he said dubiously, "Are you *sure* of this, Mistress Paradice? I beg you, if there is any doubt, please tell me. I have already had one most grievous disappointment, and I do not think I can readily bear another."

"You believed that I would prove to be your daughter, did you not?" Mrs. Paradice regarded him steadily over the rim of her exquisite blue and white cup.

"You are very like her, to one who has not met her," said Sam. "You have the same colour hair, and eyes, and she sings almost as beautifully as you do, and I – we both – allowed the power of hope to sway us into error."

"And so I was mistaken for a young girl of sixteen," said Mrs Paradice, with considerable amusement. "I am most flattered, sirs. I had thought those days long gone."

"All this is beside the point," Dark said. "You have not told us, madam, how you have come by this information that Miss Jessop is in Bristol. In fairness to her father, I beg you to tell us now."

"I very much regret that I cannot. I was given a confidence by a friend, and I will not betray it. But I know that she is there. If you make haste, you will be certain to catch her. You may take coach tomorrow morning, and be in Bristol by the end of the following day."

"Madam," Sam said, "if your information should lead to my dearest Mary, I shall always be in your debt. It will fulfil all my hopes and dreams – how can I ever repay you?"

"You haven't found her yet," said his hostess, but her smile was full of sympathy. "Pray save your thanks, Mr. Jessop, for the moment when you see her again. And if I were you," she added, with a glance at Dark, sitting watchful and suspicious next to her, "I should pay small mind to your artist friend. It is plain that he still bears me a grudge about the other night."

"And why should I not, madam, when I was manhandled by your footmen and treated with a pernicious lack of courtesy by them and by you? The only conclusion I can reach from that is that you have something to hide."

"Which I most assuredly do not! I was concerned, as any woman living alone would be, for my own safety. Now I would be obliged if you would leave, sir," said Mrs. Paradice, rising to her feet and indicating the door with an angry flourish. "I invited you here to assure you of my friendship, and to give you news of the girl you seek. No-one forced me, it was done from the goodness of my heart, and you fling it back in my face!"

"Wait," Sam said urgently. "I beg you, Mistress, please do not send us away without telling us more of Mary and where she may be found in Bristol. I am sure that if Mr. Dark is given a little time to reconsider his remarks, he will come to a different conclusion. *Please*, madam, I am sure no offence was intended. Is that not so, sir?"

There was an agonising pause. Dark was staring at Mrs. Paradice as if the power of his gaze alone could extract the truth from her, and she, with high colour and eyes bright with anger, was staring back. Then, as suddenly as if a fiddle string had been snapped, the tension broke. Dark rose to his feet and produced an entirely unexpected smile. He held out his hand to the woman standing furiously in front of him. "Madam, pray accept my most humble apologies. I doubted you, and I was wrong. For the sake of this unhappy man and his child, will you not forgive me for my boorish and impolite behaviour?"

Astonishingly, he sounded as if he meant it. Now, it was their hostess who seemed armoured in suspicion and hostility. *Please*, Sam prayed silently. *Please forgive him, and forget all about this trivial misunderstanding, so that we can get on with finding Mary!*

There was an agonising pause, before Mistress Paradice spoke, her head tilted and her jaw set in a manner which indicated that her forgiveness was a commodity most dearly bought. "Yes, Mr. Dark, I am prepared to forgive you for the delusions under which you have been labouring these past few days. Will you not sit down again, sir, and take some more chocolate? There is much that we need to discuss."

CHAPTER FIVE

'The jolting Coach'

Before dawn, the courtyard of the Bell in the Strand was a place of confused bustle and noise, erratically illuminated by lanthorns which cast huge eerie shadows across the galleried walls. The Bristol coach stood waiting in the midst of the cobbles, its ponderous bulk seeming to absorb, selfishly, almost all of the light. Sam, a seasoned passenger on all manner of stagecoaches and other conveyances, surveyed it with a sense of resignation. He disliked the tedium of such journeys, cooped up for days on end with people who might be unpleasant, malodorous, irritating or simply boring: but in the absence of wings, this was the quickest method yet devised of transporting travellers from one side of the country to the other, if they did not wish to go on horseback, which he most assuredly did not.

It was a great pity that they were too late in the year for the Flyer, but it ran only between Lady Day and Michaelmas, which had fallen just yesterday. This was the same coach and the same horses, but it set out later in the morning, at six o'clock instead of four, in deference to the dwindling hours of daylight. To secure their seats, he and Dark had spent the night at the Bell, and had been woken an hour before departure by a yawning maid. The hot coffee and fresh rolls she brought them had effectively separated Sam from his sleepiness, and now he stood in the yard, clapping his hands together in the cold air, wondering what would lie at the end of this journey. In three days, perhaps even two, they would be in Bristol. And he would, please God, find Mary before she and her lover moved on, as seemed likely.

Wondering where Dark was, he glanced curiously at the

coach, and those who would share their journey. A man in parson's black, thin and threadbare, with a sour, suspicious face, was clambering awkwardly up the steps, and he could see the dim shapes of several other people already inside. A groom was dumping the last bags into the huge wicker basket suspended behind the coach, and the maid who had woken them, still yawning, stood by the door and began to ring a handbell to warn all remaining passengers of its imminent departure.

"I thought you were in a hurry to go to Bristol," said Dark's amused voice, just behind him. "I should board now, unless you want to run behind it all the way to Brentford and beyond."

"If we leave it to the last minute," Sam pointed out, "we will have the window seats, and the chance of some fresh air."

"I bow to your superior knowledge," said Dark, walking with him to the steps. "Certainly, I would prefer to wedge myself against the side of the coach, rather than be crushed between Scylla and Charybdis. After you, Mr. Jessop."

So it was Sam who saw the other passengers first. The parson had just taken his seat in the middle of the forward-facing bench, and was looking round with self-righteous disapproval. A young couple occupied the further corner. And opposite them, next to the parson, sat a most delightful lady, neatly and elegantly dressed, a warm blue velvet mantle round her slender shoulders, and a pretty straw hat perched on the top of her soft dark hair. She smiled in welcome as Sam ducked through the door, and said sweetly, "Good morning, Mr. Jessop. How pleasant it is, to have friends share a journey."

Astonished, Sam fell rather than sat on the narrow space on the parson's nearer side. He could not help glancing at the door, and saw that Dark was similarly dumbfounded. Ignoring the inquisitive stares of the other occupants of the coach, he said to Mistress Paradice, "What the devil are you doing here?"

"Oh, dear," said the young woman, with a mischievous look of dismay. "I am *so* sorry, sir – did I not say that I intended travelling with you? That was *very* remiss of me, and I *do* most humbly beg your pardon."

There was nothing that could possibly be said to this without exposing their private business to the other passengers, and Dark obviously realised it. He sat down in the remaining space, opposite Sam, and the look he sent Mistress Paradice would have frozen the seas of Hell.

It was not going to be a comfortable trip.

* * *

The sun rose above the autumnal mists as the Bristol coach rattled urgently through the streets and out into the country. Sam, compressed into his corner seat, trying to avoid Parson Shenley's skinny elbows and the rank blast of his breath, paid scant attention to his neighbour's complaints about the journey, though he remembered to grunt pretended assent whenever a comment was directed at him. Dark, his long body compressed into the limited space next to her, had taken refuge in sleep, real or feigned. As for Mistress Paradice, she sat smiling and apparently oblivious: it was obvious that her thoughts were elsewhere. Sam, brimming with unsatisfied curiosity, wondered why she had come. Surely she could have no interest in the whereabouts of Mary Jessop, beyond the admittedly rather vague directions she had given Sam and Dark the previous day. But she must have some good reason, for no-one in their right mind would subject themselves to the discomfort, indignities and even dangers of a long journey for no purpose. He remembered Dark's suspicions, and set his shrewd mind to considering the implications. Of course there could be a perfectly innocent explanation, but in such troubled times, with Jacobite riots breaking out all over the country, and the Pretender's standard raised in Scotland, perhaps there was something deeper and more sinister lurking in this murky pot.

And he still had not properly fathomed Dark. He could guess, though, how the delectable Mistress Paradice had acquired her comfortable circumstances, for her pretty face and trim figure were obviously her fortune. Whoever her protector might be, however, he must have no idea of what she was doing. Wealthy men did not usually allow their mistresses such freedom.

Happily unmolested, the coach crossed Hounslow Heath, a notorious roost of highwaymen according to Parson Shenley, who looked unaccountably disappointed when no gentlemen of the road appeared, and rolled into Colnbrook a few miles further on. This was their first scheduled stop, and they would have perhaps half an hour to stretch their legs and take some refreshment while a new team of horses was harnessed. Sam stumbled with relief down the steps, rubbing his aching back, and went at once in search of a necessary house. At least the journey so far had been uneventful, but there were a hundred miles and many hours left. And at the end of it, perhaps, he would find Mary.

He emerged from the pungent shack at the far end of the inn's yard, doing up the last button on his breeches, and hoping there would be hot coffee waiting. In front of him, the six horses who had pulled the coach from London were being led away, their heads hanging and flanks dark with sweat, while ostlers waited with the fresh team, already harnessed. There was no sign of the other passengers, so he negotiated the crowded, muddy yard and found an open doorway leading inside.

There were two people just within, arguing in the hissing, vehement voices of those who do not wish their entire business to be heard by all and sundry. Sam was not in the least surprised to see Dark, standing with his back to the door, looming menacingly over the slight, undaunted figure of Mistress Paradice.

"It's none of your business, Madam," he was saying as Sam checked on the step. "You are not wanted on this journey."

"I'm afraid you will just have to put up with me, Mr. Dark," said Polly Paradice, quite unintimidated, though the top of her straw hat barely came up to his ear. "There is no law, so far as I am aware, which dictates that I should not travel on whatever coach I please, and so I am exercising my right to go when and where I choose." She eyed him challengingly. "In any case, you need me to tell you where Miss Jessop is."

There was a brief, heated pause. "You told us yesterday that she was living in Queen's Square, in Bristol," Dark said, as Sam listened, his heart in his throat. "Was that a lie?"

"I am not bringing you on a wild-goose-chase, sir," Mistress Paradice said. "I pray you will trust me. At the end of this journey, we will find Miss Jessop, I promise you. Have no fear, sir," she added, spotting Sam lurking behind Dark. "I am not misleading you. Once we are in Bristol, I will help you find your daughter."

"Then why did you not tell us in London, and save yourself the expense of the coach fare?" demanded Dark furiously.

"I had a fancy to go on a jaunt," said Polly Paradice, with that sweet reasonableness which, all too obviously, her adversary found so infuriating. "A lady's whim, you may choose to call it." She glanced coyly up at him, and fluttered her impossibly long eyelashes.

"I regret to say that I have no interest whatsoever in your wiles, madam," Dark said, his voice more cutting than Sam had ever heard it. "And if I find that you have been less than honest with us, I will not scruple to punish you as you deserve."

"What possible right do you have to judge me?" Mistress Paradice demanded furiously. "I am sure that you, sir, are hardly without sin. I should go in search of your breakfast, before this pointless dispute leads to something that poor Mr. Jessop may regret." She moved aside so that Dark could pass her, and smiled enchantingly at Sam. "I hope that you at least, sir, have no quarrel with my presence here."

"If you can help me find my daughter, Mistress Paradice, then you may accompany me to the ends of the earth," said Sam, with complete sincerity.

For a moment, the lovely dark blue eyes, the colour of the evening sky, or of the plant called Monk's Hood, beautiful and deadly, looked into his. There was no flirtatiousness in them now, only an expression of direct sympathy. "We will find her," she said. "But first, I am going to track down a dish of coffee and some of that cake this inn is famous for. Will you accompany me, Mr. Jessop?"

All too soon, the call came to summon them back to the coach, and they were ushered outside. For an instant, as he climbed the steps behind Mistress Paradice, Sam thought that Dark had decided to abandon the quest. But even as he sat down in his allotted place, the artist appeared in the doorway, with a face fit to curdle milk, and squeezed inside. The door was shut, the driver shouted to the horses, and with a rumble of iron-shod wheels, they embarked on the next stage of their journey.

Despite the almost constant rain that had fallen for weeks, today was fine and bright, with a chill in the air that presaged the onset of winter. Dragged by the six fresh horses, the coach lurched briskly through ruts and puddles, past trees tinged russet by autumn, and villages full of gawping yokels. After a particularly bumpy stretch, Parson Shenley expressed a wish that every important highway in the country could be turnpiked with speed, to ease travel and commerce. It was the first time he had uttered words that were not a complaint, and as this was a subject dear to Sam's heart, they fell to discussing the best means of repairing the roads. Dark, silent in his corner, made no attempt to join in, but pointedly closed his eyes, repelling all attempts to involve him in conversation with a dismissive grunt. In anyone else, Sam thought ruefully, such behaviour would have been described as 'sulking'.

Near midday they arrived in Maidenhead, where they were to dine. The coach negotiated the crowded market outside and stopped with an abrupt jolt in the inn yard. The other passengers disembarked, and Dark caught Sam's eye. "Are you hungry, Mr. Jessop? For myself, I'm pretty sharp-set, I must admit."

"Then you have not yet tasted humble pie," said Mistress Paradice tartly. "A dish not at all to your liking, I suspect. Now, are you going to unblock the way and let me alight, or have you left all gentlemanly behaviour behind?"

For a moment, Dark's face remained in its habitual stony mould. Then, with the suddenness of sun breaking through clouds, he grinned. "Not entirely, madam – though I will confess that you have sorely tried my patience today. And since you obviously have no intention of taking the next conveyance back to London, I suppose I must accept your company with good grace. So may we call a truce?"

"Very prettily put, sir," Polly Paradice said, with a dimple quivering in one perfect, peach-downed cheek. "Indeed we may. And if I promise not to be coy, or to simper, or to practice my feminine wiles on your stony masculine heart, then will you also promise not to be impolite, abrupt, and so uninformative that an oyster would seem a blabbermouth beside you?"

"Done," said Dark, holding out his hand.

After a brief, significant pause, she took it. "But can I rely on your assurances?"

"Of course you may – you have my word of honour, as a gentleman," Dark said, and Sam, seeing the uncharacteristic mischief in his face, realised suddenly that he had decided to play his beautiful adversary at her own game.

Whatever that might be, he thought as he ducked through the narrow door of the coach and made his awkward way down the steps behind Mistress Paradice's elegant figure. He had assumed that Dark was the leader of their little expedition. And instead, they were both dancing to the silent, mysterious tune of a woman who seemed to have taken their quest for Mary and turned it into something else entirely.

Dark overtook them, and went inside the inn to bespeak their dinner. As Sam hesitated, wondering if he needed to visit the privy beforehand, a loud commotion broke out at the rear of the coach. "Get out of it, you thieving little runt! God damn it, I'll break your neck!"

He turned, but Mistress Paradice was already running towards the noise. Sam followed, in time to see one of the inn's grooms flinging what looked like a bundle of rags onto the unyielding stones of the yard. But it was not a bundle of rags, because it yelped, and tried to crawl away as the man, a big brute in a leather apron, kicked it viciously in the ribs, again and again.

"Stop that! Stop that at once, do you hear, or I'll make you sorry!" Polly Paradice dodged in front of the man and, with astonishing bravado, put her small pale hands flat on his broad chest and pushed him back. "Leave him alone! You should be ashamed of yourself!"

Amazed at this unexpected onslaught by a woman who barely came up to his shoulder, the groom staggered and nearly fell. "I were only giving him a good hiding, what he deserves," he objected. "Found him in the rumble-tumble, ma'am, a-stealing of your bags."

"I never!" The bundle of rags sat up. It was a child, its face bruised and swollen, streaked with clean skin where tears had fallen, smeared with blood from a split lip and a cut somewhere beneath the lank, filthy hair. Suddenly Sam realised why the snivelling voice sounded familiar. "Gin?" he said, horrified. "What's happened?"

"I'm all right," said the boy, with some pride. "Takes more'n some cake-headed pig like him to get the better of *me*!" He tried to get up, but dropped to his hands and knees, coughing and retching.

"I'll shut your gob for you, you thieving little pikey!" the groom shouted, and pushed Polly to one side, the better to reach his victim. It was a grievous mistake, for as he lunged forward, she moved her foot to intercept him. The big man crashed cursing to the ground and lay at her feet, groaning in pain and disbelief.

"I prefer men to be properly respectful to their fellow creatures," said Mistress Paradice, her hands on her hips and her hair in dark tendrils round her face. She was breathing hard, and her cheeks were bright with fury. "If you lay *one more finger* on that child, you'll be sorry you ever saw the light of day. Now get out of my sight, or I'll tell the landlord you attacked me, and then you'll be out on the street. Go on, go!"

She was so small, so pretty, so incandescent with rage, that it might have been ridiculous, but the big groom, shaking his head stupidly, clambered to his feet and staggered off, his stockings torn and his breeches liberally smeared with dirt. At once, Polly turned and bent over the child, and to Sam's surprise her voice was not in the least sympathetic. "*Were* you nimming the bags?"

Mutely, Gin shook his head. Blood from his cut mouth

spattered the cobbles. Polly produced a fine lace handkerchief, of the kind that such a boy would delight in stealing, and dabbed briskly at the damage. He gave a muffled, involuntary whimper and then kept still, though there seemed to be more tears than before.

"Gin, what are you doing here?" Sam asked in bewilderment.

"Thought I'd like to see the world afore I die," said Gin, still with that rather desperate air of insolence. "Morning, your honour," he added to Sam. "Nice day, innit?"

"So, you've ridden in the basket from London," said Polly. She straightened up and surveyed the boy she had rescued. "If you make a habit of that, you may not have much time left to see the world. I assume you haven't paid your fare."

"Course not, but I weren't nimming the bags, ma'am, honest! Anyhow, can't hardly lift none of them, so it ain't likely, is it?" Gin stared at her with his one good eye, the other being almost lost in the puffy red flesh surrounding it. "But that bully-cock didn't give me a chance afore he lammed me." He essayed a ghastly grin, revealing several crooked teeth. "Worth it, though, to see his ugly mug when you tripped him. You're a bang-up piece and no mistake."

"And you're in trouble," said Polly cheerfully. "Here comes Mr. Dark."

Inevitably, a crowd of people with nothing better to do had begun to form around the fallen boy, staring and commenting. As Dark shouldered his way through it, Gin's face suddenly lost all its defiant bravado and the flesh seemed to shrink back against the sharp grey bone beneath. "God rat it!" he muttered, and turned his battered head away.

As a defence tactic, it was quite useless. In two swift strides Dark had reached him. He extended a long arm and hauled the boy upright. Something seemed to have happened to Gin's legs: he hung in Dark's grip like a snared rabbit, and with much the same expression on his face. "I had to come, I *had* to, Jemmy Fence was after me!"

"Oh, for God's sake!" Polly Paradice exclaimed in disgust. She marched up to them, wrenched the child out of Dark's grasp and held him, filthy and pest-ridden, close against her immaculate skirts. "Can't you all leave the poor brat alone?"

"You heard her," said Gin, rather muffled by good blue silk. "Leave me alone."

"Do you know this ragamuffin boy?" demanded the coachman, who was one of the people Dark had elbowed aside. "Has he stowed away without paying his fare? If that's so, sir, then perhaps you'd better make it good, or I'll have to take steps."

Polly glanced at Sam. He understood her look perfectly, and moved a couple of paces sideways so that he stood between Dark, now engaged in acrimonious argument with the coachman, and the woman and child. Then she lifted Gin into her arms, turned, and carried him slowly and steadily across the yard.

For a woman so small and slender, Polly Paradice concealed considerable strength in her arms, as she did in her character, and Gin was undersized and undernourished. Even so, her muscles were aching with his weight by the time she reached the stables. He had made no sound of protest as she held him, although his ribs must have been severely bruised, if not broken, by that savage kicking. She laid the child down in the clean straw of an empty stall as gently as if he had been a precious vase of the most delicate China porcelain. He did not move, and his eyes were closed. She said softly, "I'm going to find some water to bathe your face. Don't run away."

She need not have worried. When she returned a few minutes later, with a bowl and cloth and a pot of the landlady's best unguent for bruises, he was still lying exactly as she had left him, and she wondered if he had fainted. If he had, it would make her task easier. She knelt, dipped the cloth in the water, and gently wiped the drying blood away from his mouth. There was no response, and with sudden anxiety she felt for a pulse. *Of course he's not dead,* she thought with relief, feeling the strong steady beat beneath her fingers. Children like Gin were hard to kill. Survival to that age usually indicated a high degree of toughness. She knew, because she too had survived.

When she had finished with the poor battered face, she peeled back the filthy rags that might once have been a good damask waistcoat and a Holland shirt of some quality, wrinkling her nose at the sour stench. Then she paused, and the look of compassion on her face changed to something else. And in that space, the child's eyes opened, squinting dubiously up at her. "Mrs Paradice?"

"Yes. And you're Gin, aren't you? You've lit my chair a few times."

"Mrs Paradice," said the boy again, his words distorted by the swollen lips. "Just wait till I tell Pocky Tom!"

"If you live that long," said Polly. She dipped the cloth into the bowl again. "This will hurt."

"I ain't no coward – ow!" Gin screwed up his eyes in sudden pain. "Go gentle, ma'am, for pity's sake!"

"Bruised, but nothing broken, I think – you were lucky."

"Lucky!" Gin's voice whistled with indignation. "If that's lucky, I wouldn't want to be *un*lucky!"

"You'd be dead if you were," said Polly. She pulled the cork and the wax seal off the jar and scooped up a liberal helping of ointment in her fingers. "Faugh, that smells foul! So you'll never notice it."

"You saying I stink?"

"Of course you stink. So did I, when I was your age."

"You never! You're a lady!"

"Oh, I can assure you I did. I'm no lady, I'm not well-born, or rich. Once, I was very like you, Gin." She finished rubbing in the ointment and wrapped the dreadful rags once more around the scrawny white body. The seriousness in her face hooked the child's attention as she added softly, "But I was determined to make something of myself, and I was lucky. I took a helping hand and climbed out of the gutter. So can you, if you're willing."

Gin's eyes were a sort of muddy brown, at one with his hair and at odds with the bruised pallor of his face. He said hoarsely, "You saw, didn't you."

Polly nodded.

Tears had begun to slide down his face, but he ignored them. "Please, Mistress Paradice, *please* don't tell him!"

"Dark? Doesn't he know?"

Incautiously, Gin shook his head, and winced. "No, he don't, and I don't want him to neither. Nobody does. Please, ma'am, promise me you won't tell him!"

"He's sure to find out in the end," Polly pointed out reasonably. "But don't worry, I've no intention of letting him know anything more than is absolutely necessary."

Dark's voice above them both enquired caustically, "Are you by any chance, Mistress Paradice, referring to me?"

In one swift, graceful movement, Polly rose to her feet and turned to face him. Her voice absolutely controlled and her eyes bright hard chips of lapis, she said, "Leave him alone. He's been beaten half to death by that brute, and the last thing he needs is you, sir, hanging over him like a magistrate."

"Fear not, madam, I am not going to subject the boy to some heartless inquisition."

"Now," Gin muttered darkly from the straw.

"Now, or later," Dark said. "I've paid the money for carrying you to Bristol. In the rumble-tumble."

"In the basket?" Polly said, appalled. "Half his hurts come from being shaken about in there with all the bags falling on top of him."

"Perhaps, but there's no room inside the coach. And since from now on his ride will be legitimate, we can pack him in with greater care. Or shall we leave him here, to the tender mercies of those grooms?"

After a pause, Polly shook her head emphatically. "It pains me to say so, sir, but you are right. We must take him with us."

"I'm glad to hear you admit it," said Dark, with one of the lightning grins that carved deep grooves of laughter in his face, and made him look quite different. "In any case, don't forget, Gin is not some softly-reared sprig of the gentry. He's used to hardship."

"Don't mean I don't like feather-bedding now an' again," said the irrepressible urchin.

Certainly the luggage basket slung behind the coach was no feather-bed, but by the time Dark, with Sam's and Polly's assistance, had packed it with straw and rearranged the passengers' baggage so that it no longer seemed likely to topple over at the first jolt, much of Gin's usual bravado had returned and the child was sitting wedged between two boxes, eating a cold pie. Sam had procured this from the dining room, along with a basket full of food that his companions could consume on the journey, since the coach was now ready to leave and there was no time left for dinner.

It was quite plain that their fellow travellers and most of the people at the inn thought they were mad not to hand Gin over to the local constable, leave alone buy him food and pay his fare, but the landlady proved a more kindly soul: just as Polly was about to climb into the coach, she came running out with a bundle. "Here, ma'am, these were my Joe's but he's grown too big for them. They're shabby, but so much better than what that child's wearing." And as Polly took the clothes and thanked her, she added in a low voice, "You saved the poor boy's life, I reckon. I'll see that brute gets turned off without a character – I never liked him, and he knocks the horses about when he thinks no-one can see. God bless you, ma'am!"

Once more squashed into the coach, and well-fortified by as much food and drink as they had managed to swallow in their dinner break, the passengers resumed their journey. Sam distributed the enticingly aromatic contents of his basket between himself, Dark and Polly, and even gave some apple pie to the parson, who consumed it hungrily, scattering crumbs down his grimy neckcloth and across his inadequate lap. Polly, eating with rather more delicacy, wondered how Gin was faring, bounced around with the luggage in the aptly named rumble-tumble. When she had finished a very palatable mutton pasty, and fastidiously wiped the gravy from her lips with her kerchief, she turned to Dark, who was sitting opposite, his arms folded and his legs tucked beneath the bench seat, looking out at the passing scenery. "I am curious, sir, about that boy. Has he no family?"

"Gin? No, his mother is long dead, and God alone knows who his father was."

"Then you are not?" said Polly, her perfect eyebrows raised in what Sam, eating his second pasty, considered to be foolhardy provocation.

To his surprise, Dark only laughed. "No, I am not. If I had a son, I would at least ensure that he was kept fed and clothed and warm. He's a bulker."

"A bulker?" Sam asked curiously. "What's that?"

"A child who sleeps on the bulks, the wooden boards outside shops," said Dark. "They earn a living any way they can, whether honestly or, more likely, not. Like Gin, some are link-boys – others run errands or shine shoes or sweep the roads. Most of them thieve as well. Or go whoring in molly-houses. In Covent Garden, there is always something you can sell, and someone willing to buy it from you."

"But he is surely more than just your usual link-boy?" Sam enquired, taking advantage of Dark's temporary affability. "From the little I have seen of you and him together, I would say that you have some concern for him."

Obviously aware of Polly's bright-eyed scrutiny, Dark said casually, "He did me a good turn once, so I look out for him. There is nothing more to our relationship than that." He added wickedly, with a glance at the parson, "He's not my bum-boy, if that's what you're implying."

"Indeed I was not, sir," said Sam, obviously shocked, as was Parson Shenley, though Mistress Paradice did not seem in the least offended. "I was merely curious, and I apologise unreservedly."

"Don't worry, Jessop," Dark said dryly. "I've had far worse accusations flung at me, for no greater reason. No, Gin is merely a casual acquaintance, and today he has presumed on that acquaintance too far. I may live to regret Mistress Paradice's inconvenient act of mercy."

"I pray you will not, sir – not if I have any say in the matter," Polly said. She did not want to like the man, his manner could be rude and offensive in the extreme, and yet that sudden way he had, of climbing down from his high horse with a humorous word or a quick smile, was strangely appealing, giving glimpses of quite another person behind the arrogance and discourtesy. "If it is the cost of his excursion that concerns you, sir, then I am perfectly happy to reimburse you."

"I may well take you up on that offer," said Dark, who had reverted to his habitually forbidding expression. Pointedly, he folded his arms and closed his eyes, repelling all further attempts at conversation.

Sam gave her a sympathetic glance, but did not seem inclined to add anything. Parson Shenley sucked his decaying teeth and took out his tattered little book of sermons. As the Bristol coach bumped and swayed towards its next halt, Polly continued to ponder the problem of Gin. Was Dark really unaware of something that now seemed, to her, so obvious? She studied the lean, closed visage opposite her thoughtfully. It was not a face that invited confidences, or encouraged anyone to come too close. But she knew, even from her limited contact with him so far, that he was as observant and perceptive as his profession would indicate. So why had he apparently not noticed?

But of course many otherwise intelligent men, and women, were curiously oblivious to things that seemed to others plainly transparent. Even Sam Jessop, so sensible and down-to-earth, seemed to have a blind spot where his beloved daughter was concerned. Dark had evidently taken Gin purely at face value. And some less worthy part of her would enjoy seeing his expression when he found out the truth.

Smiling to herself, she addressed her mind to the question of what was to happen to the child, and by the time the coach had reached Reading, where they were to spend the night, she had resolved on a course of action. It might not be agreeable to Dark, still less to Gin, but she was convinced that it was the right thing to do.

The occupants of the Bristol coach were accommodated at the Crown, one of Reading's finest, oldest and most famous inns. Gin, who had survived the journey in the rumble-tumble with almost all that annoying insolence intact, slunk off to a quiet corner of the stables with the bundle of clothes that Polly had been given at Maidenhead. The others, being mere stage-coach passengers, expected to be served with their supper in the public dining room. To Sam's surprise, however, Mistress Paradice had a few quiet words with the waiter, money changed hands discreetly, and a few moments later he, Dark and Polly were ushered into a small private parlour, finely furnished with a walnut table and upholstered chairs, with a well-established fire burning warm and cheerful in the grate.

"You are remarkably free with your coin, Mistress Paradice," Dark said, stepping over to the blaze and holding his hands out to it.

"I beg your pardon, sir – if you would rather, I can call the waiter back and have him give us a table alongside everyone else," said Polly rather tartly. "For myself, I don't think I could bear to listen to Parson Shenley's sanctimonious complaints for a single moment longer. And if you are not of the same persuasion, Mr. Dark, then you are a great deal more tolerant than your manner would suggest."

"I am very grateful to you, Mistress Paradice," Sam said hastily, seeing that Dark seemed rather taken aback by this onslaught. "Congenial company, a good supper and an early night, what could be more pleasant? Most thoughtful of you, ma'am."

They were served with a roast leg of lamb, a splendid stuffed carp, and a chicken fricassee in the French style, washed down with plentiful wine. The Crown was noted for the quality and expense of its fare, but Sam, like Polly, was happy to pay extra for additional comfort. They ate hungrily and in silence, until the waiter came to remove the remains of their first course, and two flushed maids whisked in bearing hot pies and puddings, jugs of cream and glasses of syllabub. With the edge taken off their appetite, the travellers had leisure and energy to talk: and Mistress Paradice, with a markedly unfeminine boldness, was quick to broach the subject that had been in the forefront of her mind all that afternoon.

"Gin? *I*, have plans for *Gin*?" Dark abandoned his plum pie, a very good one flavoured with spices and port, and stared at her with some amusement and considerable condescension.

"Well, if you have not, then I have," she told him. "I have decided to take him into my household. I have need of someone to run errands."

Dark gave an astonished bark of laughter. "Take *Gin* into your household? You might as well stack all your silver on the doorstep and invite passers-by to help themselves. The child's an incorrigible thief."

"I think there is hope for him. He doesn't want to continue in his present life, I'm sure of that."

"On the basis of a few moments' conversation? My dear lady, I have known Gin for years, and a more intransigent young rogue never breathed. Why are you so concerned for the brat? Has he touched your tender female heart?"

"You condescend to me at your peril, sir," said Polly, surveying him challengingly over her wine-glass. She was so sorely tempted to tell him Gin's secret, and wipe that superior smile from his face, but she had promised the child, and she would stick to it, for she herself had been betrayed too often. "If that is what you wish to think, Mr. Dark, then you may continue in your comfortable delusion."

He laughed. "Then your generosity obviously knows no bounds."

"In that you are mistaken, sir," said Polly, flushed and very pretty by the light of fire and candle. "And perhaps you may one day discover that it does."

CHAPTER SIX

'She'll lead them with delusive Smiles along'

Bristol was the first port and city in the kingdom after London, and a place of great wealth and trade. From the hills above, it was a charming prospect, the neat green fields and market gardens sloping down to the red roofs of innumerable houses, spiked with the grey towers and spires of its nineteen churches. As travellers soon discovered, however, at closer quarters the city itself was not so enchanting. Surrounded on three sides by the winding rivers Avon and Frome, its ancient heart was packed tight with buildings like salt herrings in a barrel, all straining up from the filthy streets to the sky above. The merchants, parsimonious with space, dug vaults and cellars beneath their houses and streets to store their goods, with the result that carts and wagons were forbidden in case they fell through to the caverns below, and curious sleds, piled high with sacks, barrels or bales, ran slickly along the cobbles and wore them so smooth that wet weather proved the downfall of many unwary pedestrians.

And it was certainly wet. The coach had lumbered through innumerable potholes and ruts, puddles that were the size of young lakes, and its leather-covered body and red-painted wheels dripped copious mud and water. The second half of the journey had proved less eventful than the first, and despite the rain which fell steadily for most of the daylight hours, they had made steady progress, reaching Bristol late in the evening.

All the passengers were heartily glad to arrive safely at journey's end. The state of the roads (lumpy and bumpy), the state of his bed in the Crown in Reading (lumpy and lousy), and the breakfast (lumpy and cold), had occupied Parson Shenley, to the tedium and irritation of his travelling companions, for most of the second day. Indeed, as Dark had descended from the coach in the courtyard of the White Hart at Marlborough, where they had dined, he had glanced back at Sam and said, *sotto voce*, "I haven't often been tempted to break the Sixth Commandment, but so help me God, I wish I could wrap my fingers round that parson's scrawny neck!"

Perhaps the only member of the party unaffected by the parson's carping verbosity was Gin, perilously perched in the basket, and therefore well out of earshot. Clad in those fresh garments, which fitted rather better than the previous rags, and inadequately protected from the rain by a couple of sacks, the child still looked only marginally less disreputable than before, especially with a splendid black eye and cruelly split lip.

So it was with relief that they came within sight of Bristol, in its dusk-filled bowl of green hills and winding silver rivers, with the mountains of Wales dim and blue behind a veil of drizzle, and a lowering cloud from some of the new glass furnaces which were dotted about on the outskirts of the city. They passed through the Lawford Gate and into a bustling street, lined with shops and still crowded with people. The exhausted horses hauled the coach through the crush, while the noise of hawkers crying their wares mixed with the rumble of traffic. None of the passengers seemed to have much curiosity about the place which they had taken two long days to reach: bruised by the jolts, sickened by the swinging, swaying ride, they stumbled wearily down the steps and into the welcoming warmth of their destination.

A wash, a quick supper and a comfortable bed was all they felt fit for that night. But the next morning, well rested and refreshed by the ingestion of salty bacon, coddled eggs, soused herring and copious quantities of extremely good coffee, Sam was able to think of something other than the restoration of his physical well-being. Dark's coin had procured a small parlour for their meal: it was a rather dark and dismal room, and the fire smoked, but at least it was quiet and private.

"Well, sirs," Polly said, looking from one man to the other across the remains of their breakfast, "I take it that you do not wish to spend the whole day decorously indoors, even if it is the Sabbath. So can I count on you to escort me?"

"If it is to find Mary," Sam said, his heart leaping, "then you know that I will."

"Excellent," said Polly, rising to her feet. Today she was wearing a pretty dress of striped blue and white cotton, by some miracle hardly creased at all, and she looked as if she had spent the morning languishing at her levée, tended by devoted maids, and with a dozen adoring admirers at her feet. "And you, sir?" she added, turning to Dark. "Will you join us? Or will you continue to indulge in the sulks?"

"Sulks?" Dark had also risen: beside Sam and Polly, he seemed very tall and looming. "Madam, you are sadly mistaken. I ponder the iniquities of life, I plan complicated and devious acts of revenge, but I certainly do not sulk."

Polly smiled brilliantly at the artist. "Really?" she said, taking his arm with a boldness that rather shocked Sam. "Then you have misled me indeed, sir. I could have sworn that you were sulking, all the way from London. Ever since first seeing me in the coach, in fact. And when we found Gin, you certainly gave a most excellent impression of sulkiness. Have you ever considered appearing on the stage, Mr. Dark? For if you have not, it's a talent sorely gone to waste."

"Perhaps we ought to be going," Sam interrupted anxiously, wondering if Dark was about to explode in fury, or to laugh: it was impossible to tell which, for his expression seemed graven in granite. "If Mary is indeed here, I would very much like to find her as soon as possible."

"Then you must excuse me for a short while," Dark said.

"I have a brief errand, and someone I must speak to, an old friend. I won't be long – wait here for me." He disengaged his arm, bowed briefly and went out, leaving Polly looking at Sam with her eyebrows raised.

"What an impossible man!" she said, with a wry smile that robbed the words of any incivility. "Have you known him for very long, Mr. Jessop?"

"A few days only," Sam told her, sitting down again. He had not quite finished his last cup of coffee, and there were a couple of rashers of bacon left. "Forgive me," he added belatedly. "But I still seem to be hungry. Have you had sufficient – may I help you to a little more?"

"No, I thank you, sir, I have had enough. Lord, how tired I am, even after a good night's sleep! Some people think nothing of going from one end of the country to the other by coach, but I confess it will be some time before I consider embarking on another jaunt, for any reason save direst necessity. Perhaps we would have been better off on horseback after all – and I have been told that I look rather well in a riding habit." She glanced at him mischievously. "Are you very eager to find your daughter, sir?"

"Of course I am," said Sam, trying to eat with some decorum. "I long to see her and reassure myself that she is well and happy."

"I am sure we will catch up with her - if not today, then very soon. Don't worry, Sam – may I call you Sam? We are surely friends enough now. And you may call me Polly."

"Of course," Sam said, feeling absurdly pleased, as if she had bestowed some great honour on him.

"Thank you." She grinned, and once more he was reminded sharply of Mary. "But I have no inclination, I am sorry to say, to call Mr. Dark 'André'. Do you not find him a puzzle, Sam? He seems so daunting, so abrupt in his manner, and then suddenly you catch a glimpse of someone quite different hidden behind it, like the sun behind storm-clouds – or, more likely, those dull grey skies that stretch from horizon to horizon, with scarcely a break."

"I'm glad he isn't here to listen to you describe him so unflatteringly," Sam said, a little uncomfortable at having his friend, if Dark *was* his friend, thus freely discussed.

"I don't intend to slander him," Polly said. She was frowning, her face suddenly earnest and thoughtful. "I am sure he means well – after all, he is helping you to find your daughter, I presume out of the goodness of his heart, so he cannot be all winter weather. After he arrived at my house that first time, I took the liberty of finding out something of his past." She glanced at Sam, evidently wondering how he would receive this information. "You may think I have been prying, sir, but I was convinced that he was engaged upon some nefarious purpose, and I thought I should discover if what he had told me was correct. So I ... made enquiries."

She paused, and Sam said encouragingly, "Pray continue." He could not help being curious, and although Dark had let slip one or two tantalising hints and teasing snippets of information, yet he was still no nearer discovering much of the artist's past history, or his present circumstances. "He told me that his father was a Huguenot, whatever that is."

"Huguenots are French Protestants, driven out of France by the last King Louis. Dark's father took himself and his trade of silversmithing first to Holland, and then to London. Dark was born in Amsterdam, the second son, and he was only a baby when they arrived in England. There is an older brother who has followed in the family business. Dark was also intended for it, but rebelled, and went for a soldier in Marlborough's wars. He was hurt at one of the battles, Malplaquet I think, and came back to London penniless, for his father had disowned him. So he set himself up as a portrait painter, and he has quite a reputation." She grinned at him. "For painting an excellent likeness, of course, Sam. But I've heard he led a very wild life, for a time. You'd never think it now, would you? He is so grim and serious."

Sam thought of the whores who knew his name, and the child Gin who had once apparently done him a good turn, and could well believe it. Thinking aloud, he said, "At least if he is a good Protestant, he can't be a Jacobite spy. I must admit, the idea had crossed my mind."

"Really? No, I would never have set him down for a Jack. Parson Shenley, now, is another matter – he has 'Non-Juror' written all over him, don't you think?"

This had already occurred to Sam, who was no lover of anyone who refused to recognise the lawful authority of the new King. He said, "Certainly he looks far too poor and threadbare to have charge of any parish. But I can't imagine that he would find much of a welcome here in Bristol. The city has a long and honourable Dissenting tradition. There *are* Tories, of course, but they are very much in the minority."

"In the West Country as a whole, though, I understand they are not," said Polly. "Anyway, Parson Shenley, thank God, is no longer any concern of ours. Shall I fetch my cloak? And then we may leave as soon as Dark returns."

For Sam, waiting in a silent frenzy of impatience, it seemed an age before the familiar, black-clad figure of his friend appeared in the parlour doorway. "Ready, Jessop? Where's Mistress Paradice?"

"Here, sir," said Polly, arriving behind him. She was wearing her long, dark blue velvet mantle, the hood trimmed with soft grey fur, and carrying a matching hand muff and a folded umbrella, insurance against any rain which might dare to threaten. "We have been waiting for you this age, Dark. Poor Sam feared he might take root before you reappeared."

"She is exaggerating," said Sam, once more uneasy at her change of manner, which seemed designed to provoke Dark's temper. "Shall we go?"

"It would help to know *where* we are going," Dark pointed out. "In case this proves to be another wild-goose-chase."

"To Queen's Square, as I explained," she told him as she led the way out into the street. "And since it lies on the other side of the city, and it looks very much as if rain is about to fall, shall we step out?"

Polly walked remarkably quickly: Sam, used to women who sauntered and strolled, had to lengthen his stride to keep up with her. She seemed to know her way about, which surprised him, although he remembered that she had been born not far from here. With graceful agility, she threaded through streets crowded with people, sledges and packhorses, and although Dark's long stride remained the same, Sam soon found himself almost trotting. The day was not warm, and rain was indeed falling fitfully now, but a hot sweat broke out on his forehead, and the scalp under his wig began to prickle. He did not complain, only hurried in her brisk wake, for every step brought him closer to his daughter. Although he was not very familiar with Bristol, he knew that Queen's Square was its smartest area, a beautiful tree-shaded place inhabited only by the very rich. Why should Mary have found refuge there? His fertile imagination, still clinging to hope, supplied one possible answer. Perhaps she had left the Frenchman, and resolved to make her own way in the world. Could she have taken service with some wealthy family?

In all honesty, he could not imagine his wilful girl as a maidservant. She had been far too impatient of instruction, far too intent on her own way. *But perhaps she has truly repented*, he thought desperately. *Perhaps her experiences have shown her the error of her conduct, before it is too late.*

It was not likely. He knew Mary far too well to place much faith in such a reversal of character. But all he had left was hope, and so he clung to it like a drowning man.

Mistress Paradice led them straight down the gravel walks, under the dripping trees, to the furthest side. "Apparently it's that one," she said, indicating a most splendid building, four storeys high, ornate and extremely grand. "At least the rain has stopped, for the moment, so you won't get any wetter while you wait."

She sent them a brilliant smile, and walked towards the house. A low wall, topped with iron railings, separated it from the street. Polly opened the elaborately decorated gate as confidently as if she were a duchess, and swept graciously up to the front door, painted a rich dark green with a fanlight above. She closed her umbrella, rapped smartly on the bronze knocker and stepped back.

It was opened almost immediately by a footman in lavish blue and gold livery. He was very tall, and his powdered wig contrasted strongly with his black skin. Of course, here in Bristol, hub of the trade in sugar, tobacco and slaves, African servants were as common as in fashionable London homes. There was a brief, lively conversation, and then the footman stepped aside to let her in. The door shut behind them, and Dark and Sam were left under the dripping, gloomy trees, to await her return.

For Sam, at least, the wait was agonising. The longer Polly stayed within the house, the more likely it seemed that Mary must be inside as well: and yet he could not understand why, if that were so, they had been left to cool their heels in the square. Their vigil was largely silent, and once the first fever of urgency had subsided, Sam tried to occupy the time by pacing up and down beneath the trees, and rehearsing in his mind what he would say to Mary when he saw her. Despite everything, he would not, *could* not, be angry. He would just be so very glad that she was safe.

Dark proved to have other means of keeping tedium at bay. From his coat pocket, he produced a small flat rectangle of polished wood, put a piece of paper on top of it, and began to draw. Sam was too apprehensive, too wrapped up in his own thoughts and emotions, to pay much attention at first, but on one of his pacings he glanced over and saw that it was a sketch of the houses in the square. Evidently Dark's talent was not just limited to faces, for the accuracy was astonishing, and as far as Sam could gauge in one glimpse, he had not yet made a single error of proportion or perspective. It was a perfect representation, and yet, in the swift lively strokes that indicated the trees and sky, there was also the humanity and warmth that had been conspicuous by their absence in his manner today.

There was a sound, and he looked up, but it was a maid returning from some errand. When she saw the two men, she stopped and gave them a long, hard stare, before going into a house a few doors along from the one into which Polly had vanished some time before.

"If we loiter here much longer," Dark said drily, "we shall be taken up on suspicion of eaves-dropping." He saw Sam's bewildered look, and added, "Watching to see which houses are empty, so that we can rob them. I'm sure that Gin could give you a thorough grounding in the techniques."

"Where is Gin?" Sam asked, suddenly remembering that he had not seen the child since their arrival in Bristol.

"Oh, enjoying an undeserved rest in the inn stables, I expect," Dark said. There was a flurry of movement from his fingers and Sam, watching with fascination, saw the maidservant, nose in the air, basket over her arm and her heels kicking up her skirt, spring pertly to life on the paper, courtesy of a stick of plumbago and a wickedly observant eye.

"With a gift like that," Sam said in awe, "you could have all London at your feet."

"Instead of eking out a living in a few rooms in Half Moon Street? It doesn't seem to have occurred to you, my dear Jessop, that I might not desire fame and fortune. As long as I have a roof over my head and enough money for the necessities of life, with perhaps a little over to spend on the pleasures, then I am content."

"Don't you think it wasteful?" Sam asked, distracted from his fever of anticipation. "After all, God has given you this talent, and it's surely wrong to hide it under a bushel."

"Well, if you ever find yourself in the pit at Drury Lane, look up. No bushels there."

"You have painted the theatre ceiling?"

"Only parts of it – the parts that require a modicum of skill and the need to produce convincing representations of objects and people. Sometimes, I paint the scenery as well. It's hardly demanding work, but Cibber pays handsomely."

Beyond them, a door slammed, and Sam's head came round like a stag's at the sound of danger. He moved forward, so that he had a clear view of the green door, and then stopped.

Polly Paradice was coming down the steps, alone. She seemed to be moving with even more lightness than before, but on her pale, lovely face there lay an expression compounded at once of relief, and apprehension, and guilt. She closed the gate behind her with a soft, metallic click, and walked swiftly across the cobbles to where Sam and Dark stood together under the trees.

"She isn't there," Sam said flatly. He knew it, he had always known it, he thought with dull misery – yet another wild-goose-chase, all that effort and fear and hope expended to no purpose.

"No, she isn't," said Polly, coming to a halt in front of them. "I'm sorry, Sam – I have dragged you across Bristol in vain."

"And you knew it was in vain, didn't you?" Dark said. "You've known ever since we set out from London that Miss Jessop wasn't in Bristol – don't bother to deny it, I can see it in your face. In God's name, woman, what selfish game are you playing?"

"I'm sorry," said Polly again. "You're right – I have used you both for my own ends, and I'm sorry. I can tell you where she really is, if you want."

"And you'd expect us to believe you?"

Sam took a deep, long breath and tried to calm himself. "Polly, I don't know why you have brought us here, or raised my hopes so high when you knew it was false. But I beg you now, for the sake of the friendship you professed, to be honest with us. *Do* you, really and truly, know where Mary is? *Know*, rather than guess?"

Her eyes, that deep and glorious blue, stared into his, and he saw the unshed tears. Her lips tightened, and she nodded.

Dark gave an exclamation of disgust and caught Sam's sleeve. "Come on, Jessop, there's no point in torturing yourself further. Leave her and let's go."

"She's in Bath," Polly said quickly. "That is the truth, Sam, you may believe me or not as you choose, but she and her lover are in Bath. If we go there, we will certainly find her."

"Please," said Sam, "if it *is* the truth, why did you bring us here instead, on false pretences? What were you doing in that house? And how do you know where Mary is?"

Polly hesitated. Her eyes slid from Sam to Dark and back again. Suddenly, she seemed to come to a decision, and her shoulders squared, as if she had resolved on an unpleasant but necessary duty. "Very well," she said. "I will explain why I brought you here. Let us walk over to the other side of the square, where we will not be so conspicuous."

Sam glanced at Dark, who was still visibly annoyed. He said, "You do not have to believe her, but I do."

"Then you're a fool."

"A fool he may be," Polly interrupted, with a flash of her usual spirit, "but at least he's willing to listen. I'd rather have an open-minded innocent than a blind curmudgeon any day!"

"I take it you're referring to me?" Dark enquired chillingly.

"Of course I am. Well?" she demanded, glaring at him with an unmistakeable challenge in her voice. "Are you coming with us, or not?"

There was a pause, pregnant with all kinds of unpleasant emotions. Then she gave a little laugh, and a dismissive toss of her head, and turned away. "Come on, Sam, let's leave him to stew in his own vinegar."

But as they walked across the square, Sam heard the crunch of footsteps behind them on the gravel, and glanced back to see Dark following them. Polly must have noticed too, but gave no sign of it. She stopped in the centre of the square, where the trees shielded them from curious onlookers in the houses around, and glanced about. Then she slipped her hand inside her mantle, between the silver buttons, and drew out a thick, folded piece of paper.

"There," she said, thrusting it at Sam. "That's what I brought you to Bristol for. It might not excuse my conduct, but it will certainly explain it. Go on, Sam – read it."

Bewildered, he took the paper, warm from her skin, and unfolded it. For a moment, the hastily-written words did not make sense, and then, suddenly, he understood.

"Aloud, please, Sam, so that our sulking friend can hear it too."

There was a muffled exclamation from Dark. Obediently, Sam read.

"To whom it may concern:

I, Thomas Edwards, merchant, of Queen's Square in the City of Bristol, do hereby acknowledge the receipt of one hundred guineas from Mrs Mary Paradice, in full and final payment for the purchase of Hannah Rose, a Negro slave in my ownership for ten years.

Signed, Nathaniel Day. Witnessed, Mary Paradice, Joseph Carr."

There was a short silence. Dark said at last, "Is Hannah Rose your maid?"

"She is. She was that man's slave, but ran away. She has been living for nearly a year in mortal terror of him finding her. I promised her that I would buy her from him so that I could set her free, and I have, and I will."

"But why did you need to bring us here?" Dark demanded, and Sam noted that his voice seemed less hostile than previously.

"I did not want to carry a hundred guineas all the way from London by myself," Polly said, reasonably enough, Sam thought. "I needed an escort."

"Would not your burly footmen have sufficed?"

"I have had to dismiss Burton, for various reasons I did not trust him. Hannah begged me not to leave her alone in the house without protection in case her owner tracked her down and abducted her. So I told Evans to stay behind and keep her safe. Of his loyalty to me, I have absolutely no doubt, and besides, he is very fond of Hannah."

"You have not answered Jessop's other question," said Dark. "How do you know that Mary Jessop is in Bath?"

"As I told you in London, I learned it from a friend, and I decided to kill two birds with one stone. I am truly sorry for dragging you here, Sam, but I hope very much that you will forgive me, now that you see I had good reason for it."

"And you paid her owner a hundred guineas?" Dark queried. "That is a fortune for a slave. And in any case, I believe that any slave is free, once they set foot on English soil. You have wasted your money, and our time."

"He was going to send her back to Barbados," Polly said, and her face darkened. "He didn't want to give her up – he is a cruel man, mean and vindictive. That's why she ran away – she was beaten, locked in the cellar, and worse – much worse, I won't go into what else he did to her. Fortunately, the housekeeper took pity on her, gave her some money and allowed her to escape. She made her way to London, and into my employ. Nothing less than such a fortune would have persuaded him to sign this paper, and even then he was reluctant, although he could buy a dozen poor wretches for that price."

"So how did you persuade him?" Dark asked. "What else did you offer him, to tip the balance? No, don't tell me, I can guess."

"Dark – " Sam began, but Polly forestalled him furiously. "What are you implying, sir? Come on, out with it! Say it plain! I offered *myself!* Is that what you mean? And are you surprised? No, you are not, because you believe that a woman in my position can be nothing more than a trollop! Yes, I bought her with gold and with my favours, and I would do it again a hundred times over, because Hannah is my *friend*, and I am glad to pay the price! And in my eyes that is cause for pride, not shame. Have you never done anything for your friends, Dark? Or do you have no friends, because you have driven them all away? I make no claims for my own morality, sir, I know what I am in most men's eyes, but I will not betray friendship. Hannah trusted me to free her, and I will make it all legal as soon as I return home, and so I have no reason for apology to her. But I will apologise to you, Sam, and I hope that you will forgive me, for being so cruel, to raise your hopes and then dash them. And if you want, I will help you to find your daughter in Bath." For the first time in her tirade, her voice wavered. "I am so very sorry, but I could do nothing else, or I would have broken my promise to Hannah."

Rain was threatening again, and it was quite gloomy under the trees. Sam said, "I wish you had been honest with us, yes. I would have understood your reasons. And if you really can find Mary in Bath, I will be very grateful – but I beg you, Polly, no more lies or deceptions, for I do not think my heart could withstand any further disappointments."

"Oh, Sam," Polly said, her voice breaking suddenly. "Sam Jessop, you're a very kind man, and I thank you." She stepped forward and gave him a brief hug, followed by a light kiss on the cheek. "Believe me, if I could have thought of another way, I would have – but time was so short. And I promise to be honest in all my dealings with you in the future, and I pray most humbly that you can find it in your heart to forgive me."

"I do," Sam said at last, though he still felt raw with disappointment.

Polly smiled at him. "Oh, I am so glad. Can I have that paper back safe, before the rain ruins it? I do *not* want to go to the trouble and expense of obtaining another one."

He handed it over, and she stowed it safely within the muff. "Let us go – it has been such an exhausting morning, and I am longing for dinner and the chance of a rest. Will you do me the honour of escorting me back to the inn?"

"Mistress Paradice." Dark's voice was unwontedly subdued. "Mistress Paradice, I owe you an apology."

Polly turned and studied him. After the spilt and unhappy emotions of the last few minutes, she had now managed to regain some of her usual composure. "Yes, sir," she said coldly. "I believe you do."

There was another, supremely awkward pause. It was the first time Sam had seen Dark bested, and he looked almost sheepish – almost, but not quite. He said at last, "I have been unforgivably rude and boorish to you, not only today but on numerous other occasions. I do not make any promises that will hold my future conduct to ransom, but I would like to tender my unreserved apologies for the past and for the present." One of those sudden smiles transformed his face, and drew a reluctant answering dimple from Polly. "Mistress Paradice, I sorely misjudged you, and I am heartily and unreservedly sorry for it. Can you one day, if not today, find it in your power to forgive me?"

Polly continued to survey him. Sam, who disliked conflict and bad feeling, was relieved to see a sparkle in her eye and mischief in the lightly tapping foot. "Handsomely done, Dark," she acknowledged. "But I note that you make no promises hereafter. Am I then to infer that you reserve the right to continue to behave as offensively and obnoxiously as you have previously?"

"It is a right I must cling to, madam," Dark said gravely. "Or else I will not to mine own self be true."

"And thus you offer ample proof that too much knowledge of Shakespeare is not good for the soul," Polly said.

"As an alternative to Cibber or Manley, it will serve. Is my apology scorned, then?"

Sam glanced from one to the other, aware of the spark between them, evident in Polly's assessing, mischievous gaze, the smile hinted in the corners of Dark's long, severe mouth. A gentle rattle on the leaves above them announced the return of the rain, and she unfurled her umbrella, deliberately making him wait before turning back to him, the expensive blue velvet now protected from harm. "I make it a point *never* to refuse a handsome gentlemen," she said, with transparently artificial coyness. "Yes, Dark, of course I accept. Though if you abuse me again in such a fashion, you will not find me so forgiving a second time. You may be surprised to learn that there are limits to my patience."

"Believe me, madam, nothing about you would have the power to surprise me."

"You seem remarkably certain of that – if you care to wager money on it, I shall take delight in doing something utterly astonishing, purely for your benefit." She gave him an enchanting smile. "But I think we have stood here long enough, and I fear for the safety of my precious mantle. So now we are all friends again, shall we return to the inn before we are quite drenched? And there, we can make our plans for finding Mary Jessop."

CHAPTER SEVEN

'Remark each Walker's diff'rent Face'

The chief purpose of the city of Bristol was the harvesting and treasuring of wealth. Bath, twelve miles upstream along the River Avon, was also surrounded by hills and girded by water, but there the similarity ended. The people within its walls were dedicated either to the selling of pleasure, or the buying of it, and there was, as might be imagined, little love lost between the two places. Bristolians, proud of their mercantile tradition and their Puritan ancestors, despised the frivolous citizens of Bath: who, in their turn, mocked their neighbours for a nest of canting, money-grabbing Philistines. Everyone knew the story of Bladud, the British king who had discovered the healing properties of the waters when it had cured his diseased pigs: and everyone in Bath knew, as well, that afterwards the pigs had all gone off to live in Bristol.

In keeping with the changed mood of their surroundings, Sam thought that they made a remarkably cheerful company as they approached Bath along the Bristol road. By common consent reluctant to risk taking a coach along a highway notorious for mud and potholes, they had hired horses for the short journey. Polly wore a riding habit in the latest London style, with her dark hair pinned up under a flowing full-bottomed wig, and she did indeed look very well in it. Sam wondered where she had obtained such an outfit: surely she had not brought it with her in the two plain bags which comprised all her luggage? Yet it seemed far too fashionable to have been bought in Bristol. She also proved to be a competent horsewoman, which he had not expected. More and more, he was curious about her antecedents, but had no intention of jeopardising their new-found friendship by asking her outright. If she wanted to tell him the history of her life, she would do so in her own good time. And if not, well, it was after all none of his business.

Gin rode pillion behind her, looking very small perched on the sturdy chestnut cob. He was plainly still suffering from the injuries inflicted on him by the groom at Maidenhead, and Polly's anxiety showed in the way she spoke to him, her smiles and the tone of her voice, as if she were gentling a wild animal. And although Dark appeared unsympathetic, Sam knew that he had ensured that each night the boy was adequately fed, given a warm bed, and generally treated well.

Sam found himself liking Polly more and more, despite the way she had exploited and manipulated him, for someone who had gone to so much trouble and expense for the sake of an escaped slave must always earn his whole-hearted approval. It was an abhorrent trade, and he could not agree with those who considered Africans to be something less than human, and so treated them worse than they would a dog or a horse. He particularly despised those hypocrites who salved their consciences by baptising their slaves before they beat them, and who proclaimed that slavery produced so much profit that it must be sanctioned by the Almighty. It offended Sam's sense of natural justice and humanity, and in a perfect world he would wish it abolished altogether, despite the undoubtedly injurious effect such a course of action would have on the wealth of the worthy, rapacious citizens of Bristol.

It seemed, too, that Dark's attitude to Polly had also undergone something of a change. At supper in Bristol the previous evening, he had been far better company than Sam had ever seen him. Even the uproar in the streets outside, which proved to have been caused by the discovery of a Jacobite plot to take over the city, had not discomposed him. In fact, when an excited maid brought them the news, he went so far as to give her a shilling for her trouble, which brought a flood of delighted thanks, and further information about the wicked Jacks, and the disgraceful treasonous parson who seemed to have been behind it all.

A parson ... Sam's eyes met Polly's, gazing thoughtfully at him across the table, and he knew what she was thinking. They had both suspected that their travelling companion Shenley had been a Jacobite. Was he somehow concerned in this? And what exactly had Dark been doing in the half hour or so of his absence that morning?

Well, that too was none of Sam's business, and in any case he had no more love for the White Rose and the Pretender than any other sober Whig citizen. Dark had raised his glass and proposed a toast to King George and confusion to his enemies, and Sam had joined him at once. No Jacobites at this table, he had thought, and then caught sight of Polly. True, she was drinking obediently, but there was a lack of enthusiasm in her face that had made him wonder, then and now, just how loyal to Hanover she was.

But how could it possibly matter, he thought wryly, whether one pretty girl had a soft spot for the disinherited prince over the sea? He was supposed to be charming and handsome, even if he was a Papist in the pay of Rome and France, and his sorry situation had aroused many a young woman's compassion. Mary and her friends had sighed over his plight, but that did not make them traitors. What Mistress Paradice said and thought and did might influence those around her, but he could not, by any stretch of his imagination, envisage her as a plotter.

It was such a pleasant morning as they set out for Bath, that Sam's spirits emerged like the sun from behind the clouds, and shone all around. He loved music, and had a reasonably tuneful voice, so it seemed natural to begin *The Sweet Nightingale* as they rode, and to his delight Polly immediately joined him, improvising a perfect descant harmony as easily as she breathed. Then, evidently inspired by the avian chorus above them, she began *The Lark in the Morning*. It was a very catchy tune, and he could not help joining in: then a few bars later, another male voice added itself to the chorus. For a moment, bewildered, Sam could not think who it might be: then he followed the sound and saw Dark, an expression of ironic amusement on his face, singing surprisingly well, and obviously perfectly familiar with the words.

So, with song and merriment, and fortified by a good dinner purchased at an inn half way along their journey, they rode to Bath, passing one coach skewed sideways in a ditch, and another mired to the axles in a slough of glutinous black mud, while the horses strained to pull it clear. Sam was exceedingly glad that they had chosen to make the journey on horseback, although there were steel grey clouds beginning to pile up in the western sky behind them, and he could smell rain on the freshening wind. They arrived just as the first drops were falling, and entered through the West Gate.

Sam's business travels had only rarely taken him to Bath, and he looked about him keenly. It was a small, packed town, crammed within its ancient walls beside the same river Avon that hemmed Bristol, with tall, gabled houses, obviously centuries old. But if the buildings were no longer fashionable, the same could not be said of the people who thronged the streets, both on foot and carried in sedan chairs, the ways being too narrow and restricted to allow hackney coaches. A provincial himself, Sam knew that the lavishly-dressed men and women strolling past them were just comparatively ordinary folk aping their betters, but they certainly looked and behaved like members of the aristocracy. He had expected to see many ailing or afflicted, but everyone seemed quite healthy. Presumably the truly sick were in the sedan chairs, along with the Quality.

Once they had entered Bath, Polly had taken the lead again, and she brought them to the Bear, which lay at the hub of the town, where Westgate Street met Stall Street and Cheap Street. They had arranged to leave the horses here, and she had proposed that they try to obtain accommodation for themselves as well.

It was one of the two best inns in Bath, the other being the White Hart in Stall Street, and by the look of its handsome stone gables and liveried servants, had prices to match. Although Sam had begun his quest with a long purse, over the past few weeks its contents had rapidly diminished, but the cost of his enterprise was very far from his mind as he climbed stiffly down from his horse, pulled off his gloves and flexed his aching fingers. The only thing that mattered now was Mary. Soon, surely, *surely*, he would find her.

A very ancient ostler, tiny and wizened, had come shuffling out to take their horses, and suddenly Polly jumped down from the saddle and ran to him with a cry of delight. "Ephraim! Oh, Ephraim, I was hoping so much that you'd still be here! How are you faring?" And to Sam's astonishment, she gave him a joyful hug that, small as she was, still seemed to engulf the old man.

"Gawd help us," muttered Gin, sliding down from his pillion perch. "Surely he ain't one of her beaux?"

The ostler was staring at Polly with utter amazement on his shrivelled face. He said wonderingly, "Is it Polly? Is it little Polly, come back to us after all this time?"

"Oh, Ephraim, of course it is," said Mistress Paradice. She pulled off the thick wig to reveal her own dark hair, sliding becomingly loose from its pins. Her delight suffused her skin, shimmered in her eyes, danced in her feet. She kissed first one hollowed, bristly cheek and then the other, all the while holding his hands. "There, Ephraim, you must surely know me now! I've so often thought of you, and Kitty, and everyone.

How glad I am to find you still here!"

Behind her, Dark caught Sam's eye and raised his black brows in sardonic enquiry. As if aware of their curiosity, Polly let go the old man's hands and whirled round. Her flushed, vivid face was devastating in its beauty, and Sam saw Dark stiffen and draw breath sharply, as if he had been struck.

"Oh, Sam, I am so happy!" Reticence, artifice, sophistication had all dropped away, leaving the fresh, honest country girl she must once have been. "For this is my old friend Ephraim Jones, who was so kind to me when I was a child, and I never thought to see again."

"Ten year it's bin," said the ostler, wiping his overflowing eyes with his sleeve like a small boy. "Ten year and more since I said farewell to ee, maid, and here ee be, so pretty and so fine, my little Polly!"

"Still little," she said, beaming at him. "I never growed very much, did I, Ephraim? Even though I stretched myself every night on tiptoe, reaching up to the ceiling, until my back ached – you used to call me Farthing, do you remember? Because I was little and brown." Her voice, Sam noticed, had taken on a much more definite flavour of the West Country dialect that Ephraim also spoke.

"I remember," he said, still marvelling at her. "Little Farthing, turned into a lady!" He turned as a stout, middle-aged woman, wiping her hands on her apron, emerged from the inn door. "Looksee, Kitty, here be Polly come back to us!"

There followed a reprise of the earlier greeting, with hugs and tears and many exclamations, while more people came running out of the inn, and soon there was a cluster round Polly, and a great deal of animated talk. Dark watched for a while, his eyebrows still raised, and then, with an expressive shrug that reminded Sam sharply of his Gallic antecedents, turned away and began unloading the bags from his horse himself. Only when the rain ceased its fitful spitting and began to fall in earnest, did the group break up. Ephraim came over to take charge of the horses, and the woman Kitty ushered everyone inside the inn, still talking volubly. "It gladdens my heart to see you, lamb, so it does. And haven't you done well for yourself, all set up so smart and dashing! Have you found yourself a rich husband, then?"

"It's a story too long for here and now," said Polly. She glanced round, and gestured to Sam, standing feeling somewhat superfluous just inside the door. "Kitty, these are my friends, who have travelled with me from Bristol. We need rooms, and some refreshments, and a quiet parlour. Can you oblige, or are you full? I know how busy you can be, even at the tail-end of the Season – "

"I daresay I can find some space," said Kitty, who was evidently in authority here. Her eye travelled assessingly over Dark and Sam. "How many rooms, lamb?"

Polly giggled, an infectiously light-hearted sound. "Oh, Kitty, you've not changed at all! Just two – one for me, and one for Mr Dark and Mr Jessop. And a bed in the common chamber for Gin, the child who came with us. Can you manage it?" She grinned mischievously. "Or do I have to slip you a coin or two?"

"Lord, Poll, you don't have to do that!" cried Kitty, laughing so much that her rather small eyes almost vanished, and Sam had an excellent view of her sparsely set and yellowing teeth. "There'll always be room found at the Bear for you and your friends, and don't you forget it. Nancy," she added, turning to a maidservant just behind her, a young girl brilliant with curiosity, "show our guests to the Blue Parlour, and make the Angel and the Mermaid ready. This fine lady used to be in your position, my girl, so don't you shirk or answer back, work hard like she did and who knows where you'll end up one day, eh?"

"Yes'm," said Nancy. She ducked a curtsey and waved an

arm at the dark, aromatic warmth beyond the inner doorway. "If you please, madam, sirs, follow me, and Jack will take care of your bags."

Within a few moments, they were comfortably ensconced in a handsome private parlour, drinking chocolate and contemplating a tempting array of cakes on a big slipware dish with 'God Save Queen Anne – 1702' trailed in fat, wobbling yellow capitals around the rim. The maid bobbed another curtsey and said, blushing, "Beg pardon, madam, but was you really in my place years ago?"

"I was indeed," Polly told her, sipping the foaming, cream-topped chocolate with as much satisfaction as a cat licking up a bowlful of sweet milk. "I was maid of all work here for three years, and I'm sure Kitty drives you just as hard as she drove me."

"Yes, madam," said the girl. "But she's kind, ain't she? Not like some."

"I know," said Polly meaningfully, as if she had had ample experience of other people's lack of kindness. "You're lucky to be here, Nancy, and don't you forget it."

"I won't, madam, be sure of that," said the child respectfully. She added, irrepressibly curious, "So why did you leave?"

"Someone made me an offer that I found very difficult to refuse," said Polly, a reminiscent gleam in her eye. "And that's another thing to remember – take any opportunity that comes your way, it may never pass by you again. Now, Nancy, can you ask Kitty if you would kindly come and talk with us for a few moments, if she is not too busy? And buy yourself something pretty with this."

She gave the child a sixpence, and the little maid, blushing still more rosily and bobbing like a wagtail, took the coin with many thanks and fled. As the door shut behind her, Dark said, "It appears you have come a long way, Mistress Paradice."

"I have never hidden that fact from you," said Polly, with some asperity. "You merely failed to ask. Yes, I was a maid here – a Parish Apprentice, in fact. My beginnings were humble, Dark, but I do not think that in itself constitutes any crime."

"I never said that it did," her adversary pointed out. "In any case, the fondness with which you are so evidently regarded here does them, and you, considerable credit."

"I thought you were guilty of many things, Dark," said Polly, gazing at him thoughtfully over the rim of her blue Delftware cup. "But pomposity did not seem to be one of your sins. It seems I was mistaken." She grinned at him. With her dark, curling hair framing her pale face in damp tendrils, her rich blue eyes, the flush of her welcome still imparting a brilliant glow to her cheeks, she was an enchanting sight, and Sam felt a small, forlorn ache somewhere in his breast. *If I were twenty years younger ...*

But he was old enough to be her father, and he still grieved for his poor Susan, so he put it firmly from his mind. Dark, however, was a different matter. And with his acute eye and interest in people, Sam could see that his sardonic companion was not, despite his valiant efforts to the contrary, impervious to the charms and wiles of Polly Paradice.

"I beg your pardon, madam," said Dark, inclining his head in mock courtesy. "If I have sounded pompous, I did not intend to be. Well, then, would you prefer bluntness?"

"They do say that honesty is the best policy," Polly said demurely. "But I suspect, Dark, that for you, honesty is a scourge with which you delight in beating lesser mortals. I am surprised that you make any money painting portraits – your view of humanity seems to be jaundiced in the extreme."

"I paint what I see. And if I see too much to be

comfortable, well, the subject is perfectly at liberty to reject my view of him, or her."

"Then will you paint me, when we return to London? I will pay you well, whether I like the result or not."

"I will, madam, and I trust I will do you justice."

There was a knock on the door. With a glance at the man and woman looking at each other across the table, Sam called, "Enter!"

It was Kitty, her apron removed in their honour, and a fresh lace-edged pinner on her greying head. She bobbed a curtsey and said, "You wished to see me, madam, sirs?"

At once Polly jumped up. "Don't stand on ceremony with us, please, Kitty – I don't like to see you so! I may have fine clothes but I'm still your little Polly, and you're still the woman who was like a mother to me – so let's have no more curtseys and *madams* and *sirs*, I beg you! Come and sit down, for we need your help."

"If you say so, lamb," said Kitty. She allowed herself to be drawn to the table, and placed on the remaining chair. With an air of lively ceremony, Polly poured chocolate and handed it to her. "I remember how you love it – and how you used to put all the dregs from the pots into one and mixed it up again for all of us at the day's end. Do you still do that for Nancy and the other girls?"

"You've a long memory, lamb," said Kitty smiling. "But I was not always so kind. You had the rough edge of my tongue many times – a saucy little hoyden, you could be."

"And still is," Dark observed mordantly, from behind his cup.

"Don't mind him," said Polly, with an expressive grimace. "He is but a painter of portraits and scenes for the play-house, Dark by name and dark by nature. It is my other friend here who really needs your help. Sam Jessop has mislaid his daughter, and we think she may be in Bath."

"Ah," said Kitty. Her small, shrewd eyes travelled round the three faces and arrived back at Polly. "There's a story here, I can see. Tell it to me, Mr. Jessop, and I'll tell you whether or not I can help."

Briefly, leaving out all emotion and appeal, Sam related again the tale of Mary's disappearance and his quest to find his daughter. He omitted the Bristol episode altogether, out of respect for Polly, but Kitty was no fool: she held up her hand when he had finished, and said, "You haven't said why you were in Bristol."

Polly smiled ruefully. "Discovered! Were you trying to save my blushes, Sam? I am afraid, Kitty, that our trip to Bristol was entirely my fault. I used Sam and Dark shamefully, dragging them there by deception upon my own concerns. How did you know that we were there, then? Ah, the horses."

"Yes, the horses. We know that chestnut well, it comes to us at least twice a week in the season. But that's no matter now – what matters is Miss Jessop. You said, sir, that she may be with this man St. Clair? Who is French? What a terrible tale!" Kitty said, with warm sympathy. "You must be very anxious to find her, sir. Well, I promise I will do my best to help you. And in my way of trade, you come to know most of the visitors here in Bath. I can set enquiries in motion – "

"Please," Sam said quickly, "I beg you, it must be done with all discretion. If she once gets wind that I am here, she will surely flee again. But if I can only see her, talk to her, try to persuade her – "

"How old is she? Sixteen? Then she'll brook no persuading. No girl that age I ever knew would sit meekly and listen obediently to anyone, never mind her father."

"And Mary more than most," Sam said ruefully. "But I

have to try, for you know as well as I do, madam, the fate which will undoubtedly befall her if I do not find her and bring her home."

"I do indeed, Mr. Jessop," said Kitty, with a covert glance at Polly, who seemed to have spectacularly avoided such a fate, either from luck or good judgement. "Well, I will ask about as discreetly as I can. I know all the lodging-house keepers, and which of them can keep mum. You must describe her to me, so that I can ask them."

"I can do better than that," Sam said. He fumbled in the pocket of his coat, and handed the sketch of his daughter to Kitty. "Mr Dark was so good as to draw her to my description, and it is an excellent likeness. It will surely help your enquiries."

"A pretty girl, indeed," Kitty said sympathetically, studying it. "Thank you, sir, I will show it around. Meanwhile, your best plan will be to haunt the places of resort. The Pump Room – Harrison's Walks – the Assembly Rooms. Any lively young girl will be there, unless she is at death's door."

"And if you've any sense," said Dark, in a drawling voice that somehow implied the opposite, "wear a suit she won't recognise, and a style of wig that you don't usually inhabit."

* * *

Sam pushed a surreptitious finger beneath the curls of Polly's powdered, full-bottomed wig, borrowed for the occasion, and scratched his scalp. A ridiculous fashion, and one fast being superseded, except on very formal occasions, by tie-wigs, bob wigs, campaign wigs, any wig in fact except this hot, uncomfortable and inconvenient excrescence on a man's head. But he had never worn one, even when it was all the rage a few years previously, and so it was the perfect disguise. Mary would surely not recognise her father under something he had always derided.

But he was unhappily sure that she was not here today. The morning rain had given way to a sunlit, breezy afternoon, and the visitors to Bath had emerged like a flock of squawking bright birds to promenade in Harrison's Walks. They had all paid Nash, the self-appointed Master of Ceremonies, up to a guinea apiece on their arrival in the town, for the privilege of displaying themselves and their garments to the best advantage in front of the Quality. The cost, of course, not to mention Nash's strict rules concerning proper dress and behaviour, dissuaded vulgar townsfolk, who in any case could have a free view at any time of their betters making themselves ridiculous in the Baths. It did not discourage Sam, whose search, so long drawn out and so fruitless, was becoming an obsession. In happier times, he would have enjoyed laughing at these preposterous, painted, prinking creatures with their braying laughs and exaggerated manners, but now his eyes roved over them with increasing desperation, seeking a dark head, a girlish laugh, a light spontaneous grace.

"Dear me," said that other, wiser young woman, discreetly behind her fan. "I am so glad I was never tempted to marry the Earl who offered for me. I would have worn a hoop so vast I could not pass straight through a doorway, and diamonds so monstrous as to outshine the sun. Do you not find them ridiculous, Sam? An honest sober shopkeeper like yourself must surely have no patience with such frippery people."

"Were you really tempted to marry an Earl?" asked Dark.

"La, sir, I have had so many offers that I have quite lost count," said Polly, peeping with deliberate provocation from behind her fan, a lovely lattice of pierced ivory, exquisitely painted.

"When you are being arch and coy, madam, I find you at your most exasperating."

"Do you really, Dark?" Polly fluttered her fan at him again, her long shadowy lashes trembling in imitation. "Oh, I am *so* glad, for that is why I do it."

Dark uttered a snort of annoyance, but whether it was real or feigned could not be determined, for at that moment a gentleman strolling past them stopped abruptly, staring. He was a handsome, well-built fellow with a military air, and Polly, approving, gave him the benefit of her most alluring smile. Sam felt the corners of his own mouth curve. Sometimes he shared Dark's exasperation, for she flirted, it seemed, as naturally as she breathed, and with scant regard for the consequences.

But for once the man was paying her no heed, all his attention being focussed on her companion. "By God, it's Dark! I never thought to see you alive again! How do you do, sir, how do you do?"

"Well enough, I thank you, Beaumont," said Dark, and the two men shook hands warmly. "This is a most pleasant and unlooked-for encounter. I take it you are no longer in arms?"

"Lord, no – sadly, my elder brother died two years ago, so I came home to assume charge of the estate. And you? The last time I saw you, Dark, you were lying in that squalid inn after Malplaquet, and the surgeon had given you over. I thought you'd a day or two left at the most."

"The surgeon was incompetent," said Dark dryly.

"But not so incompetent that he killed you," Polly put in, laughing. "Or at least I assume that he did not, for certainly you can give the illusion of life, if you put your mind to it."

"Pray introduce your charming companion," said the

man called Beaumont. "Such a combination of beauty and wit cannot go unnoticed."

"Of course – Mistress Paradice, may I present my old comrade in arms, Captain James Beaumont?"

As the others conversed, Sam stared round at the crowds of strolling, gossiping people infesting the sunlit walks. Although it was now nearly the end of the Season, there must have been at least a hundred here, of all ages, shapes and sizes, but with one aim in common, to parade themselves and their airs and garments and graces before everyone else. The apparent hopelessness of his task suddenly threatened to overwhelm him, but before he could give way to despair, his arm was firmly taken, and Polly's warm and welcome voice said, "They are talking soldiery, so I have left them to it. Is she here? Can you see her?"

Sam gestured helplessly at the crowds. "I don't know. I really don't know. There are so many here, and their clothes hide so much – or she could be painted so I wouldn't recognise her, or she might be wearing a wig, like that woman ..." His voice tailed away.

"I must say," Polly remarked cheerfully, "that my dearest friend could be under that nest and I would not know her – what a fright! For myself, I would not be seen dead in it – and from all you have said of your daughter, neither would she. Here are some ladies of fashion, why not look at them carefully as they walk by?"

Half a dozen young women, decked out in all their fanciest finery, were trying to pretend that they had not noticed the two gallants, one in rose and one in blue, who were shamelessly ogling them. Sam studied their faces covertly. One too fair, one too plump, one too short, one too tall, one slightly marred by the smallpox and one with a beak, dear Heaven, that would not be out of place on an eagle, poor girl. He shook his head. "No, none of them."

"Walk with me," said Polly, taking his arm more firmly. "Let us promenade, and you can watch the women while I observe the gentlemen. There seem to be even more fops than you would meet in Will's or White's, and I find them very entertaining." And, as he still hesitated, she smiled up at him, the westering sun flushing her rounded cheeks and glowing in her deep blue eyes. "Come on, Sam – faint heart never found fair daughter. Or are you, despite everything, afraid of finding her?"

He opened his mouth to deny it with passion, and realised suddenly that she had spoken the truth. He *was* afraid. He was afraid of what Mary might do, and say, and above all of what she might have become. Mute, miserable, he nodded.

"Oh, Sam." Her voice was soft, and shook with sympathy. "We will find her, I know it, for she is certainly here. If not today, then tomorrow, or the day after, you will come down to the Walks, or visit the Baths, or stroll in the streets, and you will hear her voice and see her face."

"Polly," said Sam, bewildered by her absolute confidence. "You have never properly explained – *how* do you know that she is here?"

There was a pause. A wood pigeon, cooing rhythmically, filled the silence between them as they walked arm-in-arm beneath the limes, their leaves still summer green although it was now October. Polly said at last, "If I tell you, will you promise to keep it from Dark? I had rather he did not know just yet."

"Of course," said Sam, still confused. "But why do you not want him to know?"

"Do *you* think that he is merely an artist? Or do you think, as I do, that he is rather more than that? I made enquiries about him, Sam, if you remember. He is estranged from his family, he fought in Marlborough's wars, he lives in good lodgings and yet he seems to paint hardly any portraits. Have you never wondered where he finds the means for it?"

"Well, yes, but – "

"He's a spy," Polly said softly. "Parson Shenley was arrested in Bristol, on suspicion of fomenting a Jacobite plot. Where did Dark go yesterday morning? Was he laying information before the City authorities? I'll wager he was. I trust you are not a Jacobite, Sam, or even a Tory, because if you are then he assuredly has you marked for betrayal."

Suddenly, so many things that had puzzled Sam about his mysterious, enigmatic companion seemed to make sense. He said uneasily, "How can you know? How can you be so sure?"

"I am sure," said Polly earnestly. "And I suspect that the reason he is helping you to find your daughter – the reason he is here – is that the man she is with is a Jacobite."

The words dropped like stones into his heart, and sank there, with all their portents of future grief. Treason. Rebellion. And the terrible penalties exacted for indulging in those most heinous of crimes, with Jacobites in arms in Scotland and the North, and George of Hanover new and insecure on his throne. With dreadful visions crowding his mind, he did not realise that he had stopped walking, and that the two women overtaking them were glancing at him curiously as they passed.

"St. Clair? You mean St. Clair is a *Jacobite?*"

"Hush, not so loud. And continue walking, or we shall cause an obstruction, and then Nash will scold us. Try not to look as if Satan himself were beckoning, Sam, it is not so terrible as all that. A man may still be a Jacobite and an honest soul – it is his ideals that are flawed, not his character. And he is not St. Clair, and neither is he French – his name is Robbie Sinclair, and he is a Scot."

"This – this is too much to take in." Sam had completely forgotten to scan the other strollers: he tried to hide the extremity of his agitation, but felt the force of his confusion almost choking him. "I still don't understand, Polly – *how do you know all this?*"

"I was once well acquainted with Sinclair, and my dear friend Jenny Garnet told me where he had gone, and who he was with. Do you think it was pure coincidence brought you to Dark, Sam? Or that chance led you both to me? Hardly. André Dark is a subtle and devious man, and we would both do well to be wary of him, for he will not scruple to sacrifice either of us to get what he desires."

"I thought that he desired you," said Sam, still too shocked to be properly circumspect.

Polly laughed derisively. "I doubt he desires anything so earthly. His passions are reserved for affairs of state. He is a Huguenot, so he has a personal grudge against Popery and the Stuarts, and he has undoubtedly sworn to exterminate all who would seek to restore them to the throne."

Her certainty still troubled Sam, not least because he was tolerably sure that she had misread Dark's motives. He himself was twenty years older than either of them, and as a merchant he had long since learned to look beyond the surface of things. In the past week he had come to know, and suspect, rather more about Dark's character than that reticent and secretive man would surely have wished, and Polly, although quick and perceptive, had spent so much less time in the artist's company. That he was a spy, yes, that rang surprisingly true. But that he was completely ruthless and callous in pursuing his objectives – no, that was not right. If nothing else, there was the evidence of Gin to consider: Gin, who had been treated with unspoken but practical compassion.

He became aware that a lavishly dressed personage was standing before them, a cane in his hand. Polly nudged him surreptitiously in the ribs, and Sam bowed obediently. This ugly, black-wigged little man in the rich and splendid clothes was about his own age, or a little older, but he was also Nash, uncrowned King of Bath, and must be treated with proper civility and respect, however much Sam's own private concerns were occupying his thoughts.

"Mr. Jessop, I believe," said the great man, bowing likewise, but with far more grace and address. "I bid you welcome to Bath, sir. Are you staying for long?"

Sam smiled as if his private nightmare had not consumed all certainties, as if he were in truth the honest sober upright citizen he had always considered himself to be, rather than a man who had just learned that he was a spy's unwitting accomplice, and the father of a runaway Jacobite daughter. "A few days only, sir, at the end of the Season. We have rooms at the Bear."

"So I hear," said Nash, who seemed to have as much command of unspoken information as Polly. "And this charming young lady?"

It would have been easy to pretend that she was his daughter, but Sam was well aware that such a lie might trip up the deceiver later on, in ways that could not be anticipated, and with consequences that might be disastrous. "Allow me, sir, to present Mistress Mary Paradice, who is a friend of my daughter and therefore of all our family."

Polly, acutely aware of Nash's assessing, interested gaze, swept into a graceful curtsey, with her flowered skirts sweeping the gravel around her, and then fluttered her fan, her skin charmingly flushed with what any who did not know her might have interpreted as virginal shyness. Fortunately Nash did not seem to see anything unusual in the fact that she was being escorted by a man old enough to be her father: indeed, he engaged Mistress Paradice in affable conversation, while his eyes continued to rove over her neat figure and beautiful clothes. Sam, still dazed by the news that Mary, far from eloping with a French dancing master, had instead run away with a Jacobite Scot, registered vaguely that Nash was giving her a full account of the many and wondrous diversions to be sampled in Bath, even this late in the Season, and only belatedly realised that he was included in the flow of talk when a question was addressed directly to him.

"No, sir," he said, gathering his wits about him with a considerable effort. "Alas, I lost my dear wife two years ago."

"Indeed." Nash looked at Polly as if he suspected that she was lined up as Susan's replacement. If it were not for her alluring presence, holding his attention, Sam knew that the Master of Ceremonies would not have bothered to exchange more than the briefest of pleasantries with him. "Well, Mr. Jessop, I hope that you will enjoy your stay in Bath. May we expect you at the ball tonight?"

On any other occasion, Sam would have declined, for he was tired and the prospect of a restful evening and an early retirement to his bed was very tempting, but he could not turn away another opportunity to find his daughter. "I think you may, sir," he said.

"Excellent! And you, Mistress Paradice? Will you favour our poor gathering with the lustrous glow of your presence?" As much as a man so practised in the civilised urbanities could hunger, he lusted after Polly, it was plain to see in his small, folded eyes. So, to judge from the glances, concealed or naked with desire, of the men passing by them, did every other male here present in the Walks.

"Indeed, I would be pleased to do so," said Polly, with a modest look at her fan. "And Mr. Dark, who is the other member of our party, may also attend? That is very kind of you. So, we will meet again this evening, Mr. Nash, and my thanks for your generous invitation, sir."

"And if there is anything at all that you require, dear madam," said the Master of Ceremonies, "pray do not hesitate to make me acquainted at once with your desires." He bowed very low over her slender pale hand, innocent of any ring, and in reply Polly curtseyed as deep as she might to a king crowned in truth. Then Nash's eyes went past them, he cried, "My dear Lady Broughton!" and they could make good their escape while his attention was diverted by a more exalted personage.

"Faugh!" said Polly, when they were well out of earshot. "I know that man has done great things for the benefit of Bath – and for himself, naturally – but I still find his look raises the hairs on my neck. There is no gainsaying him when he is here, however, he reigns supreme and no-one, however great they be, can muster the nerve to contradict him. Woe betide the gentleman who dares to appear in riding boots, and I'll wager he would even scold a Duchess, were she to present herself in a morning cap or apron."

For a moment, Sam wondered how she came to know so much about Nash, and then remembered those three years at the Bear. Even in such a menial position, she must have heard all the tales and gossip about residents and visitors alike. He said curiously, "Did he have cause to recognise you?"

"Yes, he did," Polly said cheerfully. "Indeed, I am tolerably certain that he knew he had seen me before, but could not quite remember where. I served him many a time in the Bear, but then I was a child, and a lowly maid – and later, when I was in the Colonel's household in Bristol, I met him again. Have no fear, he will not denounce me for my humble origins, for I suspect his are no greater. All his interest lies in making Bath a place of resort for anyone who has the ready money to stake at his and Harrison's gaming tables, and my coin, and yours, is as good as anyone's. As long as we conform to his rules, we are safe from molestation. No riding boots, remember, or he will ask you where you have left your horse, in front of all the company."

Despite himself, Sam chuckled. They had reached the end of the Walk, and ahead of them lay a small cluster of buildings which included one of Bath's two coffee houses, as well as a parade of shops selling the kind of expensive luxury trifles that would appeal to those of taste and fashion. He turned and looked back. "Dark is still talking to Captain Beaumont. Shall we wait for him?"

"Oh, do not trouble yourself," Polly said carelessly. "He is a grown man, he can find his own way back to the Bear without our help."

"Polly, you are very hard on him, and it is not surprising that he responds in kind."

The young woman beside him tossed her head in a way that his own Mary would have employed, and her glossy brown ringlets bounced on her shoulders. "If I am cruel, Sam, then I will make amends in due course, never fear. But his arrogance does need to be taken down several pegs. Now, have you been paying attention? Have you looked carefully at all the women present?"

"I think so," said Sam cautiously. "And I am sure she is not here. But perhaps she will attend the ball tonight. If she does not ... "

Polly glanced up at him, the habitual mischief of her expression for once surrendered to seriousness. "Well, I do not think that we can raise a hue and cry. I doubt that your daughter wishes to be discovered, and Sinclair certainly will not. I suspect that they are not to be found within the walls of the town, but perhaps in some quiet lodgings in Walcot, or an out-of-the-way inn or farmhouse."

"Then how will we ever unearth them?"

"Do not despair, Sam, please. If they are anywhere in

or around Bath, Kitty will come to hear of it. And in the meantime, there is the dancing this evening, and the race meeting tomorrow."

"Race meeting? You mean, a horse race?"

"Of course," said Polly. "Were you not listening when Nash was telling me of all the entertainments presently on offer here? Tonight a ball, and tomorrow morning a puppet show, and racing in the afternoon up on Claverton Down. All the gentlemen in Bath who are well enough to ride will be there to watch, and many of the ladies too. If Sinclair wants to meet fellow Jacobites and indulge in a little conspiracy, he could not wish for a more perfect cover for his activities." She squeezed his arm lightly. "But we don't have to tell Dark that, do we?"

"I suppose not," Sam said doubtfully. Surely, surely his sweet Mary, so innocent of the ways of the world, could have no knowledge of treason or rebellion. She was Sinclair's dupe, and the sooner he extracted her from the man's dangerous clutches the better. He added, "But he will have to be told eventually."

"If he doesn't know already. Very little would surprise me about Dark." She gave Sam a wildly enchanting grin, and two gentlemen approaching nearly walked into a lime tree, so smitten were they. Indeed one of them, a very young man with a fresh high colour and a powdered wig in the very latest style, bowed so low it nearly fell off his head, and begged Polly's pardon for the intrusion, but surely she was Miss Hargreaves, an acquaintance of his sister?

"Indeed, sir," said Polly, looking him up and down as if this sort of thing happened every day, "I cannot say that I am, for that is not my name."

"Then you must forgive me, madam, for you are very much like her – only far, far more beautiful!"

"You are impertinent, sir," said Polly coolly, with a

disdainful flick of her fan. "Pray do me the courtesy of failing to trouble me again. Good day."

Leaving the crestfallen youth gazing mournfully after her, she led Sam onwards. He glanced down at her lovely face, and saw that kittenish look of satisfaction that Mary, too, could employ to great effect. Yes, Polly could be cruel, but only to those whom she considered deserving of it. To keep herself safe from predators must require a degree of ruthlessness and cunning which she must surely possess, or she would not be here, glowing and exquisitely dressed in embroidered silk: she would be plying her trade on the streets of Covent Garden.

The sun had slid behind a line of cloud advancing up beyond the western hills, and the wind was dropping. Suddenly exhausted by the events of the day, he stifled a yawn. "Shall we return to the Bear now? I for one would welcome the chance to rest for a while."

"And there I am in agreement with you," Polly told him. "Besides, we may find that Kitty's enquiries have borne fruit. And I am passing weary of these tiresome fellows ogling me. Really, people here are as rude as they are in London. Have they nowhere better to place their eyes?"

Sam doubted it, but knew better than to put his thoughts into words. "And Dark?"

"Leave him be. I can live an hour or two without him glowering at me every time I flutter my fan, and in any case that Captain may have useful information, if he asks the right questions. And to think that I was under the delusion that he had become more human since we left Bristol."

"I suspect," Sam told her gently, "that he is all too human."

"You think so? I beg to disagree, dear Sam." She smiled at him, removing the sting from her words. "Now, let us leave this place and go back to the Bear, or I shall be too weary to dance tonight."

CHAPTER EIGHT

'By happier Guidance led'

The minuet, Polly decided after successfully smothering what could have been a jaw-cracking yawn, might be all the rage at Versailles or St. James's, but it was insufferably tedious to watch. In order of precedence, one couple at a time, the dancers proceeded slowly round the ballroom while the fiddlers scraped diligently at their instruments, their steps and gestures designed to show off their glittering garments and elegant deportment rather than any particular grace or skill. She, Dark and Sam, together with Dark's old comrade Beaumont and his party, had already watched a duke, two countesses (both led out by Nash, who was an excellent dancer) and any number of ladies and rather fewer lords parade themselves, and now it was the turn of less exalted members of the company.

"I pray you, dear madam, do me the honour of standing up with me," Mr. Powell whispered urgently into her ear. He was the most handsome of Beaumont's friends, and at first she had thought his attentions quite entertaining, but he was one of those men so assured of their own attractions that they can never take no for an answer. It was a breed with which Polly was tolerably well acquainted, but even so she found the continual need to rebuff him with politeness and courtesy somewhat wearying. In fact, she would much have preferred Beaumont, but he had brought along a young woman who was apparently his betrothed, and was fully engaged with her. Sam could not rescue her, for he had planted himself in a dimly lit corner, the better to observe the company without being spotted by Mary – if she was there, which Polly doubted, since late-comers were not encouraged. Even Dark would have been better than this importunate and arrogant young popinjay, for at least he did not look greedily into her eyes, or murmur an endless stream of ridiculously overblown compliments into her shrinking ears.

The ludicrous thought actually made her smile. Unfortunately, Mr. Powell thought that this was on account of his presence, and pressed home his advantage, along with a covert caress of her shoulder. "Then you will dance, dear Mistress Paradice?"

"I regret I will not, sir," said Polly, pointedly hunching herself away from his hand. "I am somewhat weary, and wish to sit this one out." She allowed herself another yawn, which she concealed behind a flutter of her ivory fan. It was probably a mistake to use tiredness as an excuse when she had every intention of flinging herself with enthusiasm into the country dances which always made up the second part of the evening, but just at this moment she was prepared to use any means to hand to keep Mr. Powell at bay. She had never thought that she would be delighted to see André Dark approach, but the sight of his lean familiar face, as he threaded his way round the edge of the floor to their group, actually lifted her spirits, and caused her to smile more brilliantly at him than was her usual habit. "Pray excuse me, Mr. Powell," she said quickly, rising to her feet. "But I think I need a little air." She sailed past his outstretched hand as if it were invisible, and took Dark's arm.

Surprise evident on his face, he bent his head to hers, and she hissed behind her fan, "I beseech you, Dark, take me away from that booby before I lay hands on him!"

"By all means, madam, but surely you are not so enamoured of the puppy that you have to be prised away by force?"

Polly choked, and rapped his arm smartly with her fan. "You know very well what I mean, you wretch! Now pray escort me to the gardens forthwith, or I shall be forced to tell the world about your dubious habits at the card table."

"You are labouring under a sad delusion, Mistress Paradice, for I do not make a practice of haunting gaming hells."

Alerted by a richer note in his voice, Polly glanced up at him and saw that he was smiling at her. He was really very attractive when he smiled, his brown eyes almost vanished in lines of amusement, and deep grooves bracketing his long lean mouth. A small flutter began somewhere within the constrictions of her stays – she should never have asked Nancy to lace them so tight – and she could not help responding in kind. "Really, sir? Then where have you been all this inordinate length of time, when I was fending off Mr. Powell without assistance?"

"I am sure you are far too experienced in these matters to have any difficulty in resisting such adversaries, madam."

"A palpable hit, by God," Polly said. She loved this sparring, this spirited verbal cut and thrust that seemed to elevate her mind to a level of breathless invention, full of daring and wit and allusion. "I like you much better when you engage the enemy, Dark."

"Do you then consider yourself to be my enemy?"

"Oh, no, I never have done," Polly assured him. They had come to the hanging stairs which led down into the Walks, and although her hoop was not especially large, it made the descent awkward. She paused, and Dark said, "Pray allow me to precede you, madam. Then, if you fall, you will land on me."

"A consummation devoutly to be wished?" said Polly tartly. "But I thank you for your thoughtfulness, sir." She waited until he had passed her and then, with care, holding to the banisters, she descended as gracefully as she could.

Lanterns had been hung in the trees lining the Walks,

giving sufficient light for strollers to see their way, but not so many as to leave every corner of the gardens illuminated. The air struck refreshingly cool on her shoulders, and the breeze slid soft fingers through her hair, disturbing the careful curls that she and Nancy had constructed earlier in the evening. Behind them, the tall arched windows of Harrison's Rooms were brilliantly lit with myriad candles, and the sounds of the sweet, stately music of the minuet competed with the wind in the trees above them, and the distant, more subdued murmur of the river as it negotiated the town mills. There were other people in the gardens: she could hear a woman's soft laughter in the shadows at the far end, where she and Sam had walked earlier, and talked about Mary.

"It appears that Miss Jessop is not attending the ball," she said.

"So I have ascertained – though her father still seems hopeful that she will put in a belated appearance."

"I fear he is mistaken, poor man. Shall we walk? I think it is light enough for us not to run head-first into a tree."

"If he had beaten some sense into her at a young age, he might have saved himself a great deal of trouble," observed Dark dryly.

"I think that Sam Jessop is far too kind-hearted a man ever to wish to beat his daughter, or anyone else for that matter. And she has treated him with shameless ingratitude in return. Let us hope that when he finds her, he can persuade her to see the error of her ways, and to go back with him to Oxford."

"I notice you said 'when', rather than 'if'. I wish I shared your confidence. Well, *if* he finds her, you and I can return to London, and pick up our lives where we so precipitately left them," Dark said. "Which reminds me, Mistress Paradice, of the request I made earlier – will you do me the great service of allowing me to paint you?"

Polly kept her voice light and casual. "Of course, sir, so long as you do not put me in a distemper thereby."

"I hope not, although the gilding I have in mind may cause you some inconvenience."

"So long as it does not affect my skirting," Polly said mischievously, and felt an inward surge of triumph as he laughed. "Of course it will not, madam. But I must confess to a less than noble motive for my request – I have a space on the wall of my salon, if you can call the room where I hang my pictures by so pretentious a word, and a beautiful young woman will look very handsome next to all the gouty old gentlemen and pompous soldiers."

"I'm not at all sure I like the thought of spending time in such company, Dark. Are there to be no other ladies to chaperone my painted counterfeit?"

"There is my sister, but I am sure she will welcome another woman to gossip with."

"Then we can hang together on the wall and chat all day to our hearts' content. So, sir, how would you like to paint me? As a goddess in loose draperies? Or as some tragic heroine, Dido perhaps, all sighs and tears?"

"As yourself only," Dark said softly. "That is more than sufficient."

She paused, and disengaged her arm. Turning to look up at him, she could not read his expression, for the nearest lantern was some yards distant. "Are you perfectly sure? In the past, you have given ample indication that you find me at best exasperating, at worst a cursed nuisance."

"I am persuaded that you possess a few good qualities," he said: he was definitely smiling. "Perhaps I can endeavour to be more tolerant, and you may try to be less provoking. If, of course, you find that possible."

In the distance, the music had changed to a livelier tune: the country dances had begun. Suddenly, despite her worry over Sam, Polly felt impossibly light-hearted and joyful. "I doubt it, Dark," she said. "But you will just have to put up with me as I am, for I am weary of being a chameleon, changing my colours to match the person beside me. And now, sir, do you have a fancy to dance?"

"If I can find a suitable partner," he said, and at once turned to face the slender young lime tree next to him. "Dearest dryad, I beg the honour of this minuet."

Laughing, Polly tapped him with her fan. "Not that lady, sir, you'd find her much too wooden. I, on the other hand, am far more pliant."

"I don't doubt it. Will you brave Mr. Powell's importuning again? You may well find yourself making a set with him."

"I think I can bear the prospect. Are you familiar with country dances, Dark? Or will you turn the wrong way, take the wrong partner, and step on my feet?"

"I can assure you, Mistress Paradice," said Dark, grinning wider, "that I will inflict none of those horrors upon you."

* * *

By decree of Richard Nash, evenings at the Assembly Rooms ended at eleven o'clock, so the chairmen of Bath always gathered yawning outside, waiting for custom to spill out onto the Terrace Walk. Polly's sides ached with laughter, and she was hot and breathless after a most enjoyable evening, during which she had not only danced with Dark, but had persuaded Sam to stand up with her three times, until he pleaded complete exhaustion. Unfortunately, the persistent Mr. Powell had refused to take her repeated noes for answers, and was only too evidently waiting for any opportunity to corner her alone. Beaumont had issued a general invitation to the group, to return to his lodgings for some unspecified entertainment which probably included gambling and the consumption of copious quantities of port and brandy, and Sam and Dark were going, but she had already declined, largely because of Powell. She had trodden on his toes twice, most brutally with all the force of her heel, but without discernible effect: it was the first time in her life that she had wished she were heavier. Unfortunately, he had inadvertently returned the compliment, and the hem of her silver satin gown would never be the same again, were Hannah or Nancy to stitch all night at it.

He was coming towards her once more. Even the fact that she had been partnered for most of the dancing by Dark or Sam had failed to discourage him. She glanced round, saw the tall figure of the artist just beside her, and gave him her most charming smile. "For the love of God, Dark, get me a chair this instant, or I swear I shall murder that man. He just will *not* leave me alone, no matter what I do or say to him. I've tried everything short of open violence, and he still fails to take the hint."

"I could spit him for you," said Dark, giving Powell an assessing stare. "It should not prove too difficult."

"A rather drastic remedy, to be sure, though probably more certain of success than if I batter him about the head with my shoe." To her relief, a chair was approaching, and he handed her into it just as Powell came up, asking plaintively why Mistress Paradice was not favouring them with her company after all. The interior smelled strongly of stale sweat and musty leather, but at least it did not contain her tormentor. And then it was lifted with a lurch that made her wonder if the bearers had been drinking while they waited, and she was carried away back to the Bear, and her blessedly solitary bed.

Yes, she thought, as her conveyance jolted briskly along the streets, she had thoroughly enjoyed this evening, far more than she had expected. Dark had been an entertaining companion, revealing a wickedly dry and ironic sense of humour, and he had been unperturbed by Powell, when another man might have been embarrassingly protective, or even aggressive. Polly had wide experience of the half of humanity supposed to be the superior, and it had given her a decidedly cynical view of them. Most men paid only lip service to the ideals of polite society, of kindliness and courtesy and fair dealing. At the slightest opportunity, they would shed their civilised veneer and become brutes, unfit for any tolerable company. She was sure that Dark was the same as all the others: it was just that he hid his true nature better than did Powell, whose naked lust lingered in every movement of his hands and eyes, and would surely find violent expression, given the chance.

With a sigh, she leaned back against the padded silk and closed her eyes. No, they were not to be trusted, and Dark in particular, for she had good reason to know of his deviousness and lack of honesty. One day, when the time was ripe, she would confront him with what she knew. In the meantime, she would enjoy his company, take what she could from it, and never give any more than she wished.

Sam, though, was different. In an inconstant, shifting world, Sam would always be kind, reliable and fair. It was ironic that a prosperous but humble shopkeeper, despised by his superiors, was in fact far more of a true gentleman than most of those who laid claim to such status. If he were twenty years younger, she might even have been tempted to set her cap at him, for a truly good man was almost impossible to find, and in any case would never look at a woman who was almost universally considered to be no better than an expensive whore. Sam, however, valued the character within, rather than exterior trappings of wealth or breeding or reputation, and judged accordingly. Whatever she did, she knew that in him, she had found a lifelong friend.

And would he persuade Mary to come home with him? She hoped so, very much, both for his sake and for his daughter's. Yet she could not help but sympathise with the girl, who like her had found the constraints of her limited experience too great to tolerate. In Mary's place, she too would probably have eloped with the handsome and seductive dancing master. But Polly, from her advantage of ten years' experience of the world, knew that Mary's disillusionment had probably been abrupt and catastrophic.

And would a wilful, high-spirited young girl, reduced to such shame and humiliation, meekly confess her fault and return, the prodigal daughter, to her home? Polly very much doubted it.

Although she had thought that she would be more than ready for sleep when she returned to the Bear, by the time she climbed out of the chair in the inn's courtyard and paid off the bearers, she felt wide awake once more, so she went in search of Kitty, and found her in her parlour just beside the kitchen, where she could keep a watchful eye on her servants. Beside her, a small but fervent fire still flamed around its coals, and beyond the half-closed door a truckle bed, pulled up in a corner, was made up for the use of the maid on night duty, who slept there until summoned. It was now close on midnight, and round them the vast rambling bulk of the inn slumbered until daybreak. As she had hoped, Polly was given a warm welcome, and was soon sitting comfortably opposite her former employer, sipping smooth rich chocolate that had not been made from the dregs of other people's cups.

"You've come a long way," Kitty said, leaning back in her chair.

Dark had used precisely those words, but Kitty's voice held only admiration, and a certain mild envy. She smiled at the girl who had once been her protégée, and Polly smiled back. "Perhaps I have. But I have never forgotten where I came from."

"I can tell that, lamb. You never had no side to you, not like some I could call to mind. But you've done well for yourself. How much did that fine mantle cost you?"

"It didn't cost *me* anything," Polly said dryly.

Kitty laughed. "So what happened to you, after the Colonel took you into his household? Was he good to you? He said he wanted only to have you sing for him, but I can't deny I was worried, he was very much the older, his wife was long dead and you so young and pretty, I did wonder – "

"Yes, he was very good to me." Polly smiled reminiscently. "There was no impropriety, he treated me like his granddaughter. I was taught how to behave in company, how to dress and walk and dance. And he was generous, too. He asked very little of me in return, save to sing for him – he did so love me to sing, he even engaged an Italian master to give me lessons." She stared into the red heart of the fire, her chocolate cup cradled in her hands. "Do you know the story of Pygmalion, Kitty? I think he felt he was doing something the same. He took a rough, ragged, insolent child and gave her the semblance of a lady. Whatever I am now, I owe it all to him."

"Not entirely," Kitty pointed out. "I was the one who told him that my serving maid had the finest singing voice I'd ever heard. I knew he loved music, you see, and I thought he'd be intrigued. But I would not have mentioned it if I had not thought you were worth his interest, lamb. After all, there's no making silk purses out of sows' ears, no matter how hard you try. He saw in you what I saw, but he had the money, the time and the foresight to do something about it. And you had the sense not to waste the opportunity he offered. You always were one to fall on your feet, child."

"I certainly did when I was sent here, too. Not many places would treat a Parish Apprentice so well. Most of them are worked and beaten till their bones are broken. Or like my poor brother Tom, sent into a household of poverty and sickness." For an instant her voice lost its tone of light nostalgia, and trembled on the edge of grief. "A pauper's grave was all he had."

"Did you never find your sister?"

"No, although when I was in Bristol with the Colonel, I tried to discover what had happened to her. I was told that she had been accused of thieving, and had run away. I don't know if she is still alive, but I doubt it. She was so young, poor Mattie, only six years old when we were parted. At that age, she would have been too soft to bear the world's harshness for long."

"And you are different. But it comes at a price, though, don't it," said Kitty, studying her thoughtfully. "You may have fine clothes and a handsome beau, even if he does look like the back end of a thundercloud most of the time, but you're still selling yourself, as surely as any harlot."

Polly laughed. "Dark isn't my beau! Nor do I want him to be."

"Really?" enquired Kitty. ` "That's not what my eyes tell me, lamb."

"Then your eyes must be failing you," said Polly, with cheerful good humour. "I'm a light-hearted person, Kitty, you know that, I love song and laughter and merriment. Why should I wish to consort with a man who spends half his time in a temper and the other half in a fit of the sulks?"

"You tell me," said Kitty comfortably. She had taken off her worn buckled shoes, and now she stretched out her toes to the fire, wriggling them luxuriously inside red silk stockings that badly needed darning.

"And anyway, what if I am selling myself? I'm doing no more than any fine lady who brings a fat dowry to her marriage. All the world runs on commerce, Kitty, you know that as well as I do."

The older woman's only answer was a snort of derision. Polly sent her a shrewd glance, but contented herself with sipping her chocolate, which was now cool enough to drink comfortably.

"So why did you leave the Colonel's household?" Kitty pursued, her voice full of curiosity. "If he was so kind to you – "

"I didn't have much choice in the matter. He suffered an apoplexy, and died."

"I'm sorry for that, lamb."

"So was I, at the time. But that was eight years ago. In any case, he left me a little money and some jewellery, and one of his footmen had taken a fancy to me and asked me to go to London with him, and I jumped at the chance. I never did like Bristol. And in London have I lived, ever since."

"What happened to the footman?"

"Oh, he proved the first of my many faithless lovers."

"So what else have you been up to, in London?"

"No good?" Polly queried mischievously. "Oh, Kitty, I have done many things in those years – I have been a mistress to several and a lover to one, I even took refuge in Mother Whybrow's nunnery very briefly, when I grew desperate – I have sung and danced and loved and lost, and I am growing tired of it. And I am twenty-five, and soon my looks will be gone and men will be seeking younger, fresher flesh – and good luck to them, say I. Do you know what my ambition is now?"

"I'm all ears. Tell away, lamb."

"I pray you, Kitty, do not laugh." Polly looked at her very seriously over her cup. "For a while now, I have had some thoughts of opening a coffee-house."

"Nothing could be further from my mind than laughter," said Kitty, offended. "I think it an entirely sensible idea. But you need more than the will and a pretty face, my girl. You need money, and you need some skill – and not just in making coffee, either. You need the trick of making people content, whether they're your customers or your waiters."

"Oh, I know that, none better. And I know it'll be very hard work in the beginning. But I have some coin saved, and some thoughts of how to set about it. I'm not so green as I'm cabbage-looking, you know, Kitty my dear."

"Didn't think you were, lamb."

Polly smiled at her affectionately. In her three years employed at the Bear, Kitty, irascible, sharp, essentially decent and kind, had to a very large extent taken the place of her dead mother, and she would always respect her advice, however unwelcome or unpalatable. In her long life, Kitty had run three inns with increasing success, had buried two husbands and several children, was a grandmother twice or three times over, and knew more of the faults and failings and habits of man, and woman, than many philosophers. Polly knew that she owed her own veneer of sophistication and gentility to the elderly, music-loving Colonel Metcalf, who had plucked her from the Bear and educated her in the manners and refinements necessary to make her way in the world. But Kitty's practical wisdom had taught her even more valuable lessons. She had seen other girls, far surpassing her in beauty and accomplishments, waste their chances and their talents in the giddy pursuit of momentary pleasures, squandering their money playing cards and their looks and wits in drink. Inevitably they had fallen back to the squalid obscurity of the streets from which they had risen. She had observed, and vowed never to share their fate. And so far, fortune had smiled on her.

"Good," she said. "I would not have you think me a tame goose."

"Never thought you was," said Kitty, with satisfaction. "So – you plan to open a London coffee-house, do you? What does your beau think of that?"

"I told you," said Polly, hoping that her flash of irritation did not show on her face. "Dark is *not* my beau."

"Then if he's not your beau, who is? There must be someone," said Kitty, eyeing her fine lace and tender hands.

"There is no-one. Not now. And even if there were, it would be none of his business, or any man's. I have had enough, and more than enough, of being beholden to men for my bread and my gowns and the roof over my head. From now on, my life is mine, and mine alone."

"Aha – did you wrong, did he? Well, you don't seem to have done too badly out of it."

"No," Polly said, and flashed her a sudden grin. "No, indeed I have not. And now that I am a woman of leisure rather than pleasure, I can indulge any passing whim that takes my fancy."

"Does that include the ragamuffin brat at present cluttering up one of my garret beds?"

"Gin's attached to Dark for some reason I've never been able to discover, but when I return to London, I plan to employ the child."

"You're mad!" said Kitty roundly. "An urchin like that? You won't have a stick of furniture or a whole piece of china left inside a week, never mind the silver."

"You forget, Kitty – I was once in much the same position," Polly reminded her gently. "I was given a chance to raise myself, for which I shall forever be grateful. So I would like to return the favour. Is there anything wrong with that?"

"Nothing at all with your charity, lamb – but a great deal with your head."

"And on my head it'll be, if it turns out for the bad," Polly said. She looked into the fire, wondering whether to reveal more. Something in her shied away from taking her old friend entirely into her confidence. So much had happened to her since leaving the Bear all those years ago, it was utterly impossible to convey a fiftieth of the events and thoughts and changes that had transformed her from a wild, scrawny brat like Gin, into the apparently polished young lady sitting by Kitty's hearth. She added casually, "By the way, is there any word of the people we talked about earlier?"

"There are more than a score of inns in Bath, and many times that number of lodging houses," Kitty pointed out. "It will take a week to check them all. But no, there is none yet. Your Mr. Jessop will have to wait a while longer for news of his daughter – *if* she is here." She sent Polly a very shrewd glance. "You seem very sure of it, lamb."

"I am sure," Polly said calmly, and failed to elaborate.

After a pause, Kitty tried again. "Can I ask why?"

"You can *ask*, certainly, but you won't receive an answer. Let's just say that Miss Jessop and I have an acquaintance in common."

Kitty finished her chocolate and laid the cup on the warm stones of the hearth. A red-hot coal, sighing, collapsed into the embers beneath it, and she yawned suddenly. "I'm for my bed, lamb, and so should you be, if you want to keep yourself as fresh as a June rose."

"A July or even an August rose, surely – I'm hardly in the first flush of youth, after all."

"Well, you look as if you are," said Kitty, smiling at her affectionately. "And we're none of us getting any younger, are we? Anyway, I don't know what you've been up to, Poll Paradice, and I don't want to know. But I pray you, child, be careful. Just because you've always landed on your feet thus far, don't mean you always will."

"Don't worry, Kitty, you know I can look after myself."

"Yes, I do know. But there's deep water around you for sure, and I wouldn't want to see you hurt or in trouble. You're the best maid I ever had here, the quickest and the prettiest."

"And the naughtiest." She rose to her feet and stretched, cat-like, her small hands reaching for the smoke-tarnished ceiling above them. "Do you remember when I ran away to see the puppet show? You beat me soundly for that."

"You never did it again, though, did you?"

"You never *discovered* that I did it again." With her mischievous grin, Polly took the older woman by the hand and gave her a light kiss on one plump, weathered cheek. "Kitty, you saved me from poverty and despair, and I shall always be more grateful to you than I can say. Thank you."

"I'm always kind to them as deserves it, lamb," said Kitty, but her eyes had filled up. "Just don't you go and waste it, that's all. I'd love to hear of you happy and settled, with a good man and maybe a bevy of children. That's all a woman can want from life, isn't it?"

"*Some* women. Not necessarily all. Good night, Kitty, and thank you a hundred times for everything you've done."

"'T'were nothing, dear Poll," said the older woman, smiling. "No more'n anyone would have done in my place."

"Don't sell yourself short, Kitty Martin, you know there isn't one woman like you in a thousand, and I'm luckier than I deserve to have known you."

"Quit your nonsense, girl, and go to bed," said Kitty, and shooed her out of the little room as though she were still the wilful maidservant she once had been.

Later, much later, with the candles blown out in her little room off the gallery above the inn yard, Polly lay thinking about the day's events: of Sam, who both longed and dreaded to find his daughter: of Dark, whom everyone seemed to think was her lover, or wanted to be: and of Gin, caught in a cruel dilemma from which, perhaps, the child could be rescued.

But try as she might, other faces, long dead, kept crowding out the present. There was her father, his face worn and sad with a life of hard work and bitter disillusion, yet still able to smile at his children as he died. Then her mother, who had abandoned a prosperous home and a bright future to marry him, and eventually paid for her choice with her health and her life, sitting weeping in the wagon as Polly, her eldest child, tried in vain to comfort her, for no comfort could be given. Her brother Tom, ten years old, trying and failing pathetically to play the man: and little Mattie, hardly understanding what was happening to them, asking where Papa was, and when they would all go home again.

Polly had known, ever since this very different journey had begun, that coming to Bath would revive all her ghosts. She had never thought herself strong, but like Gin, circumstance had honed and hardened her, and in the end she had proved tougher than all the rest of her family. It must be so, for she alone had survived. And she was both glad, and guilty, for she had never thought that she deserved more than they. She would have given all she had, all her fine clothes and jewels, her beauty and her assurance, to see them again. And never in this world would that be possible. She had long ago accepted it, and made her own life without them: but it did not make the pain any less here and now, in the soft warm darkness of her bed.

It had been many days since tears had seeped into her pillow.

CHAPTER NINE

'New Dangers round him throng'

In Bath, stagnantly sunk within its encircling hills, the air was too warm and heavy even now, in early October. Up on the open green spaces of Claverton Down, though, the wind buffeted briskly through the grass and bustled the cloud shadows across the groups of ladies and gentlemen gathered to watch what would probably be the last races of the season. The brilliant light glittered on the gold lace and opulent jewels, worn with the carelessness of the wealthy, and danced over the glossy hides of the horses, brown and bay, chestnut and black, which had been brought here to show off their speed and stamina.

Sam, astride his willing but undistinguished hired hack, looked around at the company. The highwaymen who notoriously infested the area around the Down, and preyed upon the foolish or the unwary, would slaver at the sight of so much affluence, so brazenly displayed. Even the boldest gentleman of the road, however, would hardly dare to ply his trade here and now, in full view of several hundred people. The danger would come with the homeward ride, especially if dusk were approaching, or if they lingered too long.

Near to him, a little group of men, finely dressed with carrying voices, were debating the merits of the runners being paraded before them, and placing wagers with each other on the likely winner. Their favourite seemed to be the grey, a tall, elegant horse with a very small stable-boy perched on top, like a monkey on a branch. Sam knew little about horses, save as an occasional means of transport, and had even less interest in gambling. He prodded his dozing mount into a walk, and moved unobtrusively on. Behind him, Polly, wearing her smart midnight blue riding habit, gold braid sparkling on cuffs and hem, was acknowledging admiring glances with her usual insouciant charm, despite the presence of Dark, slouched on the big bay mare which had carried him from Bristol, close by her side.

They had agreed on their strategy that morning. Sam, who after all was the only one able to recognise his daughter with certainty, would ride casually around the race-goers, seeking Mary. Dark and Polly, a discreet distance behind him, would observe his progress. If he saw her, he would engage her in conversation, and try to persuade her to leave Sinclair and come home with him. If she refused, or fled, then Dark and Polly, whom she did not know, would follow her and try to discover where she was lodged.

It sounded far too simple for his liking. He had a sudden vision of his daughter, shrieking and furious, arguing with him while all the Quality watched with interest, and his heart quailed within him. He glanced round, and met Polly's eye. She was looking particularly fetching in the diamond light, so unkind to those whose complexions were not at their best. She smiled, and he gently persuaded his horse to move on, closer to where various groups were standing or sitting on the grass under the trees fringing the race course.

As he approached the nearest, something about the way one of the women gestured caught suddenly at his memory. It was surely nothing: a hundred girls, including the one twenty yards behind him, could converse with similar animation, could flutter a fan in just that graceful manner.

But the laugh that carried to him on the fickle wind, joyful and carefree and slightly shrill, could belong to no-one else.

Sam's heart began to thud suffocatingly within his chest. Suddenly, despite the wind, he felt the sweat break out under his thick broadcloth coat, and his eyes strained to see her better. After so long searching, so many disappointments, he could not quite believe that he only had to walk his horse forward twenty yards to speak with her.

He glanced round, and saw Polly watching him. She had evidently noticed some change in him, and had guessed the reason, for she nodded, and smiled, and made a swift little movement of her hand which said, clearer than any words, "What are you waiting for? Go to her."

He gave an answering smile, tight with terror, and then gently urged his horse forward.

There were five people sitting on the grass under a sturdy oak tree, two men and three women, evidently enjoying an *al fresco* meal. As he drew closer, he could see them more clearly. They were all young, and fashionably dressed. The men had that indefinable air about them which marked them out as adventurers, younger sons, gamblers, with eyes that were too knowing, and hard mouths. Sam noted with unease that two of their female companions would have been described by his late wife as 'no better than they should be'. One wore a most unseemly gown with a modesty piece of transparent gauze inadequately covering her ample bosom, and the other had obviously painted her face, which was also sprinkled with a variety of patches. They were both cleaving very close to the men, and giggling a great deal. He was slightly heartened to see that Mary was sitting a little apart from the others, and that her gown, while not quite so stylish as those Mistress Paradice possessed, was neither tawdry nor revealing.

So far, they had not noticed his approach. One of the men was telling a long and involved story that sounded, from the snatches Sam could hear, both malicious and indelicate. His companion kept interrupting with comments and shrieks of laughter at her own supposed wit. The other young woman, her face and neck flushed, was obviously bent on finishing the contents of her wine cup as quickly as possible.

He had dreamed about his meeting with Mary. He had imagined her always in the company of the mysterious St. Clair, or Sinclair, bold and brazen and defiant, or tearfully contrite. He had never envisaged her part of a group like this, and ill at ease in such company. With a sudden surge of anxiety and hope, he swung down from his horse, intending to tether it to the nearest available bush or post.

"Hold him for you, your honour?" said a wheedling, familiar voice. At Dark's suggestion, Gin had accompanied them up to the Down, riding once more behind Polly until the summit of the steep hill, when he had slipped off and become an unobtrusive part of the crowd. His instructions had been to keep an eye on his betters, and to do whatever might be required in the course of the afternoon. He hovered now at Sam's elbow, wearing the shabby but respectable clothes he had been given at Maidenhead. Despite these, he looked more like a scarecrow than ever, but his muddy eyes were bright with the old insolence, not to mention the prospect of earning a penny or two.

"Of course you may, lad," said Sam, smiling at the child with something approaching affection. "And watch me."

"Is that *her?*" Gin enquired nosily, gesturing with a bony elbow at the little group under the oak, so immersed in themselves that they had so far failed to notice Sam's obvious interest. "Your mort?"

"Eh? Yes, yes, it's Mary. The one in the rose-coloured gown."

"She's a rum blowen and no mistake," said Gin, with reluctant admiration. "And the Paradice could be her sister, they're like as two peas. Who's she with?"

"I don't know them," Sam said. Nor, from the look and sound of them, did he wish to become better acquainted. It was Mary he wished to see, not these dubious people who might or might not be her friends. And, with a deep, courage-enhancing breath, he thrust the reins into Gin's outstretched, dirty paw and walked forward.

The woman with the patches was the first to notice him. She stopped in mid-sentence and nudged her companion, none too gently, in the ribs. As if pulled by a succession of strings, the five heads turned to inspect him, and Mary's came last of all.

She recognised him immediately. He had time to note that her face was thinner, and that she wore a string of small pearls about her neck that must be new. Then her mouth opened wide with horrified astonishment and she sprang to her feet, tipping over the wine bottle beside her so that its contents ran like blood over the cloth spread on the grass. "*Father!*"

"Hallo, Mary," said Sam quietly, while his heart threatened to jump up his throat. "How are you?"

From the neat lawn lace-edged cap on her dark curls, to the tips of her embroidered shoes, she was radiating indignation. "What are you doing here?"

Rather belatedly, the other members of the party were also rising to their feet, staring at Sam with avid interest. He ignored them and said to his errant daughter, "I have been searching for you for so long – "

"I'm *not* going home," Mary interrupted him at once. She had recovered a little of her composure, and her full red mouth had a stubborn, wilful set to it that he recognised with dismay. "There's nothing you can say to persuade me, Father, I'm *not going back!*"

Every tendon in Sam's hands longed to seize her, to hug her close to him, and then to shake some sense into her. But he saw the obstinacy in her face and controlled his impulse.

It would do no good to engage in a public quarrel, and he had no hope of winning her over with a display of high words and paternal authority: he knew her too well for that. He added, "I have been so very worried about you, and if you wish, I will take you home."

Mary's face and figure were those of an adult, but her voice and stance were an exact replica of the small child who had been wont to shout at her nurse, "*Can't make me!*" She said again, "I'm *not* going home."

Sam sighed. All around, he was conscious of curious eyes, and the frankly intrusive stares of her companions. Keeping his voice soft and unthreatening, he said quietly, "Mary, please understand that I am not here to force you to come with me, kicking and screaming."

"Then why are you here then – *spying* on me?"

"I was concerned for your welfare. I had no idea where you had gone, who you were with, whether you were safe and happy – "

"Well, I am," said Mary belligerently. "So now you can stop pestering me and go away."

Having come so far, Sam was not to be so easily rebuffed. He said swiftly, "I have only your interests at heart. This is no place to air our differences so publicly. Will you at least do me the courtesy of a private talk?"

For a moment, her eyes flickered, and her mouth trembled. Then behind her, one of the women laughed raucously. "Giving you grief, is he? He don't know what he's dealing with."

Mary lifted her head like a hind scenting danger. She came closer to him, her back to her companions, and said in a low, hurried voice, "You're right, Father, not here, not now."

"Then you'll meet me?" Sam asked, hardly above a

whisper. "Where, poppet?"

At the old, familiar endearment, her eyes flickered again. "I don't know. It isn't safe, I can't just – "

"Please, Mary, please! I don't want to snatch you away or even scold you, I just want to talk to you – surely there can be no harm in that?"

"Don't give him the time of day!" the woman called insolently.

Sudden resolution came into her face, and she moved much closer to him. In a rapid gabbling undertone, she said urgently, "Do you know Bathampton? It's at the foot of this hill, on the way to Claverton village."

"No, I don't," Sam said, bewildered, but she had already rattled on. "Go through Bathampton and along the Claverton road. Where it runs by the river, before the ford, there's a grove of willows in a meadow – if I can, I'll be there by the trees at sunset, tonight. Just you and me, Father, no-one else. Just to talk. If – if you try to persuade me by force, I'll never speak to you again, I swear it."

"Oh, sweetheart, I would never do that, you know I would not!" Sam gasped, heartbroken. "Surely you know that you can trust me?"

The hard, mulish look had closed over her face again. "No, I can't," she said. "Goodbye, Father."

With contemptuous disrespect, she did not even favour him with a curtsey, but turned and stalked back to her companions. In acute distress, Sam watched as they clustered round her, laughing and favouring him with insolent glances. A hot flush of rage swept over him, to be followed by overwhelming sadness. What had his beloved daughter become, to consort with people such as these and ape their uncouth, ill-bred behaviour? And did she really intend to meet him alone, at such an unlikely place, when in the next breath she had addressed him with such disdain? But perhaps her show of defiance was for her companions' benefit, so that they would not be suspicious.

He turned and went back over the unheeding grass to Gin, who was still holding his horse and looking at him with a curious expression on his face. With a start, Sam realised that it was pity. Suffused with shame and misery, he snatched the reins from the child's grasp and stumbled blindly away, the horse trailing obediently after him.

"Oi!" Gin shouted, charging frantically in pursuit. "Oi, you promised me sixpence! Where's me sixpence, your honour?"

Sam halted, fighting for control. It would do no good to break down now, and give way to all the pent-up anger, grief and frustration of the past weeks. With a considerable effort, he fought the impulse to spurn the boy. His sight blurred, he fumbled in the pocket of his breeches and brought out a couple of coins. "Here. Take these."

Gin accepted them with alacrity. "Thank you kindly, your honour," he said, not without irony. "Look, here comes Mistress Paradice, and Mr Dark."

Sam glanced over to the place where Mary and her companions had been. A chatting group of gentlemen blocked his view, and might also have blocked their view of his transaction with Gin. He moved slightly to one side, and saw that they were all once more seated on the ground, and that his daughter, with an intransigence visible even from this distance, had turned her back on him and was talking animatedly to the woman next to her. The sun, now well past its zenith, stretched long golden fingers and indigo shadows amongst the race-goers as they began to drift away towards the lane that led steeply down into Bath. Sam, looking at Mary's obdurate figure, felt suddenly very old, and tired, and inadequate to the task before him. What was he doing here, as far out of his own milieu as a salmon in church? Why was he not sitting comfortably by his own fireside, with the tall silver coffee pot keeping warm on the trivet in the hearth, alongside a blue Delftware plate heaped with toasted buns oozing butter, and the maid entering to light the candles and draw the curtains?

The picture his treacherous mind had conjured up was so vivid and real that tears sprang to his eyes. He hastily brushed his hand across his face and made a valiant effort to master himself. Then, still leading the horse, and with Gin beside him, he moved towards Polly, hoping that his daughter had not realised that he had friends with him.

"Did you speak with Mary?" she asked, as he came up to her.

Sam nodded. "I did, and she proved very stubborn, but I hope that was just for show. Let us move away, so she cannot see us conversing."

On the wide but crowded sweep of the Down, it was easy to find a space to talk which was well out of sight of Mary and her group, and Sam gave Dark and Polly the outline of his encounter, and the hurried arrangement to meet later that evening.

"And do you intend to keep that appointment?" Dark queried.

"Yes, of course. Why would I not?"

"It seems a strange place for a meeting," said Polly thoughtfully. "A very lonely spot indeed. Sam, you are not to go there by yourself."

"But I must! She was most emphatic, she insisted that I come alone, with no one else, and I promised her that. If she sees I have company, she will never meet me, she will slink back to her lover and all will be lost."

"Promise be damned," Dark said. "We would not be your friends if we let you rush into what might well be a trap."

"Mary would not – "

"Oh, perhaps *Mary* would not," said Polly, with a significant look at Sam. "But we do not know about any others she may be with. You will be safest with an escort."

"But if she sees you, she will turn back and I will never have another chance to persuade her to come home."

"She won't see us," Dark assured him. We will follow you at a considerable distance. And after all, she doesn't know that there is any connection between you and us. But even if your daughter intends to meet you alone, she might be followed too, and in any case, at dusk, on a lonely country road, who knows who might be lurking."

Sam's face was still resistant, but he was obviously wavering. Polly said, "Much as it pains me to agree with him, I think Dark is right."

"For that concession, madam, many thanks!" said the artist dryly, inclining his head in her direction.

"You must let us accompany you for at least part of the way," she went on, trying not to smile. "We are only thinking of your safety, Sam. And have no fear, we will be very discreet."

"I suppose you have the right of it," said Sam unhappily, after a pause. "But there is surely no need for you to come, Polly. If it is dangerous for me, then it will also be dangerous for you."

Polly made a scornful noise. "What do I care for that? I'm not some namby-pamby little miss, am I? And I can hit as hard as most men, and scream louder. In any case, remember, I know the parts around Bathampton. You do not, and neither does Dark. What if you can't find the meeting place? I know where it is, exactly. No, Sam, I'm going with you, and there's an end to it."

"Very well," Sam said reluctantly. "I can see the sense in that. What do you say, Dark?"

"I say that I would rather have Mistress Paradice under my eye and my protection, than roaming the countryside fomenting mischief in her usual inimitable fashion."

"You are sadly mistaken, sir," said Polly. She had tried to sound severe, but her smile had broken out regardless. "I never foment mischief – I have good reason for everything I do."

"That is precisely what I find most alarming, madam."

She glanced at him sideways, slyly, from under her long dark lashes. It was a look calculated both to attract and to infuriate, and successfully, to judge from his answering grin. "I am glad to have you for my friend, Mistress Paradice," he said. "For as God is my witness, I dare not think of the consequences, were you my enemy."

"Have no fear," Polly said. "I told you, I shall never be that."

"If you're all going off to meet that mort tonight," Gin interrupted, "then you'll need someone to hold your horses, won't you."

"No," Dark said. "This is an expedition that requires speed and discretion, neither of which will be served by having you tag along with us as if we were a band of travelling players. The fewer people the better. Yes, you have had your uses today, but tonight you wait behind at the Bear. Understand? Or when we return to London, I shall put you into a charity school."

"Oh, Gawd, please, Mr. Dark, please no!" Gin cried. "I ain't going to be no charity brat, I'll die first!"

"You may yet, if you prove disobedient. I shall tell Mrs Martin to lock you up if needs be, for your own protection, and also not to listen to a word you say, for you have the devil's own insolence and you're as slippery as an eel. This evening, Sam, you may have your interview with your daughter at long last. And I for one will do everything in my power to ensure that it is successful."

* * *

Riding along the lane to Bathampton, Sam was prey to a confusing mixture of emotions: anticipation and hope mingled with dread. She would not be there: why should she be, when so evidently her new life, her lover and her friends had taken the place of her family? This was another fool's errand, and he was wasting his time.

He could not forget, though, the look in her eyes as he had talked to her up on the Down, the sensation that she was like a trapped animal, that sees the cage door suddenly opened. And if his instincts were right, he could not abandon her now.

The lane was muddy from the rain the previous day, but at least this evening was fine and dry. The hedges, spotted with bright scarlet hips and haws, hemmed him on either side, and where the low sun broke past the branches, it cast his shadow long and wavering up the low wall of ageing leaves and the spun flossy grey of old man's beard. Cows grazed in the small closes by the winding River Avon, some already being rounded up and driven back for the evening's milking. A thrush was singing the day down from high up in an ash tree beside the lane, and the sweet music, following him as he rode, offered balm to his soul.

The roofs of a village, undoubtedly Bathampton, appeared round the bend in the lane, shaggy thatch and russet tile and stone slate jumbled together. He rode onwards, between the houses and along the muddy lane, the sinking sun at his back and his elongated shadow reaching out in front of him. He had passed several people on the way, and there were more in the village, leaning in doorways, smoking pipes, or gossiping in the street. They glanced at him incuriously, and then turned back to their own concerns. Just past Bathampton, a group of children were picking blackberries from the hedgerow, and a little girl called out a greeting to him as he rode by. But no-one was following him as he rode on towards Claverton, save those two who were meant to be there. To preserve the illusion that he was on his own, he did not look back, but he knew that Dark and Polly, ostensibly out on a pleasant evening's jaunt, had ridden a hundred yards behind him, all the way from Bath. Sometimes he had heard their voices, too distantly to discern any burden of conversation. Wryly, he guessed that they would be bickering again, indulging in that barbed verbal cut and thrust in which both, curiously, seemed to revel.

It had never been Sam's way, to conduct his friendships and do his courting as if engaging with an enemy. They had probably gone at it hammer and tongs ever since leaving the Bear, and he hoped that they would have enough wit left over to watch out for footpads, highwaymen and lurking Jacobites.

As the air cooled with the onset of dusk, wisps of mist were beginning to rise from the fields beside him, and from the river to his left. Ahead, the hills were drawing close, and he knew that very soon the course of the River Avon would swing round to the right. This lane led down to a ford, climbed haphazardly up the slope on the opposite bank, and thence to Bathford. Polly had explained the lie of the land very clearly to him, and even drawn a little sketch map of the place he must find. He fumbled in his pocket and brought out the scrap of paper. Yes, he was nearly there, and behind him the sun had almost set.

The lane was gradually descending now. He glanced urgently from side to side. What if this was another vain excursion? What if the grove that Mary had described did not exist?

Then he saw the trees, close to the river on his left: a small group of ancient willows, some leaning on others for support like a group of drunkards, and sunk in the muddy soil around a small stream flowing down to the greater flood of the Avon. There were no animals in the meadow, and the ramshackle gate had been left propped open by a large stone. His heart thumping, Sam turned his horse to the side, and urged it across the rough grass.

There was no-one there. Acutely disappointed, for a moment he could not believe it. He dismounted, tied his mount to a branch and walked all round the willows. The heels of his riding boots sank in the mud, and the long leaves brushed his face malevolently. He trudged around the trees twice more, peering upwards through the boughs and into holes in rotten trunks. But no matter how hard he looked, he could find no sign that Mary had ever been there.

At last, accepting the inevitable, Sam sat down on an ancient, moss-covered log that had probably fallen when the first King Charles was on the throne, and buried his aching head in his hands. His logical, conscious mind accepted now that he would never bring his wayward daughter home, but his heart, generous, optimistic, instinctive, cried out in pain and denial.

He sat there for some time, while the sun set behind Bath in a flood of red and rose gold and deep, glowering purple. All around him, the birds sang as they prepared for nightfall. Down by the river something splashed, and a duck quacked in alarm.

It quacked again, and there were more splashes. Sam raised his head. There was still some light left, and he could clearly see a rider coming across the ford, the horse wading hock deep in the water. With a wild leap of his heart, he saw that it was a woman.

Every nerve in his body screamed at him to leap up and run to her, but with a supreme effort he kept still and waited. The woman was evidently not a practised rider: unlike Polly, she did not sit gracefully in the saddle, but held herself stiffly and nervously upright, moving in spite of the horse, rather than with it. As the animal emerged from the water, she looked around and then urged her mount up the lane.

It must be Mary, it must. Sam got to his feet and walked a few steps forward, out of the dim shelter of the trees. The movement obviously attracted the rider's attention, for she halted and looked directly at him. Then, with a rather ungainly scrabble, she dismounted, tied the horse to the gate, and walked into the meadow, holding the long heavy folds of her riding habit and her cloak clear of the grass. Halfway to the trees she stopped, and said in an uncertain voice, "Father? Is that you?"

"Indeed it is," said Sam, and the uprush of relief was so profound that he broke out into a sweat, despite the coolness of the air. He hurried forward, his hands outstretched. "Oh, Mary, my dearest girl, how very glad I am that you have come."

For a moment, she stiffened, and he thought that she might after all turn and run. Then she did run, but towards him, and flung herself into his arms with the passionate abandon of a young child who has been lost, and frightened, and now has been found.

For a while they stood together, and his own eyes were wet as he patted her shaking shoulders and hugged her close. "It's all right, poppet, Papa is here now."

At last her sobs died away and she accepted the handkerchief he gave her. As she rubbed it over her wet face, he led her gently back to the trees and sat her down beside him. "Thank you for coming," he said softly. "I very much hoped that you would."

"I'm sorry I was late," Mary said, sniffing. "It wasn't easy to slip away without being noticed." She added, with most uncharacteristic humility, "I hope you were not too greatly inconvenienced, dearest Papa."

"That signifies nothing, what matters is that you are here now. Anyway, I enjoy a peaceful ride in the country."

"Well, I most certainly don't," said Mary, with something of a return to her usual manner. "If I'd known how deep that ford was, I'd have arranged to meet somewhere else, or gone round by the other road."

"In that case, you would have had a very long ride indeed," Sam pointed out. "All the way into Bath and out again." He studied the little he could now see of her face in the dimming light. "How do you fare? Are you well and happy, my dear?"

"Of course I am," said Mary, with a confidence that did not ring true. "Why should I not be? I have money, and friends, and my Robbie, so what more do I need?"

"And do you now wish to come home?"

"No, I do not," Mary said, apparently in genuine surprise. "Of course I do not. But I *am* glad to see you, Papa. Truly I am, no matter what I said earlier. How did you find me?"

He had already debated with himself how to answer this inevitable question, and had decided to be sparing with the truth. "I heard a rumour that you had gone to Bath," he said. "And since rumour is better than no news at all, and I had no other trail to follow, I came here in hopes of finding you."

To his relief, Mary accepted this very edited version of events without further question. "I'm glad you did," she said. "But I wish you had not shown me up in front of my friends. I have been royally teased for it."

"So who are your friends?" Sam enquired, trying to sound casual. "Have you known them long?"

"They are friends of Sin – of Robbie's," she said. "They have lodgings in Batheaston. I do not know them well as yet, we have not met long, but they are prodigious lively company. Lord, how we do laugh sometimes! And Sally knows all the fashions, she has been to France. So you need not worry about me now, and Robbie takes very good care of me."

"I'm sure he does, and I'm glad of it. But what are his intentions towards you?" Sam asked, and regretted the question as soon as it was out of his mouth.

"There you go again, Papa! That's all you can ever think of, isn't it, finding a husband for me – *marrying me off!* Well, I won't have it, do you hear? I *love* Robbie, and he loves me, and we have no need of a parson to confirm what we already know. Anyway," she added, with a fine disregard for her own argument, "he'll marry me one day – there's no hurry, I'm only sixteen."

Never had her essential naïvety and innocence been more apparent. His heart wrung for her sake, Sam said gently, "But what if – if for some reason neither of you can help, he does not marry you?"

"Don't be ridiculous, Father, of course he will." Mary sprang to her feet, her wild energy barely contained within her slender frame. "I told you – Robbie loves me. I say he *loves* me! That's all you need to know, so there's an end to it. I don't want to discuss it any more." Her arms resolutely folded, she flounced out from under the trees and stood with her back to him, glaring at the river.

Sam knew he must accept defeat. If Mary, in order to salvage her pride, secretly wanted him to extract her from a situation that had become intolerable, and carry her back to

Oxford ostensibly by force, she was certainly concealing it very effectively. With an inward sigh, he heaved himself up from the log and approached her. "Mary, sweetheart – "

She paid no attention to him. Instead, she was gazing intently at the river. The light was fast draining away from them, but he could see, as she had seen, that there was another rider crossing the ford.

"It's Robbie," Mary whispered. "I know it's Robbie. He must have followed me."

Fear was plain in her voice. Sam put his hands protectively on her shoulders, and said softly, "Come back into the shadow of the trees, and perhaps he will not realise we are here."

"Don't be silly, Papa, of course he will, my horse is tied to the gate," Mary pointed out. Under the stout broadcloth of her riding coat, he could feel her shivering. "But perhaps he will not mind," she added, with transparently false brightness. "After all, if I tell him you're only my father, how can he object to our meeting?"

So Robbie was evidently prone to jealousy. Sam's heart sank, but he took his daughter's arm and led her forwards, to meet the man who had halted by the gate and was staring at them.

"Mary? Is that you? What in God's name are ye at?" The harsh question rang out across the grass. "Come here now, lassie."

She cast an anguished glance up at her father. Sam bent, and whispered, "Don't worry, poppet. If you don't want to go back to him, I shall tell him so straight – and I am your father, so he can't argue with that."

"You don't know Robbie," said Mary despairingly. "If he wants something, he takes it." As, indeed, he had taken her.

"Come *here*, girl!" It was not a voice that brooked any disagreement.

Sam squared his shoulders and laid a hand on the plain, reassuringly solid hilt of his sword. Despite his brave words to Dark in London, he had little idea of how best to employ it, but the steel under his fingers was enormously encouraging. He said, "It might be wise, sir, to be more courteous when speaking to a young lady."

"Really? And what would ye know of *ladies*, sir?"

The sneer raised the hackles on Sam's back, but he kept his temper well under control. "More than you do, it would seem," he said mildly.

Mary's lover surveyed him with contempt from his horse's back. Sam returned the look with interest. The dying light showed him a tall and well made man with a pale, oval face, unfeasibly handsome: just the type, he thought bitterly, to sweep a naïve young girl off her feet and elope with her. His coat was trimmed with gold braid and his wig was fashionably powdered, even for a hasty ride in pursuit of his errant mistress. "And who may ye be?" he demanded.

"I am Mary's father."

"Her *father?* That's rich, that is!" The young man threw back his head and shouted with mocking laughter. "Ye don't expect me to believe that! Don't deny it, ye had an assignation with her."

"Robbie, I *swear* to you he is my father," said Mary plaintively. "I just wanted to see him and assure him that I was safe, that's all – I never meant any harm by it, I promise you – "

"Then why did ye not come to the house, sir?"

"But you told me never to bring anyone back to the house, or say where we lived," Mary complained, an unbecoming whine tingeing her voice.

"And so ye must arrange to meet him in secret – skulking about the countryside as if ye had something to hide! Do ye want suspicion to fall on us?" As his anger increased, so did the strength of his accent, and Sam, who had met few Scots, strained to follow the sense.

"No – no, Robbie, of course I don't," Mary stammered, beginning to cry. "I thought – I thought there would be no harm in it – he is my father, after all – "

"Your *father,* is it?" With a sudden swift movement, the man leapt down from his horse and strode up to Sam. He was also wearing a sword, a very much more splendid weapon, and his hand rested menacingly on its hilt. "I beg your pardon, sir, but I find that very hard to believe. Did ye want a tumble with the little trollop, then? A man your age should be ashamed of himself."

"My daughter is no trollop!"

"Is she no'? I see it differently, sir. Yes, I do." He thrust his head forward, daring Sam to respond, to give him some excuse to join battle. "Shall I tell ye what we do together, she and I, in our bed? And then say she's no trollop."

"Robbie!" Mary wailed. "Robbie, please, he *is* my father – don't say such dreadful things, I beg you!"

Sam felt a rising sensation of panic. The belligerent Robbie obviously intended to provoke a fight. Where in God's name were Dark and Polly, following him to guard against just this eventuality? He knew he must control his temper, for Mary's sake, but in the face of such a vile onslaught it was desperately difficult.

"Ye paltry wee man," said Robbie, advancing. He was six inches taller and doubtless many years younger, and despite all his brave intentions, Sam found himself taking an involuntary step backwards. "Ye wouldna frighten a mouse! Why don't ye crawl back under your stone, eh, wee man?" He poked a contemptuous finger into Sam's ample chest. "Away wi' ye, and leave us be, eh? And she barely more than a child, young enough to be your daughter!"

"She *is* my daughter," Sam said. A man less wise would long ago have risen in anger against this monstrous provocation, and despite his efforts he was feeling the urge to do as this sneering young cockerel wanted, and begin the fight. Dark should be here, he should have been watching, ready to intervene, but there was neither sight nor sound of him, or of Polly. Where were they, when they were so desperately needed? *Where?*

CHAPTER TEN

'Their Swords the Strife decide'

Polly had mounted her hired horse in the yard of the Bear with a most pleasurable sense of anticipation, which for various reasons she concealed to the best of her significant ability. The skies were still a fragile, opalescent blue, a lovely evening for a ride in the country. And of course, Dark would be with her. Only a few days ago, the thought of his company would have filled her with annoyance, so grim and unpleasant had he seemed. But lately she had begun to see another side to him, a side which he had kept well hidden at first, but which had a tendency to emerge at the most unexpected moments. He interested her: she wanted to see more of the witty, sardonic man who had been so surprisingly entertaining at the ball.

Besides, she had the power to make him smile: Kitty, bless her, had been right.

She arranged the voluminous folds of her cloak and riding habit to best advantage, and turned to see what Dark was doing. He was talking to Gin, who stood slouched by the horse, wearing a most mulish and sullen expression. But Gin would do as Dark said, and Polly had also had a quiet word. The relationship between the urchin and the artist interested her too: once back in London, she would have to find out more about that.

"If you do not make haste, sir, it will be nightfall before we leave this place," she said. "I have been ready this past age, and Sam is long gone."

"Then why are you lingering here?" Dark asked, raising his eyebrows. "Let us go."

Leaving Gin scowling after them in the yard, under Ephraim's watchful eye, they rode out into Stall Street. The way was cluttered with pedestrians and sedans, but a long way ahead Polly saw Sam's sturdy back, unobtrusively clad in good russet broadcloth, almost at the bridge. Smiling, she caught the eye of two young men just passing, and acknowledged their open interest with a modest inclination of her head.

"Are you ogled by *every* man you meet?" Dark queried in apparent surprise, as they negotiated the crowds. "It must be very wearisome."

"Indeed, sir, I do find such exaggerated interest passing tedious," said Polly, with a mischievous sideways glance. "Lord, sometimes I can hardly move a step outside my door for the multitudes that swarm around it, hoping to ascertain the neatness of my ankle, or to earn a glance from my languishing eyes."

"Sometimes, Paradice, you are quite shameless."

"I thought that was a requirement of my profession."

"A songbird surely need not be so."

"Am I a songbird? I thought I was something else entirely. And to judge from your evident disdain since the earliest days of our acquaintance, so do you." She lifted her chin, well aware of his scrutiny, and steered her horse round a sedan that was proceeding in erratic, zigzag bursts, as if the person within was almost too heavy for the chairmen to lift.

"I humbly beg your pardon for that, madam. I know that my manners have at times been unforgivable."

"No, they have not been, for I have forgiven you. We are friends now, are we not? And we are riding out in a common cause, to help Sam."

"Although he will probably have no need of us."

"Do you really think so? Many of the country inns and

taverns around Bath harbour unscrupulous servants who are in league with footpads and the like, and tell them about the movements of wealthy travellers in return for a share of the mint. Claverton Down in particular is notorious. There are very rich pickings to be had."

"I am well aware of that. And have no fear, Paradice, I have no intention of letting any footpad come anywhere near you."

"Oh, I have no fear of any *footpads*," said Polly demurely. "My escort is far more dangerous."

To the sound of his laughter, they crossed the bridge, and then turned left along the meandering lane that followed the course of the Avon eastwards, beneath the bulk of the Down. In contrast to the thick, squalid air of Bath, corrupted by the sulphurous fumes of the waters and concentrated by the surrounding hills, the evening breeze here was fresh with the invigorating scent of damp soil and wet grass. The hedges were studded with scarlet hips and haws, brilliant lamps against the weary green of leaves almost ready to turn and fall, and the gleaming floss of old-man's-beard laced like silver thread in a tapestry through the foliage. Although much of her life had been spent in urban surroundings, Polly had passed her early years in the country, and she breathed deeply, savouring the difference.

Close to the city, there were other groups taking the opportunity for a ride or a stroll at the end of the day, and most of them gave Polly at least a second glance as she rode past, well aware of the pretty picture she made with her dark blue habit, the long velvet mantle draped over the horse's rump, and the dashing tricorne hat. If her escort was indeed dangerous, he gave no sign of it: relaxed in the saddle, he answered her bantering questions about his art with rare good humour, and yet gave nothing of any note away.

"And will you hold to your word, to paint my picture?"

she enquired.

"Of course I will, Paradice. I make promises so rarely that I am always concerned to carry them out to the letter. As I said, I need something decorative to enliven my wall and entice prospective customers."

"And enticement is my business," Polly pointed out, without rancour. She peered at the road ahead. "How long since we last caught sight of Sam? He seems to have vanished."

"A while ago, I must confess. You said you knew these parts – is there a danger that he may have turned aside and we did not notice?"

Polly shook her head. "Oh, no – unless some madness has prompted him to ride up onto the Down. There are no turnings now until we reach Bathampton, which will not be long – can you see the smoke rising behind those trees? And the side roads there all head up onto the hill. Beyond the village and near to the river and the ford, he said."

"I bow to your superior knowledge, madam. But shall we give the horses a run, all the same? If, of course, you are equal to a canter."

Polly rose joyfully to the bait. "I'll have you know, Dark, that I am more than happy to accept the challenge – follow me if you dare!"

Neither of their mounts was especially speedy, but Dark's was a large, ponderous beast with feathery heels and thick legs, and to Polly's delight her chestnut soon drew ahead. As she turned the next bend in the lane, she saw Bathampton in the distance and, just reaching the first houses, the plodding and unmistakable figure of Sam Jessop. Aware that she should not get any closer, she pulled her reluctant horse to a halt and turned, waiting for Dark, who had failed to urge his mount out of a lumbering trot. "You are very slow, sir," she said, sending him her wayward, mischievous grin. "Pray hurry yourself, sluggard, or we shall be benighted before we come to the meeting place."

"Beware, madam, you may find you go too far," Dark warned her, but the corners of his mouth had turned upwards, and although his face was very grave, his eyes were dancing. "Pray, how do you know just what will be the most provoking thing to do or say?"

"Long study and practice, of course," Polly said. She leaned forward and patted her horse's steaming neck. "I am glad to learn that my efforts have been worthwhile."

"Indeed they have. Now let us be off, or we shall lose sight of him again."

"There will be no danger until after Bathampton, I am sure," Polly said reflectively, as they moved on. "This is a comparatively well-used lane, but once it leaves the village, it can be quite lonely, and night is drawing on."

"Do you think he is walking into a trap?"

"No, I do not. But I would much rather be safe than sorry. I like Sam very much, and I would not have any harm come to him for the world."

The village sat smoking quietly in the lee of the Down, with the broad sweep of the river in its green water meadow beyond it. As they approached, a cow's horned head appeared through a gate in the hedge just ahead of them, followed by the rest of it, and then the heads and bodies of its companions, all eager to reach their stalls to be fed and milked. Within a few moments they had filled the roadway, urged on by a small child waving a stick. A wave of remembrance filled her, and she halted her horse, smiling, as the torrent of beasts blocked their path. Long ago, she had been just such a child, and the memory was at once sweet, and very bitter.

"We will lose him altogether if these infernal animals

do not get out of our way," Dark muttered beside her. He fidgeted impatiently in the saddle, and called out to the child. "Hey, you! Hurry yourself – we want to pass!"

The boy turned and stared at them insolently. He had fair hair and a round, flushed face, but the expression on it was very reminiscent of Gin being impertinent. "Can't go no faster," he said. "You'll have to wait."

"Don't fret," said Polly soothingly, laying her gloved hand on Dark's arm. "I'll handle this." She had a quick glimpse of his surprised expression, and then she rode forward. "Child, perhaps this will help clear the way."

She always carried some coins, and the half crown she held out to the boy was generous in the extreme: it would take Gin, with a link, several nights to earn as much. The boy grinned delightedly and capered about, waving his stick. Miraculously, like the Red Sea, the bony brown backs of the cattle parted, and like a female Moses, Polly swept grandly through, with Dark, once more discomfited, following in her train.

They had not been held up for very long, but there was no sign of Sam in the narrow village street, and Polly did not want to ask any bystander if he had come through in case she aroused suspicion: after all, Mary and her lover might be lodging here. Anyway, she knew for certain where he was heading.

"Dark?" she said, once they were well clear of the houses. "If we do not wish to be seen, I suggest we dismount and tie our horses to that tree."

"And then proceed on foot?" said Dark, with a sly glance at her. "Leaving our mounts, of course, at the mercy of any passing footpad or highwayman. It would probably be more sensible to go a little further before we dismount."

With a charming smile, Polly acknowledged it, and

they rode cautiously along the rutted, muddy lane. It was sometimes difficult to see beyond the overgrown hedges, and the light was failing fast, but her eyes scoured the fields on either side, watching for signs of life other than the ubiquitous sheep, and at last found what she was seeking.

"There they are," she said, pulling on the reins. "There, see, to the left by the river? That's surely Sam, and there's a woman with him."

"Thank God she turned up. Let us hope that he can persuade the little minx to go home, and then this caper can come to its proper conclusion. I have business back in London that needs my attention."

"Do you? That is strange, Dark, I was positively convinced that you had come on this journey out of the goodness of your heart. Have you not enjoyed yourself? Has it not been a most entertaining experience?"

"Madam, I have been dragged round Bristol on a wild-goose-chase, I have disported myself in Bath in front of nincompoops who should have been exposed at birth, and I have somehow endured the most blatant exploitation of my goodness of heart, as you put it, by a young woman who most emphatically should know better."

"Are you by any chance referring to me, sir? Am I then to collect that this whole episode has been little better than a nightmare, and that you blame me for it?"

"Of course I blame you for it," said Dark, grinning at her. "But I shall not have my retribution just yet. I prefer to choose a suitable time and place."

Something had happened to Polly's chest, inside the stiff cloth of her coat and within her constricting stays. But she met his clear, challenging gaze without flinching, or with any spurious feminine modesty. "Then I shall have to be on my guard," she said lightly. "For I am sure, Dark, that you will expend a great deal of time and effort in devising a suitable vengeance, and I shall look forward to thwarting you at every turn."

"Then let battle commence. Everything is fair in war, so it's said – and I carry the scars to prove it true."

So do I, said Polly, but to herself.

He was still looking at her, and she said, "Perhaps you are already thinking of how you will paint my portrait. Are you planning to make it satirical? The unrepentant Magdalene, for example, or Jael slaying Sisera?"

"What an excellent idea. I must admit, the thought had not occurred to me. Well done, Paradice, you have solved a dilemma. You may arrive at my lodgings barefoot, clad only in your shift, and with your hair flowing loose."

"And with the multitude following me, eager to glimpse more than just my ankle," Polly said dryly. "I should stop the traffic in the Strand." A movement in the murky distance caught her eye: she paused, narrowing her gaze, and then said quietly, "Who is that?"

Dark's attention had been concentrated on her, but he turned his head to look at the third figure which had suddenly appeared by Sam and Mary. Abruptly he dismounted, pushed his mount's reins into Polly's hands, and said sharply, "Stay here. Don't move."

She stared in alarm as he ran down the lane, his hand on his sword to keep it from clinking in the scabbard, his booted feet soundless on the soft grass of the verge. Then she kicked her foot out of the stirrup, disentangled her other leg from round the pommel, and slid in a flurry to the ground. It took only a moment to find a suitable branch to which she could tie both horses, and then, with her skirts lifted well clear of the mud, she hurried disobediently in pursuit.

By the time she reached the gateway into the field, where another horse was tethered, she could hear Sam's voice, hoarse and urgent. "She *is* my daughter! That is the *truth*, I tell you!" But in response came the harsh rasp of a sword being wrenched from its scabbard, and a woman's scream. "Robbie, *no!*"

The light was now so poor that it was difficult to make out exactly what was happening. She could see the sharp glint of steel, saw Sam stumble backwards, his daughter clutching at him. Then Dark running across the grass towards them, his own weapon in his hand, shouting, "Put up your sword, sir! *Put it up*!"

Her heart pounding wildly, Polly stared into the gloom, her eyes wide as if she could suck in the scene in front of her and somehow make sense of it. Metal clashed, and clashed again. The girl clung to Sam and wailed. Frantic with the desire to do something, anything, Polly ran from the gateway towards them. Her heel caught in a tussock of grass and she fell with a squelch into the mud, losing her hat. She scrambled to her feet with all concern for dignity vanished, and stumbled the remaining yards to his side. "Sam! Sam, are you hurt?"

"No – no, I'm quite unharmed," he said breathlessly. "Where were you? I thought you would never come – that man's quite mad, there's no reasoning with him, he won't believe I'm Mary's father – "

"He's not mad!" the girl moaned. She was still grasping Sam's arm, and sobbing in terror. "He'll kill me – he'll kill all of us – oh, Papa, take me away, please, take me home!"

Her decision had been reached rather late, but at least, Polly thought grimly, it had been reached. "You heard her," she said urgently to Sam. "Go on, remove her now, before she changes her mind again, the silly little baggage."

"Who are you?" demanded Mary indignantly. "How

dare you insult me?"

"Never mind who I am," Polly said. "Just go, before he realises what's happening – I don't know how long Dark can hold him off."

In the gathering dusk, fighting with swords on the soft uneven ground that was full of unseen hazards, it was not a contest full of finesse. Dark had possessed the momentary advantage of surprise, but Mary's lover was fuelled by rage and jealousy, and he hacked savagely at his opponent's blade, driving him back across the grass towards the trees. Sam's horse, unnerved by the shouting, snorted and stamped fretfully as they came closer. Appalled, Polly said desperately, "Sam, take her away, *now*!"

"But we can't just leave him," Sam protested indignantly. "We must do something to help him – " He broke off as his horse, maddened by the approaching conflict, plunged sideways. Something broke with a crack that echoed across the field, and the frenzied animal sprang away from the trees in blind panic, straight at the swordsmen.

As if watching the action in a play, Polly saw Dark shouldered aside by the stampeding horse, saw the sword slash at him as he fell, heard the Scotsman's crow of triumph. She could not move, but Sam gasped in horror and ran forward, shouting and waving his arms. A shapeless sprawl on the ground, Dark did not appear to be moving.

"Stop there, wee man, or I'll serve ye likewise," said Robbie, and the intention to do murder was plain in his voice. "D'ye hear me? I said stop!"

"You've killed him!" Sam shouted furiously. "You lunatic, you've killed him – I'll fetch the constable, have you hanged for this, you murderer!"

The other man laughed, a chilling sound. He began to walk towards his own horse, which stood a few yards off, restive and waiting. "Shout all ye like," he said. "You'll never catch me, nor your lassie neither. Mary!"

Beside Polly, the younger girl made no sound save for a sobbing moan. While Sam bent over the man on the ground, Sinclair reached his horse and leapt into the saddle. He called again peremptorily. "Come here, lass! Now or never!"

But it was Polly who suddenly broke into a ragged, stumbling run across the grass, leaving Sam and Mary and Dark behind her by the willows: and Polly who stretched up a hand to grasp the one reaching down for her, and was pulled roughly up behind Sinclair. He dragged the horse's head round, and drove spurs into its sides so that it leapt back through the gate and along the lane towards the river. Sam, kneeling beside Dark and trying to find some way to help him in the gloom, heard the urgent splashes as they plunged across the ford: and then silence, save for the owls in the wood.

* * *

Polly's cheek hurt where it chafed against the harsh cloth of Sinclair's coat, her wrist ached savagely from being grasped to haul her up behind him, and her fingers, clenched desperately around his waist, were taut with cramp. She had often ridden pillion before, but not at this speed, and not without a pad to stop her bouncing on the animal's round, slippery rump. Every leap of the horse, every swerve and change of pace, seemed likely to throw her from her precarious perch. But she clung on, with all the strength at her command, knowing that if she fell off at this speed, she would probably be sorely hurt. And even more to the point, she would never know where he had his lair.

The broad river lay across their path, palely reflecting the dim sky above, and the horse plunged in. With a sob, Polly tightened her hold, and somewhere within the broad back in front of her, a laugh emerged. But he said nothing, not even a word of encouragement to his mount, which was struggling through the swirling water. It was deep: she could feel it pulling at her trailing mantle. Her skirts were all bundled up around her calves and thighs, and she was acutely uncomfortable. But still she gripped his coat as if it were all that saved her from drowning, and shifted her position slightly so that her seat was not quite so insecure.

Snorting, the horse increased its pace as the further bank approached. Beneath her, its hindquarters bunched and it sprang up onto dry land. Sinclair dragged sharply at the reins, and turned in the saddle to look behind them. Polly did not dare move her head, but presumably there was no sign of anyone following, for he laughed again, a carefree, triumphant sound, and kicked his mount into a trot.

Polly was feeling safer now that the initial effort of keeping her grip and her balance had succeeded. She had time to think, and to plan. Coldly and clearly, her brain made the necessary assessments and calculations, yet she also felt a deep, taut fury, very similar to the rage that had consumed her on the day when, a scrawny ragged child, she had faced the implacable might of the magistrates and pleaded for their mercy on her family. They had shown none, and neither had Sinclair, when he attacked Sam, and cut Dark down. If Dark was dead ...

She would not think of that. He had surely survived much worse, and he must survive this. But if he had not, vengeance lay easily to her hand, and with utter ruthlessness, she would take it.

The horse slowed, and began to ascend. Within the limited confines of her vision, Polly peered through the darkness. They were on a lane or track which led up through a thick belt of low trees and scrub. This must be Bathford Hill, which loomed above the village on the other side of the ford. Where was he going? It surely could not be far, for she did not imagine that Mary would have had the courage or the initiative to ride more than a short distance alone, at dusk, to her rendezvous with Sam. She could not remember what lay up here, whether there were any houses, a farm perhaps, or an isolated alehouse or tavern of the kind that sensible people avoided if they could. Such a place, if it existed, seemed their most likely destination.

The prospect should have filled her with dread, but did not. She had no fear for herself. She had taken the chance that offered when she, rather than Mary, had grasped Sinclair's hand, and in doing so had accepted whatever danger lay ahead. A wild impulse had propelled her forward when he called, and she had hardly dared to believe that her ruse had worked. But in the gloom and confusion it was quite probable that he had no idea that Mary had not been the only woman in the field, and not only were they very similar in appearance, but they both wore sombre colours and long dark cloaks. Certainly he did not seem to have realised that he had the wrong girl behind him.

Once more, he reined in the horse and twisted to check that there was no pursuit. It was growing cold, and Polly felt the night chill strike her right through her thick velvet mantle and the sturdy cloth of her riding habit. She could not suppress a shiver, and Sinclair laughed again. "Dinna fret, lassie, we'll be home and in the warm soon enough. I can see the lights."

He shook up the horse and it began a steady, jolting trot that seemed to rearrange all her innards and propel her stomach upwards into her throat. Hooves thudded on soft earth and then abruptly, slipping a little, rang harshly on stone. The final lurch almost unseated her, and then at last, blessedly, the animal beneath her came to a halt, breathing hard. As she urgently collected her scattered thoughts, Sinclair dismounted and lifted his arms up. His voice was brusque. "Stir yoursel', woman! Or do ye want to stay there all night?"

Polly jumped down. Without gentleness, he set her on her feet and then, gripping her arm above the elbow, propelled her towards the dim building by which they had halted. She had time to glimpse a single wavering light in a small window downstairs, and then they were inside a night-black porch and he was fumbling with the door latch.

All this time, during the frantic ride, she had not spoken, knowing that her voice would surely give her away. But now the reckoning was upon her, and she marshalled all her spirit and resolution. There was a battle to be won, and she was determined to be the victor.

The door opened, and he pushed her through it. Beyond lay a dimly lit hallway, with an uneven stone floor, walls panelled in blackened, mouldering wood probably two centuries old, and a door on either side. Distantly, a woman's voice sounded. "Who's there?"

"Sinclair!" the man beside her called back. "And I've found her!"

With a sudden, swift movement calculated to draw his attention, Polly put back the hood of her mantle and smiled challengingly up at him. "Have you, indeed?"

The Scotsman's astonishment was absolute. He gaped at her in bewilderment, his eyes bulging. Usually he was regarded as a very handsome man, but at this moment he looked like one of the gargoyles on the Abbey church in Bath. A strangled sound came from his throat, but nothing else that was intelligible.

"Well?" Polly enquired. "Aren't you pleased to see me, Robbie Sinclair?"

Belatedly he found his voice. "*Polly*!"

"Indeed it is," she said coolly. "Did you mistake me for your infant mistress?"

"What in the de'il's name are *ye* doing here?"

"I was hoping that you would answer that question. You brought me to this God-forsaken place, after all."

"I – I – "

"What's the matter, Robbie? You're never usually at a loss for words."

With a considerable and obvious effort, Sinclair managed to master himself. He said, "I left ye in London."

"I know you did. How many months ago now? In June, I seem to remember. Waiting for your return grew passing tedious."

"Ye lacked for nothing," Sinclair said harshly. The single candle, reflected in his eyes, seemed to turn them red. "I left ye well provided. Ye can have no complaints on that score."

"No, I have no complaints on *that* score," Polly agreed. Despite the soft, muted light, she seemed to blaze with assurance, as brilliant and implacable as a diamond, and as beautiful. "But I grew curious. Why were you absent so long? And without a word, too, Robbie."

"It was dangerous to write, ye know that as well as I do, darling Poll." His voice lingered affectionately on her name. "If wishes had been all, I would have sent you a dozen letters every day."

"But instead you remembered me so well that you found a replacement for me within a few weeks – a replacement ten years younger." Polly's voice snapped suddenly, like a whip. "You like women with dark hair and blue eyes, do you not, Sinclair?"

He was beginning to recover some of his composure

now. "I dinna ken what ye mean, Poll."

"Oh, don't come the innocent with me, Sinclair, I know exactly what you've been up to. I know who Mary Jessop is, and what you did with her. So let's have no more lies, shall we?"

"Och, Poll, you're mistaking the issue. Mary was a diversion, no more. How could she possibly compare with ye? A child hardly out of the schoolroom – "

"With sweet firm untouched flesh and a mind eager to be moulded to your desires," Polly said contemptuously. "You stole her from her loving, respectable home and ruined her, all for a *diversion?* I thought you were an honourable man. It seems I thought wrongly. You are no better than any of the other worms in breeches who slither about the earth and pretend to superiority over women."

"She wanted to come with me, she implored me – it was pitiable – I could not refuse."

Polly's laugh indicated what she thought of that. "I can well imagine it. 'Oh, dearest Robbie, take me with you, I will *die* if you leave me behind!' So you took her away and gave her what she thought she wanted. And then, too late, she realised that she did not."

"She's a little trollop," Sinclair said angrily. "Ye saw that – making assignations in a field wi' a man old enough to be her father!"

"Robbie, he *is* her father."

There was a brief, significant silence. "How do ye come to be so sure of that?" Sinclair demanded at last. "What were you doing in that company? And how did ye know about Mary and me?"

Beyond his shoulder, a door opened and a woman's voice said, "Will you be wanting supper, sir?"

Sinclair turned. A grossly stout woman, wiping her

hands on her apron, had appeared in the hall. Her small bright eyes fastened curiously on Polly, and she bobbed a very brief curtsey. "I thought you said you had found her," she said to Sinclair, with a look that had more than a trace of insolence about it.

"I was mistaken," said Sinclair, breathing hard. "I'll have supper for two in my chamber, Bet, this instant, and no more questions or it'll be the worse for ye, understand?"

"Yes, sir," said the woman, with a venomous glance, and waddled out.

As the door shut behind her, Sinclair turned back to Polly, his cheeks flushed and his eyes hot. "I'll not have her knowing our business, d'ye hear?"

His face was pushed close to hers, and his spittle struck her cheek, but she did not flinch. "Then if I were you, I should moderate my voice," she pointed out mildly. "I should imagine you can be heard in Bath, if not Bristol."

He raised his hand then, and she thought that he might give way to his fury and strike her, but still stood her ground, her perfect brows raised, her eyes bright. "Then let us go upstairs," he said at last, his teeth clenched. "We have a great deal to talk about, madam." He grabbed her arm, but she shook herself free with a lithe, contemptuous twist and stalked ahead of him to the stairs leading upwards. "Take your hands off me, Sinclair, you do not own me. Remember that, if you please. I am not your property."

"Are ye no'? When I paid for the roof above your pretty head, and the clothes on your back, and your servants and footmen and that fancy blackamoor, and your siller and gold and jewels? You're as much mine as any African slave, madam, and ye'd do well to remember *that.*" Without gentleness, he put his hand on the small of her back and pushed her onto the first step. "Up, woman!"

Polly gathered her skirts and climbed the narrow, uneven stairs. They curled round to the left, and emerged onto a passageway with several doors off it. Every board seemed to creak and groan as if even her slight weight was too much for them to bear. The naked stone walls were smeared with green mould, and a single tallow candle, placed smoking and malodorous on a window sill, gave more light than she would have wished. Sinclair pushed past her, opened the nearest door and held it ajar with a mocking bow. "Pray enter my apartments, madam."

Her chin haughtily high, Polly swept into the room. Ancient hangings covered the walls, the window was shuttered against the night air, and a starveling fire glowered reluctantly in the grate. She noticed a woman's clothes, presumably Mary's, draped untidily over a plain wooden chair. A small, battered box, perhaps for writing materials, lay on an oak table, its top scored and pitted with much use. There was a four-poster bed that looked as if the canopy might collapse on its occupants if they did anything more energetic than lie absolutely still, and the mattress was undoubtedly crawling with bugs and fleas. Two pewter candlesticks shed a guttering light over all, and there was a pervading musty smell of damp bedding, mould, stale sweat and dirt. Polly wrinkled her nose in distaste. "Faugh, what a stink! Can you not even keep yourself clean, without me to nag you?"

"I mislike the place as much as ye do," said Sinclair. "But needs must. This place is isolated and the woman discreet. She should be, I have paid her enough."

"A shame, then, that she did not provide furnishings that do not look as if they will collapse from the woodworm at a touch. Is it safe to sit down, do you think?" She poked a dubious finger at the rickety chair, and gingerly lowered herself onto it. The legs creaked, and the seat settled a little under her, but it held. Secure and confident, Polly surveyed her former lover and said, "Did Mary like her pretty love-nest, then?"

Sinclair flushed. He said defensively, "She had no complaints."

"Yet she wanted to go home with her father. You called her, and she refused to come."

"Ay, so she did – but *ye* came in her stead." In one long stride, Sinclair was standing over her, and Polly, who was beginning to regret her decision to sit down, had to tip her head back to look up at him. "I'll ask it again – how in God's name did ye find me?"

She had known he would persist, and had her answer ready. "You have not been especially discreet, Robbie. Jenny told me that you had found another love, and one of her cousins knew where you had gone with her. Then Mary's father came looking for her in London. His friend thought that I might be the girl they were seeking."

"Ye flatter yourself, madam. Even in the softest candlelight, ye would never pass for sixteen again."

"So you descend to insults now? You left me with words of love, but a few days later you were enticing an innocent young virgin into your bed. Well, now you will have neither of us, for she is returning to Oxford with her father, and I am going back to London, and if I never see you again, Robbie Sinclair, it will be a day too soon."

"But Poll – I thought ye loved me!"

"I was mistaken," she said coldly. "And for sure you have never loved me."

"And what will ye do? Everything you have is mine – "

"No, it is not. My heart and soul are mine alone, and you have never possessed them, nor has any man. You are deluding yourself if you think that I will sacrifice all pride and dignity to a love that never existed, for the sake of some pretty jewels and a comfortable lodging. It's false coin, and I will have no more part of it."

In the silence, there was a blunt tap on the door. Sinclair swung round angrily. "Now what?"

The fat woman shuffled in, bearing a tray. "You wanted your supper, didn't you, sir? Then here it is." She set it down on the table, pushing the box out of the way. Sinclair snatched it up before it could fall on the floor, and put it on the bed. "Get out," he said tersely.

"Very good, sir," said the woman insolently, and withdrew. Polly, looking at the greasy, scrawny joints of chicken and coarse grey bread, was glad that she had already eaten that evening. There was also a squat green bottle that presumably contained wine, together with two plain lopsided glasses. Sinclair poured the contents of the bottle into these and held one out to her. "Will ye no' at least take a drink wi' me?"

She could smell the thin, sour liquid and shook her head. "No. I will accept nothing else from you."

"Then I'll have that mantle off your back, ye thieving trollop!"

He put the glass down and lunged at her, but Polly was too quick for him. Before he could grab her, she had dodged round the table, and surveyed him coldly. "You're no better than a thief yourself, Robbie Sinclair. If he who paid for it owns it, then everything I possess properly belongs to James Stuart."

As she had known it would, that gave him pause. He stared at her, breathing hard, his eyes wild with fury. She pressed home her advantage. "Wouldn't your masters like to know what you did with all that gold, Robbie?"

"There's enough arms and powder stored in Bath to fuel

the rebellion in the West," he said indignantly. "That's what I did with it!"

"But not with all of it. The rest paid the rent on the house in Flying Horse Court, and bought my fine clothes, and yours, and that gold-hilted sword, and the blood horse you ride, and I cannot think that Ormonde will approve. How does the purchase of a blue velvet mantle for your mistress further the Jacobite cause, Robbie?"

Once, he had been charming, attentive, entertaining company. Despite her earlier words, she had truly thought that she loved him, so she had accepted his gifts and his protection because she was a woman alone, and because she had vowed long ago never to descend again into the abyss of poverty and powerlessness. But she had discovered, when she learned of his betrayal, that sometimes a price can be too high.

His face had changed. It lost its anger and became focused, calculating. His eyes, nearly as blue as hers, narrowed suddenly. "Are ye by any chance threatening me, sweet Poll?"

Then she realised the danger she was in. She had reminded him of how much she knew. How ruthless was he? How devoted to the cause he professed to revere? How far would he go to protect himself and the rebellion he was nurturing in this squalid place?

In the tense silence, she heard a horse approaching the house. Its hooves clattered on the cobbled yard, and then someone knocked quickly on the front door, a distinctive pattern, three double taps in quick succession.

"Stay here," said Sinclair. "We'll finish this later." He strode to the door. "I'll no' tolerate anyone, man or woman, who puts the Cause in danger, understand?"

"All too well," said Polly, but the door had already slammed shut behind him. With horror, she heard the sound of a key turning, then his footsteps running down the stairs.

For an instant, panic threatened to overwhelm her. She was trapped, he would come back in a few minutes and kill her, she had seen it in his eyes ...

Polly sucked in several very deep, deliberate breaths and mastered her terror. He was not some mad assassin, he was Robbie, until very recently her lover, and she knew him better than that. He was wild, reckless and dishonourable, as his seduction of the innocent Mary proved, but surely he was not a murderer. At this moment he might think that he wanted to kill her, he was so furious with her, but she was sure that she would be able to calm him down and talk him out of it. In any case, it would not be in his interests, and Robbie's interests had always reigned supreme.

Below, the door opened and closed, and she heard voices receding. Whoever his visitor was – probably another Jacobite agent – he was not going to bring him upstairs. So she had time: time to think and to plan. Time to escape, if she could.

Swiftly and silently, she crossed to the door and gently checked it. The lock seemed secure, and in any case, getting out this way would mean negotiating those stairs, with every groaning step betraying her. The only other alternative was the window. Polly went over to it, lifted the bar on the shutters, and opened them. The hinges had been greased, and there was no sound. Behind them was an old-fashioned stone mullioned window, glazed in tiny, lead-framed panes of thick glass. One side was fixed, but the other was a casement. She undid the catch and very carefully pushed at it. For a moment it stuck, and then with a sudden jerk the frame freed itself and swung outwards, nearly pitching her forward onto the sill.

Cold air rushed at her, and the soft sounds of the night. She thrust her head out and looked down. The window gave onto the back of the house, and as it was built on a slope, the drop this side was much less than it would be onto the stones of the front court. Her eyes, straining through the gloom, made out some straggly bushes and long tufted grass. If she could squeeze through the gap, and hang by her fingertips from the sill, she would have a fall of a few feet at most. The window was small, but so was she. Polly stepped back and surveyed it judicially. Yes, it was surely possible, but only if she removed some of her voluminous petticoats and her mantle. She was still young and supple, in spite of Robbie's insults, and as a child she had been an agile hoyden, climbing trees and larking about with her brother and sister.

There was one last thing to do before she left. Polly turned back into the room and picked up the little wooden box on the bed. She tried the lid, but it was locked.

She heard a sudden sound outside the door: someone was coming up the stairs. She stiffened, listening intently, and then put the box down, crept forward, and picked up one of the dented pewter candlesticks. Hot stinking tallow dripped onto her hand, but she ignored the pain. If she stood behind the door, she would be able to smash it down on Robbie's head before he had a chance to do anything to her ...

It was the slatternly woman. Polly heard the floorboards protesting all the way past the door, and muttered complaints. "Says he'll want me later! And never a please nor a thank you neither! Who does he think he is? No gentleman, that's for sure!"

The voice faded away into the distance, and a door shut with an ill-tempered smack. Somewhere, deep within the house, she thought she could hear Robbie's voice, and another man's answering it. With luck, he would be busy for a while yet with his unexpected visitor. Her heart thumping madly and her palms greasy with tallow and sweat, Polly put the candlestick down, lifted up the trailing wet hem of her riding skirts, and unfastened the petticoats beneath them. She stepped out of the fine creamy lawn and lace, leaving it in a heap on the floor, and dropped her mantle on top without a twinge of regret. She had been very fond of that garment, but now her freedom and safety were far more important. Then she pulled out one of the long pins holding up her hair, and turned her attention back to the box.

She had been taught this skill by one of the other girls at Mother Whybrow's, and it had proved far more useful than anything else she had learned at that very dubious establishment. It took perhaps half a minute of gentle probing and testing, no more, before there was a small positive click, and she was able to raise the lid. Inside, a corked bottle of ink and a couple of pens lay on top of a thick pile of papers. Polly lifted out the contents and laid them carefully on the table. She glanced through the documents, selected a few, rolled them up small and inserted them with great care down the neck of her riding coat, so that they nestled inside her stays. Even more carefully, she replaced the rest, put the quills and ink back on top, closed the lid of the box and used the pin to reset the lock. Then she put it back on the bed exactly as Robbie had left it, before turning once more to the window.

If anything, it looked even smaller than it had done a few minutes ago. Ruefully, Polly assessed her chances. If only she had not eaten such an excellent and filling supper before riding out. Four chops, some chicken, and the better part of a very delicious apple pie had enlarged her to the point where she had had to ask Kitty to loosen her stays more than a trifle. Would that ensure that she was trapped here, in this foetid room?

Not if I can help it, Polly said to herself, with determination. She dragged a stool over, and used it to help her clamber up onto the deep stone sill. Then she took a firm grip of the stone mullion, and slid her legs through the window.

But her skirts, bunching up around her, had increased her circumference so much that she quite blocked the opening.

There was no room to squeeze her arm round and pull them free. Again, panic surged up, but she squashed it ruthlessly. Things could be worse, at least she had not gone headfirst. If she had, she could imagine Robbie striding in, seeing her wedged in the window with her rump bare to the four winds, and taking lecherous advantage of her humiliating plight. The thought was at once ridiculous, and extraordinarily motivating.

"God damn him for a fornicating deceitful thieving rogue!" Polly muttered through clenched teeth, and with all her strength gave one last frantic squirm. Her naked skin scraped agonisingly on the rough pitted stone, there was an arm-wrenching jerk, and then, scrabbling in a most undignified way, she lost her hold and slid feet first through the window.

Fortunately, it was not far to the ground, but still the shock as she hit the earth jolted sharp pains up her feet and legs. She crouched on the grass trying not to whimper, and wondering if the sound of her fall had been heard. But there were no shouts, no running feet, not even a barking dog. Of course, in this lonely place, a dog would advertise any visitor across the whole valley. Polly would have laid a handsome wager on there being no dog. The people here wanted their activities to remain unnoticed.

Painfully, she stood up. Nothing seemed to be broken. She hobbled a few experimental steps and then, her skirts gathered in her hands, crept cautiously along the back of the house and round the corner.

Slabs of soft yellow light shone from a window a few feet in front of her. Instinctively, Polly ducked down. She was just crawling past when she heard Robbie's voice, shockingly loud, and apparently right above her head. "So, all's ready. It must be soon, or we'll lose any advantage we have left."

His companion's voice was far less distinct. Polly,

frozen beneath the window, heard only the words, 'great risk'.

"And when was plotting rebellion not a great risk, eh, Mr. Dunn? What do ye think we're planning, a tea party for ladies? Don't make me laugh, laddie!"

She did not dare to move. He must be standing at the window. What if he leaned out to close it, and saw her?

The man Dunn said something in an aggrieved tone. To her intense relief, Robbie's reply was just as unclear: he must have turned back into the room. Polly scuttled forwards until she reached the next corner, and peered cautiously round it. Yes, there was the front of the house, as she had expected. A lantern had now been hung outside the porch, and cast an inadequate light across the uneven cobbles. She glanced quickly up at the sky. There was a three-quarter moon somewhere behind those thin scudding clouds, but the air smelt damp and cold, and she could hear the wind fidgeting restlessly in the trees beyond the courtyard. Rain was coming, without a doubt, and there were upwards of three muddy, murky miles back to her warm bed in the Bear. Moreover, she was wearing riding boots, and the stiff leather would be most uncomfortable for walking any distance. Either she would have to suffer the blisters, or go barefoot.

Something large moved just outside the limits of the lantern light. For a moment her heart lurched with apprehension, and then she realised that it must be Mr. Dunn's horse. She slunk along the wall of the house, ducking down below each of the windows, although they were unlit, until she reached the porch. There was a sturdy dark coloured cob tethered to a ring in the wall. It raised its broad white face at her approach and snuffled at her softly. Another horse stood beyond, and her eyes, now accustomed to the gloom, recognised Robbie's fine chestnut.

Prigging prancers was a capital offence, but somehow Polly thought that neither Dunn nor Sinclair would care to notify a magistrate of their loss. Using her hands and the murmur of her voice to soothe and reassure, she moved between them. Yes, they were both still saddled, and their riders' negligence was to her advantage. Very slowly and carefully, she untied first the cob, since it seemed likely to be the most docile, and then the chestnut. The white-faced horse's whiskers tickled her face as he nuzzled hopefully for a titbit, and his warm aromatic breath sent a great tide of nostalgia surging through her. As a child, she had been good with horses, and she had never lost the knack. She took both sets of reins tight in her hand, and led them quietly out of the yard. Behind her, no window was opened, and no-one shouted. The rain was falling steadily now, obscuring any sound they might make. When they had gone well beyond reach of the lamplight, she kilted up her trailing skirts as best she could, and scrambled up onto the cob's broad back. Of course it was a man's saddle, so she must ride astride, but there was no-one about to be shocked at such brazen behaviour. She found the stirrups, pulled her skirts down to cover her legs, and then clicked her tongue at her mount. With a willing obedience that cheered her heart, he moved off at once, and the chestnut, feeling the tug on the reins and averse to being separated from his companion, followed them. She gave a gusty sigh of relief, for without the horses, Robbie could not pursue her. For the moment, she was surely safe.

CHAPTER ELEVEN

'Safe from nightly Harm'

Polly had worried about losing her way, but the moon made a brief appearance at last, and showed her the bare shoulder of the hill, and the distant pale ribbon of the river below. Downwards, and a little to her right, a dark smudge and a few faint lights marked the position of Bathford, snuggled beneath the down. Surefooted in the mud, the cob strode down the rutted track, and Sinclair's horse paced effortlessly beside him.

Dogs barked in the village as she approached. She had thought of riding round through Batheaston and along the northern bank of the Avon, thus avoiding the ford, but she did not want every householder in Bathford coming out to see what was amiss, so there was nothing for it – she would have to brave the water. It lay before her, deep and fast-flowing, a dangerous and formidable barrier, but her fear of it was less than her fear of being pursued and caught.

"God damn him," Polly muttered again, and set her horse at the ford.

The cob, wonderfully game and undaunted, waded straight in without a qualm. Sinclair's horse obviously did not fancy the thought of crossing it for the third time that night, for he baulked at the edge, pulling the wet reins out of her hands. As she cursed him, he turned and plunged back along the lane, snorting in fear.

Good riddance, Polly thought robustly, and urged her mount onwards with soft words of encouragement. "Come on, boy, not far to go, you can do it!"

They were nearly at the further bank when there was

a sickening jolt and suddenly the cob lurched sideways. Polly grabbed at the pommel, missed, and made a frantic clutch at a tuft of coarse mane. Underneath her, the horse struggled in the water, and she felt the cold fingers of the river pulling at her heavy skirts. She had lost the reins, both stirrups and almost her seat, and she was surely going to fall in and be dragged under. Desperately she flung herself forward and tried to link her hands round the cob's neck. The water was icy cold, and she could feel the strength of the current swirling round them as the animal fought to stay upright. With a last violent effort, his scrabbling hooves struck solid ground and he heaved himself back onto the shallower bed of the ford. The lurch was too much for Polly's precarious balance: with a total lack of grace and dignity, she slid down the cob's side and fell with a heavy splash into the freezing, rushing river.

She had assumed it would be deep, so she was not prepared for a landing in less than a foot of water, with the hard stones of the ford bruising her rump. The dark bulk of the horse staggered overhead, and for a dreadful instant she thought that he would come down on top of her, but he found his footing and hauled himself up onto the bank. The wet reins flapped past her, and she made a wild grab for them, missed, overbalanced and found herself on all fours with the icy Avon surging around her, while her mount galloped off into the gloom.

"And I hope you go for knackers' meat!" Polly yelled at the departing cob. Mindful of the splashing water endangering the precious papers inside her stays, she tried to struggle upright. It was hard to keep her balance in the strong current, and her skirts seemed to be demonically determined to pull her over. Cursing the horse, Robbie, Sam, Dark, Mary, and anyone else who could possibly be responsible for her plight – everyone, in fact, except herself – she dragged the hem of her habit up out of the river, and waded desperately towards the bank. She fell again, twice, and snared her skirts on something sharp sticking up out of the water, probably a root. At last, abandoning all dignity, she crawled out onto dry land, which proved to be thick and slippery mud, and lay there gasping and shivering with relief at the nearness of her escape. If she had landed in the deeper water, she knew that she would have drowned, for she was unable to swim, and her skirts would have dragged her down.

But she could not lie there all night. Gritting her teeth, grimly determined, she rolled over and sat up. Careful exploration confirmed that the papers were, miraculously, still dry. She hauled her boots off in turn and shook them upside down. That got rid of most of the water, but when she put them back on they were cold and clammy, and the leather had shrunk. To compound her misery, the rain began to fall harder, hissing on the surface of the river and stinging her face, and there was an ominous mutter of thunder in the distance. Polly stood up, draped her soaked, trailing skirts over her arm, and set off down the muddy lane towards Bathampton. Very soon she passed the open gateway into the field where, an hour or two before, Dark and Sinclair had fought, perhaps to the death. She peered into the gloom, but there was no sign that anything untoward had ever happened in that dim, featureless meadow.

If he was dead, she had her revenge ready. It would not bring him back to life, but at least Robbie would not escape scot-free.

After a hundred increasingly agonising yards, she stopped and took the boots off. They had been expensive, so she tucked them under the other arm and proceeded barefoot, after throwing her ruined stockings over the hedge. Despite the thick sludgy mud squelching up around her toes, she felt far more comfortable, and she was tolerably certain that now she must be safe from pursuit. Robbie might not even have discovered her escape yet. And if the farm did possess other horses, he would not know which way she had gone, and in the dark there was no means of tracking her. He might guess that she would be making eventually for Bath, but she did not think that he would risk trying to waylay her at the entrance to the city. A Jacobite spy would hardly wish to draw attention to himself, however compelling the reason. And quite possibly he would not notice the theft of those papers for some time.

No, he would dismiss her escapade with a worldly laugh, and forget both her and Mary in the excitement of plotting rebellion. She knew him too well. He loved women, but they were only pleasurable adjuncts to the mainspring of his life, to be picked up and discarded at will. He had always underestimated her, and with luck it would prove to be his downfall.

The storm broke in earnest just as she reached Bathampton. It ensured that dogs and villagers did not notice her bedraggled figure as she trudged along their mired street in torrential rain, but suddenly the ceaseless battering of wind and water and sound was more than she could bear. A flash of lightning above the down revealed a barn in the next field. She climbed up to the top of the gate, fell painfully down the other side, and hobbled into the dark dry space within. Another momentary flare showed an empty cobbled floor, and in the corner a generous heap of straw, as welcome as any feather bed. Cold, dripping and desperately weary, Polly sank down onto the prickly mound and fell almost instantly asleep.

* * *

In these troubled times, with rumours of Jacobite conspiracy and invasion flying like chaff in the autumn winds, the gates of Bath were closed every evening, and opened again at dawn. The usual collection of market traders, farmers, travellers and merchants streamed through in the early light, together with less desirable elements – beggars, vagabonds and sundry criminals, bent on milking the wealthy inhabitants of the city with as much panache, if rather less lucratively, as they were fleeced at the gaming tables by Nash and his cronies. It was impossible to stop all of them, and the gate-wards never usually tried very hard: a torrent of foul abuse would be the least reward for their pains. But the young woman limping at the end of the draggle-tailed crew had already attracted a following of jeering urchins, and no wonder: her garments were crusted with mud and filth, there was a huge rent in her skirt which revealed a tantalising glimpse of bare thigh, and her hair, matted and tangled with straw, coiled in filthy snakes on her shoulders. Sensing the prospect of sport, the undersized youth who had opened the gates stepped in front of her. "Where d'you think you're going?"

Polly stared at him coldly, her blue eyes like chips of sapphire. "Out of my way," she said, with a calm that belied her inner fury. "Or it'll be the worse for you."

The young man laughed mockingly. "Fine words from such a drab," he sneered. "So what are you going to do to me, eh? I know what I'd like you to do to me." His eyes stripped her foul clothes from her with naked lust, and he licked his lips. "This groat says you'll suck my cock and – "

Polly hit him with a strength that was considerably enhanced by rage. Amid the derisive cheers of the onlookers, he staggered back in astonishment, his mouth suddenly a mess of blood. She pushed past him, her trailing skirts gathered in her hand, and stalked doggedly up Southgate, still pursued by the crowd of children. Her knuckles were bleeding and her whole arm tingled from the force of the blow, but she did not regret it in the least. She would have liked to do the same to Robbie, but the pimply youth had proved an adequate substitute. Ignoring the urchins, as she had done since acquiring their company close to the city, she concentrated on preserving her dignity as best she could, given her dreadful appearance and the fact that her feet, slopping about inside the cold wet riding boots which she had thought best to put back on before entering Bath, had been rubbed raw.

And here was the Bear, a blessedly familiar haven, and for the first time her mood of angry and determined stoicism faltered. Up until now, all her energy and will had been bent first on escaping from Robbie, then on the struggle to avoid drowning in the river, and the long, miserable trudge back to the city once dawn had woken her from her exhausted sleep in the barn. But in the next few moments, she would find out whether Dark was alive, or dead. And a terrible apprehension welled up in her, for she very much wanted him alive, and yet she feared that he was not.

The first person she saw as she walked under the arch into the yard was Ephraim, backing a grey horse into the shafts of a carriage. He stared at her in disbelief and then, still holding the horse, shouted across. "Poll? Where ee bin, maid?"

"Several places I would rather not have been," Polly said grimly. Her feet were almost unbearably painful, not least with the prospect of imminent relief, but she hobbled over to her old friend. "Ephraim, did they come back? Mr. Jessop and Mr. Dark?"

"Oh, aye, so I hear, and a young lady with them," Ephraim said. His washed out grey eyes, old but still observant, assessed her extremely disreputable appearance. "You bain't looking so trim, Farthing," he pointed out. "Surgeon be inside, I'd ask him to look ee over nif I were ee."

"The surgeon?" Polly's heart lurched, but she made strenuous efforts to conceal the rush of hope within her. "Who is he seeing?"

"That long grim black-haired fellow," said Ephraim, with a shrewd glance at her which revealed that he had perceived rather more than she would have wished. "At death's door he looked when he came in, so I d'hear."

"Oh, sweet Jesus," Polly whispered, her hands flying to her mouth. "Thank you, Ephraim," she added, and limped into the inn as fast as her abused feet would allow her.

The stairs loomed in front of her, and coming down them, solid and reliable, was the very welcome figure of Samuel Jessop. Panting, Polly stopped, and found that her voice, usually so fluent, had suddenly deserted her. "Sam?" she gasped. "Oh, Sam, how is he?"

"Polly!" He stopped abruptly and stared down at her with obvious relief. "Thank God you're safe! But what on earth has happened to you?"

"Never mind that! Dark - how does he do? Ephraim said ... " She stopped, struggling for composure, and then added, "Just tell me, please, Sam - is he going to die?"

"Die? Who, Dark? No, of course he isn't - just a scrape along the ribs, it's a nasty scratch but if it takes no infection he'll be right as rain in no time."

"Oh, thank God," Polly said. And suddenly, to her surprise and horror, her legs gave way and she sat down with a thump on the bottom step and put her head in her hands, trying desperately not to weep.

"Polly, please, my dear ..." Sam sat down beside her and put a hesitant hand on her shoulder. "You're soaked, you look terrible – what happened?"

His kindness almost undid her, but she marshalled her strength and lifted her head with a smile. "I'm sorry, Sam, I'll explain soon enough. But I must see Dark now."

"The surgeon is with him – he may not welcome visitors – "

"He'll welcome me when he hears what I have to tell him." Polly stood up. Every bone and muscle in her body shrieked in protest, but she ignored all the aches, and the pain in her feet, and began to climb the stairs. The chamber that Dark and Sam shared was the second door on the left: as she reached it, a small grey man in a very exuberant wig emerged, his thin, sallow face full of satisfaction. He stared at her dishevelled state with his eyebrows raised, and his omission of a bow spoke eloquently of his opinion of her. To Sam, puffing up behind, he said with a smile, "Yes, he will do very well now, sir. I have applied a poultice, strapped up the wound and let five ounces of blood, and I would now prescribe a day of rest, maybe more. Rest, sir, is most efficacious in these circumstances. And with your leave, I will call again tomorrow, to change the dressings."

The two men exchanged bows and the surgeon clattered away down the stairs. Sam was still looking at her as if he could not quite believe his eyes, so she gave him a tired, encouraging grin. "Pray knock on the door, Sam – I fear it would not be quite proper for me to do so."

"But you heard what the surgeon said – he needs rest, can it not wait until later?"

"No, I regret it cannot, Sam," Polly said. He was still staring at her like a booby, so she turned and rapped smartly on the door. Without waiting for an answer, she lifted the latch and walked straight in.

Dark was lying propped on a multitude of pillows. He looked pale and very tired, and the lack of a wig and the soft fuzz of brown hair on his head made his lean face seem surprisingly young. At Polly's entrance, he sat up abruptly and then fell back, wincing. "Paradice! I'm very glad to see you safe, if not exactly sound."

"I could say the same of you." There was a chair by the bed, and Polly sat down on it, trying to disguise the utter relief of taking the weight off her feet, while Sam shut the door. "I have come to give you these papers."

With considerable aplomb, she undid the top two buttons of her riding coat and plunged a hand into the depths. Dark watched with interest. "If you have any need of assistance ..."

She glanced up and met his eyes, which were bright and amused. "Indeed, I do not, sir," she said, with a return of her cool, slightly insolent manner. "For here they are, and I am handing them over to you, because you are the person most qualified to make use of them."

She withdrew a small tattered roll, and laid it on the bed within his reach. It was damp, but the writing, although smudged, was still legible. At the top of the outer sheet could plainly be seen the words, *'List of those Gentlemen loyal to the Cause around Bath.'*

"There you are," Polly said. "You are a government spy, are you not, Dark? Then for God's sake take these documents and make good use of them, because I have gone to considerable trouble to obtain them, and I have no intention of returning them to their rightful owner."

Dark was staring at her as if he could not credit what she was saying. Suddenly impatient, she leaned across and pushed the papers under his hand. "*Read* them, you purblind fool!" she said fiercely, and sat back, watching keenly, as at last he obeyed her and unrolled the sheets, still warm from her body. He gave the top one a swift glance and then raised his eyes to her. There was genuine, frank astonishment in his face, and also burgeoning respect. "Just *where* did you get these, Paradice?" he demanded. "From Sinclair? Did he not object?"

"He may not have discovered, even now, that they are missing," Polly said. Briefly, she recounted the tale of her night's adventure, though she omitted the full indignities of her fall into the river and the prolonged and painful struggle back to Bath. Dark made no expression of sympathy, or praise. He bent his head once more and gave each paper a quick but thorough perusal, before speaking again. "So these were in his writing box? I did not know you could pick locks, Paradice. The list of your hidden talents is remarkably long. I shall have to explore them fully at some future date."

"Pray do not trouble yourself," Polly said briskly, but she had seen the look in his eyes and concealed a smile. She added, "So what will you do with them?"

"I should very much like to be told exactly what these papers contain," Sam said, obviously unable to suppress his curiosity any longer. "In God's name, what is in them, Polly?"

"A list of the names of all the Jacobite sympathisers around Bath and further afield in the West Country. Together with the total quantity of arms which each has stated he is willing to supply, and the whereabouts of a considerable store of gunpowder and muskets secretly held within this city. In the cellar of a house near the Eastgate, to be precise."

She paused, and Dark filled the astonished silence. "These three pieces of paper are enough to hang anyone whose name is mentioned on them. And Sinclair." He glanced up and met Polly's eyes. "Sinclair was your lover, was he not? The mysterious man who kept you in such style? I am beginning to see the picture. Did you know that he was a Jacobite?"

"I lived under his protection for nearly a year, of course I did. He did his best to persuade me of the justice of his cause, and at first I believed him, but then I came to see that it was a foolish dream. I tried to talk him out of it, but he would not listen. And then he told me, in June, that he was going away on the King's business."

"The King being James rather than George, I take it. But *you* are not a Jacobite?"

"I certainly am not. If I were, would I have gone to such trouble, and put myself in such danger, to bring you those papers?"

Blue eyes met brown again, and held. “I think you have too much sense to be involved in plotting treason,” Dark said dryly. “But what of your faithless lover? Do you really want him to end on the scaffold?”

“Robbie is a gambler by nature, he knows the risks he runs. I had little sympathy for him, even before I saw what was in these papers, because of what he did to Mary.” She glanced at Sam, who was staring at her in astonishment. “Which reminds me, where *is* Mary?”

“Asleep in your bed,” Dark told her. “Exhausted, devastated, and reluctantly considering repentance. Sam was remarkably restrained, in the circumstances. Most fathers would have taken a stick to any daughter who’d led them such a dance.”

“I am just so glad to have her safe,” Sam said. He looked anxiously at Dark. “What will you do with those papers?”

“Are you worried that they will incriminate Mary in some way? I’ll set your mind at rest, there does not appear to be any mention of her. And with luck, there’ll be no reason to connect her with Sinclair. If I were you, Sam, I would book two seats on the next coach to Oxford and take her home before she decides she wants to go back to him after all. Is it generally known amongst your acquaintance that she ran off with him?”

“No, fortunately, it is not. I gave it out that she had gone to stay with relatives in the country. The servants know the truth, of course, and my brother and my nephews, but we kept it as quiet as possible. I still had hopes that she would return to me, and that a husband could be found for her.”

“Well, with luck your discretion and prudence will ensure that her reputation is undamaged,” Dark said. “Assuming, of course, that *she* can be persuaded of the wisdom of discretion too.”

“I will do my best,” Sam told him. “But you still haven’t

answered my question, Dark. What will you do with the papers? Will you lay them before the authorities?"

"That might not be wise," Polly said. "You'd be surprised how many people hereabouts are sympathetic to the Jacobite cause."

"If the length of this list is anything to go by, there must indeed be a considerable number. No, I have no intention of handing these over to the City fathers – many of them are probably named in them. But Beaumont told me that there is a regiment of horse and two troops of dragoons on their way to Bristol, under the command of General Wade, and they should now be within a day's ride of us. He's probably the best person to act on that information. So if you will excuse me, Paradice, I must now get dressed."

"Did you not hear what the surgeon told you?" Sam demanded. "You must rest, or you will re-open the wound. You can't go riding out in pursuit of this regiment, it would be madness in your condition! Surely it can wait a while – or I can go in your stead."

"No, you can't. What of Mary? And I know Wade, he is an old comrade, so he will see me without delay. Do you want to give these men, not to mention Sinclair, the slightest chance to escape justice? Listen to me," Dark said, and his voice was low, savage and passionate. "If they have their wish, this land will be plunged into a civil war just as bitter and bloody as the one your grandfathers fought. Do you want that? Do you want to be persecuted because you refuse to hear the Mass? Do you want your free worship forbidden, your home ransacked, your goods pillaged and your womenfolk abused by brutal soldiers? That is what happened to the Huguenots in France under King Louis, including my own family. It will happen here under King James, if you let it. Even if he himself wants to embrace toleration, the French and the Pope will not allow it. And the people of England will rise up to defend their religion." His eyes glittered with anger. "Have you ever seen a sacked town, Jessop? Women ripped up, children raped, old men hacked to death? Believe me, if you had, you would think the execution of a few misguided Jacobites a small price to pay for peace under George of Hanover."

The silence was brief. Sam, looking suddenly sickened and weary, passed a hand over his face, and shook his head. "No," he said at last. "No, you have the right of it. I see it must be done, however squeamish I may feel about the whole sordid business. You may risk your health to give those papers to General Wade, and if the men named in them are taken up and hanged, I will tell myself that it is for everyone's good in the long run. But you cannot expect me to welcome their deaths."

"Why not?" Polly demanded. "Sinclair tried to kill Dark, and you. Indeed, he would not scruple to kill anyone who stood between him and his precious Cause. I was his mistress for nearly a year, and even so, last night I feared that he would kill *me*."

"I am touched by your concern for my welfare, Sam," Dark said. "As for you, Paradice, I shall be most careful not to risk offending you in the future. After all, Robbie Sinclair is about to discover that hell indeed hath no fury like a Paradice scorned, and I do not wish to suffer the same fate."

"I did not do it for revenge," Polly said. "I did it to stop rebellion, for the same reasons as you, Dark." Successfully disguising the pain of her blistered feet, she rose from the chair. "And now, gentlemen, I will leave you and seek somewhere quiet to rest after my exertions of the night. No, Sam, don't worry, I won't disturb Mary – I shall ask Kitty for a bed somewhere for a few hours."

"Paradice – "

"Yes?" She paused, looking back at Dark. One of his rare smiles lit his face suddenly, and he held out his hand. "Thank you, Polly, for what you have done."

Flushing, she turned back to the bed and took it. The pressure of his fingers was firm and friendly. "I thank *you*, sir," she said, with a quick, mischievous grin. "For having the courtesy to keep yourself alive. I had all but convinced myself that you were dead."

"So it was not purely to prevent rebellion, then?"

Close to, his eyes were not completely brown, but interestingly flecked with green and amber. She shook her head, smiling down at him, and two pieces of straw and sundry fragments of chaff dropped onto the coverlet. *"Purely?* Purity had nothing to do with it, Dark."

"It never seems to, where you are concerned," he murmured slyly, his fingers still curled around hers. "I shall have to remember that in future. In order to attract a woman's interest, arrange to appear dead."

"It is not a method which I can recommend using very often," Polly said, her voice as caustic as his could be. "Your credit might expire rather quickly, even if you do not. Now, if you will both excuse me, I will go to repair the damage to my energy and my appearance. I wish you good luck and good speed, Dark, and my thoughts will be with you. Until later, sirs."

It was curiously difficult to withdraw her hand from his, and almost as hard to curtsy to the two men with grace and dignity, and leave the room as if there were no raw, bleeding blisters inside her riding boots. But at last, washed, her feet anointed and bandaged, changed into a clean shift and tucked up in Kitty's own bed with the landlady's avid curiosity still largely unsatisfied, she was able to fall asleep in comfort.

There was one certainty, though: whatever she was suffering now or in the future, it was nothing compared to the fate which her actions last night would inflict on Robbie

Sinclair.

* * *

The sudden clash of bells woke Polly with a start from a most unpleasantly vivid dream, in which Robbie was pursuing her with murderous intent. Her heart was pounding wildly, and her shift was damp with sweat. She gulped air in deep, shivering breaths until she had attained some measure of calm, and could think clearly.

As far as anyone could think, when the bells were ringing. Every church tower in Bath, the Abbey and St. Michael's and St. James's, must be vibrating with the cacophony until the stones were in danger of cracking. This was not the decorous peal rung to welcome Lord This or Lady That, bringing valuable prestige and generous purses to the city. This noise screamed danger, and panic.

Her nightmare forgotten, Polly sat up abruptly. Something had happened. Had the rebellion begun? Had Robbie discovered the theft of his papers and decided on one mad, reckless throw, to take Bath for the Pretender? It would be entirely in character, for whatever else he was, he was no coward and no ditherer.

She leapt out of bed and found, neatly folded on a chair by the window, a pair of stays, her blue flowered wrapping gown, stockings, shoes and a frilled cap. With hands that shook and fumbled, she dressed quickly, while the bells rang on and on, wild and frantic with terror. Then she went in search of someone who could tell her what was happening.

The inn was empty, doors open, fires untended. In the kitchen a bowl lay smashed on the floor, its contents splattered over the tiles. With a terrible presentiment of doom, Polly went out into the yard. It was empty, and the noise of the Abbey bells, virtually overhead, poured down all around her. She ran to the stables, hoping Ephraim would be there soothing the horses.

She entered the dim space, and saw him further down the row of stalls, trying to calm the chestnut she had ridden from Bristol. The nearest box, though, was empty, save for a heap of clean straw, and on it a small, curled figure, sharply familiar. Although she could not see Gin's face, the scrawny shoulders were shaking with sobs.

Polly stopped precipitately in the doorway, stared, and then walked inside. She had to kneel beside the child before her presence was noticed. With a jerk, one grimy arm went up to wipe a face that was wet and slobbery with tears. "What's the matter?" she yelled.

The bells stopped halfway through her question, leaving her bawling the final word into a breathless, painful silence. "Thank God for that," Polly said. Her head was still ringing, and so were bells more distant, probably St. James's down by the South Gate, but at least the Abbey and St. Michael's were quiet now. "Gin, what's wrong?"

"Dunno," said the child, with a pitiful attempt at unconcern. The filthy sleeve had left a smear of dirt, tears and snot. "Nuffink."

"Nonsense," Polly said briskly, glad of something to divert her attention from what might be happening in the city. "You don't cry without good cause, do you, Gin? So what's happened?"

"Told you. Nuffink."

"Is it something to do with Dark?"

"Nah," said Gin, snuffling, and then spoilt it by adding immediately, "Do you know where he is?"

"He's gone on an important errand," Polly said. "I'm

sure he'll soon be back." Her heart ached for this child, so sharp and cocksure, and yet so vulnerable beneath the bravado.

"But he looked like he was dying!" Gin cried suddenly. "He came back with that Mr. Jessop and some little smock and he couldn't hardly walk and they fetched the surgeon – so why's he gone? I stopped him killing himself once, I ain't going to watch him doing it again!"

Polly stared at the child. "You stopped him killing himself?" she said softly. "When was that, Gin?"

"Dunno. Three or four years back, in Queen Anne's time it was. Lit him down to Temple Stairs, and he would've jumped in the river if I hadn't hung onto his legs and stopped him, an' made him see sense," Gin said, with a note of pride. "That was when he began to look out for me, an' I looked out for him."

Polly was silent. Surely Gin could not be telling the truth? She could not imagine that someone as arrogant and self-assured as Dark might be tempted to take his own life. She said at last, "You must have been mistaken, Gin. I cannot imagine him being brought so low."

"You don't believe me, do you?" Gin said wearily. "' God's own truth, though, I swear it. Blind drunk, he was, and set on ending it all, just 'cos some moll he loved had done him wrong. So I clung onto him and wouldn't let go. He cursed me then, but he thanked me the next day." The child stared up at Polly's white face, defying her scepticism. "As God's me witness, cross me heart an' hope to die. That's why he don't let no woman near him now, case they does the same what she did. It ain't you he's been angry with, it's her, because I reckon he thought you was the same. And you ain't."

"Well, he has nothing to fear from me," Polly said. "I have no intention of coming near him, now or in the future. A curled hedgehog would be more approachable."

Gin surveyed her shrewdly. "And that ain't God's truth,

I seen the way you looks at him, and him back."

"Then your eyes must be deceiving you." Polly got to her feet. "Well, we can't stay here all day. I want to find out why the bells were ringing, and exactly what is happening."

"Oh, I know that. General Wade's come to take them Jacks, o' course," said Gin scornfully.

"Wade? He was supposed to be going to Bristol."

"Well, he must've lost his way, then, 'cos he's almost here. Horse and dragoons and all, within a mile of the Northgate, and everyone's in a terror because they think he's going to sack the place." Gin also scrambled up, with rather less grace, and wiped away the remaining tears with the other sleeve, compounding the dirt. "You won't tell Dark what I said, will you? He'd never want it known."

"Oh – no, of course I won't," she said. Her mind had been in such a ferment of anxiety and guilt that for a moment she had wondered what he was referring to. "Don't worry," she added reassuringly. "When I wish, Gin, I can be as close as an oyster on the seabed. Shall we go find Mr Jessop now? Perhaps he will have some news for us."

"He must be out there, with the rest of Bath, to see what's afoot." Gin gestured at the arch leading to the street beyond the Bear. "You'd best stay here, you'll get your toes trod on else."

"I'll do my best to avoid such a terrible fate," said Polly. "Come, you can be my escort."

Despite the child's obvious reluctance, she towed Gin out into the yard. They crossed to the gateway and peered cautiously out into Cheap Street. The staid and venerable city of Bath was in uproar. At least the raucous bells had ceased, but the clamour in the streets was almost as violent. People of all degrees from beggars to lords surged to and fro in the road, shouting, screaming, or just hurrying by with looks of urgency and desperation on their faces. She saw two opportunistic pickpockets at work, and a boy riding on a man's shoulders who snatched someone's wig, slid down like an eel, and vanished into the crowd almost before the victim had clapped his hand to his suddenly unprotected head. But before she could launch herself and Gin into this maelstrom of humanity, to her intense relief Sam and the young woman who must be his daughter emerged from it, both rather flushed and dishevelled.

As they came under the arch, Polly stared at Mary with considerable interest. This was the first opportunity she had had for a good look at the girl who had been mistaken for her, and on the whole she was not offended by the error. Sam's daughter was undeniably a beauty, and she would be enchanting if she bothered to smile. In contrast, Sam was beaming with relief. "Polly, my dear, I am so glad to see you safe and sound. I feared you might venture out into the crowd on your own, and it is dangerous in the extreme – one poor lady by the Guildhall was nearly trampled underfoot, and was taken up in a dead faint."

Polly's interest in Mary was returned: the girl's bright blue eyes were resting on her suspiciously, and she turned to Sam and said bluntly, "Papa, who is this woman?"

"Why, this is Polly, I have spoken to you of Polly, who helped me find you – I told you about her this morning, did I not? She has been very helpful – if it had not been for her, I could never have rescued you."

To judge from Mary's expression, this was not an act deserving of any thanks. "But she does not look in the least like me," she said resentfully.

"Indeed I am sure I do not," Polly said, recognising at once that responding to such open hostility in kind would lead to all sorts of trouble. "For you are much younger and prettier than I am. It was uncommon foolish of Dark to make such a grievous error."

Sam threw her a grateful glance. She added, "But we can't conduct a conversation here – shall we go back inside the Bear?"

"That will be safest, I feel," Sam said. "We do not know what Wade's purpose is, in coming here. If they intend to secure Bath for the King, there may be unpleasant scenes. Soldiers have their duty to perform, and it is not something for a gently reared young lady to witness."

"I'm not a *child*!" Mary cried indignantly. "I'm a *woman* now, Papa, and I'd be glad if you would treat me like one."

"I for one am retreating inside," Polly said. "There must be someone to give us dinner – are you not sharp-set, Miss Jessop? I know I am. And doubtless we will learn what is happening in due course." She wondered how much Mary had known of Sinclair's plot. It seemed incredible that anyone who had been in his company for two months could still remain in ignorance of what he was doing, with his squalid hiding places, his dubious accomplices visiting at odd hours, his insistence on secrecy: but Sam's daughter, although blessed with beauty, seemed very obviously too self-absorbed to have inherited his perspicacity.

Mary was studying her suspiciously. Polly returned the scrutiny with her most charming smile. "That is such a pretty necklace you are wearing," she said. "I do love pearls, and those are so well matched, both in size and colour."

As she had expected, the girl took the bait at once. She stroked the gleaming little beads with a loving, complacent hand. "Yes, they are, are they not? Robbie gave them to me."

Just as he had given Polly the magnificent sapphire necklace and earrings, chosen to mirror her eyes, which lay in pride of place within her jewellery box at home. If

Robbie's affections could be measured in jewels, then she was undoubtedly the victor. It was an unworthy thought, but satisfying.

Dinner would be late, they were told by a scared Nancy, and there was only bread and cold meats and cheese and the remains of a beef pie and the apple tart, because the cook and his boy had gone off into the city when the bells started and had not yet come back, and Kitty had gone to her daughter, who was near her time and of a fearful disposition. Mary discovered a small rent in her dress and ran upstairs to change it, which surprised Polly: surely she had not brought any baggage with her from Sinclair's hideout?

"Your friend Kitty recommended a woman who always has gowns for sale," Sam said, seeing her looking puzzled. "We visited her after breakfast and bought two. She could hardly wear her riding habit, after all."

"Of course not." Polly took Sam by the arm and drew him into the little parlour where they were to dine. The table had already been laid, for three, but the fire was a dead heap of ashy coals and the window needed cleaning. Beyond it, in the yard, she could see Gin unobtrusively lurking near a gathering of half a dozen or so maids and grooms, who were obviously taking the opportunity to discuss the news without interference from Kitty's sharp tongue. When the door was safely shut, Polly said, "Is it true, that Wade is coming?"

"Oh, yes, there's no doubt of it. He's been sighted coming over – Kingsdown, is it? Yes, Kingsdown. And making good progress. I expect he'll be here very shortly."

"And do you think Dark is responsible for his sudden change in direction?"

"I don't know. I haven't seen him since he rode out this morning." Sam looked at her with affection, and something akin to bewilderment. "Polly, my dear, I have so much to thank you for – but what will you do now? For if Sinclair is taken up – "

"Then it will be my doing. Yes, I know. Do you think I don't feel guilty?" Polly demanded fiercely. "I loved him once, or I thought I did. He was good to me, at first, he showered gifts on me – but then he betrayed me with Mary, and what he did to her was unforgivable. It's one thing to install a woman of the town – and yes, Sam, that is what I am – as your mistress, but quite another matter to seduce and abduct a malleable young girl still in the schoolroom, just as a pleasurable way of passing the time in Oxford while he was organising rebellion. When I thought we loved each other, it was easy to be caught up in his enthusiasm for the Pretender – why should we have Farmer George on the throne, who can't speak a word of English and has no sensibility, when we could have English-born James, whose inheritance was stolen from his father?"

"That is one way of looking at it," said Sam drily.

"I know. I am playing devil's advocate. If I had stopped to think, if I had not been blinded by my affection for Sinclair, I would have come to the same conclusion as you and Dark – that even if James *is* the rightful King, the price to be paid for putting him on the throne is too high. I don't care that he is a Catholic, nor even that he hopes to regain his throne with French help. But there are many people in this land who *do* care, and so passionately do they care that there would be another civil war. My grandmother told terrible stories about what happened then. And there may still be fighting, if Wade does not stamp out this rebellion here in Bath before it has a chance to begin. So that was why I stole those papers – I suspected Sinclair might have some evidence of his plotting with him, and I was right."

"Was it really?"

Polly grinned at him ruefully. "Partly, I confess it was. And partly because I thought that he might have killed Dark.

And I wanted revenge for that."

Perhaps wisely, Sam offered no comment. She gave him a sharp glance, and continued. "Dark is safe, but Sinclair certainly intended to kill him, and I cannot forgive that either. He could come crawling back to me on his knees and I would not let him through my door, because I can never trust him or his empty promises again."

"But do you want to see him hanged? A traitor's death is a terrible one."

"Frankly, Sam, I cannot find it in me to care. He has made his bed, and must lie in it. But so far, he has managed to escape any consequences. He is devoted to his Cause, but he is even more devoted to Robbie Sinclair. I doubt they will catch him. He always seems to lead a charmed life, however little he deserves it."

"As for the other Jacobites, if they are taken in arms, the government may make an example of a few," Sam said thoughtfully. "But they will probably ensure that the rest cool their ardour in prison for a few weeks or months before being quietly released and told to behave themselves in the future. It may be a different story, though, in Scotland and the North Country. The rebellion there seems in full flood."

He turned to gaze out of the grimy window, and Polly went to join him. The gaggle in the yard had dispersed, but she could see that the street beyond was still thronged with people. "Are you returning to Oxford tomorrow?"

"Yes. There is a private coach going back empty to Abingdon, we have taken seats on that, and we will hire horses for the final distance. With luck we should be home by nightfall. And you? Will you wait for Dark?"

Polly turned, laughing, and shook her head emphatically. "Indeed I will not. There is bound to be a stage for London, Wade or no Wade, and I intend to be on the first one that leaves. I have been thinking of Hannah, and how desperately she wants to be free, and it would not be right to keep her in such suspense any longer. And I shall take Gin with me, I have promised to give the child a position. I think it's thoroughly deserved, don't you? Someone gave me a similar chance, long ago, and I took it and made use of it, as Gin surely will."

"I hope so," said Sam. He paused, and then said quietly, "I have had much talk with Mary. I don't think she realises, even now, that you were also Sinclair's mistress. She merely thinks that you were mistaken for her because of your similar appearance."

"Or not so similar," said Polly, with a wry face.

"Yes. I apologise on her behalf for that. Mary has always been more forthright than is proper, or indeed wise. No, I am certain that she does not know, and I think it best that I keep her in ignorance. She is already suspicious of you, and the part you have played."

"I am aware of that." Polly grinned at him. "You're a good man and a good friend, Sam Jessop, and even if our paths never cross again, I shall always think of you kindly."

"And I of you," he said, and she saw with affection that there were tears in his eyes. "Dear Polly, you and Dark between you have brought me my heart's desire, and I shall be grateful for ever."

At that moment, the door crashed open and Mary whirled in, clad in a cheerful striped yellow gown that did not suit her complexion. "Papa!" she cried. "Is there no dinner yet? I am so ravenously hungry, I declare I could eat a horse!"

PART TWO

London
1715-1716

CHAPTER TWELVE

'At first a Beggar's Brat'

Polly had only been absent from London for ten days, but most of those ten days had been so crowded with event and emotion that the coach's erratic progress along the familiar streets seemed to be the protracted return to reality from a particularly vivid dream. She had the nearside window seat, and as she gazed through the mud-splashed glass at the crowds in the Strand, the hawkers and whores, the chairs and wagons, beggars and street children and the old woman with clawed hands who sold apples from a hand barrow by the Exeter Exchange, she felt a vast sense of homecoming. This was her world, in which she moved as easily and surely as a fish in the sea. By comparison, Bath and Bristol seemed slow, provincial places, steeped in petty morality and petty squabbles.

It was raining, and she asked the coachman to stop near Flying Horse Yard and let her off. Somewhat to her surprise, Gin was still with her. She had wondered whether the child would panic at the thought of a settled, respectable life as a servant, and flee back to the dangerous camaraderie of the streets: but when she checked the rumble-tumble behind the coach, the small pinched face scowled back at her from under a wad of sacking, presumably in the hope of keeping off the rain. "I'm still here," Gin said belligerently. "Did you think I'd run off?"

"Not at all, for I know you have more sense," Polly said briskly. "We're almost home. You will take my bags."

Gin clambered stiffly out of the basket and hobbled a few steps. "I ain't no bleeding Samson. Can't you find someone with muscles?"

"I said – you will take my bags." Polly's tone, of intent, tolerated no argument. If Gin were to become her servant, the child would have to act on orders without complaint or question. A masterless link boy was answerable to no-one, and that peculiar relationship with Dark had accustomed Gin to far too much freedom. It was best to get used to the restrictions of this new life now, for if she was hard on the child, Hannah would be far harder.

Gin sent her a mutely appealing look, which she ignored. Her luggage was heavy, but not impossibly so, and that scrawny frame disguised considerable strength. Grumbling curses, the child stamped over to the two bags and picked them up, while Polly unfurled her umbrella and set off for Flying Horse Court.

It was not far, and she had brief leisure to think again about what might await her there. If Robbie had escaped Wade's soldiers, would he have risked fleeing back to London, to settle the score with his treacherous mistress? It would be perfectly possible for a single, well-mounted horseman to overtake the lumbering stagecoach. But if he had managed to evade capture, he would surely have ridden north to join his fellow Scots. The latest reports, which she had heard on their journey from Bath, spoke of the Pretender's armies gathering in Scotland for the march south. If they had planned to link up with the rebels in the West Country, they would be sorely disappointed. She hoped Robbie would consider warning them of the failure of his plotting to be far more important than chasing after his errant former mistress.

So she had reasoned, all along the slow, muddy, jolting road back to London, and she knew that it was most unlikely that he would be waiting for her at the house they had once shared, but even so, her heart was thudding with apprehension as she knocked on the door, ready to run if Sinclair was indeed inside.

But the door opened, and there was her maid, her dark face shining with delight, as it surely would not have done had Robbie returned. "Oh, madam, you're back! How glad I am to see you safe and sound!"

"And I am so glad to see you."

Hannah shut the door and turned back to her mistress, hope and apprehension struggling on her face. "Oh, madam, tell me please – did you –"

"Yes, I did," Polly said, smiling. "He agreed to sell you to me, and tomorrow we will go to that lawyer I found, and have the paper drawn up, signed and witnessed. It will have all the force of the law, and it will guarantee your freedom. Guard it well."

Hannah stared at her mistress while the tears poured down her face, apparently unnoticed. "Truly? You really have done this for me?"

"Yes, my dear friend. Nathaniel Day, may he be forever cursed, has relinquished all claim to you. Tomorrow, you will be free to come and go and live your life as you please, just as I am."

At last, realisation was beginning to dawn on Hannah's face. "And the paper – that will be all the proof that I need?"

"Yes, it will," Polly said softly.

"So I will no longer be a slave?"

"When first you entered this house, you left slavery behind. The document I give you tomorrow will confirm it. No-one can ever possess you again. You are safe from him, and from anyone else who would seek to own you."

Hannah seemed to become aware of her tears for the first time. Blindly she scrubbed at her eyes with her apron. "I can't believe it," she said at last, on a sob. "Even now, I can't believe he won't come after me."

"I swear to you that he will not. You will have your freedom, and no court of law in the land can say otherwise. Oh, Hannah, dear Hannah, what else to I have to say that will convince you? You are free, you are *free*! So shall we have some chocolate, to celebrate?"

"I'm sorry, madam," said Hannah, still drying her eyes. "I'll go and see to it directly."

"No, you will not," Polly told her, laughing. "For tonight, Hannah Rose, *I* shall do the serving, and *you* shall be the lady. No, don't protest – I shall hear no argument. Is the kettle hot?"

"Simmering over the hearth, madam," Hannah said. A hesitant smile of pure delight began to break out across her face, as if the full impact of her new status was only now striking home. "And I bought some more chocolate just this morning. The house is all in good order, madam, kept waiting for your return. I pray it'll be to your satisfaction."

"Of course it will be, I trust you completely," Polly said. She untied the strings of the plain plum-coloured wool mantle she had bought in Bath – she still regretted the loss of that blue velvet – and hung it on the peg next to the mirror. "You are the most efficient person I know, so how could everything not be fine? Let us go and make that chocolate, at this precise moment I could kill for a cup of it."

A repressed cough attracted their attention. Gin had slipped unobtrusively into the house behind Polly, and now stood in a dim corner beside her bags. "What'll I do wiv these?"

"Lord above, madam!" cried Hannah in astonishment. "What on earth is that?" She peered at him more closely and then drew back with a look of distaste. "Ugh, he stinks! However did he come to sneak inside? I'll send him packing at once!"

"No need, Hannah," said Polly calmly. "This is Gin, a former link boy, to whom I have promised a position here as my servant."

Hannah stared with hostility at the ragged scrawny figure, and Gin glared defiantly back. "That's right," the child said belligerently. "I've come up in the world, I'm a *servant* now."

"Then you'd better mind your manners," said Hannah sharply. She glanced at Polly, her eyebrows raised. "Haven't I seen him somewhere before, madam?"

"Gin has lit my chair several times, and came with us to Bristol and Bath. Don't worry, Hannah – under that most unprepossessing exterior beats a heart of only slightly alloyed gold. I think there is some potential in the child."

"That's a deal more than I see," Hannah said suspiciously. "So are you capable of turning spits and running errands and sweeping floors, brat? Or will you be gone with madam's silver by this time tomorrow?"

"I ain't no thief," Gin whined. "Cross me heart."

"Well, you could have fooled me," said Hannah, folding her arms. Polly suppressed a smile. Her maid's bark was very much worse than her bite, but Gin was not to know that, and it would do the child no harm at all to start this new life in full awareness of what it entailed.

"I think that by this time tomorrow, you'll be so hard at work that you won't have the energy to speak, let alone abscond with all our goods," she said. "Hannah has a sharp tongue to lick you into shape in short order. You can start by taking my bags upstairs, Gin – my chamber is behind the first door at the top, on the left. Then you may come down to the kitchen and have some supper."

The child's mouth opened for another whine, before catching sight of Hannah's frown. "Yes'm, very good'm." And with a great show of weariness began to clamber up the stairs, dragging the bags rather than carrying them. As soon as Gin had vanished into the gloom, Polly took Hannah by the arm and hurried her along the narrow passage-way leading to the kitchen at the back of the house. The night was drawing in fast, and the fire cast a warm, rosy and infinitely heartening glow over the dark room. Polly, her spirits high, settled the other woman onto the shabby cushions of the settle by the hearth, and grinned at her. “Stay here, Hannah, while I wait on you, and don’t you dare move!”

“It don’t seem right,” said the maid, reluctantly sitting still while Polly bustled about the kitchen, finding the rosewood chocolate caddy, setting a small pan of milk on a trivet in the hearth, and putting two blue Delft china cups and saucers on the scrubbed table.

“Of course it’s right. You know me, Hannah, have I ever been one to stand on ceremony and act the great lady? I think of you as my friend as well as my maid, so why should I not do this for you? The world is not turned upside down for ever, come tomorrow it will have righted itself back again.” She spooned the ground chocolate into a tall silver coffee pot, and dived swiftly to remove the pan of milk before it boiled over.

“That’s as maybe,” said Hannah, watching Polly as she worked, the soft golden light from fire and candle enhancing the pure and lovely lines of her face. “And what of that child, madam? You can’t seriously suppose that a little ragamuffin like that can be made into a respectable servant.”

Hannah had always been plain-spoken: it was one reason, out of many, why she had been forced to run away from her owner. Polly smiled. “I’ll put a year’s wages down, if you like,” she said. “If Gin is not transformed into what is appropriate by next Easter, you may have seven pounds.”

“And where’s the money to come from, now *he’s* gone?”

Hannah’s mistress poured the hot, foaming milk into

the pot and fetched a wooden spoon. As she stirred, she said, "There is still plenty left. And anyway, to my mind he has forfeited it. Let me tell you what happened in Bath."

The story, somewhat expurgated in certain details, did not take long, and Hannah listened with her mouth pursed in emphatic disapproval. "Forgive me, madam," she said at last. "But I always thought he was no good, that one. You wept when he left – don't deny it, I saw your red eyes – but it was the best for you, I reckon."

"I know that now," Polly admitted. She added a beaten egg and a generous pinch of cinnamon to the chocolate, and stirred again. A delicious smell filled the warm air of the kitchen. "And to my way of thinking, that money has become mine."

"Some folk might have other ideas."

"And who is to gainsay me? The Pretender can hardly come storming in with a magistrate to accuse me of theft. Sinclair squandered fully half of it on himself and on me, and much of what remained was spent on arms and supplies for his failed rebellion in Bath. I took some to buy you, but there is still nearly two hundred pounds remaining." She paused, her face glowing not only with the candlelight. "Think, Hannah, how that could transform our lives. I could open a coffee-shop, a respectable place where gentlemen could read the news and talk into the night, I would not be beholden to anyone, no man would rule me – I would be free, Hannah, as free as you are!"

"Didn't know you wanted to be *respectable*," said Hannah, looking at her doubtfully.

"Oh, I have no intention of trudging to church three times on a Sunday and joining the Society for the Reformation of Manners – never fear on *that* score! But I have a great wish to be myself, Hannah, to be witty and wise and engage a little in the worlds that interest me – of artists and actors, writers and men of affairs, to be able to listen to their talk and contribute some thoughts of my own. And how else can a woman like me, with no birth and only a little education, do that save by running a coffee shop or a tavern? Look at Jenny Mann."

"'*Jenny Mann, Jenny Mann, she don't love the warming pan,*'" her maid quoted in a soft sing-song. The lady in question ran a very successful establishment at Charing Cross, famous as a haunt of the Whigs, hence the reference to the warming pan in which the baby Pretender had supposedly been smuggled into the birthing chamber back in 1688. Hannah added doubtfully, "But she ain't young and pretty like you, madam. She's fifty if a day, and she's got the clout to keep her house respectable. How will you fare?"

"Thank you for that 'young and pretty'," Polly said, smiling at her. "Oh, I expect there will be plenty of yearning young gallants trying to persuade me into their beds, but I shall be very firm with them. After all, if my coffee-house is a success, I will not need to offer myself in return for their money. And I shall not be the only one in the shop, after all. There will be you, for a start – you *must* be my partner in this venture, Hannah, you make such wonderful coffee, I've never tasted better."

"Thank you, madam," said the maid, smiling with shy pleasure.

"And Gin, and two or three pot-boys, and a stout fellow to keep the door and deal with troublemakers. Perhaps Will would take that position, he's reliable and trustworthy. I assume all was well while I was away?"

"Yes, madam, no trouble at all."

Polly poured the steaming liquid into the cups, and scattered a pinch of ground chocolate on top of the froth. "Where is that child? It surely does not take that long to find my chamber and leave my bags."

"Perhaps he's run off with them," Hannah suggested. "It might be well to go see where he is. I don't trust that sort further than I can see 'em."

She insisted on accompanying Polly, and they left the kitchen in search of the errant Gin. The hallway was well lit, but the upper part of the house was quite dark now, and silent. Hannah had brought a carrying candlestick with her, and climbed first, frowning, the pewter clasped tight in her fist as if she was prepared to use it as a weapon. She lit the lights in the landing sconces, and then, with Polly beside her, cautiously opened the door to the main bedchamber.

It was a pleasant room, freshly decorated in carnation and pale green, with a table and stool, a clothes chest and hanging pegs, and a wide comfortable bed with tapestry curtains depicting, in voluptuous detail, the story of Leda and the Swan. Polly's bags had been dumped down on the matching counterpane, almost obscuring the concupiscent leer on Leda's plump face, and beside them, quite covering the swan's outstretched wings, lay Gin, fast asleep.

"Lord!" said Hannah scornfully. "Hasn't he got more sense, the ragamuffin brat? He'll ruin that counterpane, and how much did it cost? And I don't doubt he's got fleas, madam, if not worse."

"It'll brush off when it's dry," said Polly, looking down at the sleeping Gin. The candlelight gave the white, shifty face a fleeting illusion of colour and innocence, all too soon dispelled when the child gave a great start and jerked upright, eyes wild. "Wha' – what's doing?"

"It's all right, Gin, you were asleep. We wondered where you were, so we came to find you."

"You thought I'd run away, didn't you," Gin said challengingly. "Like I said, I ain't no thief, not now. I know which side me bread's buttered, don't I? I ain't going nowhere."

"Get off that bed directly, you impertinent brat," said Hannah, folding her arms and fixing the child with a look that would have shrivelled anyone less cocksure. "First things first, boy. There's supper downstairs, and then a good thorough wash in the bathtub. I'm not having you making this house lousy, not when I've worked so hard to get it nice and clean."

"A bath?" cried Gin, in the unmistakable shrill tones of panic. "You ain't going to *bath* me, are you? That'll kill me for sure!"

Hannah reached out and hauled the child off the bed. Polly noted that the swan now had a large damp stain on its white breast. Her maid was a tall woman, strongly built, and beside her, Gin looked as insubstantial as a rather grey and mucky cobweb. "Then you'll just have to be killed," she observed, regarding her captive with disfavour. "Now get your rump downstairs before I speed it on its way with my foot."

Always keen to avoid chastisement, Gin scurried hastily out of the room, and they heard steps rushing headlong down the stairs. Polly looked at her maid with affection. "You've certainly put the fear of God into the child, Hannah."

"Does no harm, madam," said Hannah, dusting her hands. "Lord, if he's ruined that coverlet, I *will* kill him. I'd best go and fill that tub, before he spreads his muck all round the house."

"A good idea, but shall we have our chocolate first? And before you bath Gin, there is something you should know."

As she told her, the maid's face split into a delighted grin. "You don't say, madam! Well, who'd have guessed it? I wouldn't, that's for sure. Well, well. And this artist fellow, does he know?"

"No, I'm sure he doesn't, and I can't wait to see his face when he finds out. I've enjoyed taking him down a couple of pegs already, and a couple more won't do any harm."

Hannah, shaking out the dampened counterpane and draping it over the chest to air, gave her a suspicious glance. "Thought you said you was done with men."

"Oh, I am, I am. But a little dalliance here and there, a touch of flirting, some merry banter, well, it all adds spice to life, don't you think? And it's not as if I'm beholden to him. If anything, it's the other way around."

Hannah, not in possession of the full story, and unaware that Dark was, if not a Government agent, as near as made no difference, merely grunted. "I'll set a fire for you in here later, madam," she said. "That'll help dry the coverlet. So where is this artist cove? He didn't come back with you, then?"

"Oh, no, as far as I'm aware, he's still in the West Country. Shall we go and have that chocolate, before it cools completely? And I must make my plans."

"Plans, madam?" queried Hannah, as they descended the stairs, their vast shadows flickering behind them.

"Oh, yes, we have a lot to do. Most important of all tomorrow, as soon as maybe, we shall visit that lawyer and have your certificate of freedom drawn up, so all is legal. Once that is done, I shall go find a discreet and reliable goldsmith where I can bank the rest of those guineas. Then I must make enquiries, to discover if there are premises suitable for a coffee-house anywhere within half a mile of here. And Gin must be properly clothed, and I must lay in a better winter mantle, oh, there are a thousand things all to be done, I shall hardly be finished before next week. And then ..."

She paused before the kitchen door, which was half open. Inside, Gin sat hunched on the floor by the fire, hands clasped round skinny legs, staring sleepily into the flames.

"And then, madam?" Hannah prompted her.

"And then," Polly said, laughing, "then, I think I shall

have my portrait painted!"

* * *

Several weeks after Polly's return from Bath, Flying Horse Court was dozing somnolently in the transient warmth of the morning sun, a rare sight so late in this October, which had generally been very wet and windy. A playful breeze scattered dust and leaves along the cobbles, while above the roofs the bright blue sky was becoming hazed over with high, thin cloud, a sure sign of more rain later in the day. A stray dog scratched itself in a patch of sunlight, pigeons cooed and called from the rooftops, and a maid shook a mat briskly out of a window, showering fluff and dirt on the pavement below. Two women, obviously met while returning from shopping in the Strand, gossiped amiably further up the Court, their baskets and bags on the pavement around them. The door of the furthest house opened, and a very small maidservant emerged, struggling with an overflowing pail of soapy water. She dumped it with an ill-tempered splash on the top step, took a scrubbing brush almost the length of her scrawny forearm, and knelt down beside the bucket.

A tall gentleman, dressed in shabby black with a dark tie-wig, turned into the Court and walked briskly past the women to the end house. They turned to stare at him curiously, for he was not at all ill-looking, though rather grim of face, and then whispered to each other slyly, with delighted grins peeping out from behind their hands. The little maidservant lifted her head and watched him approach. She put the scrubbing brush down and got to her feet, wiping her hands on her apron. A near observer might have seen a flush on her thin cheeks, but her eyes sparkled with sudden mischief. As he paused at the foot of the steps, looking up at her, she bobbed a rather clumsy curtsey and said chirpily, "Can I help you, sir?"

Dark stared at her, frowning. He said, "Is your mistress at home?"

"I'll see, sir," said the maid, with another bob, and paused, seemingly in expectation. As the artist said nothing further, she turned and went inside, leaving the brush and bucket on the step, formidable obstacles to his further progress. Female voices could be heard within, and then the maid reappeared, looking very grave and demure. She was wearing a plain blue cotton gown, rather too big for her, and the hem had obviously been hastily cobbled up. Her cap was a little askew, and her hair snaked untidily beneath it: as if conscious of the fact, she put a hand up to pat it, and said, "Yes, sir, she is at home and will receive you."

"But you did not ask my name," said Dark, still staring at the girl. "Haven't I seen you somewhere before – good God, it's Gin!"

A gleeful grin erupted on the maid's face. "I was wondering when you'd notice! Took you long enough, didn't it?"

"*Gin!*" said Dark, in utter astonishment. "What in God's name are you doing dressed like that?"

"Cos that's how I *should* be dressed," said Gin, with some scorn. "Ain't you never realised? And you an artist an' all, ain't you supposed to be *observant?*"

"Jane!" Hannah's voice was sharp, and she walked briskly out onto the step beside the child, frowning. "I have told you time and again the proper way to talk to your betters. Now put that bucket to one side so the gentleman won't fall over it. I want those steps white as snow in half an hour, understand? And then you can take the coals upstairs to madam's chamber."

The old habit of mutiny died hard. Gin opened her mouth to protest, transparently thought better of it, and hauled the bucket out of Dark's way. Still with an expression of complete bewilderment, he walked past her and into the house.

Polly was waiting for him in her pretty parlour. The fire burned brightly, the tabby cat sitting before it, and the air was scented with the rich fragrance of hot coffee. She smiled at him, and held out her hand. "Dark! I am so glad to see you. How do you do? When did you return to London?"

"I do very well, thank you," he said, and lightly kissed her cheek. "I came home yesterday, quite late."

"Have you breakfasted? Would you like some coffee, at the least? Hannah is an expert, she brews the best cup in town. Sit down and tell me all that has happened – I am burning to know what you have been doing in the last few weeks."

"That can wait," Dark said. He did not take the proffered chair, but remained standing, staring at her. "Tell me about Gin. I met him, or her, on the doorstep. Is it really true?"

"That your link-boy was all the while a girl? Yes, it is."

"I still can't believe it. *Surely* I would have noticed –"

"Why should you have? She made a good boy. I don't think anyone suspected."

"Then how in God's name did you find out?"

"At Maidstone, remember? When that man beat her. A few months ago, there would have been nothing to see, but now her breasts are beginning to grow. I took off her shirt to tend her bruises, and it was obvious. She begged me not to tell you, and I did not. But I promised to help her, and I could not have her as a male servant." She gave him a mischievous smile. "Before long, tongues would have started to wag. And she was happy to become a girl again, in exchange for a home, and security."

"Good God," Dark said again. He sat down abruptly in

the chair. "But why, *why* in Heaven's name pretend to be a boy?"

"Oh, use your common sense, Dark," said Polly briskly. "Her mother was a whore, raddled with drink and the pox, and so desperate for money that she tried to sell her to some gentleman who liked pullets. Gin's no fool, she could see what was going to happen to her and she didn't want it. And for a girl, there's no alternative but the streets. A charity school wouldn't have her, a trull's daughter, and in any case she said she would have died rather than enter one, they seemed to her like prisons. Nor would any respectable house want her for a servant. At least if she was a boy she could sweep the streets, carry links, run errands, and she'd be safe from men if she kept away from Clare Market and the molly houses. And so she ran away, stole some old clothes and changed her sex."

"I've known him – *her* – for more than three years," Dark said. "So how old is she? She always claimed not to know for certain."

"Fourteen or fifteen, I think. She was an infant when Queen Anne was crowned, she said that her mother used to tell her how she held her up to see the procession."

Dark was silent for a moment, shaking his head in amazement. "Fourteen or fifteen years old. And as wise, sometimes, as an old crone. Paradice, you have done a deed of great and unwarranted kindness in taking her in."

"I was left as a child to the mercy of strangers," Polly said. "I know how it feels. I wanted to give her the chance to defy her fate." She grinned suddenly. "And how she has cursed me for it, these past few weeks!"

"She was never one to mince her words, and Hannah had to take her to task for it, just now."

"Poor Hannah! She was very reluctant to take Gin under her wing at first, but now I think she quite enjoys licking her into shape. She calls her Jane, which I think must be her real name, and she stands absolutely no nonsense. And if you think that we are hard on Gin, well, it is a hard world, Dark, and she must learn to be obedient and polite and behave properly, or she will share her mother's fate. And however much she may grumble and rant, Gin herself is aware of it. She has tried very hard so far to please us, and for the most part she has succeeded. She has two pounds a year and her keep and clothes. I was given the opportunity to drag myself out of the gutter," Polly said fiercely, "and I will not deny the same chance to Gin. One day she may marry well and become a lady of leisure – and don't dare laugh, why should she not? With some flesh on her bones and a less abrasive manner, she might even become pretty. If she needs a reminder of the fact that it is possible to rise above your beginnings, then she need only look at my example."

"I thought you rose lying on your back, Paradice."

Polly glanced at him. "Yes, of course I did, and I know that in essence my calling was the same as Gin's mother's – but there is a degree of difference, is there not? I am now the same age as she was when she died, but I have every intention of living for many years yet. I was helped, I was given chances, and she was not. Gin may stay a maidservant all her days, or she may become a rich man's mistress, as I did, or she may catch the notice of some nice steady tradesman and marry him. It matters not to me what she does, so long as she has the opportunity to defy and defeat her destiny, and be happy."

"I'm not at all sure that many would agree with you," Dark pointed out. "Many would say that she must stew in her fate and accept it."

"Did you? Did I? Anyone of spirit must kick against what is allotted to them, if they do not like it. I admit that Mary Jessop did, and has suffered for it, but then Mary Jessop is a spoilt brat who has squandered all the love and opportunity that children like Gin have been denied, for the sake of a stupid infatuation."

"You are a harsh judge, Paradice."

"I had a family once – I had parents who loved me, and a good home, and a rosy future, just as she had. And it was all taken from me, through no fault of my own. *Now* do you understand why I have little sympathy for Mary Jessop? And before you mention it, I would have as little sympathy had she run off with a man quite unknown to me."

He had no time to make any comment, for the door opened and Hannah entered, bearing a tray laden with a steaming coffee pot, cups, a small silver jug of cream, a dish of sugar and a plate of cakes. She gave Dark a suspicious glance, but decorously set everything out on the table and waited, the empty tray in her hand.

"Is Jane still labouring over her steps?" Polly asked her, with a quick smile.

"Indeed she is, madam." Hannah's impassive face began to curve slightly, as if concealing amusement. "We'll make a good servant of her yet, I think."

"I heartily hope so. Keep her nose to the grindstone and she'll have no chance of mischief. Thank you, Hannah, that will be all. If I need anything else, I shall ring for you."

"Very good, madam," said the maid, and withdrew.

As the door closed behind her, Polly began to pour the coffee. "Do you take sugar? Cream? I can recommend the cakes, they come from the little confectioner's in the Strand by Charing Cross. And now," she added, handing over the aromatic dish of coffee, from which gossamer wisps of steam curled enticingly, "pray, do tell me what has happened in Bath. All we knew was that Wade entered the city and caused a great deal of panic. I heard that there was a quantity of arms and horses seized, and some arrests, but I took the opportunity to leave first thing the next morning, so I don't know any more details." She hesitated, and then added quietly, "Did they catch Sinclair?"

"Yes, they took him up, and Dunn, the man who visited him at the farmhouse while you were there – and a Colonel Lansdon, Sir George Brown, and sundry other local gentlemen, including the owner of the farm. Of course the real ringleaders, Wyndham and Packington and the rest, were arrested three weeks ago, and are now safe in custody in London. I expect that is where the Bath rebels will be sent." He glanced at her over his coffee cup. "But Sinclair did not remain captive for long. Whatever else, he's a bold and enterprising rogue – apparently he climbed down a drainpipe and escaped. I expect he's gone north to join the Scots. Are you glad?"

Polly grimaced. "Do you want an honest reply?"

"I have long since ceased to expect anything of the sort from you, dear Paradice."

"Then whatever I tell you is bound to be disbelieved, so I will stay silent."

When it became clear that she meant it, Dark sipped his coffee and continued. "They found a hundred horses in the fields around that farmhouse, and another hundred scattered in various places nearer the city. There was a hogshead of basket-hilt swords, and six chests of muskets, with another five in that house by the Eastgate, along with the gunpowder. They had even hidden three pieces of ordnance in a barn, under a heap of hay. Your Sinclair had also ordered more arms from France. If Ormonde had not panicked and fled months ago, if he had kept his nerve and stayed to lead them, the King might now be faced with a huge rebellion in the West as well as in the north and in Scotland. They had plans to seize Bristol and Plymouth too, and I think Oxford was also involved, but General Pepper has occupied it with his dragoons, and made it safe. His Majesty may not know it, Paradice, but his throne is a great deal more secure because of you."

"Am I then to expect an invitation to St. James's?"

"Only if you wish it. Farmer George is even duller than ditchwater, if that were possible, but the Prince of Wales is an affable fellow, and his wife is lively enough."

"Well, if I go, I doubt I shall be the greatest whore there," Polly commented. "But I do not want my part in all this known, do you understand me, Dark? I don't care a jot what becomes of him now, but I have friends who would not understand my reasons for betraying the rebellion."

"Well, it was not your information alone which helped Wade," said Dark. "True, he turned aside to Bath because I took the papers you found to him, but when he arrived there, a man called Ralph Allen, who I believe is the postmaster for the city, provided further details of the plot. Apparently he had become suspicious and opened some letters. So thanks to him and to you, the West has been secured for the King. It is a great service, Paradice, and if I drop a word in certain quarters, you could be well and discreetly rewarded. Allen will surely benefit, why should not you?"

"No," Polly said at once. "I have plans for my future, and they do not depend on any royal remuneration."

Dark looked at her enquiringly. She held herself straight and proud under his gaze, though her skin tingled and her breath faltered. "Now that Sinclair has gone," he said, "surely you cannot stay here. The rent must cost a fortune."

"It is paid until Christmas, but yes, you are right, I do intend to find somewhere else." She paused, wondering how much to tell him. Of course, he would discover her plans when she opened her coffee-house, if not before, but she did not want him to guess about the Jacobite gold. True, it was now safely lodged with a discreet banker in Cheapside, rather than heaped in a locked wooden chest in her closet, but if the money did not belong to the Pretender, it did not belong to her either. Dark was an agent of King George, and he would surely consider that the gold was due to the Crown.

But of course he himself had just told her that she had done that Crown considerable service, and since she had rejected any thought of open reward, she might as well take that money in lieu. The thought made her feel much happier, and she smiled, the dimples puckering her cheeks. "Dark, do you know of any premises that might be suitable for a coffee-house?"

"A *coffee-house?* My dear Paradice, you are surely not thinking of opening a *coffee-house?*"

"You make it sound as though I wanted to open a Covent Garden nunnery," Polly complained. "I have done with being beholden to men. Either they die or they betray you, and in any case I am no longer so young and dewy as I used to be."

"Not all men are so vile," Dark said softly, and his eyes held hers. "Do not reject us entirely, Paradice. And in any case, you do yourself a disservice, as your mirror must daily inform you."

"I am twenty-five, I have been the mistress of six different men, and I have also spent a brief while in one of those nunneries, so I know how the cards are dealt, and my hand is almost done. Yes, I could doubtless attract another cully and then another, but it would grow more and more difficult, I would become more and more desperate, less discriminating, and where would I end? Where Gin's mother ended, dead in the gutter. So I cast around for another source of income, and decided on a coffee-house. I have some money saved, and Hannah makes the best coffee in London, as I am sure you will agree."

"Indeed I do, but there are hundreds of coffee-houses, all struggling for custom. It's not a path to quick riches."

"If I wanted quick riches, I'd buy a lottery ticket, or invest in stock, or some hare-brained scheme to mine gold in Brazil. I only require enough to live on in comfort, and to put by a little for my old age. It's all I have *ever* wanted, Dark – the means to be comfortable, and safe. I thought I was safe when I was a child, and I was wrong."

"You haven't told me exactly what happened to you."

Polly looked at him thoughtfully. She knew much about Dark from her own enquiries, and from Gin, but there was still a great deal that was mysterious about him, and that added spice to her feelings. She did not wish to make him such a gift of her own past that she was no longer an enticing enigma, and in any case the wounds, though ancient, had never entirely healed. She shook her head firmly. "Nor do I intend to. That water has flowed under the bridge and out to sea long since, and my business now is with the present, and the future. So, will you give my enterprise your blessing, Dark?"

He gave her a rueful glance that liquefied her bones. "Of course I will. But you must do something for me in return. Shall we agree on a date and a time for you to sit to me, for your portrait?"

Polly smiled at him. "Certainly I will, when I am not scouring the streets around Covent Garden looking for suitable premises. I have prepared myself for a long quest, for I am not interested in shacks or hovels. I intend to open my new coffee-house – to be called the Paradise, naturally – in a handsome, well-built establishment, with at least one good-sized room downstairs, if not two, and living space above for me, and Hannah, and Gin. I shall serve coffee and tea and chocolate, and spirituous liquors in moderation – Hannah has a most excellent recipe for Arrack Punch. There will be prints and paintings on the walls, and a roaring fire to keep the coffee hot, and perhaps some cakes and refreshments as well, depending on the premises and on what my customers might want, and sometimes I might divert them with a song or two. I shall stock *The Daily Courant* and *The Flying Post* and the other papers for those who wish to keep up with the news, and I might even be persuaded, for a small consideration, to take advertisements from reputable practitioners in medicine, or peruke-makers."

"And artists?"

"Do you know any reputable ones?" Polly enquired slyly, arching her exquisite brows. "For I am sure I do not."

Dark grinned at her, his eyes crinkling with amusement and the lines deepening around his mouth. "I do not either, so perhaps you'll have to omit the artist. Unless you plan to hang a splendid portrait of yourself above the hearth, of course."

Polly pursed her lips in apparent thought. "What a most excellent idea! Though I do insist on appearing in respectable attire. Your notion of depicting me as a penitent Magdalene might not sit too well with the atmosphere of a coffee-house."

"Don't worry, I have had a much better idea. How if you sit at a table, as we are now – Hannah can pour your coffee, and Gin can hover in the background with a tray. Does that appeal to you?"

"I have never seen a portrait like that," said Polly doubtfully. "But on the other hand, I haven't seen many portraits at all ... oh, yes, to have Hannah and Gin with me, I would like that above all things! When shall we start?"

"Would tomorrow suit you? The light in my painting room is best in the morning, so how does ten o'clock sound? And then you will have the rest of the day to seek out the perfect premises in which to serve your coffee."

"It would suit me very well," Polly said. It was much sooner than she had anticipated, and she did not feel quite ready for this: she needed to sort out her feelings and decide whether she wanted a pleasurable flirtation with Dark, or something more. But on the other hand, she longed to see a portrait of herself with Hannah, and the sooner she found herself a suitable place for a coffee-house, the better: she did not want to fritter away her gold on another quarter's rent. So she gave him, by design, her most entrancing smile. "Thank you, Dark. I shall look forward to it, very much."

CHAPTER THIRTEEN

'The subtil Artist'

Polly had never visited an artist's painting room before, and she had no idea what to expect. To begin with, she was somewhat taken aback by the elaborately bewigged footman, clad in a livery of sickly carnation and yellow, who opened the door to her. He asked her business in unctuous tones, and ushered her into a surprisingly spacious hallway, where he took charge of her mantle, muff and hood.

"Who's that, John?" It was a harsh, imperious voice, and it seemed to come from a room to the right.

"A young lady, ma'am, a visitor for Mr. Dark."

"Well, show her in, you soft-brained widgeon!"

Polly could remember the artist mentioning that he lodged at the house of an elderly lady. She glanced at the footman's professionally wooden face: he was obviously quite accustomed to abuse from his mistress. "If you will please to come this way, Mistress Paradice," he said smoothly. "Madame Rousselle wishes to see you."

The parlour was much larger than her own, with a marble fireplace and two tall windows looking out onto the street. Most of the space was taken up with a vast four-poster bed, draped with ancient and mouldering tapestries whose covering of dirt entirely failed to conceal their astonishing lewdness. Even in Mother Whybrow's, the decorations had not been so explicit. Propped on a lavish array of pillows and bolsters, her withered dugs almost exposed by a wanton déshabillé that had been fashionable forty or fifty years ago, reclined an elderly woman in a bright scarlet wig. Perhaps she had been beautiful once, for the bones of her face were still good, but the shrivelled skin which covered them was caked in thick white and red paint, so that now she looked like a grotesque in one of Powell's puppet shows. Only her eyes, voraciously curious, still contained some vestige of youth.

"Mistress Paradice, ma'am," said the footman, with a low bow. Polly, well aware that she was being assessed and judged, produced a sweetly graceful obeisance and stood demurely under that avid gaze, her hands clasped and her head slightly tilted in expectation.

"Very pretty," the old woman in the bed commented, her accent that of Southwark rather than France. "Almost as pretty as poor Nelly. You have more style than she did, though. A drab she was born and a drab she remained to the end of her days, despite all her fine clothes and jewels and her royal lover. You can't make a silk gown out of linsey-woolsey. John, don't stand there staring like a fat-arsed doodle, go fetch Dark!"

"Yes, ma'am," the footman murmured, and withdrew. Madame Rousselle extended a skeletal grey arm, the ancient skin drooping loosely from the bones, and beckoned her closer. "Come here, child, and let me get a good look at you. Yes, very pretty indeed. Is he your lover yet?"

"I have no lover, madam," said Polly calmly.

"Oh, I daresay you have none *now*," said the crone, looking at her knowingly. "But what of the future, eh? Not to mention the past. A long past, I'll wager. You're no drab, but you're no lady either. So why are you here, if he ain't your lover?"

"He is to paint my portrait," Polly said. She was glad she was no longer wearing her new winter mantle: despite the frosty chill outside, the fire burned so hot that she could barely breathe, and the air was filled with the musty stink of age and dirt and stale urine.

"Your portrait, eh?" said Madame Rousselle, with a

cackle. "To hang in his chamber, or in yours?"

"In mine, madam."

"Hm. For God's sake come *closer*, girl, how am I expected to see you properly in this light when that smarmy apology for a footman hasn't lit the candles?"

"Your eyesight seems excellent to me, madam," said Polly. The old woman was unsavoury and offensive in all departments, but she could not help admiring her stubborn refusal to be cowed by old age and infirmity. She walked to the side of the bed, and immediately regretted it, because a skinny claw promptly seized her wrist. "Plenty of flesh on your bones," Madame Rousselle said approvingly. "Gentlemen like flesh on a woman's bones. Plump bubbies and a trim waist and generous hips, that's what they like. When first I appeared at Drury Lane, I was in a breeches part, and only a blind man could have taken me for a boy. You've been on the stage too, I hear?"

Polly did not ask how she knew. She let her wrist lie still in the old woman's painful grasp – her nails were long, and unclean, and dug into her skin – and said, "I have sung occasionally, and most recently I was at Lincoln's Inn Fields for one or two nights, not long since. But I have never been persuaded to act."

"Though Rich asked you, I expect. Don't look so surprised, girl, I know everything that goes on. Once I was as famous as Mrs. Oldfield or Mrs. Santlow. Every night they had to turn people away. All the women aped my speech and my gestures, and all the men wanted to bed me." She gave a lascivious giggle, grotesquely inappropriate for a woman her age. "King Charles himself came to see me, and he saw a deal more of me later that night. How the Castlemaine was jealous! She threw plates, she wept and stormed, but for three long weeks he wanted Marie Rousselle instead. Three long, lewd, lecherous weeks." Her voice tailed away as she contemplated her vanished triumph.

"Indeed, madam," said Polly politely. The grip on her arm had slackened, and she gently withdrew it, resisting the temptation to rub the pain away.

"Indeed," said the crone, coming to life again with a snap. "What's he been telling you, eh, pretty Mrs Paradice? That I'm a senile old hag who peddles a pack of lies?"

"He's told me nothing of the sort," Polly said, with perfect truth.

"I'm glad to hear it. Well, it ain't a pack of lies. King Charlie did bed me, we made the beast with two backs time and time again." She gave Polly a sly look. "And if you don't believe me, well, look around you, girl. This is *my* house, *my* footman, and *my* bed. A very generous man, Charlie Stuart, gave me everything I asked for, even the roof over my head. Only one regret - he never gave me a child. He was even more generous to his bastards. I'd have been a Duchess, and my brat a Duke. Still, a house and a bag of diamonds and rubies ain't so bad for a few weeks on your back, eh, girl? If only you could find a lover so free with his mint."

"If only," Polly agreed. To her relief, there was a knock at the door, and the footman entered. Behind him, the colour of a shadow, came Dark, though at first she did not recognise him: instead of his usual brown tie-wig, he was wearing a dark blue silk turban, of the sort affected by gentlemen with artistic or literary pretensions, when indoors. He bowed most politely to Madame Rousselle, and then to Polly. "Good morning to you, Paradice. I suspected I might find you here."

"You thought you'd smuggle the girl upstairs without letting me look her over, eh?" said the ancient. "Well, nothing gets past *me* in this house, oh no! You can't pull the wool over *my* eyes. So when are you going to vault her, eh?"

Polly glanced at Dark, but his face was perfectly

straight. “Is that any of your business?” he enquired.

“You live in this house, don’t you? Then of course it’s my business. Be sure to come and tell me all about it when you’ve swived her. You can both go now - you’ve tired me out.” She gave an exaggerated, theatrical yawn and leaned back against the pillows, the scarlet wig slightly askew. “John? Where’s that looby gone? Where’s my draught? Fetch it this instant, or you’ll be out on the streets without a character!”

“I do apologise for Madame Rousselle,” said Dark, as they climbed the stairs. “As you have probably guessed, she was born plain Mary Russell. She is a relic of a less polite age, and I hope she did not shock you.”

“Of course she did not,” Polly said. “Though I confess to being a little surprised by her.” This was a considerable understatement, for she found the old woman both interesting and repellent, and her relentless and salacious questioning had, as Madame probably well knew, struck a nerve. “How do you come to lodge in her house?”

“Oh, we have many acquaintances in common through the Drury Lane theatre. She and I suit each other very well - I give her an endless source of gossip and interest and she gives me a roof over my head at very reasonable rates. True, some of my more respectable clients have been a little taken aback by her forthrightness, but –“

“You do not have very many respectable clients,” Polly murmured mischievously.

Dark laughed, and threw open the door at the head of the stairs. “Welcome, Paradice, to my own domain.”

Polly had never been in an artist’s lodgings before, but this room, hung with pictures, was more like the gallery in a country house. There was no easel, no classical statues and drapery to serve for a background, and no sign of work in progress. Looking about her, she said, “This is not your painting room."

"Your powers of observation do you credit, Paradice. No, it is not. I had this chamber fitted out to display my work to discerning patrons."

"Then all the pictures are by your hand?" Polly walked over to the nearest. A plump, brown haired woman in a dark red dress reclined against a tree. She held a rose in her hand, and her warm eyes smiled out from the canvas. "Dark, I am exceedingly impressed. She looks as if she were about to speak to me!"

"My sister, Bonne," he said. "She graciously agreed to let me hang it here. Unlike the rest of my family, she is an enthusiastic supporter of my painting."

"Is she your only sister? She does not much resemble you."

"She is very like our mother, whereas I favour my father. And yes, she is my only living sister. I also have a brother, but he disowned me long since." He glanced at her. "That is his loss, not mine. Bonne lives in the country, in Richmond, with her husband and children. I do not see her very often, but we have remained friends."

Polly wondered if his sister sent him warm stockings and urged him to eat regular meals and go to bed early. Looking at the kind, rather maternal face, she could well imagine it. Smiling, she examined the other portraits. Most were of single men and women, in a variety of poses, but there was a group of gentlemen poring over a map laid on a table, and another depicted a young couple, obviously newly married, gazing at each other fondly. "I am surprised that they did not keep this to hang in their parlour," she said, admiring the intricate details of the woman's flowered silk petticoat.

"He died of a fever, not six weeks after the wedding. She did not want any reminder."

There was a small, awkward pause. Polly said lightly, "If you have entertained the notion that showing me these pictures will dissuade me from sitting to you, and thus release you from your obligation, well, you are sadly mistaken. I am even more determined to have you grant me the immortality of paint."

"Then if you will step this way, Paradice, we may begin."

They climbed another flight of stairs, and another. These houses in Half Moon Street had been built fifty or sixty years ago, when space had not been so much at a premium, and they were well-planned and generously proportioned. Polly guessed that Madame Rousselle and her staff occupied the ground floor and basement, leaving Dark the rest of the house. Presumably his private quarters lay on the floor above the display room, and his studio was to be found in the garret, high under the eaves. Polly paused at the top of the stairs, warm from the exertion, and waited expectantly as he opened the door and ushered her within.

The smell struck her first: a mixture of pungent oils, throat-catching fumes, and gentler, more fugitive fragrances. She coughed involuntarily, and put a hand to her mouth.

"I apologise for the stench – I shall open a window. You will, I hope, find that you soon become accustomed to it."

Polly could not imagine this being possible, but she nodded, and wiped her watering eyes. With her vision cleared, and breathing through her mouth, she was able to look around. The room obviously took up the entire space at the top of the house: she could see the marks where the flimsy partitions normally used to divide the area into servants' chambers had been taken down. There was a small fireplace at either end of the room, in which some coals glowed sullenly, and on both sides three dormer windows, set into the sloping roof. Dark opened one, and a wave of cold air charged in, making the hairs stand up on her arms, but at least dissipating the smell. Lengths of heavy velvet, in a wide variety of colours, hung from a pole across one of the corners, and an ancient urn, a plaster pillar and a small marble sculpture of some Greek god that she had seen, greatly enlarged, in several of the portraits downstairs, were placed together by one of the windows, along with several wooden boxes of varying sizes, and a yellowed globe. Next to the nearest window stood an easel, burdened with a canvas, and Polly walked forward to inspect it.

To her surprise, there was a scene already sketched out upon the pale grey ground. The ghostly shape of a woman sat at a table, one hand raised as if in gesture, or drinking tea from an invisible cup. Beside her stood another woman, her head turned to look out at the spectator. Above them, swooping lines of the same thin light brown paint indicated the presence of swags of drapery.

"But you have started it!" she said.

"Certainly I have. Knowing your contrary and fickle nature, I did not wish to waste time. I feared that you might change your mind."

Polly looked at him, her eyebrows raised. "You have so much to learn about me, Dark," she said. "And what would you do if I did not like the pose?"

"I would change it. At this stage, indeed at any stage, it is not especially difficult. The paints are thick and opaque, you can put almost any colour over another, though there are a few which do not go together. Orpiment, for example, ruins almost any colour that is laid on top of it."

"I have no wish to be browbeaten with the minute details of your methods," said Polly. "I merely desire you to paint my portrait. Where shall I sit? You have sketched in a table, but alas, there does not seem to be a table here."

"Never fear, we do not need one. This, my dear Paradice, is the alchemy of the painter's art. Do you wish to look even younger and more beautiful than the charming reality? I can oblige. Do you wish to appear as a vestal virgin, or Diana the huntress, or a vengeful Amazon? I can arrange that too. Whatever you desire in your picture, I can supply. You may have a multitude of different tables - polished oak, gleaming walnut, or fetchingly draped with that white figured damask. Which would you prefer?"

"Whichever will best suit the picture," Polly said. "Is it true that Kneller only paints the faces of his portraits, but has all the rest done by a drapery-painter?"

"It is indeed. He also has wig-painters, hand-painters and tree-painters. I, on the other hand, being a jack of all trades and unwilling to subscribe several hundred guineas a year to a drapery specialist, am forced to brush every inch of the canvas myself. So if my portrayal of the table or your gown leaves something to be desired, you may take the painting away and give it to one of Kneller's men to be improved."

"There will be no picture at all if we do not start it," Polly pointed out. "I am not wholly a lady of leisure, Dark, and although in the normal run of things I would be happy bantering here all day with you, I have affairs that demand my time. So shall we begin?"

The morning passed swiftly, and agreeably. She was placed on a comfortable, high-backed chair, told to arrange her skirts so that her quilted petticoat and rich velvet gown could be seen to best advantage, and sat very still while Dark, a curiously exotic figure in his turban and an old embroidered night-gown, squeezed a variety of colours out onto his palette, selected a couple of brushes, and began to work. A multitude of questions sprang to her mind. How long had he been an artist? Had he received any training? Did he have any assistants to prepare his colours and canvases, if not to help with the actual painting? And how many of these sessions would be required before the portrait was finished?

Only the last of these conformed to her self-imposed restrictions about prying too closely into his life, so she waited until he was engaged in mixing the little glistening coils of colour on his palette, and asked him.

"Oh, at least half a dozen," said Dark, looking at her over the top of his easel, then glancing down at the palette again, as if matching paint to skin. "Kneller, for example, usually needs just one sitting from the life, but then of course he is only painting a small oval on a large canvas. After that, the picture is completed by his assistants – of whom I was one for a time, some years ago."

"But you do not appear to have any assistants. So how do you prepare your paints and canvases?"

"I have neither the time nor the inclination to grind my own pigments - it's a long and tedious task at best. I use the colourman in Long Acre, and he also sells canvases ready primed, stretched and cut to size. All I need do is mix the colours, and apply them. And there is a boy who comes in to help me when need arises."

For Dark, he was being remarkably informative. Taking advantage of his temporary laxity, Polly said, "And do you sell many portraits?"

"Enough." Dark was working the brush briskly over the area where she presumed her face must be, in swift bold strokes, glancing first at the canvas, then at his subject. "And of course there is also my work at Drury Lane. I make a living, that is all. But then I have no desire to keep my own coach or retire to some mansion in Chelsea." He gave her a sly, provoking smile. "Like you, my needs are simple."

That room downstairs, with the carving and expensive paintwork and gold leaf, must have cost a good many portraits. Polly ignored the jibe. "So – you were one of Kneller's assistants. Before that, someone must have taught you to paint?"

"I chiefly taught myself. My father was a silversmith who wished me to follow in his craft, and would have forced me to learn engraving and design, but I was a rebellious brat and would have none of his plans for me, so I fled to the Army for a number of years, before deciding to turn to painting. Have you heard of the Academy? It was founded by Kneller some five or six years ago, and meets in a house in Great Queen Street. If you pay a guinea subscription, there you may draw and paint figures from the life, and meet with other artists and students. Face painters are of course not so highly regarded – in fact I've heard them called phiz-mongers, as if they were selling cheap goods in the market – but it gave me some opportunity to learn new methods and styles." He gave her a long, judicious stare. "Your face is very pleasingly proportioned, did you know that, Paradice? Almost a paragon of perfection."

"Perhaps that is why I am considered to be a beauty, sir," Polly said, with a deliberate flutter of her eyelashes. "So as well as Sir Godfrey, the great man, you have met other artists?"

"Yes, I have – you may have heard of Thornhill, who has won the commission to decorate the inside of the dome at St. Paul's. He is chiefly a history-painter, he does not demean himself by doing portraits, unless the subject is very great or very rich. Jervas, Laguerre, Gibson, Laroun –"

"None of those names means anything to me," Polly confessed, with a smile. It was strange, she thought, how in this chilly, rather bleak room, with its pungent aromas and its jumble of props and accessories, a new dimension to their relationship seemed to have emerged, based on a friendship of equals. The looks he gave her were purely professional, his manner entirely devoid of hostility or disrespect. He might have been painting one of his artist friends, rather than a beautiful woman to whom he was attracted. And he was attracted to her, she was certain of that, as surely as she knew she was attracted to him. Yet now it was as if he had set all thoughts of lechery aside, to concentrate on his art, and she found the idea very encouraging. In her experience, lust soon died, and love had proved a fickle jade. Friendship was what she valued most, and if there were indeed to be half a dozen more sittings, beside those needed for Hannah and Gin, then there would be ample opportunity for that growing friendship to flower. And when the portrait was finished, she planned to ask him to do a sign for her coffee-house, which should ensure that their meetings were even further prolonged.

With a secret smile of anticipation, she looked forward eagerly to the days ahead.

* * *

"I regret to inform you, madam, that Mr. Dark is not at home today."

The pang of disappointment that shot through Polly's breast was painfully acute. She would have died, however, rather than reveal this to Madame Rousselle's poker-faced footman, and so she said lightly, "Oh, is he not? Perhaps I have mistaken the date."

"You have not, madam, but he is unable to keep the appointment for your sitting today. He has asked me to give you this note."

The thick scrawl had been done in charcoal and considerable haste, and was virtually unreadable. Polly managed to decipher it, with some difficulty, while the footman pretended not to be interested.

'*Paradice. My apologies, but I had quite forgot that urgent business commands me elsewhere. If you would seek me out, ask Gin where I am usually to be found on this day. Dark.*'

What was so significant about this day? Polly stared at the writing in bewilderment, and then remembered. It was the fourth of November, the late King William's birthday, and always an occasion for Protestant rejoicing, particularly as the traditional celebration of the discovery of the Gunpowder Plot took place on the fifth. She tucked her paper into her muff, and nodded to the footman. "Thank you. I will not trouble Madame Rousselle, unless she particularly wishes to see me."

"Madame is at present being blooded, and is not receiving visitors today," the footman informed her lugubriously. To her considerable relief, he ushered Polly out into Half Moon Street, with her curiosity thoroughly aroused, and the whole day in which to satisfy it.

This would have been her fifth sitting for Dark, and she had been greatly looking forward to it: moreover, he had promised her that afterwards, he would accompany her as she inspected potential premises for her coffee-shop. So far, despite a thorough and dispiriting search that had taken in the entire length of the Strand and Fleet Street, not to mention all of Charing Cross, Westminster and Whitehall, she had failed to find anything suitable. Sometimes the downstairs rooms were too small, or the living quarters cramped: several places had looked as if only the expenditure of vast sums would render them fit for habitation: and the only one in any way fit for her purpose, in a plum position hard by Northumberland House, was within sight of four popular coffee-houses, including the famous Mann's.

Polly, walking briskly back to Flying Horse Court to quiz Gin, pondered the problem. The Strand was one of the principle shopping streets in London, and premises there would attract a considerable passing trade, but rents were correspondingly high. The same applied to Charing Cross. There was no doubt that the sort of clientele she wished to attract - the artists, writers, actors, poets - were largely to be found in and around Covent Garden itself, but of course the popular Will's and Button's, both in Russell Street, were already haunted by the likes of Addison and Steele. Opening yet another coffee-house in the immediate vicinity would be an enterprise surely doomed to failure. She did not wish to go much further afield – towards the Temple she would attract only earnest young lawyers, St. Paul's was the haunt of the clergy, and in the City there would be a superfluity of merchants and stock-jobbers. None of these groups seemed likely to provide the lively company and good conversation that she craved.

But somewhere near, surely, was the house of her dreams: well maintained, needing perhaps only a lick of paint and a few days' work by a competent carpenter: sited just off a busy area, easy to find and yet not demanding the huge rents of premises on a main thoroughfare: close to the theatres and the bustling life of the city without treading on the toes of more established and popular coffee-houses. She would find this place, sooner or later, and it would be her own Paradise.

Mrs. Garrett, who came in most days to cook, sat at one end of the kitchen table, jointing a chicken, while opposite her Gin scoured pewter plates until they shone like silver. In her reduced circumstances, with the Jacobite gold now to be jealously conserved rather than spent, these two, along with Hannah and her remaining footman Will Evans, were the only servants Polly possessed, and in consequence her formerly well-ordered household was beginning to look a little blurred with dust around the edges.

Gin's hair was growing fast, and with occasional washing no longer resembled a hank of old bristles. There had only been a few lice on the last combing, performed by Hannah with her usual ferocity, to the accompaniment of smothered curses and squawks of pain. Even with the constriction of her stays, the child's sex was now becoming apparent, and there was a flaring of pimples on her nose and chin. She must still be nagged to keep herself clean, and to behave with proper decorum, but the painful lessons were being slowly learnt. Polly noted her sore, reddened hands and hardened her heart. In just such a fashion had she been taught the essentials of womanhood: to work, to obey, and never to complain. Later, she had joyfully broken all those hated rules, and she suspected that one day Gin might also kick over the traces: she, too, possessed the spirit and intelligence to make something more of herself.

"I want a quick word with you, Jane," she said. "I trust she can be spared for a few moments, Mrs. Garrett?"

The cook, with a sniff – she did not care for Gin, who failed to match up to her exacting and impatient standards – agreed grudgingly that she could, and Polly bore the child off to her parlour.

Stand still and straight, speak only when you're spoken to, never out of turn, don't wipe your nose on your sleeve, don't scratch yourself, keep your eyes lowered, always address your betters as 'ma'am' or 'sir': Polly could almost see Gin's lips move as she recited to herself the servants' litany that she herself had had drummed into her by Kitty, all those years ago. She smiled at her. "Don't look so alarmed, you've done nothing wrong – the reverse, in fact."

"I ain't frit," said Gin, with a flash of the old insolent spirit, that she would never have dared to disclose to Hannah or Mrs. Garrett. "Ma'am," she added, as an afterthought.

"I need your help," Polly went on. "I need to find Dark, and according to the note which he has left for me, you will know where he is today."

"Will I?" Gin looked startled. "Ain't he at his house, then? Ma'am."

"No, he is not. And today is the fourth of November. Old King William's birthday," she added, seeing the girl's obvious bewilderment.

"Why didn't you say so?" demanded Gin, her face clearing at once. "He'll be at Whitechapel, then, making his skyrockets. He always makes skyrockets for Gunpowder Plot Day, and King George's birthday, and Queen Bess's day an' all."

"*Skyrockets?*" Now it was Polly's turn to feel bewildered. "I did not know he made skyrockets – is it not very dangerous?"

"Yes – ma'am – that's why he makes 'em at Whitechapel and not at Half Moon Street," Gin explained, as to one very lacking in intelligence. "In case he blows himself up."

"Dear God," said Polly, stunned. "How on earth did he learn how to make skyrockets? Surely it's a very specialised business?"

"When he was in Marlborough's army, from the Firemaster. They're powerful good rockets, showers of gold and silver like rain! D'you mind them on the river at the Peace? They were his."

It was two years ago and more, but Polly remembered the absolute and transitory beauty in the night sky, doubled by reflection in the shimmering black water of the Thames beneath. She had not cared for the noise, the crackles and bangs, but she had been entranced by that splendour.

Gin was looking cunningly at her: she added, in a wheedling tone, "Do you want to go to Whitechapel, then? Ma'am."

"I certainly do," said Polly briskly, and rose to her feet. She pretended to think. "But how will I find the place ... "

"It ain't that easy, but I knows it, ma'am," said Gin, with a sly glance. "I could show you where it is. We could go in a hackney, it ain't so far – "

"Very well, Gin, you may accompany me," said Polly, with an inward smile. What child would not leap at the opportunity for a jaunt through the City streets, when the alternative was to sit in the gloomy kitchen all day, polishing pewter and scouring dirty dishes under Mrs. Garrett's gimlet eye? "Fetch your warm cloak and hood, and look sharp about it."

Half an hour later, they were rattling eastwards in a hackney. Gin, it was plain, had never been inside such a conveyance before, but Polly strongly suspected that in the past she had frequently hitched an illicit ride by clinging onto the sides or the roof. Her thin cheeks flushed with excitement, she peered out of the window at the shifting, cursing, shouting crowds.

There was much traffic in the Strand and along Fleet Street. Many people wore orange ribbons, in honour of Dutch William, and in a couple of places they were piling up old wood and rubbish to make bonfires. She heard shouts of "Hanover!" and "Down with the Jacks!" There was a mood of excited expectancy in the faces outside, but it was not all so light-hearted: they passed one man, foolishly wearing a white rose to signify his allegiance to the Pretender, who was being efficiently beaten for his presumption by half a dozen supporters of King George.

Polly's habitat was the area around the Strand and Covent Garden: she knew all the houses and alleys, both respectable and notorious. As they went further east, the scenery became much less familiar. She had been to the Tower, of course, and several times she and Robbie had taken a boat downriver to Greenwich to see the Hospital there, and wander in the park: but these streets were foreign territory for the most part, and she was glad that Gin, at least, seemed to know where they were bound. When the hackney driver stopped by Aldgate, she hopped out to give him precise directions, and then climbed up beside him on his perch, leaving Polly in sole possession of the inside, with its ripped leather upholstery and stale, unpleasant aromas.

The child's rather raucous voice accompanied them under the Gate and along Whitechapel. Here the close-packed houses, courts and alleys of the city began to thin out, and there were glimpses of green fields and windswept trees between the buildings. It had begun to rain fitfully, and Polly heard Gin shouting exhortations to the straining horse. With a lurch, the hackney turned right, down a narrow lane, and then came to a halt.

"Here we are," Gin said, appearing suddenly at the window. "Shall I tell him to wait?"

"That won't be necessary," Polly told her. She gathered her cloak closely about her and, with a glance at the glowering sky, stepped down from the carriage and looked around. The way was lined with old houses, gabled and half-timbered as all of London had been until the Fire, hugger-mugger with tall buildings in clean red brick, with sash windows and pedimented doors. The lane forked just ahead, one way continuing between terraces of newer houses, the other striking left across open fields on which cattle and horses were grazing.

"Where are we?" Polly asked, fumbling in her pocket for a couple of shillings to pay the fare. As the hackney moved off, Gin said, "White Horse Lane. That way leads back to Goodman's Fields, and over there, no, there, beyond them cattle, is Hangman's Acre."

"So where is Dark to be found?"

"He's in that stable," said Gin, pointing to a long, low brick building, comparatively new, with a tiled roof and a few small windows, which stood further down the lane. "It ain't a palace, but it's dry and safe and if he *does* blow himself up, he won't hurt no-one else. Shall I go knock on the door, ma'am?"

"You may," said Polly, for the wind was increasing, whipping maliciously down the narrow lane and blowing a stinging scatter of raindrops against her face. "Be as quick as you can."

With her own mantle clasped tight around her, the girl ran up to the door and hammered briskly on it. Polly followed more slowly, feeling curiously apprehensive about this encounter. True, in his note Dark had plainly encouraged her to visit, but there was the matter of the skyrockets. Gin's relish when she talked of the danger involved in making them was evident, but that did not mean that she was exaggerating the risk. Gunpowder could not be trifled with.

The door opened, and there was Dark, warmly clad in his usual black. At the sight of her, he smiled, and bowed her into the gloom beyond. "Paradice! This is an unexpected pleasure."

"You did invite me," Polly pointed out. The floor under her feet was flagged with broad slabs of stone, and it was breathtakingly cold. Her breath steamed white in the icy air, and her nostrils, assaulted by a pungent and unidentifiable aroma, recoiled in disgust. She sneezed violently, and had to fumble in her pocket for a handkerchief.

"Indeed I did, but I never thought you would actually venture forth on such a miserable day. Obviously I underestimated the strength of your curiosity."

"Obviously." Polly blew her nose, wiped her wet eyes, and looked around her. It was a small room, occupying probably about a quarter of the entire building, and lit by a couple of small high windows. There was a hearth, but it was swept clean and bare, and there were no candles. Of course, lighting any flame in such close proximity to gunpowder would be the height of folly, hence the bitter cold.

A long workbench took up the length of the wall under the windows, and was strewn with a variety of objects: many long pasteboard tubes, twists of paper and short pieces of cord, bundles of sticks, a set of weights and scales and a nest of brass measures and spoons. Below the bench, scarcely visible in the shadows, rested a variety of small barrels and boxes.

"I regret I am unable to offer you any refreshments," Dark said. "But as you can see, there is no fire here."

"A wise decision," Polly commented. "I am sure there is an inn or chophouse close by, that will furnish us with dinner if we require it. So where are your skyrockets?"

"Ah, so Gin has told you what I am about. The finished ones are stacked over there, against the wall. A couple of men with a handcart will come for them in the morning, and take them down to Tower Hill. There's a huge celebration planned for tomorrow night, with music and ox-roasts and barrels of beer."

"And skyrockets," said Polly, walking over to the bench. Gin, who had evidently seen it all before, stood by the door and yawned behind her hand. "Let us hope it stops raining, or your display will be spoilt." She picked up one of the empty tubes. "Do you put the powder in here?"

"Yes, along with whatever makes the coloured stars when the rocket bursts in the sky. Charcoal or iron filings for yellow and amber, verdigris gives a sort of pallid green, not very satisfactory, and if I add extra sulphur to the gunpowder there will be a shower of white stars, rather pretty. And there is also the powder to send the rocket into the sky, the powder that makes it burst, and a timed fuse to set it off, preferably before it falls back to earth and lands on your head." He grinned at her. "Rockets are not simple constructions."

"I never supposed they were," Polly said, putting the tube down. "I never supposed they were safe, either. How do you still come to have your full complement of limbs and eyes and digits?"

"Because I am careful. And because I was taught well."

"By the Firemaster of England himself!" said Gin, coming to life from her post by the door. "Mongsewer Borgard."

"Yes, *Colonel* Borgard was my tutor, when he returned from the Spanish wars some years ago. I expressed an interest in fireworks, and he imparted the basics. After all, as an artist, I am not unfamiliar with the use of chemical colours. I would love to be able to produce a skyrocket that showered crimson or scarlet sparks, but so far I have failed to discover any substance which will oblige me."

"You'll blow yourself to Kingdom Come one o' these days," said Gin, with gloomy relish. "Nuffink left of you but little pieces."

"What a cheerful optimist you are to be sure, child!" Polly said lightly, though she could not help but agree with her. "Well, I am chilled to the very marrow standing here, Dark, what do you say to a hot dinner in some welcoming tavern or coffee-house? There must be some here, even in this benighted spot."

"I am nearly done," Dark said. "I contracted with the magistrates of Tower Hamlets, who are organising this celebration tomorrow, for half a hundred skyrockets, twenty-five white and twenty-five amber, and there are just five more amber left to fill. Will you wait?"

Polly's hands, tucked inside her fox-fur muff, were numb and blue, the tip of her nose was tingling and her toes, cramped inside thin kid shoes, seemed to have lost all feeling, but she nodded. "So long as you do not mind if I tramp up and down to keep warm. How have you managed not to turn into an ice statue, working in here for hours with no heat?"

"Like the Arctic Bear, I am extraordinarily hardy." He began to scoop the grainy powder from a half-empty barrel onto the scales. It was a tedious process, precise and thorough, but Polly's attention did not wander. She studied his neat, deft fingers as they sorted and weighed and poured, and wondered what they would feel like on her naked skin. The thought made the hair rise on her arms, and pleasurable sensations glowed in her loins. He glanced at her as he rammed the powder home in the tube, and to her mingled pleasure and chagrin, she blushed.

"I have had a letter from Sam Jessop," Dark said, apparently taking no notice of her brief embarrassment. "He sends you his kindest regards, and so does Miss Mary. She is overjoyed to be home, and has been a properly penitent and dutiful daughter. He has high hopes of finding her a suitable husband in the near future. Indeed, his eagerness to have her off his hands seemed to inform every line."

"That is not very fair," Polly pointed out. "Sam loves her dearly, and he only wants the best for her."

"Although, as she is in many eyes soiled goods, he will probably not achieve the match for her that he had hoped."

"He seemed to think that word of her escapade had not gone beyond his family and household. Anyway, I know that all he desires is her happiness, and she was not happy with Sinclair, that much was painfully obvious, despite her denials."

"Well, neither were you."

Polly opened her mouth to deny it, then closed it again, for she knew it to be true. No, she had not been happy – but then simple happiness, for a woman in her position, was almost unattainable, for every liaison was precarious and true love or commitment, on either side, a rarity she had not yet encountered. She had enjoyed Robbie's flattering attentions, the gifts, the life of luxury he had given her, but not the feeling that she must walk round him on tiptoe for fear of rousing his unpredictable anger. In the bedroom, he had at first been exultant, glorying in his ability to pleasure her, and she had believed he truly loved her, as she believed that she loved him. With the cruelty of hindsight, she knew that she had wilfully ignored the signs that now seemed very obvious. She had thought that he was worthy of her, and it had been humiliatingly painful to discover, with the news of his seduction of Mary Jessop, that she had been wrong.

"At the time, I supposed that I was," she said at last. "But I realise now that I was merely deceiving myself, just as he was deceiving me. And any happiness I did feel has been tainted beyond repair by his infidelity."

The look he gave her was intensely sympathetic, almost as if he understood her feelings. Polly remembered Gin's casual account of how he had also been cheated by a faithless lover, and wondered if, in the improbable guise of this gaunt, untidy and secretive artist, with moods apparently as changeable as any weathercock, she had at last encountered a man of sensibility and kindness.

It did not seem very likely. She had never been lucky in love, though each encounter had left her better off, in the material sense, than the one before. Now, by most people's standards, she was a woman of substantial means: but although that stolen Jacobite gold would buy her a measure of security, the bulwark against poverty and degradation she had always craved, it would never bring her true happiness. And perhaps nothing would.

"Ain't you nearly finished yet?" whined Gin, shivering by the door. "I'm perishing here!"

"Quiet, brat, or I'll send you outside." Dark was carefully pouring the precious, deadly mixture into the final tube. He rammed it home and tucked in the fuse. "There. Done. Well, Paradice, will you do me the honour of allowing me to escort you to dinner? The Green Dragon is just round the corner, and can furnish a tolerably good table. I have taken the liberty of bespeaking a private parlour with a roaring fire, in happy hopes of your company."

"Your presumption is astonishing," Polly said, with her most charming smile. "So how could I possibly refuse? Lead on then, Dark, and quickly, before we catch our deaths of cold in this place."

CHAPTER FOURTEEN

'Kindlers of Riot'

Eventually, that blazing fire thawed them out, and the hot mutton broth, well seasoned with a rich Madeira gravy, quickly disappeared, along with the steaming vegetables and fresh bread and the dish of mussels and oysters, poached in wine. Outside, the light was already waning, and the maid had lit the candles. The food glowing warmly in her stomach, Polly rose reluctantly to her feet. "I must go – I had arranged to look at a house this afternoon, and even if I grew wings, I would not reach it by the time appointed."

"Where is it?" Dark asked her, rising also. "I will escort you, if you wish."

"It's just off Fleet Street, near the Temple. I have no great hopes of it, but perhaps it will prove to be just the place." She grinned at him. "You see, Dark – despite everything that fate flings at me, still I am the optimist."

"Are you not perennially doomed to disappointment, then, Paradice?"

"Of course I am, but I cannot help always hoping for the best, that is my nature. Now, let us find Gin, and go."

Her maid had taken a rather less sophisticated dinner in the kitchen, and there were still smears of mutton fat round her mouth as she followed them out into Whitechapel. It had stopped raining, and in the west the setting sun had emerged, flooding the wet street with a sinister yellow light, while to the south, the quarter moon was already beginning to glow between the fleeing clouds. There were few people about, and the shopkeepers nearby were already putting up their shutters.

"There ain't no hackneys in sight," said Gin, looking up and down. This was hardly surprising: although there were seven hundred licensed in London, most of them congregated in the centre and west of the city, and here on the eastern periphery they were few and far between. Dark extended his arm to Polly, with a smile. "I knew it. Well, the evening has not turned out too badly – shall we walk? After spending all day inhaling gunpowder, I feel in need of some fresh air, however cold and damp."

It was an easy and leisurely stroll back along Whitechapel to the entrance to the City at Aldgate. Nearly two miles still lay between them and their destination, but Polly felt refreshed and invigorated by their dinner. Her arm rested lightly on Dark's, and the hood of her mantle was thrown back, exposing her face to the interested gaze of male passers-by, but she ignored them disdainfully, as if she were a respectable woman out for an evening walk with her husband.

The thought made her smile. In no way could she be considered respectable, nor did she wish to be. Respectable females did not spend time in the company of artists with dubious pasts, nor did they wish to open coffee-houses. Respectability, for Polly, was not something to which she aspired, but to be avoided at all costs, for it was both a restriction of her freedom, and an obstacle to her desires. In any case, why should she, with her own far from lily-white history, wish to ape those who would loathe and despise her for what she once had been?

No, she was entirely satisfied with her present lot, if only, if *only* she could find a place for her coffee-house.

By the time they passed the Royal Exchange, it was almost dark, and the streets were full of people hurrying home, or to taverns and cookshops for their evening meals. Although the street was lit by lamps at every doorway, and light poured out from the windows on either hand, she glanced enviously at those with the forethought to hire a link-boy to illuminate their path. But of course Gin, stumping doggedly along just behind them and probably grumbling under her breath, was no longer in a position to oblige.

Ahead of them, the crowds were growing thicker, and there seemed to be some shouting. Her companion paused, and Polly took the opportunity to bend and adjust her footwear. A man jostled her as he pushed by, and she overbalanced and almost fell. Gripping Dark's arm to stay upright, she said breathlessly, "Is there something happening?"

"I don't know." He glanced down at her, and in the light from a shop window she saw the flash of his smile. "But at this time of night, I have no wish to avoid trouble by trying to negotiate the back streets."

"And fall into far worse trouble, probably," Polly said. "I shall rely on you for my protection, Dark."

"I hope that your trust will not be misplaced," he said, and his hand touched hers briefly, before he turned to Gin. "Stay close, understand? And if you lose us in the crush, you may go straight back to Flying Horse Court – that is bound to be quicker than trying to find each other in the confusion."

"I can look after meself," Gin whined indignantly. "I don't need no molly-coddling."

"Just as well – because you won't get any. Shall we move on?"

The disturbance seemed to be taking place where Poultry joined Cheapside. There were hundreds of people here, many of them sporting badges obviously intended to represent white roses. There was much shouting and cheering, but in the general hubbub it was hard to discern any words until a huge man with a red, sweating face reeled against them and thrust a tankard under Dark's nose, bawling, "Drink a health to

King James!"

Somewhat to Polly's surprise, her companion obliged, tipping the beer down his throat and handing it back with a comment that was lost amid the noise around them. The fat man staggered on, apparently oblivious to the fact that his tankard was empty, and Dark put a protective arm around her shoulders, while attempting to steer a passage through the bawling, shifting crowd. A hackney was trying to force its way past, and she saw it surrounded by a yelling mob who pulled the driver from his box, while others opened the doors and ordered the occupants to declare their support for the Stuarts. For the first time, Polly felt a twinge of alarm. The mood of the crowd was rapidly becoming ugly, and it would not be long before the gathering became a riot.

Opposite Old Jewry, a vast bonfire had been lit in the wider space by the junction with Bucklersbury, and its red, flickering light cast a sinister glare over the mob as it screamed its loyalty to the Pretender, the High Church and the Duke of Ormonde. Another howl of rage greeted the arrival of a crude effigy, being carried aloft on the shoulders of the crowd. From the hook nose and paper crown, this was obviously intended to represent King William.

Dark was shouting something at her. She strained to hear what he was saying, and he bent down to bawl in her ear. "When the Whigs at the Roebuck hear about this, there'll be hell to pay. Let's find a way out of this rabble before it all turns into a battleground."

That was certainly easier said than done. The mob, drunk and belligerent, now blocked Cheapside from wall to wall, bawling insults at the effigy and surging to and fro at random, like currents in a storm-tossed sea. Polly was jostled, bumped, squeezed till she could hardly breathe, her feet trodden on innumerable times and her person groped in a most intimate way by fingers that seemed to sneak bodiless out of the press, to fumble at her breast or waist, and retreat before she could locate their owners. But Dark had her hand tightly in his, towing her remorselessly through the crush, although sometimes she felt as if her arm would be ripped from its socket as the swirling mass of people around them threatened to pull her out of his grasp.

They had managed to struggle past the corner with Old Jewry, and the press of people seemed to be declining a little, when a great howl went up ahead of them. "The Whigs! The Whigs are coming!" Immediately the crowd surged forward again, roaring defiance. Polly felt her hand torn from Dark's, and in the wild, flickering light from the bonfire, she could not see where he was. But she was small, agile and utterly determined, and she used her hands and heels and elbows to punishing effect. Breathless, she gained the refuge of a doorway hard by Queen Street, with steps up to it that gave her a few precious inches of vantage point above the heads of the mob. There was no sign of Gin, but Polly had few fears for her: the girl had lived on the streets of London all her life, she knew every alley and court, and she was quite capable of looking after herself.

Further down Cheapside, yells and screams announced the arrival of the pack from the Roebuck, a tavern notorious as a haunt of the wilder Whigs. Furious at the insult offered to their beloved King William, they waded into the Jacobite mob wielding clubs and staves, with shouts of "Hanover!" and "King George!" Battle was joined with a vengeance, and Polly watched from the steps, in an agony of fear and impatience, her eyes hunting for a glimpse of Dark amongst the hurly-burly in the street below her. Suddenly it convulsed and spat him out at her, his coat ripped and his wig askew. Behind him, close enough to pierce the pandemonium of violence, a voice roared, "I know him! He's a filthy Whig!"

"Dear God," Polly said, on a sob, and she turned and

hammered on the door. Of course it remained firmly closed: the occupants, if they were within, would have been mad to open up with a riot right outside. Dark grabbed her by the shoulder and pulled her away, just as something soft and foul smacked into the brickwork beside her, spattering her cloak. "It'll be cobblestones next," he said. "Come *on!*"

Before she could protest, he had dragged her back into the crowd. A fist came out of the struggling mass and hit Dark in the cheek. His head jerked back from the blow, and then he retaliated with a savage punch at the nearest face. The man's nose dissolved in a spray of blood, and the men around them howled in fury like a pack of wolves. In terror, Polly realised that she and Dark were no longer part of the mob, but its prey.

If she fell now, she would be trampled underfoot and killed for sure. Dark, relentless, was using brute strength to force his way through the press, one hand grasping hers, the other laying about him with the flat of his sword. Behind them, the roars of their pursuers rose to a pitch of ferocity. She saw the entrance to Queen Street on their left. Thank God, Dark was heading for it. Suddenly they were on the edge of the crowd, dodging knots of onlookers clustering on the corner. She glanced wildly over her shoulder and saw a group of men thrusting through the mob. One saw them, and pointed, his mouth open, soundless in the din, to cry havoc. She wrenched her hand free of Dark's, picked up her skirts, and ran full pelt along Queen Street.

Of course, he was forced to follow her. A narrow alley opened up on the right, and she ducked down it. Only one or two lamps glowed here, giving intermittent illumination. The hunters were following, but some way behind. Despite her fear, Polly's mind was working quickly and efficiently, just as it had when Robbie had imprisoned her in the farmhouse. Her wooden heels rattled on the cobbles, her breathing seemed to fill the air. The alley turned right, then left, and flung them out into Bow Lane, slipping down towards the wharves and warehouses lining the river. There were shops and coffee-houses here, but nothing to offer them shelter, for the prudent occupiers had kept their windows shuttered and their doors fast against trouble.

"Where – are – you going?" Dark demanded breathlessly. The echoing sound of footsteps crashed along the alley they had just left, and someone bawled, "There he is! And his whore!"

The tall bulk of St. Mary-le-Bow church loomed up above Bow Lane, on the corner with Cheapside. "Follow me!" Polly gasped, and sprinted towards it without waiting to see if Dark would obey.

The moon was too far from full to cast more than a vague light on the churchyard, which was notorious as a haunt of street-walkers and their clients after dark, and even the uproar in Cheapside had not deterred the most brazen of them. She brushed past one couple doing their business on a table tomb, and from the urgent grunts and groans coming from the shadows, more still were at work under the walls of the church itself. Dark caught up with her, and put his hand on her shoulder to slow her down. "Paradice! What in God's name do you think you're doing?"

"Take your coat off."

"*What?*"

"I said, *take your coat off!*" Almost sobbing from exertion and urgency, she pulled at his sleeve. "They said I was your whore, well, act as if I am." She unclasped her mantle and hurled it away. "Here. *Here*, you fool, against the wall, in the shadow. They'll be here any minute – for God's sake, Dark, what are you waiting for?"

As if he had only this instant realised what she was proposing, Dark ripped his torn coat from his back and dropped it neatly onto a headstone, where it hung with an incongruous, faintly jaunty air. The rapid tread of running feet, and shouting, bounced around the walls of the church. With a swift, decisive movement, he turned to her and pushed her up against the rough stone. "Like this?" he said in her ear, his breath hot on her face, his hands at her breast, and then his mouth found hers.

She must keep her wits, or they would be lost: and yet she was lost, lost to everything save the feel of his body crushing hers against the wall so hard that it was difficult to breathe. Someone shouted, "Where did they go?" It sounded alarmingly close: she pulled her mouth away and peered round his shoulder. There were dim shapes blundering about the small churchyard, curses as one of them fell over a stone, and an indignant stream of epithets from one of the whores and her client, violently interrupted.

Somehow, he had managed to loosen her stays, and his hand slipped inside her bodice. A man of considerable experience, then. His fingers felt icy on her warm flesh, and her nipples hardened from the cold, and also from pure, piercing desire. *Dear God,* she thought wildly, *in a moment I'll be having my chimney swept out, with the men who wanted to kill us not ten yards away still searching!*

But her body, starved for too long, was almost out of her control. With a desperate effort she turned her face away so that she could see beyond him, and at that moment a man ran round the corner of the church and almost fell into them. With a fury born of terror, she shrieked at him with a venom that Gin would have envied. "Go boil your prick, you scurvy Whig!"

"King James!" the man cried indignantly, and Polly echoed him with fervour. "God save him! Ormonde and King James!"

As if in answer, a great roar smashed the air. Without

any further word, the man turned and ran out of the churchyard towards the battle in Cheapside. She saw the couple on the tombstone rise up as if at the Last Trump and walk off in different directions, she to Bow Lane in search of further customers, he in the direction of the riot. Someone shouted, “They’ve captured King Billy!” and for a moment the churchyard was full of rushing, stumbling, shouting men: then abruptly they were alone.

A cool tendril of night air, noisome and rank, lifted Polly’s hair. Suddenly her knees wobbled, and she clung to Dark for support. At once he said, his mouth against her ear, “Paradice? Have they gone?”

Weak with utter relief, she leaned her head against his shoulder. He repeated his question, louder, and she managed to nod assent, her forehead rubbing against the harsh wool of his waistcoat. But they could not stay here, it was far too dangerous, and besides, she longed for the safe refuge of her house, and her bed.

Did she want him to share it? She only had to crook her finger, she knew, to have him there, beside her, around her, within her, and she desired him so much – but she had told herself so often and so sternly that she neither wanted nor needed yet another lover, that even the urgent pulsing of lust could not quite drown out the small voice of reason, that dictated caution, prudence, withdrawal.

“Come on.” His voice was more gentle than she had ever heard it, and waves of heat coursed over her face and washed her body. “Let’s go, before they return.”

“Yes.” She took a deep, shivery breath, and stepped slightly away from him, smiling rather shakily. “But not before I find my mantle. I don’t want to lose another one. And besides, I’m frozen.”

Fortunately, it was lying next to the headstone that

carried Dark's coat. He laid it tenderly on her shoulders, and fastened it over her bodice. Only a few minutes before, he had been fondling her breasts, and the memory made her shiver again, with desire rather than the cold. Impulsively, she turned and put her hands on his shoulders, looking earnestly up into his face. In the gloom, she could not discern his expression, and she said, a little hesitantly, "Dark – thank you. I think I must owe you my life."

"You're wrong, Paradice – it was your quick thinking saved us." She heard his rare, deep chuckle of amusement. "I doubt any Billingsgate whore could have sounded more convincingly abusive than you did when that Jack discovered us. You should apply to Cibber for a part at Drury Lane."

His arms were encircling her, holding her close to him. It was strange, for they were both mature, experienced people of the world, but she felt suddenly as shy of him as any sheltered virgin. She said softly, "A church wall is a rough place for a wooing – will you come home with me?"

There was a pause. She heard him draw breath, as if surprised, and added, more lightly, "Though of course you may be a better actor than any Rich has yet discovered."

That made him laugh again, and his arms tightened around her, drawing her closer still. "No, Paradice," he said, his voice suddenly rough. "No, I was not acting. Were you?"

"You know I was not."

"Then, yes, if you truly wish it, I will come home with you. Or you may come home with me. That might be preferable, if you do not wish your affairs to be conducted under the gimlet eyes of Hannah and Gin."

That was true, but neither did she fancy walking past Madame Rousselle's impassive, knowing footman, or being subjected to the old harridan's lewd questions. The very thought of it was pouring a douche of icy water on her feelings.

The moment was slipping away, she could sense it trickling past her like a stream through her fingers, and suddenly she could not bear to let it go.

"I know a place," she said quickly, before caution could overcome this wild, reckless, insane decision. "It's not far, will you come?"

"Only if you promise I won't be knocked on the head, or robbed, or both," he said, and kissed her. "Sweet Polly Paradice, why do I still not entirely trust you?"

"If you do not trust me," Polly said, with a flash of vivid anger, "then you may go back to Half Moon Street and forget that you ever saw me. What do you think I am, a common buttock with a twang lurking in the shadows to rob you? If you went alone to this place, yes, you would be risking your purse if not your life, but with me you'll be quite safe." She stared up at him challengingly. "Well, Dark? You can trust me, or you can forget all about me. Which is it to be?"

"Oh, Poll," he said, and his voice was suddenly filled with an intensity of longing that raised the hairs on her neck. "Oh, Poll, I am sorry – I do trust you, God knows we have been through enough together – so lead on, my dear, to this place that you know, and I will try not to lay lecherous hands on you till we are safe inside."

Like a whirlpool, the riot in Cheapside had sucked in all the shifting, nefarious population of London's streets, those intent on robbery, theft or picking pockets as well as men who just wanted to take part in the violence and law-breaking, whether in support of the Pretender or of Hanover. And of course a disturbance of this size would be too much for the Watch to deal with, so they were probably lurking discreetly in their cabins, hoping to avoid the summons. The narrow streets, lanes and alleyways between Cheapside and the Thames were almost deserted, the law-abiding hidden safe behind their firmly bolted doors and shuttered windows. At a brisk walk, Dark and Polly skirted round the broad space of St. Paul's churchyard, so bustling and crowded by day, now quite empty. To judge from the noise behind them, the Whigs from the Roebuck were winning the fight, and the uproar rose to fever pitch. Several men ran past, eager to join battle before the riot should end, but no-one pursued them, though Polly noticed that Dark paused several times to glance over his shoulder.

Down Ludgate Hill they went, and over the Fleet Bridge. Now there were more people in the streets, several hackneys, a couple of chairs, and taverns and coffee-houses doing thriving business. Half way along Fleet Street, Polly stopped, looking up at her companion. Since Bow Churchyard, they had hardly spoken a word, being both intent on getting as far away from Cheapside as possible, but now she said softly, "We are nearly there. Are you sure?"

For answer he laughed. "Am I sure? Does the sun rise in the east? Is the Pretender a milksop and Farmer George a hoer of turnips? Of course I am sure. Lead on, Paradice."

She turned, taking him by the arm, and led him to the corner of Water Lane. Now was the test of his desire, and his trust: few people dared to venture down here, and fewer still at night. She felt him balk, and turned. "I promise you, it isn't far."

"*Alsatia?*" Dark said in disbelief. "Do you expect me to follow you into *Alsatia?*"

"I said that you would be safe with me," Polly reminded him, her eyes sternly fixed on his. "And you said that you would trust me. Well, now's the time to prove that you do."

Before them, the narrow slot of Water Lane seemed to pour its blackness and despair out into Fleet Street, infecting the passers-by so that most of them walked on the opposite pavement. Down that dim thoroughfare lay the maze of squalid alleys and courts with the reputation of being the most lawless district in all London, despite its small size and proximity to the lawyers of the Temple. Although the ancient rights of Sanctuary had been removed nearly twenty years ago, old habits died hard amongst thieves, and vast numbers of them congregated here in garrets and cellars, emerging to rob and beg from those who were more fortunate. Shadows lurked down there, a woman was singing drunkenly and off-key, and she could also hear the brutal sounds of a fight, and a distant scream.

"Follow me," Polly said. She picked her skirts up and away from the wet filth heaped in the gutter, and turned towards Alsatia.

For several heartbeats, she thought that it must hang in the balance: that she had misjudged him, and that he would fail this final test. Then André Dark was suddenly at her side, and with one hand on his sword, and the other grasping hers, walked with her into Water Lane.

It was not far to the house she sought, the place where she had briefly plied her trade when her first lover had abandoned her to the tender mercies of a brothel-keeper. But it was nested so deep within the tangle of alleyways that although she had thought she knew exactly where it was, she nearly made a wrong turning. The moon did not penetrate here in this narrow street, with the tall houses on either side crowding out the sky, but there was light from the windows of the taverns and cookshops which clustered at the top end of the lane, nearest to the respectability and bustle of Fleet Street. Further down, the darkness was almost complete, full of scarcely glimpsed shapes and indistinct noises. Then she noticed the stone post at the corner of Hanging Sword Alley, and slipped into its sly maw. She counted two doors along, and stopped before the third.

"So," said a low voice in her ear, "is this where I may

enter Paradise?"

Despite the sinister sounds, and the noisome stench seeping up from the aptly named Dung Wharf, by the river, Polly was conscious of a great feeling of exhilaration. Smiling in the dark, she knocked on the door twice, then twice again. His arms were round her, and he was nuzzling her cheek. A hot surge of arousal flooded through her as she felt his hands caress her bare flesh, just above the rim of her loosened bodice. If there was no answer, or Nan was no longer here, she did not know what she would do, for she could not bear to wait any longer.

In the shadows behind them, something stirred, and Dark swung round, his hand ready on his sword. There was a scuffling sound, and an indistinct shape scuttled down the alley to be lost in the gloom. Within the house, Polly could hear music being played, rather well, on a viol or fiddle. It was an incongruously comforting sound in such a mean and sordid place. Before she could knock again, the door opened the merest sliver, and a sullen, unenthusiastic light from a single candle shone on them. "Who's that, and what d'you want?"

"It's Poll, Nan, remember me? Poll Paradice."

There was a startled pause, and then the crack widened very slightly. "Well, strike me dead," said the shape holding the candle, in tones of total astonishment. "I thought you was far too high and mighty ever to show your face here again, Polly. Come down in the world, have you? And who's your cully?"

She glanced up at Dark, whose face was perfectly composed. "He's an artist."

"An *artist*, eh?" said the shadowy Nan, as disapproving as if Dark had admitted to matricide. "Well, if you makes it worth my while –"

Polly had expected this, and slipped a couple of generous coins into the outstretched hand. The door creaked reluctantly open, and Nan was revealed to be a scrawny, hunchbacked woman, probably far younger than she appeared, with a huge purple portwine stain disfiguring most of her face. She grinned up at Dark, disclosing a sparse collection of decaying teeth. "What sort of an *artist?*"

"One who paints pictures," Polly said. "Is there any other kind?"

"You tell me," said Nan, with a sly chuckle. "Well, don't stand here letting all the warmth out, come in."

Polly and Dark stepped past her into a narrow hallway. A rickety flight of stairs led up into the gloom. The music had stopped, and somewhere, in this house or one very near, she could hear the sounds of rhythmic copulation. Before Nan could shut the door, a man stumbled down the stairs, his hands fastening his breeches, and blundered past them into the night. A woman's voice shrieked something unintelligible from above, and the next instant a painted girl, half naked in a torn shift and unlaced stays, pelted down in urgent pursuit.

"Good riddance," Nan observed, slamming the door shut behind them. "You want a room, Poll? It'll cost you."

"A clean one," said Dark, with a look on his face that Polly realised, with some surprise, was intense amusement. "If you have such a thing."

Nan looked from one to the other, and sneered. "You've picked yourself a topper here, Poll," she said with derision. "*Clean?* In Whitefriars, with the lay-carts passing by all day? Do me a favour!"

"Your *best* room, then," Polly said. "Is this sufficient?"

Nan examined the proffered half crown closely, and then tucked it into her scrawny breast. "Next floor, front," she said tersely, jerking a thumb upwards. "There's a fire lit. And for another shilling I'll bring you breakfast in bed!"

"That won't be required," Dark told her gravely. He gestured towards the stairs. "Will you step this way, Mrs. Paradice?"

Wild mirth bubbled up inside her. Evading his hands, she turned and ran upwards, hearing his footsteps pursuing. She remembered where the door was, and reached it just before him. As she lifted the latch, he was upon her, and they stumbled together, breathless and laughing, into a small square room, lit only by a cheerfully glowing fire that had probably been made with coals stolen from the wharves at the end of Water Lane. It was hot, and smelt frowsty and stale, but at least there was no really foul taint in the air, and a surprisingly large and comfortable-looking bed occupied most of the space.

Dark kicked the door shut and turned to her. His breath was coming in gasps, and his face was bright with hilarity. "This is a common cunny-warren! What have you brought me to, Poll Paradice?"

"The pinnacle of passion, I hope," she said. Holding his gaze with hers, she stepped lightly backwards until she touched the bed, and then untied the strings of her mantle. It dropped to the floor, and she smiled at him. "Unlace me?"

"Of course I will," he said. "For I would much rather embrace your naked flesh, skin to skin, than feel you all boxed in with those damned stays ... turn round, Paradice, so that I can reach."

She obeyed, and stood with apparent docility as he unfastened first her fine woollen gown, and then the padded whalebone and linen stays that caged her body and imprisoned her breasts. The touch of his hands, stroking and caressing her as they performed their task, was as arousing as she had imagined, and she shivered with desire, the waiting only serving to feed the fire of anticipation. Gown, stays, petticoats, hoop all slithered down over her body to lie in a heap around her, and then she turned to face him, clad only in her soft linen shift, so fine that the darkness of her nipples, and the patch of brown hair around her groin, showed faintly through it. Polly stood quite still, breathing rapidly, and saw his intent, avid gaze travel over the firm contours of her body beneath the thin cloth. She was proud of her round, high breasts, her slim waist and curving hips, and revelled in his obvious admiration.

"A paradise is the ancient Persian word for a garden, did you know that?" His voice was rough with desire, and as he spoke he was taking off his coat and waistcoat, dropping them beside her clothes. "And you are a peach, delicious Poll, a wonderful scented juicy peach of a woman, you are superb ... and I want to savour you, and taste you, and bring you delight."

The memory of his words, and the tone of his voice, and the look in his eyes, stayed with her as he kissed her slowly at first, tenderly exploring her mouth and then her body, his lips sidling lower, his hands slipping the shift off her shoulders until her breasts were exposed, caressing her with his hands and tongue until her bones seemed to melt and her loins were on fire, while she, also expert at undressing a lover, unbuttoned his breeches and slid her hand inside. He gasped then, and she pushed herself onto him brazenly, too desperate with lust and longing to care now for anything save the immediate fulfilment of desire. They fell back onto the bed, twisting round so that she was astride him, riding him as his hands cupped her breasts and squeezed her nipples, and the wild sensations, ascending with every movement, made her sob as their power soared and burst inside her like a skyrocket, in spears of brilliant delight.

She was lying on top of him, and her shift was soaked with sweat, and his arms were close around her. "You're weeping," he said, and laughed rather shakily. "Was it truly so terrible?"

Mute, racked with feelings she hardly recognised, Polly

shook her head, while the tears poured from her eyes and her breath came in huge, gasping sobs. Never, in the years since she had ceased to be a virgin, had she been overwhelmed by this storm of desperate emotion. She had had many lovers, she had experienced pleasure countless times, and yet it seemed, in this hot squalid room, that all her past life had been wasted and squandered with false coin, for this, here and now, was the true gold.

Gently, Dark rolled her over, taking her with him, and sat up, still cradling her in his arms, as if she were a child. "Poll, darling Poll, what is the matter?"

Now, if ever, was the moment to cast aside all the secrecy, the layers of sophistication and wit and elegance with which she had cloaked her true self, and reveal to him the workings of her heart and her soul. Almost, she did: she opened her mouth to speak, but he was already saying, his voice comically rueful, "And to think that I prided myself at being good at the game."

And so she could laugh, and let him dry her tears, and persuade him, not that he needed much persuasion, that she wished to repeat the experience as quickly as possible. This time, the urgency was replaced by a fierce, lingering explorations of each other's desires, using hands and mouths alike to discover the secrets of arousal, and the climax, when at last she could resist no longer, was deep and prolonged and wonderfully intense.

She slept afterwards, and woke to an unpleasant itching sensation. The fire had almost expired, and there was very little light left in the room. "Hell and damnation!" Polly said, sitting up abruptly. "This lousy bed's full of bugs!"

"What did you expect?" said Dark drowsily beside her. "This is Alsatia, not St. James's."

"I expect they've got bugs a-plenty in their beds too."

Polly leapt out onto the floor. "But these ones are *ravenous!*" She ripped off her shift and capered energetically about the room, slapping at as much of her skin as she could reach, while her lover, still on the bed, shook with silent laughter. "Do you *know* how fetching you look, Paradice? If you do not cease this instant, I shall be forced to leap on you again."

"Don't you dare," Polly said, picking up her shift and shaking it vigorously. Then she held it over the sulky fire, as close to the embers as she could, and to her satisfaction several small black specks plummeted into the coals, to be instantly consumed. "Good riddance. You may be still wearing your shirt, Dark, but I'm sure they'll soon find a way inside it, and then you won't laugh so loud. Shall we go home?"

"If you wish." In the dim light he was looking at her, a lazy expression of amusement curving his long thin mouth, and deepening the lines around it. "To our separate beds, I take it?"

Polly had wriggled back into her shift. The fire behind her outlined her shadowy shape, the trim curves and prominent breasts: suddenly aware of it, she bent down and picked up her stays. "Yes," she said. "I think so, don't you?"

"And what of tomorrow night? You may have brought me here tonight, Paradice, but I'm damned if I'll be dragged down to Alsatia again, however luscious and tempting your enticements. I prefer a bed without bugs, in a house that isn't full of whores and thieves."

"Then neither of our establishments can meet your exacting requirements, in one particular if not in another," Polly pointed out tartly.

Dark got up from the bed and, unasked, began to lace up her stays. He bent and kissed the nape of her neck, a wonderfully gentle, tender gesture, and her skin tingled all over in response. "Dear Paradice, will you come with me tomorrow, and see my skyrockets?"

"Only if you can promise me that there will be no more riots. A little tighter, if you please – there, that's it. Now my gown. You would make an admirable abigail, Dark, have you never thought of applying for such a post?"

"I shall give it my earnest consideration. What complicated garments you ladies do wear – they must surely be designed on purpose to ensure chastity. I cannot promise that there will be no riots, but I can assure you that you will be safe. There will be so many loyal citizens out to watch, that the Jacks won't dare to put in an appearance. And afterwards, we can lodge at an inn I know of, close by."

"Will they not mind you bringing your whore there?" Polly's tone was light, and full of self-mockery, but she was watching his face closely.

"My dear, you are not my whore."

"Am I not? What am I, then?"

"My lover, surely," said Dark, and took her in his arms. "In any case, it is an establishment where they know not to ask questions. Not highly respectable, but clean and very comfortable."

"No bugs?"

"I doubt it extremely. The landlady is so fierce, none would dare invade any mattress on the premises. Oh, Poll, the thought of waking up with you, warm and lazy in the morning, is so alluring I can hardly wait."

"Neither can I." Suddenly serious, she stood still, her hands on his shoulders, and looked earnestly up at him. That grim, hostile Dark of their earliest acquaintance might never have existed, save in her memory: this man, his face full of laughter and his eyes bright even in the faltering firelight, appeared hardly more than a boy. She said, "I will make no promises, and demand none from you. We both know what we are. But whatever happens in the future, Dark, I will always want you for my friend."

"And I you, Paradice." He smiled down at her. "Never, surely, was a woman more aptly named."

"It was my father's name," she pointed out. "And he, poor man, spent all his life searching and longing and yearning, and never found it."

"Well, I have. And I am only sorry that my cross-grained and contrary nature prevented me from discerning your qualities when first we met."

"Well, now we have both discovered our error. And I have never been one to waste much time on futile regrets. Today is all that matters," Polly said softly. "For who knows what tomorrow will bring?"

CHAPTER FIFTEEN

'The dang'rous Flame of Love'

Polly lay back in the warm, scented water and closed her eyes. The aroma of sweet herbs and oils tickled her nose, and she inhaled deeply. A feeling of voluptuous languor had descended over her in a soft and sensuous cloud. This was a luxury indulged in much too rarely, though she was a regular visitor to the Duke Street Bagnio on ladies' days.

She thought of Dark, and that squalid little room in Alsatia that had indeed proved to be the entrance to paradise, and her whole body grew warm with memory and anticipation. She had had lovers who were more handsome, lovers who were more conventionally charming, lovers who made great show with wealth or influence or display. But none of them had aroused the glorious, exquisite pleasures of last night.

"Madam?" Hannah had come back into her bedchamber. "Will you require more hot water?"

"No – no, thank you," Polly said, her eyes still closed and her mind floating deliciously amidst the warmth and fragrance. "I shall get out soon. What is the time, do you know?"

"Past three o'clock when last I looked, madam."

Dark was calling for her at four. Polly sat up abruptly in a surge of water, lethargy transformed in an instant to energetic eagerness. "As late as that! A towel, please, Hannah, and my robe – I must be dried and dressed in less than an hour."

"It's all slopped over the side now," her maid grumbled, helping her to rise. "There'll be drips in the parlour, I shouldn't wonder."

Polly, wrapped in a large white towel and rubbing at her wet tangled hair, grinned at her. "You have got a fit of the grumps! Has Gin – I mean Jane – been troublesome again?"

"No, madam," said Hannah. She picked up the embroidered silk banyan, made like a man's but long enough to trail on the floor, that had been laid out ready on the bed.

"Then what is wrong? Oh, Hannah, I have known you a year and more, I can tell when you are unhappy. Surely we are friends enough?"

"It's not my place to say anything, madam."

Whenever Hannah took refuge in rigid formality, it was a sign that she was deeply disturbed. Polly exchanged the towel for the robe, and tied it tightly around her waist. "That's nonsense, Hannah, and you know it. Please tell me what is troubling you."

Her ruffled pinner perched on top of her plaited and twisted hair, her striped calico dress as neat and fashionable as any her mistress wore, the maid possessed no air of servile inferiority. She said at last, frowning, "I thought you were finished with men, madam."

Polly stared at her in genuine astonishment. She had said nothing of her exploits the previous night, and although Dark had escorted her home, it had not been particularly late, and they had said goodbye on the doorstep. For a moment she felt irritated: surely her affairs were her own business, and nothing whatsoever to do with Hannah. "How on earth did you know?" she demanded at last.

"I know you, madam," said her maid. Her dark eyes rested anxiously on Polly. "Will you go into his keeping now?"

Suddenly, Polly guessed the reason for her concern. She said quickly, "Don't worry, Hannah – I have no intention of giving up our plans for the coffee-house."

"You may find he has something different to say about that," Hannah pointed out, with a sniff. "Most gentlemen prefer their mistresses to be their own private property."

Polly shook her head vehemently. "We have shared a bed, Hannah, you were right about that, yes. And it's more than likely, I hope, that we will do so again, many times. But – but no promises have been made. He knows I wish to be independent of any man, and he respects that."

Hannah's response was a contemptuous snort. She turned away to the walnut hanging robe where her mistress's clothes were kept, and took down the plain dark grey woollen gown that Polly had chosen as being most suitable for a November evening spent watching a pope-burning and skyrockets. "Men are all the same," she said over her shoulder, giving the skirts a particularly vigorous shake. "What they say and what they do are two entirely separate things, and I don't reckon this artist of yours is any different."

"Perhaps he is not," Polly said. "But at least I go into it with my eyes open. Dear Hannah, I know you only have concern for me, but pray credit me with the wit to look after myself. This is an agreeable interlude, an affair of mutual pleasure, and no more."

"If you say so, madam," said Hannah, slapping the gown onto the bed and glaring at it as if it alone were responsible for all the ills in the world. "But when it all turns to tears, don't say I didn't warn you."

An agreeable interlude it might merely be, but later, when Dark knocked at the front door, Polly's heart leapt like a deer. She glanced into the mirror to check that her hair was still securely pinned up underneath her cap, gave each glowing cheek a pinch to raise still more fresh colour in them, and fastened her winter mantle firmly under her chin.

"Mr. Dark, madam," said Hannah with a scowl, and stood aside to let him into the hall.

In the hours since she had last seen him, he seemed to have taken on a mythic quality in her mind, for the reality was at once more substantial, and less daunting. He bowed low to her, with the sly, wicked smile that she found so attractive. "You astonish me, Paradice. I deliberately arranged a time much earlier than necessary, in the full expectation that it would take you another age to make yourself ready – and I find you champing eagerly at the bit!"

"I humbly present my apologies, sir," Polly murmured, sweeping him a graceful curtsey. "Perhaps I should go back upstairs and undress."

"Only if I can watch."

Acutely conscious of his teasing, provocative gaze, and of Hannah's almost tangible disapproval, Polly shook her head. "That will not be necessary. Surely it does not matter if we arrive early?"

"You disappoint me, Paradice. But, no, it does not. I had thought to go by water, as it is not yet dark, and the tide is right, so we can shoot the bridge in comparative safety. Are you agreeable?"

Hannah, who hated the river, was gazing at him in horror, but Polly, seeing the challenge in his eyes, rose with delight to the bait. "Indeed I am, sir. Shall we go? You may lock the door behind us, Hannah, I shall not be home tonight."

There was a boat waiting for them by the stairs at the end of Salisbury Street. It was some time since she had made a journey by river, and her heavy, voluminous skirts and mantle robbed her of her usual agility, but she took the waterman's proffered arm and managed to step into the boat without too much undignified wobbling. She sat down in the stern, and Dark took his place beside her. The little craft rocked again as the man climbed in and picked up the oars. One strong shove pushed them away from the stairs, and a few more powerful strokes propelled the boat out onto the Thames.

Here, the wind blew strongly and coldly at their backs, and Polly folded her mantle tightly about her, in case it should break free and provide an unwanted sail. There was not much room on the narrow seat, so she and Dark were pressed close to each other, and she was acutely aware of the warmth of his body and hers, mingling where they touched. Above them, the waterman had fixed a lantern to a pole, to light their way and warn off other boats as it grew dark. The rising tide, beating against the wind, made the water choppy, and tiny drops of ice-cold spray spattered her face.

"Will the wind affect your skyrockets?" she asked Dark, as the boat pulled past the *Folly*, a floating gambling den and place of assignation moored off Somerset House. Snatches of wild music and raucous laughter whipped around their ears as it fell astern.

"I hope not," he said, with a candid grin. "For what goes up must inexorably come down, or so Sir Isaac tells us. And I have no wish to shower you, or the rest of the crowd, with burning debris – or to set fire to the Tower."

"That is a relief," said Polly, snuggling surreptitiously closer, while his arm slipped round her waist. "And at least it isn't raining."

"It will afore dawn, I reckon," said the waterman, plunging the blades of his oars deep into the murky water, while a motley collection of debris – pieces of driftwood, part of a barrel, the bloated corpse of a puppy – jostled the boat. "I can smell it on the wind."

Polly found the view of the city from the river perennially fascinating. Even in this sullen, murky light, the bright red brick of the walls and roofs seemed to glow from within, and she loved the contrast between the jumbled mass of buildings and the soaring spires and towers of the churches pricking the skyline. Over all, like some noble galleon, sailed the great silver bulk of St. Paul's, its leaden dome almost the same colour as the clouds behind it. The south bank, with its fringe of houses and wharves and warehouses, and the fields and market gardens beyond, was much less interesting, so she concentrated on noting the famous landmarks as they passed. There was the Temple, most of its buildings bright and new after their destruction by the Great Fire fifty years ago, and immediately after it, appropriately marked by the great mound of dung at the laystall at the bottom of Water Lane, she could see the huddle of squalid houses, courts and alleys that comprised the district of Whitefriars, popularly known as Alsatia. Somewhere in that shadowy maze lay the house in Hanging Sword Alley where she and Dark had lain last night, and her whole body glowed like the sunset with the thought of it.

They passed the place, surrounded by timber yards, where the Fleet Ditch poured its noisome stream into the Thames, and drew level with St. Paul's. Now London Bridge lay ahead, blocking their path. Sensible people, wishing to travel further downstream, disembarked at Old Swan Stairs and walked round to Billingsgate to resume their journey, for shooting the bridge at most states of the tide, when the water poured through the piers in a mad wild cataract, was a highly dangerous enterprise. Many watermen, not to mention their passengers, were drowned every year, though that did not stop young bloods, eager to show off their bravery, attempting the feat on a regular basis.

But this evening the tide had now almost reached equilibrium, with just a demure swirl of current around the nineteen piers holding up the bridge. Polly had never done this before, and despite Dark's obvious confidence, she could not help feeling apprehensive as the great bulk, with its burden of ancient and more or less decrepit buildings, loomed closer. They were past Old Swan Stairs, so it was too late to turn back. The waterman kept glancing round as he rowed, steering for one of the gaps fairly close to the shore. There was nothing coming the other way: several swift strokes set the boat on its course, he shipped the oars to avoid fouling the piers and the submerged starlings on which they stood, and they glided effortlessly beneath the bridge. The water rippled gently along the craft's side, and the sound was echoed and amplified by the ancient archway above them. Polly glanced up, seeing the crazy ramshackle penthouses and sheds built perilously far out from the stone parapet. She imaged the people walking only a few feet above her head, shopping or going about their business, and completely unaware of their passage below. The thought gave her a thrill of furtive excitement, and she shivered.

"It's all right, we're nearly through," Dark whispered, and she jabbed him indignantly in the ribs with her elbow. "Did you think I was frightened? You have much still to learn about me, I fear."

"And how I relish the prospect of coming to know every inch of you better," he said softly, and his arm tightened about her as the boat emerged safely on the other side, to a chorus of whistles and hoots from some urchins hanging over a gap in the wall of houses. *So much for my imaginings*, Polly thought wryly, as a few handfuls of thrown filth spattered the water behind them.

"Well, when I'm an old hag I can tell my grandchildren, if I ever have any, that I shot the bridge," she said cheerfully. "I shall give them to believe that it was a raging torrent only negotiable by the skill of the waterman, and that I was in mortal peril of drowning. And how will they know any different?"

With the bridge safely behind them, the oarsman put

his back into his stroke, and now wind and tide were as one, conspiring to sweep the boat past Billingsgate and the Custom House. There was such a crowd of shipping, unloading at the wharves below the bridge, that Polly could hardly see the warehouses behind the mass of spars, masts, rigging and furled sails. Beyond, at Tower Stairs, a dozen or more boats were queuing to land, so Dark told the waterman to go on past the Tower, pale and sinister to their left. Already a considerable crowd was gathering on Tower Hill, eager for good positions, and a band playing hautboys and kettledrums had struck up the familiar and Protestant strains of *Lilibulero*. From within the fortress a lion, unimpressed, set up a dismal roaring in counterpoint.

"Where are you planning to fire the rockets?" Polly asked curiously, turning to view the arena as it receded into the dusk.

"On the wharf. With luck, the wind should take the debris out over the river. It would spoil the celebrations somewhat if half the spectators were killed or injured by falling fireworks."

"Certainly it would," Polly agreed, matching his dry tone. "Or, heaven forbid, if that lion were to be inconvenienced."

Iron Gate Stairs was quite deserted, and the waterman skilfully steered his craft towards it, judging wind and tide so exactly that the boat kissed the wet, splintery wood as gently as a feather. Despite her protests that she did not need assistance, Polly was helped to disembark, and stood, vibrating with concealed excitement, on the cobbled surface of the wharf. The narrow streets and alleys of St. Catherine's lay at her back, and before her, beyond the cranes and warehouses around the stairs, was the broad space of Tower Wharf, familiar yet strangely altered. Curious, she walked forward while Dark was paying the waterman. The cobbles seemed to have grown an array of spikes like a hedgehog's, and several men were moving purposefully through them, carrying what looked to be sticks. As he joined her, she turned to him. "Are those your skyrockets?"

"Yes. They must be fastened to sticks to fly successfully, and set into the ground so that they are in the right position when they are launched. Surprisingly," said Dark, in the dry voice, full of suppressed amusement, that she was coming to know so well, "it has proved somewhat difficult to find volunteers willing to hold the sticks in the air while they are lit."

"A wonder, to be sure."

"Indeed. Well, Paradice, I must ensure that everything is set out according to my instructions. If you are willing to wait awhile – by Traitor's Gate is a sheltered spot, though somewhat inappropriate – then I pray you will excuse me while I check my rocket army's dispositions."

She stood, unwontedly obedient, in the lee of the great towers, and watched as he went over to the strange *cheveux-de-frise* between wall and water. Because of the wind, and the risk, there was little light save from glass lanterns, although over on Tower Hill the crowd was supplied with torches, and bonfires were already ablaze. Dark moved quietly amongst the ranked rockets, talking with his assistants, bending now and then to examine something. She had never seen him interact with others in this way before, friendly and efficient, with no arrogance, no bullying, no hint of grimness. It warmed her through and through, for she sensed that this was the real Dark, and that the armour of hostility in which he had cloaked himself was merely a disguise, a defence against the world.

Someone came running along the wharf, there was a huddled conference, and then he came back, recognisable from his height and the black skirts of his coat flapping briskly as he walked. "We have been ordered to commence the show shortly. Will you come with me towards Tower Stairs? It's a little further away, just in case anything should chance to go awry, and you will have an even better view."

"Your wishes are mine to obey," she assured him, mischievously demure, and at his laughter reached up on the tips of her toes and kissed him. Then he ushered her past the high walls of the Tower to the warehouses at the further end, where a small man wearing a round hat pulled firmly down over his head, and carrying a lantern, was waiting for them. Beyond, the fringes of the huge mass on Tower Hill could be seen, torchlit and jostling, some staring eagerly down the wharf, their curiosity kept at bay by a stalwart row of men, some armed with staves and cudgels.

"Jacob here will stay with you while they're fired," Dark said. "Look after her, Jake, and make sure she doesn't get up to any mischief."

"Gawd, sir, she don't look like butter would melt in her mouth," said the small man, with a grin. "Don't worry, I'll guard her like she was one of me own girls."

"In that case," said Dark drily to Polly, "you can kiss all your freedoms goodbye. Jake has six daughters and keeps them closer than a Sultan's harem. Enjoy the spectacle, Paradice!"

At the fireworks display in honour of the Peace of Utrecht, she had watched at a considerable distance. Now, as the boy with the slowmatch lit the first fuse, and the rocket screamed skywards trailing a vast shower of shimmering lights, she could not help flinching, although she hoped that Jacob would not notice. Then it burst above the Thames in a cascade of golden stars, and a huge wall of cheering erupted from Tower Hill.

Before the last sparks had died, three more skyrockets had soared into the air and exploded above them with a sharp triple bang that could barely be heard above the crowd: then more, and more, and more, so that the dark river blazed with reflected brilliance, silver and amber, gold and bronze, brimstone and sulphur, while the cracks of each report seemed to reverberate inside her head, and she pulled the hood of her mantle tight around her ears. It seemed to go on forever, the sparks so dazzling that even when she squeezed her beleaguered eyes tight shut, she could still see them.

Then abruptly it was over, a momentary and absolute silence after the battery of sound, before the spectators roared their applause. Her ears ringing, her eyes watering, Polly cheered as loudly as the rest, until her throat was dry and rasping with the effort. As the music struck up again, a hand touched her sleeve, and she jumped.

"It's only me, Paradice," said her lover. "Do you have such a bad conscience, then?"

"I have no conscience at all, you should know that. Dark, that was utterly spectacular and wonderful and I do not think I shall ever be able to see or hear properly again."

"Eh?" He cupped his hand round his ear, and she shouted at him until she saw his grin and realised that he was making game of her. She slapped him playfully on the shoulder, and for answer he grabbed her round the waist and kissed her so thoroughly that she forgot all about Jacob, watching with a good-natured leer on his face.

"Shall we go dine?" he murmured at last. "I have bespoke us a private room at the Vine in the Minories. Unless, of course, you have a fancy to see a Pope-burning."

"Certainly not. I have had more than my fill of riots and fights and bonfires. And I very much like the prospect of that dinner at the Vine, not to mention what may follow, so lead on, Dark, and please do your best to escort me well away from any riots tonight."

"Your wish is my command," he said, with a bow, and although she could not see his face in the gloom, she could tell from his voice that he was smiling.

* * *

"What is your pleasure today, madam?"

Polly, seated at her parlour table contemplating fresh warm rolls and a steaming pot of fragrant chocolate, smiled at her maid with unalloyed delight. "Well, Hannah, I hope to finish my breakfast first. After that, an hour or so with Jane, teaching her her letters."

"And that's a waste of time," said Hannah bluntly. "What would a little ragamuffin like that want with learning her letters?" The weeks since Gin had joined the household had not greatly softened her apparently unsympathetic attitude to the girl, but Polly knew that, like Dark, much of her gruffness was put on.

"She is no longer a street child," she pointed out, breaking a roll. The heady steam wafted out, and she inhaled appreciatively. "Your baking is as wonderful as your coffee, Hannah."

"I do my best, madam," said the maid, not in the least mollified by such a transparent attempt at pacification. "And after your hour of fruitless toil?"

Polly grinned at her. "I have an appointment with Dark at eleven, or thereabouts. And so have you."

"*Me?*" Hannah's look of utter astonishment made her seem suddenly much younger. "Whatever would he want with me, madam?"

"He wants to paint your portrait. It is to be a group portrait, Hannah, they are becoming all the rage apparently. I believe it is called a conversation piece. In the picture, I am sitting at a table very much like this one, drinking chocolate, as I am now, and you are sitting at the table too, pouring a cup for yourself." She had asked Dark to alter the composition, wishing herself and Hannah to be on a more equal footing, and he had readily obliged.

"Oh, madam, no-one's ever wanted to put me into a *painting* before!"

"Nor me," Polly pointed out, spreading butter on her roll. The bread was still hot, and the yellow lump turned glossy and liquid under her knife. A drop fell on her plate, and she dabbed it up with her finger and licked it off.

"Is it difficult, madam, to be put in a picture? What do I have to do?"

It was at moments like these that Polly was reminded, very sharply, just how thin was the veneer of Hannah's self-assurance. Within the narrow limits of the household, and her duties outside it, she was confident, brisk, even rude. But if presented with anything out of the ordinary, anything that required independent thought, she tended to panic. Polly knew that it must be the result of her miserable years of slavery, in Barbados and then in Bristol. And yet she could not have been entirely cowed by her experiences, for somehow she had mustered the courage and initiative to escape.

"Very little," she said lightly. "All you have to do is to sit as still as possible, while he puts your likeness on his canvas. And you need not worry, he won't shout at you if you move."

"That ain't what I'm feared of," said Hannah, her abandonment of her normally precise grammar an indication of how deeply she was moved. "I just – oh, madam, no-one ain't ever thought so much of me before! Putting me in a picture! Are you really sure you want a blackamoor in your portrait, madam?"

"I want *Hannah* in my portrait," Polly told her firmly. "Because you are my friend, as well as my servant. And I plan to have him put Gin – Jane – in it also. Don't you dare pull that disapproving face, Hannah Rose, it ill becomes you."

"What's she going to do in this conversation piece, then? Stand in the background waiting to help herself to the silver while we're not looking?"

"The silver will all be on the table, so the question will hardly arise. In any case, Jane is no longer a street urchin, just as you are no longer a slave. Who knows, Hannah, one day your efforts may turn her into a first-rate maidservant."

"Birds will fly upside down first," Hannah said darkly. "Oh, she works hard, madam, I'll grant you that, but such a look she gives you when you dare to tell her off, it'd curdle your blood! You can't make a silk purse out of a sow's ear, and she's more of a sow's trotter than a sow's ear."

"That will be all, thank you, Hannah," said Polly, praying that she would be able to keep her face straight until the maid left the room. It was a close-run thing, but she managed it, just, until the door closed and she was able to giggle quietly into her chocolate cup: and to wish, suddenly and piercingly, that André Dark was sitting on the other side of the table, to share her mirth.

Nearly two hours later, she and Hannah set out for their appointment with him. It had been a trying session with Gin, who remained unconvinced of the value of literacy, and had to be bullied and cajoled into co-operation, with the promise, dangled temptingly before her, of as much gingerbread as she could eat, as soon as she could write her name unaided. At first the child had been cock-a-hoop, until Polly added that the letters G-i-n would not be sufficient, and that her full and correct name was required. "So it will be Jane ... Jane ..."

"Just Jane," the girl said helpfully. "Ain't got no more

names. Never have had."

"Of course you must have a surname, everyone does. If your parents were married, you have your father's, and if they were not, then you take your mother's name. Surely you must know what that was?"

But Gin patently did not. Other people had addressed her mother as 'Mag', but if she had ever known any further details, she had forgotten them. At last, seeing her mulish, sullen look, Polly said, "Well, we must give you some surname, for London is full of Janes, and you cannot be distinguished from them else. You can choose one for yourself, if you like."

"Summink what's short and easy to write," Gin muttered.

But she had remained indifferent to all suggestions, and in the end Polly had given up and set her to work sweeping upstairs, while she and Hannah went off to Half Moon Street for their sitting with Dark. At present it did not matter in the least what surname Gin took, and surely inspiration would strike her eventually.

It was a cold, blustery day, and the weather seemed to be settling maliciously into winter. Even hooded and cloaked and masked against the wind, Polly's appearance was striking enough to attract notice, for her head was high and her blue eyes sparkled behind the black velvet mask. She was well aware of male eyes following her as she walked along the Strand, with Hannah just behind, but their open admiration and comments no longer induced the glow of complacent satisfaction. Now she only wanted one man's gaze, one man's regard, and very soon she would bask in the warmth of his desire.

But Madame Rousselle's footman, opening the door to Hannah's knock, had most unwelcome news. "Mr. Dark has asked me to inform you, madam, with great regret, that he is not at home."

"What do you mean?" In the shock of disappointment, Polly heard her voice as an ill-tempered squawk. "I have an appointment with him, for eleven o'clock today."

"Indeed you have, madam, but unfortunately Mr. Dark finds himself unable to keep that appointment. He presents his most profound apologies, he is utterly desolated, but – "

"Where has he gone?" Polly demanded.

"He was called away on urgent business, madam, and I regret to say that he gave no indication of his destination. More than that, I am not at liberty to say."

Polly could imagine the look of acute disappointment on Hannah's face. She mastered herself with an effort, and said with laboured politeness, "Did he say when he would return?"

"I regret to inform you, madam, that he did not – to me, at any rate."

In another moment, she would be forcing his hypocritical regrets back down his throat. "Then perhaps Madame Rousselle might know." Suddenly decisive, Polly swept past the footman and into the spacious, familiar hall. "Pray announce me."

"I regret to inform you, madam, that Madame is not receiving visitors today."

"A pox on your mealy-mouthed regrets!" Polly cried in a passion. "I only wish to know where he's gone, for God's sake, not conduct a three hour prayer meeting!"

The footman, with a supercilious smirk, opened his mouth to deny her yet again, and was forestalled by a peremptory bark behind him. "Oddsfish, John, you witless widgeon, leave your stalling and let her in!"

Madame Rousselle was not in her bed today. She

stood in the doorway, a grotesque scarlet-wigged scarecrow supported on one side by a stick and on the other by a rather blowsy, plump young maidservant with a pert and knowing face. “Good morning, Mistress Paradice. Had a wasted journey, eh? No matter, I feel like a good gossip. John, you whoreson slive-andrew, go get some tea, good and strong mind you, none of your dregs nor dishwater! Come in and sit you down, and we will have a splendid cosy chit-chat.”

Cosy was not at all the word which Polly would have associated with the fearsome old harpy, but since this was obviously the only way of arriving at the truth, she allowed herself, like a wary fly, to be ushered into Madame Rousselle’s parlour and shown to one of the red velvet upholstered chairs on either side of the uncomfortably hot fire, while Hannah, her face stiff and shiny with disapproval, was borne off to the kitchens.

“You’re looking somewhat peaky and wan,” said her hostess, lowering herself stiffly into the other chair. “Suffering the pangs of love, eh?”

“Of course not,” said Polly, smiling with what she hoped was perfectly opaque self-possession. “Love, as you must know, is a luxury not available to women in our position.”

Madam Rousselle uttered a snort of contempt, and banged her stick on the floor. “John? John! Where’s the rogue got to now? Sukey, go tell him I want that tea on the table this instant, or he’ll be turned off without a character.”

“Yes’m,” said the maid, with a simper and a bobbed curtsey, and went out.

“I’m surrounded by simpletons,” Madame said, before the door had closed. “That blackamoor of yours looks a good reliable sort, how much d’ye want for her?”

“Hannah is a free woman, madam, not a slave, and so is not for sale.”

"Hm. Pity. I could do with an honest servant – or a slave, I'm not choosy, ha ha! Mine think they can rob me blind and run off with the silver, but they soon find they've bitten off more than they can chew. Sukey came out of the Bridewell, and she knows I'll put her back in there or in Newgate if she steps out of line. You been in the Bridewell, child?"

Polly was on fire to discover where Dark had gone, but if she was to learn anything at all, she must humour the old hag. She shook her head. "No, madam, with great good fortune I have managed to avoid it."

"Indeed you have. I've been asking about you. One of Mother Whybrow's pigeons, weren't you?"

"For a very brief while, when I had ended with one keeper and before I acquired another."

"Yes." Madame Rousselle stared at Polly, assessing every detail of her appearance, from her neat dark hair, simply dressed under a lace-edged pinner, to the toes of her blue kid walking shoes. "And I'm sure you had no difficulty finding a cully then, pretty little thing that you are, but it won't get any easier, I can promise you that. How old are you?"

"I am not sure that is any of your business," said Polly, trying not to sound too pert.

"Twenty-five or thereabouts," Madame continued, ignoring her. "Is that a blush? Then I'm right. So you've decided on Dark for your next beau, eh? Well, you won't have much change out of him, he's as poor as a church mouse."

"It may surprise you to learn, madam," said Polly, keeping her temper under a tight rein, "that I am not interested in any wealth that Mr. Dark may or may not possess."

"And he ain't so obviously a young girl's dream either," the old woman observed maliciously. "Though I grant he's personable enough when he troubles to smile. So how does he dance the mattress jig, eh? Does he ring all your bells?"

Polly was very far from being a prude, but she found this coarse and unrelenting prurience offensive. She said, "I beg to remind you, madam, that it is my affair and not yours."

"Hoof!" Madame Rousselle raised her painted eyebrows. "We're very hoity-toity today, aren't we? I'll draw my own conclusions. Ah, Sukey, put it down on the table. So that I can reach, you stupid child. Yes, there. Come on, girl, you know how to pour two dishes of tea! Without a drop spilt, without a *drop*, d'ye hear me? That will do. Now go."

With a sly, resentful glance from lowered eyes, Sukey swept out. Madame leaned forward to hand Polly a delicate teacup of very expensive porcelain. "Impertinent girl. But then so are you. That's what I like about you, child – you ain't some milk-and-water miss who can't say boo to a goose, you ain't afraid to speak your mind and you've got a head on your shoulders. I hear you're thinking of opening a coffee-house."

"It was either that or a whorehouse," said Polly, looking her straight in the eye.

The old woman, spooning vast quantities of coarsely grated sugar into her tea, which was swimming in cream, cackled appreciatively. "And you'd rather stay on the right side of the law, would you?"

"That has nothing to do with it. I have had my fill of whoring. In my sadly declining years I see little future in it."

"Ah – so you want a respectable old age, do you? Well, you won't get it with Dark, I can tell you that. You know what he is and what he's done, do you?"

"I have no idea," said Polly, opening her eyes innocently wide. "But whatever it is, I could not care less. He is a diversion, no more."

Madame's eyes must once have been as blue as Polly's own. They were yellowed and faded now, but they were still very sharp. "Have you told him that?" she demanded.

"Of course not," said Polly blithely. "Since I am sure it is mutual. A brief dalliance for both of us, that's all." She sipped her tea, wishing that she could be somewhere, anywhere else, than in this roasting stuffy room, drinking liquid that in spite of her hostess's orders might as well have been scalding hot dishwater, and having her most private affairs probed so intimately and mercilessly by this raddled old harridan who seemed to know neither shame nor courtesy.

"'Methinks the lady doth protest too much'," Madame Rousselle quoted. "Or you wouldn't be so keen to learn where he's gone. Well, I've a good idea of it, girl, but I ain't telling you, because if I did I'd put him in danger, and then I'd have no-one to pay the rent. All *you* need to know is that someone came hammering on the door for him at dawn, and he packed a bag and called a hackney and went, with no word as to when he'd be back." She set down her cup with a vigour that slopped greasy tea all over the stained damask cloth, and gave Polly a gleeful smile. "So if he's 'just a diversion', why do you look as if you've lost all you own?"

At once, Polly sat up straighter and squared her shoulders. "You think so?" she said coolly. "I am merely concerned for my portrait. It remains unfinished, and my maid was supposed to sit for him today. She is sadly disappointed at such a waste of her valuable time – as indeed am I."

"Really," said the old woman, fixing her guest with a sardonic eye that indicated that she did not believe a word of it. "Well, that is his affair. If he wants to waste time and paint to no purpose, who am I to prevent him? He's always been a law unto himself. If I were you, girl, I'd forget all about him and concentrate on your coffee-house." She leaned forward, with a waft of musky perfume overlaying the reek of an unwashed decaying body, so that Polly had to force herself not to recoil. “And I may know just the place for you.”

“Do you?” said Polly doubtfully, for surely Madame Rousselle had not set foot outside her house for years.

“I do.” The old woman sat back, beady-eyed with satisfaction. “Well? Ain’t you going to ask me where it is? Or do you think I’m a foolish old hag with no knowledge of how the world wags these days?”

“Of course not, madam.”

“Hoof. You lie very well, girl, but not quite well enough to gull me. John’s uncle died last week, dropped dead of an apoplexy, and he could give me twenty years,” said Madam Rousselle, with ghoulish satisfaction. “So his landlord is looking for another tenant. He won’t care what you do to the place, so long as it don’t cost him anything, and he gets his rent paid on time. Mind you, it won’t be in good order, knowing old Tom Archer, he took to the bottle after his wife ran off. But a sturdy hard-working girl like you won’t have any trouble setting it right.”

“And where are these premises?” Polly enquired, careful not to look too interested. It sounded little better than a hovel, and it was sure to be somewhere totally unsuitable - the Ratcliffe Highway, or Thieving Lane, or even, heaven forbid, the wilds of Hackney.

“In Covent Garden, King Street, two doors up from the Essex Serpent, backing onto Paul’s Churchyard. John’s uncle was a stay-maker - a *respectable* stay-maker, and that’s a rare breed these days, little better than pimps, most of ‘em. They’re built good and generous, if I remember right. Sal Fustilugs used to lodge in one of them, when we trod the boards together.”

“I think I recall the place,” said Polly. She was tolerably

certain that the house in question was the one with windows so dirty it was impossible to see through them. But King Street, which led into the Piazza, was an excellent location. There were few coffee-houses in the immediate vicinity, and it was not far from Drury Lane. She said, "Is the whole house for rent, or just a few rooms?"

"Oh, Tom had all of it," said Madame Rousselle. "Though I did hear he let rooms out, to them as weren't too fussy about the stink and the dirt. You'll have a deal to do to make it clean and trim, girl."

"I'm not afraid of hard work."

"Didn't think you were. Anyway, you'll want something to take your mind off Dark. Two weeks scrubbing floors and smoking out bugs should cure you of him. Good luck to you," said her benefactress, with a look that was almost approving. "There's more to life than men, and you've realised it in the nick of time. None of 'em are worth the candle – not even King Charlie, God bless his lewd and lecherous soul!"

CHAPTER SIXTEEN

'Tho' Fortune yield ye Captive, ne'er despair'

Polly found, as that cold, wet autumn deteriorated into a freezing winter, that the mood in London matched her own: uncertain, nervous and hectic. As news and rumour swept the streets, telling of rebel victories, or rebel defeats, in the north, the adherents of both sides paraded and rioted and fought one another outside the Roebuck, or on Cornhill, or Smithfield, making the nights bright and dangerous with bonfires and tumult. The processions of warming pans and effigies for burning, accompanied by *Lilibulero* on fife and drum, marched triumphantly along Cheapside and Holborn, to St. James's, and back along the Strand and Fleet Street. The activities of the Jacobite supporters were necessarily more furtive, and mainly restricted to attacks on the Whig mug-houses, the clubs scattered about the city where loyal Hanoverians met to organise their parades and drink confusion to the Pretender and all rebels. There was one in Long Acre and another in Tavistock Street, both close to the Piazza, and Polly took care to keep herself and her servants within doors after dark.

Despite her dislike of Madame Rousselle's manner, and her doubts about being in the old woman's debt, she had taken the house in King Street with alacrity, for she could see tremendous potential in its location, if nothing else. It was not an obvious plum, being absolutely filthy, and home to a dozen disreputable sub-tenants who objected strongly to being evicted. Polly could have employed a gang of stout fellows with cudgels to get rid of them, but the modest outlay of a crown apiece was just as effective, and much less violent. On Saturday, the twelfth day of November, she took complete possession of the place that she hoped would soon become the coffee-house called Paradise.

Standing in the squalid front room, she knew that she should have been filled with triumph, but was not. It was a week since she had last seen Dark, a week since they had spent that wonderful second night together at the Vine, and had raised each other to a peak of wild passion that she, even with all her experience, would never have believed possible. She had imagined then the days and nights stretching out before them, in which they could drink each other until desire died, as it inevitably would: a dalliance, true, but so intense, so urgent that she had not dreamed it would end so soon.

She still had no idea where Dark had gone, but it must be to do with his work as a spy. Madame Rousselle had hinted that it was dangerous, so it could be connected with the situation in the north, where the rebels, marching from Scotland, had reached Lancashire, and were supposed to be expecting many reinforcements from the Catholics in the area. She knew, rationally, that for him there must be much greater matters afoot than an affair with an attractive and accomplished lady of pleasure, but all the same she begrudged his disappearance, and the abrupt and unheralded manner of it. Even if he could not divulge the nature of his business, she thought resentfully, the very least he could have done was to leave her a note of apology.

"Lord above, madam," said Hannah, looking round in frank disgust, "it looks like a litter of pigs have been living here – and smells like it, too!"

Polly was very glad that there was so much work to do, for it distracted her from brooding too much upon Dark. She had the help of Gin and Hannah, of course, and of various women and craftsmen who came in to wash and scrub, repair and replace, but every day the house echoed to the thump of her broom and the clatter of her pail, mixed with her brisk and forthright instructions to her minions. And every night she sank into her bed in the house in Flying Horse Court and slept in the dreamless stupor of total exhaustion.

So she had no energy to think about anything save for her coffee-house, until news arrived in London. It was passed on by the carpenter she had asked to look at the battered staircase. "There's word from the north," he said as soon as he had crossed the threshold. "Ain't you heard yet, ma'am? They're saying the rebels in Preston have surrendered with hardly a shot fired."

"Are you sure?" Polly asked. "We have had so many wild reports and rumours over the last few days, that I no longer know what to believe."

"Well, that's what they was saying in the mug-house last night," said the carpenter, putting down his bag of tools and surveying the broken banisters and crooked treads with a gloomily professional eye. "But it ain't necessarily true, of course. That's worse than what I thought, ma'am, I'll have to replace most of it or you'll find yourself falling head over heels before long."

The repair would be expensive, but Polly agreed to it immediately, her mind whirling. If – *if* –it proved to be true, then Robbie would be a prisoner once more, or a hunted fugitive. The ignominious end to the Jacobite cause did not trouble her: she had only become involved in it for Robbie's sake, and she could see now that it had been an enterprise doomed to failure from the start, dogged by bad luck, incompetence, corruption and downright treachery, not least her own. And of course Dark, too, might have been involved – had he not fought in Marlborough's wars? Would he have rejoined the King's army? She wished that Madame Rousselle had never uttered the ominous word 'danger'. Otherwise, she might have imagined him presiding over a relative's sickbed, or taking the waters at Tunbridge Wells, unlikely as it might seem. But he had been a soldier, and he spied for the government, and she feared for his safety. He had cheated death, several times, but sooner or later, his luck might run out. And she could not bear the thought that their liaison, that had already brought her such joy, might be over before it had properly begun.

More news was disseminated via the government press over the following days. The rebellion in Lancashire had come to an ignominious end, and further north, the Duke of Argyll had engaged the Scottish Jacobites at a place called Sherriffmuir, and defeated them. In London, the general feeling amongst the supporters of Hanover was one of relief, and Polly, hoping that Dark was no longer in peril, sang as she worked, wielding a whitewash brush like brilliant moonlight across the grimy walls, so that slowly, reluctantly, the shape and form of her Paradise began to emerge from the cobwebs and dirt. Reports began to circulate about the Jacobite prisoners taken at Preston and Sherriffmuir, who were apparently being sent south to London for trial. Polly, up to her ears in organising shelves and deal panelling, nevertheless took note of it. She wondered if Robbie were amongst them: and she wondered still more, through the long, bereft nights when she was not too tired to lie awake, when Dark would return. Apart from anything else, her coffee-house needed a sign: a naked man and woman, she had suggested to him at her last sitting, chastely clad in leaves, amidst a wonderfully flowery garden. And who better to paint it, than her artist lover?

But November reached its cold and miserable end, and there was still no word from him. Some Jacobite officers who had tried to stir up rebellion in Oxford were executed at Tyburn, dying with great courage and resolution, said their sympathisers, though those of the Whig persuasion preferred to call it obstinacy. And on the ninth day of December, the main body of Jacobite prisoners captured at Preston was marched into London.

Polly had refused to go and gawp and jeer and watch the mob pelt them with missiles, telling herself that she was above such morbid curiosity. But the day after the captives arrived, Hannah, returning from the market in the Piazza laden with vegetables and a huge basket of fine ripe apples, brought with her a familiar face, though one which Polly, her time entirely taken up first with Dark, now with her coffee-house, had not seen since the summer.

"Lord above, Poll Paradice!" cried an astonished voice. "What in heaven's name are you doing here?" And Polly, wreathed in cobwebs and smeared with dust, came down the stairs to find her old friend Jenny Garnet in the hallway.

Long Jenny was an actress at the Lincoln's Inn Fields theatre, the latest move in a career even more disreputable than Polly's. She was twenty-nine, though very few people were aware of her real age, a tall, lean young woman who, seen across the street or on the stage, might be taken for a radiant beauty. At close quarters, however, the radiance could be seen to owe more to artifice than to nature, and the abundance of red-gold curls gleamed a little too harshly in the cold winter light. Like her friend, she had paid her dues at Mother Whybrow's establishment, where they had first met, but she was also a competent performer, with a capacious memory and a drawling, expressive voice. Polly regarded her rather warily, for Jenny, with her Jacobite connections and loose tongue, had learned a few months ago of Robbie's seduction of Mary Jessop, and had lost no time in informing his mistress of his betrayal. There had been harsh words, and they had parted on bad terms because Polly had refused at first to believe the news of her lover's infidelity.

But the other woman was smiling warmly at her, and she said with relief, "I'm so glad to see you, Jenny. And I'm heartily sorry for what I said to you, when last we met."

"So I should hope," said her friend. "Do I take it that

you now accept that he is a lying cheating rogue who doesn't deserve to kiss your feet, let alone any other part of you?"

"My eyes have been opened, thanks to you," Polly told her. They embraced affectionately, but Jenny drew back at once, wrinkling her nose. "Faugh! You didn't have that from any perfume bottle! And you look like a drab!"

"Dear Jenny, as flattering and tactful as ever," said Polly, grinning. Her friend habitually spoke her mind, being too lazy, as she always put it, to go to the trouble and inconvenience of lying, and as a consequence had suffered for it in the past. "Are you still at Lincoln's Inn?"

"Indeed I am, for want of a better offer, though Cibber has been sniffing round. I declare, I might be tempted, if I fall out with Rich."

"Is that likely?"

"La, Poll, you know me!" Jenny was well aware of the shortcomings of her wayward tongue. "But for the moment, it will suffice. He keeps asking me if you'll sing for him again. Says he'll pay you double what he did last time. I said I'd speak to you when I saw you next."

"You can ask," Polly said. "But I only sang to ward off boredom, and perhaps, if I'm honest, to place myself in the market again. Since then, as you can see, my situation has changed somewhat, and now I have other irons in the fire."

"So I can see," said Jenny, looking round with her thin eyebrows, plucked into an improbable arch, raised even higher. "Lord, Poll, what is all this? What are you doing here? Are you reduced to scrubbing and cleaning for a living?"

"Not directly. Welcome, dear Jenny, to the Paradise Coffee-House, where the finest brew in London may be had, along with the best conversation and the liveliest wit."

The tall woman stared at her in astonishment, and then

let out a most unflattering hoot of laughter. "*A coffee-house?* Now I know you've run mad. Why work all your fingers to the bone when you could crook one of them and have another beau to set you up in style?" She leaned a little closer, picked a cobweb off Polly's cap, and said slyly, "I heard you've a French phiz-monger dangling at your heels. Why not take up with him?"

"Because I have set my heart on this. And besides, what would I want with an artist?"

"He could paint a flattering portrait of you, to hang in your parlour."

"He has," said Polly, thinking of that unfinished picture, gathering dust in Dark's deserted painting garret.

"Well, artists are never rich, are they?" Jenny was looking round the gloomy hall with bright-eyed curiosity. "Saving Kneller, of course. So, will you show me over your *coffee-house*, Poll? I confess I am dying of curiosity."

With a smile, Polly obliged her. Despite the interruption in her work, she was pleased to see her friend, who was always good company, even if some of the things she said were unwelcome. Knowing her essentially kind heart, Polly was prepared to ignore her candour, although she had to admit to herself that Jenny's astonishment at the news of her treasured project had hurt.

At least the house was no longer the squalid, dilapidated wreck that she had taken over only a few weeks previously. The stairs had now been repaired and painted, the battered panelling replaced, and the floor in the front room scrubbed and sanded. The carpenter and his apprentice, a sallow, pock-marked boy, were busy constructing the corner bar from which Polly or her assistants would dispense (assuming that the licence was granted) fine wines, spirituous liquors and a punch made according to a secret recipe from the island of Barbados, Hannah's birthplace. The fireplace had been enlarged and altered to provide a place for the pots of chocolate and coffee to keep hot, and the broken filthy windows had been reglazed, letting in a thin veil of chilly winter light. Without furniture, the room looked surprisingly spacious and airy, and there was a strong but pleasant smell of fresh paint and sawdust.

"Very fine, I must allow," said Jenny, looking round with her eyebrows arched still higher. "But it will not seem so large once the tables and benches are all set up."

"Perhaps not, but there will also be the back room and there is more space in there, since it has no bar. Come and take a look."

It was some time before Jenny had seen enough to satisfy her curiosity. "For of course I have never been in a coffee-house before, though I have often peered through the windows. How unfair it seems, that we women are permitted to dine in taverns and inns, but if we dare to walk through the door of a coffee-house, we are instantly rebuffed."

"Well, that is precisely why I am setting up here. I have always longed to be part of the wit and society and conversation that men take for granted, and yet Button's or Mann's would not let me in, for fear my feeble female intellect would pollute their high-minded talk."

"Or for fear that they might be accused of running a whorehouse," said Jenny drily. "And from what I've heard, some places are little better. The Blue Posts in Exeter Street, you surely know it? A bevy of pretty girls to serve the customers, and not only with chocolate. You'll have to take care that your Paradise does not acquire a similar reputation – after all, you do have some small fame in this town, aside from your singing."

"A reputation must be earned," Polly reminded her.

"And once the gentlemen have realised that neither I nor my servants are for sale along with the coffee, those who want whores will go elsewhere – there's plenty of choice, after all. And if any trouble threatens, I have a stout man to keep order – Will Evans, my footman."

"I remember him well," Jenny said warmly. "Welsh, was he not? A most handsome creature, if your taste runs to muscle."

"You may nip any such ideas in the bud now, Mrs. Garnet, he is sweet on my maid Hannah. No, mine will be a respectable house, quiet and sober."

"Then I have no hope of being admitted," said Jenny, with a wistful look round at the pleasant, bare back room, with the tall sash window giving view directly onto a small yard with a privy, while beyond it lay the trees and headstones of St. Paul's churchyard.

"Of course you will be admitted – but as the price of letting you in, you must take a turn at serving the gentlemen. Or do you consider that to be beneath your dignity as a lady of the stage?"

"Certainly I do not," Jenny cried, with a look of fierce delight. "I shall be happy to assist you in your venture, Poll, you know that. And now I must take my leave, it is almost dark – how I hate these cold grim days!"

They walked to the front door together, and Polly was about to open it when her friend said suddenly, "La, I had almost forgot – your coffee-house drove it quite out of my head! Have you heard about the Jack prisoners?"

"No-one can talk of anything else, it seems," said Polly drily. "They came into town yesterday, apparently."

"And what a spectacle that was – the whole of London lined their route, either to throw white roses or rotten eggs.

My Cousin Thompson has a shop in Holborn, and I went to watch from her window."

"Which cousin is that? The one with seven children, or the one who was found in a molly-house wearing his wife's petticoats, or the miser who won a fortune on the Lottery and lives on bread and cheese?" Polly enquired mischievously. Jenny had lived in London all her life, and seemed to be related to half the city, from link boys and whores to prosperous drapers and even a former Lord Mayor. Most were devoted adherents of the White Rose.

"None of them. She's a widow, sells snuff and tobacco and teas and such things. Does a roaring trade."

"In snuff and tea and what else?"

Jenny cackled. "I'll have you know, she's very respectable."

"So why is she on such friendly terms with you?"

Jenny punched Polly playfully on the arm: it would leave a bruise. "She thinks I'm a respectable woman too. Don't laugh. But I must tell you, the prisoners passed right by her door, and guess what? Amongst them was your handsome Robbie, large as life and sitting his horse like a king, despite all the jeering."

"He's not mine anymore," said Polly, knowing that he never had been. "But thank you for giving me the news, Jenny, and thinking so kindly of me. Do you know where he was taken?"

"To Newgate, so I understand. So are you going to visit him in prison with money to bribe the gaoler to keep him in comfort? Or smuggle in a file or a set of keys for his escape?"

"I do not care a single fig for Robbie Sinclair," Polly said vehemently. "I am *not* going to visit him, and I'm *certainly* not going to help him to escape."

Jenny's sharp dark eyes studied her. "Lord above, are you still fond of him?" she demanded, as triumphantly as if she had found a pot of gold. "I've called you many things in my time, Poll Paradice, but never a fool before. Why waste any more time on that rogue? He was born to be hanged, and by the look of it he soon will be. Forget Sinclair, that's my advice, you've got that artist fellow now, where's he?"

"I don't know," Polly said tersely.

"Oho, so that's the way the wind blows! You're thinking kindly about Sinclair again because the other one's left you."

"That's absolutely not true," said Polly. "I shall be more than happy if I never clap eyes on Robbie again."

"Oh, don't try to pull the wool over my eyes, I know you too well! You haven't had much luck with men recently, have you, Poll? No wonder you're thinking of retiring from the game." She waved a hand round at the coffee house. "Believe me, respectability ain't all it's cried up to be."

Polly wondered how anyone could misunderstand her so wildly. She felt that if Jenny did not leave now, she would do or say something completely unforgivable, and she did not want to estrange herself a second time from one of her closest friends. "I beg your pardon, Jenny, but it is growing late and I still have so much to do here, I must get on. I'll send word as soon as the coffee-house is open – are you still in the Cook's Court lodgings?"

It was snowing freely when her friend finally left. Polly vented her anger and frustration in a vigorous bout of cleaning – never had window glass been so clear – but even that did not dispel her feelings. With Hannah and Gin, she walked back to Flying Horse Court, the thin flakes stinging her face under the hood. By the time they reached home, the tears were cold on her cheeks, but they were not shed because of Robbie Sinclair.

* * *

The note arrived the next morning, delivered by just such a street child as Gin had lately been, undersized and filthy and shivering in the cold. Hannah took pity on the brat and brought him in for hot broth and a toast in front of the kitchen fire, while upstairs Polly, frowsting by her own hearth with her cat Sly snug on her lap, beheld with a sinking heart the once splendid flowing hand, now decidedly shaky and full of blots, gracing a grubby piece of paper that had obviously been torn from a book. She knew exactly what the message would contain, and so it proved.

'Newgate, the condemn'd Hold, in Haste.

My dearest Poll, I am held in this vile Prison, barbarously threaten'd with Irons, and due to be moved to the Common Side unless you come swiftly to my Aid, for there is no other Soul in all the World who can help me in my Plight. I am in most sore and urgent Need of whatever Succour you may bring, for the Damp and Cold and Stench of this Place have brought on a severe Chill, which is like to settle on the Lungs and cheat the Hangman of the Life of your most humble, devoted and faithful Friend and Servant,

Robert Sinclair

I do most heartily and desp'rately beg and beseech you to act on this at once, darling Poll, or I fear it will be the End of me.'

Her first impulse, immediately obeyed, was to screw up the paper and hurl it into the fire. She was not his dearest, or his darling, and never had been: nor had he ever provided her with devotion, never mind faithfulness. But it was entirely typical of Robbie to gloss over such trivial points when in dire need. And he was probably right that she was the only person he dared contact in London. All the others were doubtless either walled up with him in Newgate, or were lying low, fearing that if they drew attention to themselves, they would join him there.

The Common Side, as she well knew, was where the poorest prisoners were kept, those who could not afford to pay for better accommodation. A friend from Mother Whybrow's had briefly lain there, in a squalid cell little better than a hole in the ground, with twenty other women. The vile reek had made even the strong-stomached Jenny retch. By no possible effort of her imagination could Polly picture Robbie, with his fine clothes and arrogant airs, brought so low as to share a heap of stinking straw with a score of verminous criminals. Surely he must have some money with him, enough at least to pay for better lodgings?

It was, of course, no more than he deserved. He was a rebel taken in arms, a false deceitful rogue, a man emphatically unworthy of her thought, let alone her affection. But, she realised, his self-conceit was so great that he must still think, despite everything, that she would immediately forget all the wrong he had done her, and rush to his rescue. And until she disabused him of that idea, he would never cease to pester her. Moreover, there would be considerable satisfaction in telling him exactly what she thought of him. She might not be able to penetrate that vast arrogance, but she would dearly like to try.

Her decision made, for good or ill, she dressed in a plain gown of dark blue wool, such as a servant might wear, with a cheap, worn, coney-fur muff and her old frieze mantle, for despite the thin sunshine, it was very cold outside today. She told Hannah that she had business in the City – her maid would hardly approve of her actual destination – and she took Gin as her escort. The girl, with her quick wits and bounteous knowledge of street life, might prove very useful.

She summoned a hackney to Newgate, and bade it halt a short walk away. Then, with her maid scurrying behind her like a malevolent familiar spirit, she made her way up to the gaol, beginning to have second thoughts about the wisdom of this coming encounter.

Newgate prison was, quite literally, a gate: one of the many that led into, or out of, the City of London. The gatehouse itself, straddling Newgate Street, had reputedly been built by the famous Dick Whittington, several hundred years before, but the Great Fire had wrought considerable damage and the handsome renovations, including the arms of the City carved above the gates, offered a cruel contrast to the terrible conditions within. Polly had often passed it by, never without a shiver, and she had twice ventured inside to visit prisoners: as well as her acquaintance from Mother Whybrow's, who had spent several days incarcerated on suspicion (afterwards disproved) of stealing a watch, a man who had briefly been Jenny's lover had been taken up for a highwayman and kept here in irons until his execution. She retained vivid memories of the stink, the drunkenness and despair, mixed with a hectic forced hilarity that was as chilling as the rictus grin on the face of a dying man. There were women aplenty in Newgate who could have been her: women who from ill luck, or lack of opportunity, or sheer desperation, had descended to this hell. It was a salutary reminder to her of her own good fortune, and of what might await her if she made a wrong choice.

As the grim bulk of the gate loomed up to block their path, she wondered again why she had come. There was plenty to keep her busy, after all: they were due to move out of the house in Flying Horse Court after Christmas, and all her possessions, ornaments and furniture needed to be packed up carefully for the jolting wagon journey over to King Street. There was also much still to be done at the coffee-house, and she had not yet got around to employing any potboys to serve the customers. She must find a supplier for tobacco pipes, and place an order for the *Flying Post* and the *Daily Courant*, and get coals in against the winter weather, and a myriad other trivial things which, like cards in a pack, must be carefully placed together to make her grand edifice. She paused as a laden cart rattled past, rather too close, and for a moment the temptation to turn her back on Newgate, and on Robbie, was so strong that she almost succumbed.

"Here, watcher waiting for?" demanded Gin, in her usual whine. "Make up your mind, you going in or not?" At Polly's glare, she turned a deep shade of red, bobbed a hasty curtsey and muttered, "Beg pardon, ma'am."

"You still have not learned a proper respect for your betters, have you, Jane?" said Polly warningly. "And it will go hard for you if you do not. Now remember what I told you – stay close by me, and keep your eyes open and your mouth shut. I don't want any trouble."

It had snowed the previous night, and some had drifted in the icy wind, to lie softly heaped in the shadows. They crossed the street, avoiding the puddles where it had melted. There was a small group of idlers loitering outside the prison, some obviously there because they had nothing better to do, others, in hoarse and desultory voices, proclaiming their loyalty to Hanover and their hatred of the Pretender. Despite her plain respectable garb, Polly drew several loud and derogatory comments, but she ignored them and hurried up to the gate, Gin so close beside her that their mantles swirled together as they walked.

It usually cost sixpence to visit a prisoner, but the turnkey informed her, with lip-smacking relish, that because of overwhelming demand he had been forced to raise his prices. After all, as he pointed out, William Pitt, the governor of Newgate, had paid five thousand pounds for his post, and must recoup his outlay as best he could. So Polly handed over a shilling, careful not to let his greedy eyes fall on the rest of her coins, and said that she wished to see Captain Robert Sinclair.

To her considerable surprise, she was escorted not

to the Common Side, which lay on the north of Newgate Street, but to the Master's side on the south. They passed along narrow corridors lined with chill, sweating stone, encountering numerous prisoners as they went, for no-one here was confined in the hours of daylight, and could come and go as they pleased, provided, of course, that they did not stray beyond the bounds of the prison. Many of them must be Jacobites, and she heard the familiar accents of Scotland, as well as the blunt vowels of Northern England, for numbers of the rebels had come from Lancashire and Northumberland, where Papists were common. Defeat and capture had not affected their manners, and they bowed and saluted her as she passed by. Their courtesy touched her, for whether or not she agreed with their politics, they were still men, husbands and fathers, brothers or sons, as subject to human virtues and failings as anyone, and as deserving of compassion.

They came at last to the Press Yard, in the south-eastern corner of the prison, where the more fortunate prisoners were permitted, on payment of a considerable fee, to take leisure and exercise in the open air. It was a very constricted space some fifty feet long by seven feet wide, and despite the cold it was crowded with men, and some women. Trestle tables had been set up, people were drinking, playing cards or dice, reading from dog-eared pamphlets or strolling up and down. There were even two men playing with battledore and shuttlecock. If it had not been for the high bare walls and barred windows, she might have thought herself in the yard of some prosperous country inn.

"He'll be hereabouts somewhere, madam," said the turnkey. "If you wish me to point him out to you ... " He made a significant gesture with the fingers of his hand, and Polly shook her head. "You need not trouble yourself, sir, I'm sure I will come across him soon enough."

The man turned away with evident disappointment,

and much grumbling. Gin glared after him. "Thieving shabaroon!"

Fortunately, the turnkey did not hear her. Polly pulled her recalcitrant maid close, and said in a forceful whisper, "I had thought you more sensible than that! I have no wish for us to be thrown out, after going to all this trouble. Or worse, taken to the Waterman's Hall, have you heard of it? No feather beds or close-stools or fine white bread there, and a most evil band of hell-cats for company."

"He wouldn't," said Gin, but her voice lacked all conviction and bravado, and her face had lost colour.

"Oh, yes, he would, so keep quiet," Polly told her. "Now go and wait for me over there in that corner. And don't let anyone come too near you – this may be the Press Yard, and mostly full of the better sort, but a Jacobite is just as likely to be a thief as any other man, especially when he's desperate."

She watched, frowning, as Gin sullenly obeyed her, and then turned to study the prisoners again. Many of those near to her returned her gaze with interest, and one, a middle-aged man in a rather battered tie-wig, came up to her, bowed, and said politely, "May I help you, madam? Are you seeking someone?"

"I'm looking for Captain Sinclair, but I can't see him – he sent me a note saying that he would be placed on the Common Side, so the turnkey may well have made a mistake in bringing me here."

"I can assure you, madam, that he has not," said the Jacobite, with a smile. He had a soft, musical accent that she could not place exactly, though it reminded her a little of Robbie. "We have most of us been brought here to the Press Yard, though it has cost us dear – some of us have funds enough to pay the garnish and lodging for those who have not. There is your Captain Sinclair, in the blue coat, playing at dice."

CHAPTER SEVENTEEN

'And for the public Safety, risk thy own.'

The crowds shifted, and Polly saw Robbie sitting at a table with several other men. The board was crowded with flagons, bottles and glasses, and all of them were smoking pipes. They might have been taking their ease in a coffee-house or tavern: indeed, as she watched, a burst of laughter came from them, followed by a brisk rattle of dice.

A wave of anger swept over her. She thanked her informant and marched across to the table. Robbie, his back to her, did not see her approach, for he was too busy sweeping a substantial pile of silver coins into his coat pocket. His companions had noticed, though, and she saw them nudging each other and grinning. One looked up, his face flushed with wine, and winked at her with lascivious intent.

Before Robbie could realise that she was right behind him, she said with a pathetic catch in her voice, "Such a sad sight! My heart bleeds for your misfortune, Captain Sinclair, sick unto death, confined so close in the Condemned Hold, and cruelly laden with irons!"

Her former lover turned so fast that the last of the shillings scattered clinking over the stone paving. At once there was a scramble as less scrupulous prisoners leapt to retrieve them, and despite his shouts of protest, within a few seconds every coin had disappeared, and the successful inmates were discreetly melting into the crowd.

"For God's sake, woman, what are ye about?" Robbie demanded. He rose to his feet, a trifle unsteadily, and glared at her. "Ye've no call to come in here and startle a fellow out of his wits – now I've lost close on twenty shillings because of ye!"

"You'll lose more than that if you speak to me in such tones," said Polly forcefully. "So I suggest you moderate your voice and your words, sir, or I shall leave this place forthwith – without giving you what you deserve."

Several men guffawed, and she heard someone suggesting, in the coarsest possible terms, the precise services which she might render. Robbie flushed, and whirled round, his hand seeking his sword before he realised that he no longer had one. Even without a weapon, his fury seemed to have some effect, and the muttered comments and laughter died abruptly away.

"Any more o' that talk and I'll see ye in hell, Tam Maclean," he said savagely. "Understand? Now get out of my sight before I forget that I'm in respectable company."

A brief turmoil in the crowd indicated that the foul-mouthed Maclean had prudently taken his advice. Sinclair stood with his fists clenched, glaring round at the remainder of the prisoners. Evidently he had something of a reputation for belligerence, for after a brief pause most of the men began to drift back to their previous concerns.

"Will you no' take a seat, madam?" With exaggerated courtesy, Robbie wiped a rather dirty kerchief over a rickety stool and proffered it to her. "I'll call for wine."

"Pray do not trouble yourself," Polly said coldly. "I shall not be staying long in this place. After all, you plainly no longer require my assistance."

With an obvious effort, Robbie put a lid on his anger and set himself to be more agreeable to her. "Ah, Poll, dear lass, I did not mean it. Ye came up silent behind me, and I was alarmed." He added, with a pathetic look, "Ye canna imagine what it is like, in this hell-hole –"

"Oh, I know all about conditions in Newgate," Polly said. "But this is neither the Condemned Hold nor the Common

Side, you are neither in irons nor sick unto death, and you seem to be doing perfectly well for yourself without any help from me."

"I was desperate when I wrote that letter," said Sinclair, his voice quivering pathetically. "Ye canna conceive of the horror of that place, with neither light nor air, and the wolves circling round, demanding payment for everything – twenty guineas for the privilege of not being kept in irons, the same again to enter the Press Yard, eleven shillings a week for rent, and then they had the gall to ask for twelve bottles of wine for garnish last night, and I had no money to pay for any of it, save in promises to the tapster and those kind comrades who were so good as to advance me the wherewithal to buy myself a measure of comfort – oh, Poll, for God's sake have pity on me!"

"So how did you come by the wherewithal for a game of dice?"

"I was lucky – I had a few small coins, and a good run."

Or they were loaded, Polly thought, but wisely did not say so.

"But it will not see me through more than a day or two." He glanced round at the company within earshot, and then gave her a significant look. "Poll, I grow cold out here, this is my summer coat and lets the chill through – will ye no' come inside, out of the wind, and we may talk some more?"

He so obviously assumed that she had obeyed his request that despite her anger, she might have laughed. Before she could respond, though, he took her arm in a tight grip and steered her away from the curious crowd around the table. "The tap-room has a fine fire, so we'll be warmer and more comfortable. Oh, Poll, I canna tell ye how good it is to look on your sweet face again!"

He could not possibly appear so pleased to see her if he suspected her of betraying him to the Bath authorities.

She remembered that he and his accomplices had been arrested soon after her escape, so it was quite likely he had never realised that his papers had been stolen. And Dark had mentioned that the Bath postmaster, Ralph Allen, had also given information about the conspiracy to General Wade. Presumably Robbie ascribed his initial capture to this mischance, and she would not risk arousing his suspicions by gratuitous mention of the subject. She said, "Were you captured at Preston?"

"Preston? Oh, aye. A sad business, that was. But that was the second time. Did ye no' hear that I was taken first at Bath?"

"No, I did not." She tried to remove herself from his grasp, but he was too strong for her. Despite his apparent affection, she could sense the power and menace in that grip. If he attempted to do her real harm, would anyone come to her rescue? Remembering the scene around the table earlier, she suspected, with alarm, that there was a real danger they would not. For the moment, she must appear to be compliant, although she did not like to think what he might do, once he realised she had brought no money. She had been beyond foolish to come here, and even more foolish to believe that she would be able to have the last word.

"I am sorry I had to lock ye up," Robbie went on. "But I was expecting company, and I didna wish ye to be seen. Then ye made away before I could explain." He stopped by the door to the tap-room, and regarded her sorrowfully. "And ye took my horse!"

"Did you get him back? He got away from me by the ford." Polly glanced at him uneasily. She added, "He's a fine animal."

"Aye, he came back, but the soldiers were hot on his heels. God alone knows where he is now. In some fine Whig gentleman's stable, I dinna doubt, a reward for loyalty to Hanover." Robbie looked around quickly and then bent his head close to hers. "Seeing ye again, Poll," he whispered, his breath hot and wine-laden against her skin, "has put me in mind of what we used to do together, remember? Oh, I'm aching for ye, Poll, it's been so long. How about it, eh? I can slip the turnkey a shilling so we're not disturbed –"

Her instant revulsion lent her strength, and she pulled her arm abruptly out of his grasp. "*No*, Robbie," she said vehemently. "Those days are gone. I am your mistress no longer, and after I leave here, I want nothing more to do with you. Do you hear me? *Nothing*."

She saw the flash of raw anger in his eyes, and stepped back, but even in his half-drunk state he knew better, now, than to give way to it. "Come now, lass, that's no way to talk," he murmured coaxingly. "You're my girl, Poll, ye know ye are, there's never been anyone but ye, lassie –"

"What about Mary Jessop?"

He looked at her blankly. Polly elaborated. "You must *surely* remember her. Pretty little chit, dark hair, blue eyes, sixteen years old. The girl you lured away from her father in Oxford and ruined. Or have you seduced so many innocents that you've forgotten which one she is?"

"Oh, her. She bored me with her whining and her jealousy. You're the only lass for me, Poll, I swear that's the truth."

"*No*, Robbie. You're a liar, a cheat and a brute, you've shown me your colours plain, and they are not pleasant ones. I thought I loved you once, but I was a fool to think you could be trusted."

"There's another, isn't there?" Robbie's voice roughened, and his face grew redder still. "There must be – who pays your rent now, eh? Who puts the fine clothes on your back, and pays for your handsome house and your servants and your life of ease? A woman like ye wouldn't last an hour without a man's siller, so who is he?"

"There is no-one else," Polly said, through gritted teeth. "Do you think I would wish to take up with another man, after the way you have treated me?"

He made a sudden lunge for her again, and before she could move beyond his reach, he gripped her arm and wrenched her close to him. "*Liar,*" he hissed. "Who is he? Because when I find out, lassie, I'll carve his balls off him and feed them to the dogs."

She had thought she could handle his rages, as she had done before, but here in front of her was the real Robbie Sinclair, all the insouciant charm vanished, and it frightened her. He laughed. "That's more like it! Not so brave now, are ye, Poll? So where's my coin, eh? Hand it over, or it'll be the worse for ye."

Desperate to put him off, she said, "Not now in the open, there are too many people to see." As indeed there were: a swift glance round had revealed several interested pairs of eyes upon them.

Robbie obviously saw the sense of that, for he propelled her, none too gently, towards the tap-room door. "In here. It'll be busy, but there's no' much light and plenty o' smoke, and most of 'em will be too shotten to see what we're about."

She had just enough wit left to turn and beckon to Gin. Fortunately the child was watching, and scurried over to take up a position just behind Polly. Robbie did not seem to notice her. "Ye'll take a glass or two of wine, Poll? Or brandy, to warm ye? I can stand ye that, as thanks for your kindness." He leered at her, and she suspected that he was hoping that she would prove more accommodating after a few drinks.

The taproom was crowded with prisoners, and their friends and kin. Polly had wondered why so many were outside in the cold of the yard, but she realised now that they must have wished to escape from this stifling atmosphere, thick with the fumes of stale sweat, stale wine, and other, even less pleasant aromas. With the hand that was not imprisoned by Sinclair, she took her scented handkerchief from her muff and pressed it to her nose. He had spied a vacant table and bench in a dark corner, furthest from the hearth, and led her over, excusing himself as they negotiated the throng, many of whom seemed to be maudlin drunk. Someone began to sing a mournful air, and the tune was taken up by many of his comrades. It was a strong, attractive melody, and at any other time Polly would have been interested in learning the song, but she had no wish to consort with any of the prisoners: she would need all her wits about her to escape from this frightening situation without him harming her.

He pushed her down onto her seat, a rickety stool, and stood over her. "Stay there while I get the wine. Here, Black? This doxy has something for me." He smirked. "And though she's no' disposed to be friendly just now, she's come to see me, and that's proof she's still mine, eh, Poll?"

Polly turned, to see a man sitting a few feet away at a nearby table, and felt the pit of her stomach change to ice. Even in a plain brown coat, his scalp roughly fuzzed with short hair, she would have recognised him at the ends of the world.

It was Dark.

Not by one minute flicker of his eyes did he betray the fact that he knew her, let alone that they were lovers. He had obviously not shaved for some time, and his roughly bearded chin and jaw, together with his bare head, gave him a disreputable, even a sinister appearance. If she had encountered him in some of the more depraved parts of London, she would have assumed he was a roarer, out to rob someone and none too gentle about how he did it.

As she was all too well aware, Robbie could change his

mood in an instant, and he had presumably now decided that, with her effectively at his mercy, and the coin imminent, he could afford to be more amiable. With exaggerated courtesy, he gestured to Dark. "My good friend, Andrew Black – may I present Mistress Paradice, another dear friend o' mine?"

Somehow, she rose to her feet and managed a bobbed curtsey without falling over, though her knee-joints felt as if they were made of string. He bowed, and gave her a cold smile. "I am delighted to meet such an enchanting lady."

"She's come to offer me some help wi' the garnish," said Robbie, beaming at Polly, who was wishing she could somehow cut off his damning flow of talk. "What a lovely and generous woman, eh?" He put an arm round her shoulder and squeezed her in proprietorial fashion. "She was mine once, ye know, Black – and I have hopes I'll win her back, for the very fact that she's here with her coin proves she's sweet on me yet. What say I slip the turnkey a shilling later, Poll, and we can go up to my room – I willna say my cell – for a little talk, eh? Or even more – I'd love to dance the reels of Stumpie wi' ye again, for old times' sake."

God only knew what Dark was thinking: there was no sign of anything in his face except polite interest. Fortunately, it was plain that Robbie had not recognised him, for in their fight in the field at Bathampton, it had been too dark to distinguish the details of a face. And without a wig, a man could look completely different. Desperate to escape from this appalling situation, she said quickly, "The wine, Robbie?"

"Oh, aye, lassie, I hadna forgot. I'll get it for ye now." To her utter relief, he turned and began to make his way back to the bar at the other end of the tap room.

But Dark had not returned to his table: instead, he came up to her, his face set in the implacable hostility of their earliest acquaintance. "So, Paradice," he said, very softly. "What comfort do you plan to give to your Jacobite lover?"

The tone of it raised the hairs on the back of her neck. Polly gripped her hands together and dug her nails into the palms of her hands. She said, also very softly but savagely, "I have *not* given him any assistance, and he is *not* my lover!"

As if she had not spoken, he went on. "He seems to have plenty of money without your contribution. Did you know that all the tender-hearted Jacobite females in London have pawned their jewels and sold their treasures to keep your Sinclair and his comrades in fine state? Perhaps he's putting it by to bribe the turnkey to look the other way when he leaves. Or, more likely, he's spent it on fine wine and good food and fancy women. Perhaps he'll spend some of it on your favours."

"I told you – I have *not* helped him! Now stand aside and let me go, before he comes back." She glanced at the bar, seeing Robbie engaged in talk with the tapster, and then turned back to him. "I will not ask what you are doing in Newgate, Dark, for it is obvious to me, if not to your supposed comrades. For the love of God be careful!"

"I need no advice from you, madam. Good day to you."

He turned away before she could say more, and besides, Gin was pulling urgently at her sleeve. "Madam, let's scarper, before he comes back! Come on, let's *go*!"

She had already noticed another door, presumably leading to the main part of the prison. Now, with her maid at her side, she hurried towards it, evading drunken hands put out in the hope of detaining her, not daring to look back. To her relief, she reached it and went through. Beyond lay a long bare passage. Uncertain which way to go, she paused, then turned to the right, and in that instant a hand gripped her shoulder so painfully that she gasped, and pulled her viciously around. "So, my pretty," said Robbie menacingly, "trying to run away, are ye? Where's my coin?"

"You let go of her!" Gin cried, and ran at him, but he

pushed her away so violently that she fell to the floor with a cry of pain. Sinclair turned back to Polly. "*Give – it – to – me*!"

"I have no money for you," Polly said. She was frightened of the look on his face, but also furious at his attack on Gin, who was still on the ground. "I have never had any *intention* of giving you any. I came here to tell you that I will never help you again, never believe you again, never give in to you again, never *see* you again. Is that plain enough for you?"

"Oh, ye're wrong about that, lassie, because I *will* see ye again, once I get out of this hell-hole, and when I do, ye'll wish you'd never been born, ye false deceiving strumpet! So ye'll get the coin and bring it to me *now*, or it'll be the worse for ye, understand? There's half a fortune left, it's *my* money, and I *need* it." He shook her, to make his point. "Twenty guineas should suffice for now. And bring some of your clothes too, wi' that white paint you use on your face – "

"*What*?" Polly could hardly believe her ears. "Why would you want my clothes?" Even as she spoke, she knew why. "You mean to escape, dressed as a *woman*? But you're nearly six foot in your stockings - and you need to shave twice a day! My petticoats would barely hang down past your knees!" She tried not to think of Sinclair, tall and broad-shouldered and brutally masculine, flouncing effeminately past the guards in her pretty blue flowered wrapping gown, but it was impossible. Mad laughter bubbled wildly up in her throat, threatening to choke her.

Robbie had always hated being the subject of ridicule. He thrust his face so close to hers that his spittle sprayed her skin. "You'll laugh on the other side of your face before I'm done with you, you bitch! I'm no' spending more time in this hell hole, I'll be deid if I do!" She could see all the tiny black hairs sprouting on his chin, and the bloodshot veins in his eyes. "They'll hang me for sure if I face trial. Already they've threatened me wi' death if I dinna give evidence against my comrades. And there's a spy in here, everyone knows it, and some are saying it's me. If I stay, I'll be hanged or murdered in my bed – one way or another, I'll die if I don't get out of here!"

His furious agitation was extraordinarily convincing, even if she had not known that he spoke the truth: there was indeed a spy amongst the Jacobites. And unlike Robbie, she knew who it was. A chill of foreboding slithered over her skin, but she would not give in. "Then you must seek help from elsewhere, Robbie Sinclair, because as sure as I'm standing here with your foul breath on my face, you won't have it from me!"

"You bitch! I'll throttle the life out of you!" His hands closed round her throat, and she kicked out at him as fiercely as she could, making contact with his shin so hard that it jarred her foot. Behind her, there was a shriek of rage, and Gin hurled herself into the fray, using fists and feet to furious effect. Taken by surprise, Robbie staggered back, releasing his hold, and Polly seized her chance. "Run!" she cried, and with Gin beside her, turned and fled down the corridor.

Above the noise of their feet, she could hear Robbie shouting, and then other voices, also urgent. As they reached a corner, she glanced round before the turn, and saw him remonstrating with a group of his fellow prisoners, who appeared to be restraining him from pursuit. Even such a brief look told her that Dark was not amongst them.

To be sure of safety, though, they kept running, though more slowly, until they reached the outer gate. Once they had left the confines of Newgate, Polly paused to lean against the outer wall and take great gulps of the free fresh air. She felt sick and her legs could hardly hold her upright. Only now, when it was all over, did the fear and panic rush in and threaten to overwhelm her. The rough stone was gritty against her cheek, and she pressed her skin closer, using the pain to bring herself back to normality, or what might pass for it.

“Ma’am! Ma’am, are you all right?” Gin was urgently plucking at her sleeve. “What is it, Ma’am?”

“Don’t worry, child,” said Polly. With an effort, she smiled down at the girl. “I’m fine now. It was just a passing dizzy spell. I assure you, I shan’t keel over in the street.”

“You don’t look fine,” Gin said suspiciously. “You look like you’d had the fright of your life.” She stood on tiptoe and added in a hoarse whisper, “It’s Dark, ain’t it? Don’t be frit, he can look after himself. But he’s mighty friendly with your Sinclair, ain’t he?”

“I know. That’s what worries me most.” Polly pushed herself away from the wall and brushed her mantle down. “Thank you,” she said, turning to Gin. “I couldn’t have got free of him without your help.”

The girl was red faced and still breathless, but her eyes were glittering with triumph. “I kicked him square in the cods, Ma’am! He’ll be walking bow-legged for days!”

“He deserved it, and much more. I was a fool to think I could best him.” She glanced at Gin, and gave her a rather shaky smile. “As you probably thought from the start.”

“It ain’t my place to say so, Ma’am,” said her maid, but she was grinning. “But we bested him together, didn’t we? And hanging’s too good for him, I reckon.”

“I reckon so too,” Polly told her. She could see that several passers-by were looking at her curiously, and a well-dressed gentleman paused, obviously wondering if this was an opportunity to accost her. “Come, girl,” she said, loudly and confidently. “Let us go home.”

Her legs moved apparently of their own accord, while her mind frantically assessed the possible outcomes of this unfortunate encounter. Dark was playing an incredibly dangerous game, and the slightest slip could have fatal consequences. It would be so easy, in the confines of the Press Yard or the taproom, to stage a brawl in which he could be stabbed or beaten to death, and in the confusion the perpetrator need have no fear of discovery. Newgate was a violent place and murder was common, even amongst the better sort of prisoners.

But he could not have known that she would visit Sinclair, and even in the shock of meeting her, his mask had never faltered, and no trace of recognition had shown on his face. It was, obviously, not the first time he had engaged in such deception. But in that brief, forceful conversation with him, had she unwittingly given her relationship with him away? She did not think that Robbie, at the other end of the tap room with his back to her, would have seen them together, but other prisoners must have done so, and might tell him. Would Robbie realise that the man he had befriended was not only a government spy, but his former mistress's current lover? He was a very jealous man, as she had good cause to know, and nor would he scruple to do murder in the service of his pretended king.

She was so distracted that she tried to cross the Strand without looking, until Gin yelled at her in alarm, and a hackney driver swore at her, but still her unpleasant thoughts whirled wildly round inside her head. Dark's suspicion had taken her aback, but she could not blame him: what else was he to think, when he discovered his mistress apparently in the act of giving aid, and perhaps more than aid, to her former lover?

I only have myself to thank for my predicament, she thought, as she and Gin finally reached the relative safety and tranquillity of the house in Flying Horse Court. *I was such a fool, I should never have responded to Robbie's note. All I have done is to make him angry and, much worse, suspicious. And if he ever discovers who and what Dark is, he will surely kill him.*

"Say nothing to Hannah about this," she urged Gin as

they approached the front door. "She has never cared for Dark, or Sinclair, and she will have no sympathy for either of them, besides scolding me for a purblind fool."

"I won't," Gin assured her. "And please, Ma'am, *please* don't think of going back."

Polly gave her a reassuring smile. "Don't worry, the hounds of hell would not drag me in there again, and I would never put Dark in further danger. In any case, Sinclair is a vicious and violent man, a rebel taken in arms, and he thoroughly deserves whatever fate is waiting for him."

"And *that's* true enough," Gin said decisively. "I wouldn't care if he and all them Jacks was to rot in there for the rest of their lives! And good riddance to 'em!"

CHAPTER EIGHTEEN

'Upon his Brow sit Jealousies and Cares'

It was as well that Polly's preparations for opening the coffee-house were taking much of her time, for she had no leisure to worry too much about Dark, and what might be happening to him, should his duplicity be discovered. Determined not to let her thoughts dwell on him, or on Sinclair, she occupied herself with essentials, like coffee, coals, pipes and cups, and in packing up her belongings ready for the move.

As Christmas approached, the weather turned even colder. The Thames had frozen over, and a Frost Fair had sprung up on the ice: Polly would have liked to have visited it, but had no time for pleasure. Fortunately, she had already ordered extra supplies of coal, to be delivered both to the house in Flying Horse Court and to her new premises in King Street, and was very glad of her foresight, for the price was now soaring like one of Dark's skyrockets. She had saved herself a considerable amount, and could pile the fires high with a cheerful glow of satisfaction. Memories of her poverty-stricken childhood still haunted her: she hated above all things to be cold.

Unfortunately, the icy weather meant that the coffee-house called the Paradise did not open its doors for business until the New Year. More snow fell to add to the heaps already clogging the city streets and pavements, and the bitter winds and heavy frost continued. Polly was disappointed, but there was nothing she could do to influence the weather, so she determined to be philosophical about the delay. In any case, she was glad to have so much to do, for the more she thought about what might be happening in Newgate, the more she was filled with dread.

And there was no way of finding out, short of returning to the prison, which she could not do. Nor would she go round to the house in Half Moon Street and submit herself to another inquisition from the scurrilous tongue of Madame Rousselle. In her busy daylight hours, she gave a splendidly convincing picture of a worldly, careless, heartless woman. At night it was a different matter. However hard she worked, she found sleep evading her: she would lie awake in her bed, her body aching for Dark so fiercely that she must curl herself into a ball around her pillow, every muscle wound as tightly as an overstrung guitar, consumed with longing and ashamed of her need.

But then after Christmas the delay vanished, the coals were delivered, the house-painter finished his work downstairs, and a possible date for the opening of the coffee-house came rushing upon her with exhilarating speed. In the sudden whirl of activity, she could think only of the long-awaited fruition of her plans and dreams.

Word of the new coffee-house in King Street had been assiduously spread around the theatrical community by Jenny Garnet, and when Will Evans drew back the bolts on a cold dark morning, the second day of January, he found half-a-dozen impatient customers outside, all eager to sample what was said to be the best coffee in London, and catch sight of the beautiful nightingale Polly Paradice. By nine o'clock there was no space on any bench, and the two pot boys, Dan and Joe, former colleagues of Gin, were sweating profusely as they dashed from fire to table, filling cups, supplying pipes and tobacco, distributing glasses of hot rum punch. Polly had ordered a basket of fresh rolls to be sent round from the baker in Hart Street, for this house, unlike the last, had no oven, and these proved exceptionally popular. "Selling like hot cakes, madam," Hannah reported, with a delighted grin.

It had taken a great deal of very hard work to

transform the filthy, derelict house into this clean, fresh, inviting establishment. Upstairs there was still much to be done: Polly's bedchamber wanted new panelling, the fireplace in Hannah's room smoked abominably and there was a week's worth of work left for the painter. But they had moved in three days ago, earlier than she had expected, and the place was now more or less comfortable. She had been heartened by the eagerness of all her friends to help: even Jenny, so idle and languid, had taken her turn with unloading the wagon, and had hung up all the curtains, although, coming from a house with much larger windows, they trailed on the floor. Fires were lit and sweet oils sprinkled on the flames to dispel the last lingering whiff of damp, and Polly's tabby cat, Sly, gave the move her satisfied approval by curling up in front of the hearth in the upstairs parlour as if she had lived there all her life.

While Hannah, Will Evans and the boys did the real work downstairs (Gin was above, dusting and polishing, having shown a most uncharacteristic reluctance to appear in her new incarnation in front of Dan and Joe), Polly presided at the bar, the centre of attention. This was more a matter of calculation rather than any desire to have men flocking around her: she was too experienced now in masculine ways to gain much pleasure from courting such cheap popularity. But she knew that the coffee-house needed custom to survive, and that in these early days, before attendance became a matter of habit, the more people her presence enticed through the door, the better. Once they had tasted Hannah's coffee, rich and aromatic without the bitterness that was the result of too much boiling, or her Barbados Arrack punch, which slid down like mild milk but with a warming kick at the back of the throat, they would, she was sure, return again and again, whether she was behind the bar or not.

And in the meantime she must practise her feminine charms on the men clustered about her, she must smile sweetly and banter with them and perhaps – for some of them were particularly insistent on this – even give them a song. "Keep 'em dangling," Hannah had advised last night, as the two women had discussed their plans for this momentous day. "Let 'em think they might get under your guard –"

"You mean my petticoats!" Polly smiled, her hands cradling a warm cup of chocolate, while Sly, seeking greater comfort than the hearthrug, purred contentedly on her lap. "Have no fear of that, Hannah, have I not said often enough that I am done with men?"

"Save one," her maid muttered into her own cup. "But he's gone off with no word nor leave – just like all the rest of 'em!"

There was a gleam in Polly's eyes as she looked across at the other woman. "My affairs are my own, Hannah, where they concern matters of the heart. In all other issues, you may freely offer your advice, and it will be taken, or rejected, just as freely. You know that, do you not? But do not presume to judge my choice, or my rejection, of lovers." She grinned suddenly. "Even if I say that I have done with them, you should not take too much notice."

"If you say so, madam," said Hannah, with an answering smile.

Now, listening to the laughter, the compliments, seeing the flushed, eager faces of the men around her, Polly knew that there was only one person whose praise and approval she craved, and yet she feared that by going to Newgate, she had wrecked their affair before it had barely begun. Dark had obviously completely misunderstood her reasons for going there, and she did not relish the prospect of explaining them to him, when even to herself, they sounded ridiculous and even vindictive.

"Madam! Madam Paradice!"

It was Evans, who had been lurking discreetly in a

corner, poised for any trouble, although at this time of the morning it was hardly likely: his chief usefulness would come after dark, when half-drunk men might wander in from the Essex Serpent or other local taverns and try to take liberties or cause a disturbance. She realised that she must have been smiling and nodding vaguely as the conversation surged around her, while lost in her own thoughts. "Yes?" she enquired, trying not to look too startled.

"A boy brought this for you, madam." The doorkeeper heaved a large flat parcel, wrapped in rough sacking and tied with string, onto the bar counter. Polly grabbed an empty cup before it could be swept onto the floor: Evans was large and willing, but also uncommonly clumsy. "And gave me this to give to you." Amid ribald comment, she was passed a letter, folded and sealed and inscribed, *'For Mrs Paradice, the new coffee-house, King Street by the Piazza.'*

"He didn't wait," Evans said, in answer to her enquiry. "And I didn't go after him, madam, I reckoned you'd want to save yourself a penny or two."

"That doesn't matter. I know who sent it." Polly paused, her hands on the string and her heart thudding suddenly. It was obvious to her, and to Hannah who had left the coffee pots and was standing on tiptoe behind the crowd of curious customers, what it must be. And the thought came to her, that perhaps this gift meant that he was prepared to accept that her visit to Robbie had not been an attempt to win her old lover back, and had forgiven her.

She folded the letter and put it in her pocket for later perusal: she had no intention of reading something so private under the avid gaze of her customers. Then she untied the string and carefully drew the sacking aside. Within, lay a flat board, perhaps two and a half feet by two, and brightly painted. A man and a woman stood amidst a luxuriantly fertile garden, surrounded by flowers. The man was tall and in a state of nature, his modesty protected by a strategically placed rosebush. The woman, also naked, possessed a head of hair so magnificent as to rival Lady Godiva's, and with similarly concealing effect. With a mischievous smile, she was proffering him not an apple, but a coffee pot, and from the expression on his face, he was delighted at the prospect. Instead of the snake, a gleaming scarlet ribbon writhed around the tree beneath which they both stood, and upon it, in gleaming characters enhanced by real gold leaf, was written, 'Paradise'.

An extraordinary wave of emotion swept over Polly, leaving her face flushed and her eyes filling. It must have taken some considerable time and effort to produce something so delightfully accomplished, and surely it could not have been painted in Newgate. Did this mean that his task there, whatever it was, had ended? And how, *how*, could an artist of such sensitivity be a creeping, sneaking spy?

"Oh, madam," said Hannah, peering through the thicket of heads, for many customers had now left their benches and were craning to catch a glimpse of the mysterious package. "It's your sign, ain't it? The sign to go above the door. It's come at last!"

Somewhere amidst the turmoil within her, Polly found room to be grateful for her maid's quick wits. Of course, she must give the impression that this was not a wonderful and unexpected gift from an absent lover, but an ordinary signboard that had been ordered weeks ago. "I had forgotten all about it," she said, smiling. "The painter's done well, hasn't he? That will look quite splendid, hanging above the door."

"What's on the other side?" demanded a young man with a beaky nose and a very elaborate wig, who had been chief amongst her admirers. "Turn it over, Madam Paradice, I beg you, so that we can see!"

In her confusion, Polly had forgotten that a signboard

would, of course, have two faces. She looked at the young man's eager expression and realised that he was hoping for an image more risqué than the chaste Adam and Eve under her hands. And it would be just like Dark to have this respectable pair on one side, advertising good coffee, and a rampant couple on the other, indicating a bawdy-house.

"I pray you, madam, turn it over!" cried several voices, and with a certain trepidation, she did so.

She need not have worried. There was the beautiful garden, even more crowded with flowers than before, and decorously seated at a table in the midst of it was the same couple, now clothed, he in a coat of brilliant red, she in a gown of sapphire blue almost identical to the one which Polly was presently wearing. The coffee pot stood prominently between them, and they were each lifting a cup to their lips. She could not help laughing aloud with pleasure at the conceit, and her customers echoed it.

"And so your coffee has wrought a miracle," said another, older man, who reminded her a little of Sam. "Behold – it clothes the naked and civilises the savage!"

"Then the blackamoor must have been given a dish or two," said someone in the crowd, and Hannah flinched. Polly said loudly and clearly, "Have you all enjoyed your coffee this morning, gentlemen? Is it not the best in Town? Come now, don't be shy – tell me the truth. Is it good?"

A chorus of voices assured her that it was. Polly continued. "Well, I must inform you, gentlemen, that if this sign is correct, why then my maid was the civilising influence on *me*, for it is her coffee you have been drinking, and the punch is made to her recipe as well."

Everyone in the room looked with interest at Hannah, and Polly feared for an instant that she would flee in embarrassment. But her maid's confidence had grown greatly since she had been given her freedom, and she merely gave a broad smile and a bob of acknowledgement, before turning away to busy herself with the coffee pots in the hearth.

Now all the talk was of the sign and, not without some misgivings, Polly allowed it to be passed round and examined. Several customers asked her who had painted it, and she prevaricated. "The name escapes me now – he was recommended to me by a friend."

"He's made an uncommonly handsome job of it," said Beaky Nose, to the eager agreement of those around him. "It will look very splendid hanging above your door, Madam Paradice. Why not get your man to put it up now, so that everyone in King Street can have the benefit?"

Of course, once the idea took hold, there was no denying them. Evans went off to borrow a ladder, while a crowd of enthusiastic customers swept Polly out into the street. After the hot, comfortable fug within the coffee-house, it seemed breathtakingly cold, and more snow was beginning to fall, dusting the icy pavements and drifting over her dark hair like a net of pearls. There was a bracket already over the door, with brass eyes waiting to receive the links of chain screwed into the top of the sign. Evans set the ladder against the wall and climbed carefully up, carrying the board, while the few people abroad on this freezing day came over to watch. Out of the corner of her eye, she saw a tall figure in a black coat loitering in a doorway on the other side of King Street, and her heart leapt, but at that moment Evans finished his task, to loud cheers, and began his descent. Once he was out of the way, the sign could be seen in all its glory, the gold leaf catching the limited light and gleaming amidst the rapidly falling flakes.

"Ain't it beautiful, madam?" said Hannah beside her, and Polly nodded, her heart full and aching. "A picture fit for a palace."

"And uncommonly skilfully painted, for a sign," said

Beaky Nose, sidling closer to Polly. "More than a journeyman, I would warrant."

She looked round, wondering if it was Dark she had seen, but there was no sign now of the man in the black coat. An icy wind gusted round her skirts, and she shivered. "Shall we return to our fireside, gentlemen, now that the sign is put up? I for one have no wish to freeze to death!"

Some of her customers took this opportunity to leave, but about a dozen or so returned to the warmth of the coffee-house, and a fresh pot that Hannah had already set to steep on the hearth. There were several newcomers, too, and they looked round appreciatively at the cream painted panelling, the two long tables lined with benches, the newspapers and pipes strewn about, even the ill-printed advertisement for the corn-cutter who offered his services in many establishments around Covent Garden, announcing that he would be available here every Wednesday morning between the hours of nine and ten. To Polly's secret relief, Beaky Nose joined a little group clustered together on the further bench, deep in animated discussion about something in *The Flying Post*, while Joe brought them coffee and fresh supplies of pipes and tobacco. From her vantage point behind the bar, she could see little of the street outside, and in any case the windows were misted over from the snug warmth within. She wondered if that tall man in black had truly been there, or whether he was a figment of her imagination, conjured up by her thought and her longing.

She poured punch for a wizened old man with the brown leathery skin of one who has spent much of his life under a harsh sun. He beamed at her as he sipped it. "I haven't tasted anything so fine since I was a young man in Barbados! Does your blackamoor hail from there?"

"I believe Hannah was born on the island, yes, sir."

"A slave, was she?"

"She was, but I have given her her freedom," Polly said.

To her pleased surprise, the old man smiled even broader. "That's good. It never seemed right to me, that one man should have ownership over another, as if a human being was no better than a chair or a cow - and any fool can see that she's no more a savage than I am. Free 'em all, that's what I've always said, and be damned to those greedy, hypocritical plantation owners. Your very good health, ma'am, on this cold morning."

"And yours, sir," said Polly, giving him her most brilliant smile. Unexpected kindness always had the power to lift her spirits.

Much later, when business was less hectic and the snow, falling thickly outside, had driven many customers home, she left Hannah in charge and ran upstairs to open the letter unseen. Her heart thudding anxiously, she slipped her thumbnail under the seal and opened it.

It was brief, and the phrasing was as taciturn and hostile as their conversations during their earliest acquaintance.

'Paradice,

I trust this meets with your satisfaction. There are matters which need discussion between us, and therefore if I do not hear from you to the contrary, I shall wait upon you tomorrow morning at ten o'clock.'

And he had signed it, curtly and impersonally, with the four thick black letters of his surname.

Tears came to her eyes, and she brushed them roughly aside, ashamed of her weakness. It was dangerous to allow him so much mastery over her emotions, but even the thought of him brought a glow to her loins and set her skin tingling with anticipation. Yet still her mind kept returning to the man who could lurk amongst people who trusted him, spying and sneaking and ultimately betraying them. Would he betray her too, as every one of her other lovers had done? For now, her most difficult task would be to conceal just how powerfully she was in thrall to him. In the end, she had never expected to be anything other than alone, fighting for survival in a world ruled by men.

She slept very little that night, most of which was spent rehearsing, as thoroughly as any actress, how she could explain to him that she had visited Sinclair in Newgate to put a final end to their relationship, and that she now realised that it had been a mistake to do so. The scenes played out in her imagination had many variations, but all ended in the same way: and by the time the dawn light crawled reluctantly past her shutters, her heart was filled with dread.

There was a little brass clock on the mantelpiece above the hearth in the coffee-house: never had its hands crept so slowly by. Polly could not prevent her eyes from straying to it every time she had the leisure to do so, which admittedly was not often, for the place had been full since eight. Despite the weather, which continued bitterly cold, the business of the town had almost returned to the usual, and in any case a place where you could sit by the fire all day for a few pence, was a good refuge from the freezing winds outside. A part of her mind had noted several faces familiar from the previous day, together with many new ones, so evidently the word was spreading. The old man from Barbados was here again, and had engaged Hannah in conversation. Polly was relieved, for her maid had given her several suspicious looks, as if she guessed something of the turmoil within.

At last, the hands passed ten. The door opened, but it was only Beaky Nose, with his over-eager smile pinned rakishly to his undistinguished face. Polly told her fluttering heart to be still, and forced herself to be pleasant without making him assume that she would invite a more intimate acquaintance. Eventually he took his cup of punch and went over to join his friends by the hearth, and as she turned to check the clock yet again, Dark walked in.

As he came up to the bar, she wondered why he looked different, and then suddenly realised that he was wearing a paler wig than was his normal habit. He asked her casually for a cup of punch, while his eyes studied her closely, and while she was pouring it, he leaned a little nearer and asked quietly, "Is the sign to your liking, Paradice?"

"It is indeed," said Polly. "And has been much admired, for it is beautifully painted. Thank you, Dark, it was a most splendid gift." She gave him a tentative smile, which was unreturned, and passed him the cup. "That will be fourpence, sir."

"I am glad you like it. And you received my note? Good. Then may I beg the privilege of a conversation in more private surroundings? There are matters which I would very much like you to explain. If you are able to, of course."

Polly glanced significantly round the room, which was still crowded. Dan came up for some more pipes, and she paused while he was extracting them from the box on the counter. When he was out of earshot, she said, "I am not sure that I have anything to explain."

"Oh, I think you do. A betrayal of trust always requires an explanation – if, of course, there *is* any explanation."

She stared at him indignantly. Surely he could not really believe she had succumbed to Sinclair's blandishments? And yet, remembering Robbie's gross, tactless talk, she realised with dismay that he did.

"And sometimes," she responded, "things are not always as they seem, and one should not take them at face value."

"I agree. Which is why I have suggested that we talk it over upstairs. And perhaps sooner rather than later? I have much to do today."

"I am sure that you have. For example, there is a certain portrait you have been working on, and it would be a crying shame to leave it unfinished, especially as I have reserved just the right space for it there, to the left of the fireplace." She gave him a wide, challenging stare. "I am sorry to say that Hannah has quite taken against you. Have you not seen the fearsome looks she keeps sending in your direction?"

"Compared to the Stygian depths of your gaze, Paradice, Hannah's glares are as innocuous as a baby's."

To her dismay, Polly could not quite prevent an upward twitch of her lips. What was happening to her? She wanted to lean over the counter and kiss him, then and there with her servants and all her customers looking on, but she had no intention, yet, of succumbing to her baser desires. If she wanted an easy life, she would have to be discreet. And whatever the outcome of the coming 'discussion', it would do him no harm at all to make him realise that she was not some subservient little lapdog who would come running at his beck and call, and never dare to say no.

"On the other hand," she continued smoothly, "I may have other plans for that space. There is a man in the Piazza who sells all kinds of engraved pictures, very cheap. I have a fancy for some scenes from antiquity, full of bold heroes and voluptuous, scantily-clad maidens." She glanced at him. "After all, why go to the expense of one painted picture when you could have a dozen prints for the same price?"

"If you really think that, Paradice," said Dark, "then I have truly been wasting my time with you. Fortunately, I can tell when you are being infuriatingly provoking. Shall we go upstairs before your woman there turns me to stone?"

"Her name is Hannah. I thought you knew better than that, sir."

"I thought I knew a great many things about you better than I find I do." Dark's tone held flat hostility. "Now, madam, unless you want all our private business conducted in this rather public place, I suggest we withdraw to your parlour."

Gin was in the hallway, sweeping up the mess brought in from outside. She bobbed a curtsey, and gave Dark a very sharp glance, which he returned, unsmiling. "Are you behaving yourself?" he enquired.

"Yes, sir," said the maid shortly.

"And are you happy here?"

Gin's wide, startled eyes flashed up at him in the gloom. "Course I am! D'you take me for a noggin? I know which side me bread's buttered, even if you don't!"

There was a brief, pungent silence. "And just what do you mean by that?" demanded Dark.

"*Nothin',*" said Gin, and attacked the floor with her broom so vigorously that straw and crushed cinders flew in all directions.

"That will be enough, Jane," Polly said. "You may go help Hannah at the bar."

"Oh, ma'am, do I have to? Joe and Dan won't stop calling me a molly."

"They are silly boys and you should pay them no attention. I shall speak to them later. In there, if you please, Jane."

With a look of sullen belligerence, Gin pushed her broom into a corner and stamped resentfully into the coffee room. Polly did not dare to look at Dark. Instead, she turned and made her way up the stairs to her parlour.

Gin had banked up the fire, and it smouldered as sullenly as she did, with an evil plume of deep grey smoke ascending the chimney to contaminate the air outside. Polly shut the door behind them, and turned to face Dark. Her heart was shaking within her, but she kept her face calm and unemotional. "We do not have very long, and you were a trifle late," she said.

"Was I? Still, as they say, better late than never. Would you like to explain yourself, Paradice?"

"I confess, I have no idea what you mean by that." Polly surveyed him warily, but his face was as closed and hostile as it had been during their earliest acquaintance. Trying to ignore her deep sensation of unease, she added, "Do I take it that you object to my visit to Newgate?"

"I thought you had been enlightened, Paradice, as to the true nature of your Jacobite lover and his tawdry cause. Yet you visit him in Newgate, to offer him assistance – and you alone know what else you offered, for, as you confessed to me not so long ago, there is little you will not do to help a friend." He folded his arms and surveyed her. "So, let me see if I have this aright. You have been secretly bringing comfort to a Jacobite taken in the act of rebellion – and moreover, a Jacobite who is your lover."

"*Used* to be!" Polly cried indignantly, but he ignored her. "So what prompted you to conduct yourself so recklessly? Mere sympathy for a suffering prisoner? Unlikely, since you never do anything that is not to your advantage."

"Dark, that is grossly unfair, and you know it."

"Do I? Think of the dance you led poor Sam in Bristol."

"If you will take the trouble to search your memory," said Polly, her mouth dry, "you will recall that escapade was not to my advantage, but Hannah's. As to Sinclair, well, I know you might find this difficult to understand, but when I received his message, I knew that his conceit is such that he would never cease pestering me if I did not tell him, once and for all, that our affair was at an end. And that I would not take up with him again, were he the last man on earth."

"And did you tell him? Because he followed you out of the taproom, and I did not see him again until next day – when he was at pains to tell me what the two of you had done, with so much detail and so much relish I could barely restrain myself from striking him. What was the name of the dance? The Reels of Stumpie, was it? More commonly known, I assume, as the Beast With Two Backs."

Polly stared at him in horror. "He lied to you! Dark, you cannot possibly believe I would do that! He laid hands on me, I had to fight him off and run."

"Was that before or after you gave him the coin he asked for?"

"I did not give him *anything*! I had no *intention* of giving him any help whatsoever! That was why he threatened me!"

"Of course, he would ask you for money, because he knew you had plenty of it." Dark waved a hand round at her pretty, comfortable room. "Where did it all come from, I wonder?"

"I had some saved up," Polly said, her heart pounding so hard that she felt it might burst through her bodice. "And a legacy at a very opportune time."

"A legacy, eh? I doubt it. Sinclair is a Jacobite agent, sent from France to incite and fund rebellion. For that he'd have needed gold, and plenty of it. Now he's in prison, and can't touch it, but his loving mistress can. So that's what he wanted, isn't it, madam? But you had none left, because you used it to open your coffee-house. Does he know about that, I wonder? What have you told him? Ah, I have it now – that must be why you refused to help him escape. After all, if he were let loose in London, he might realise just what you had been doing with the Pretender's gold."

Polly had risen from her chair. She could see her reflection in the mirror above the plain marble chimneypiece. All the colour had fled from her face, leaving the paint, which she had thought so subtle and flattering, standing stark on her skin as if she were in truth a drab off the streets. There was no point in denying anything, for he had come at the truth exactly. She said, "That is why he asked me for help in the first place, for he looks on it as rightfully his." Her mouth twisted in a sudden, bitter smile. "After all, it paid the lease on the house in Flying Horse Court, and a thousand other things. The Pretender did not know, when he gave his gold to Sinclair, that so much of it would go to keep him and his mistress in fine style. And surely you would rather that, than on guns and arms for James Stuart? In case you had forgotten, I did George of Hanover sterling service, a few months ago. Some might say that this is merely a just reward for my efforts on his behalf."

"Some might say. Your Robbie assuredly would not. In fact, if he were to discover exactly what you had done with his master's guineas, then I dare say his rage would know no bounds. He is something of a hothead, is he not? I can quite see him putting his hands round your throat in a fury."

As indeed he had. She said, with something of Gin's bravado, "I am not afraid of Robbie. He is all bombast and bluster."

"Is he? *Is* he? I could tell you some things about your Captain Sinclair that would chill your blood. It would be as well for you, madam, that he never leaves Newgate, and never discovers that you have betrayed not only his cause, but himself."

"He will be tried, and probably transported," said Polly, praying that her words would come true in due course. "He has made his own bed, and must lie in it."

"And so must you."

The harsh words hung in the air, his judgement on her, and if she were honest with herself, no less than she deserved. She said, spreading her hands in helpless appeal, "What does it matter now? What harm has been done? Yes, we embezzled the gold, but that has damaged only the Pretender and his cause, and you can have no objection to that. And whatever twisted tale your jealousy has woven, I am *not* his lover, and I did *not* give him any help, so you can have no quarrel with that either."

"Come, madam, I know better than anyone how devious you can be," said Dark contemptuously. "Yes, you are utterly delightful between the sheets, you could give a sultan's harem lessons which would make them blush, but look beneath the skin and you find only a self-seeking callous little trollop."

"No!" Polly cried. "No, Dark, that is a heinous lie and you know it!"

Dark's eyes seemed to bore holes in her heart. He said, his voice low and impassioned, "You have betrayed me and my trust."

"No, she ain't!"

They had been so intent on each other that neither had noticed the door open. Polly turned, startled, and saw Gin standing on the threshold, her pointed face scarlet with indignation. The girl went on, her voice rising hotly. "That ain't true! She ain't like that other lying jilt, so don't tar her with the same brush!"

"I don't recall asking you for your opinion, Jane," Polly said. "Do I collect that you have been listening at the door?"

"And what if I have? Ain't no crime, is it?"

"It is in polite company. Now leave us, Jane, before I am

compelled to shout at you."

"I ain't going," said Gin mutinously. "Not till you've seen sense, the pair of you. Madam went to Newgate cos he asked her to, *begged* her to, but she didn't want to, and she didn't like it, and she only went the once, so why are you treating her like she's committed high treason, eh?"

"I trusted her. She told me Sinclair meant nothing to her, yet the next minute she went to him in Newgate, and gave him comfort. How can I believe what she says, when she denies she's his lover?"

"I have told you, *over* and *over*, he is my lover no longer!"

"And he told me you were."

"She ain't no whore!" Gin shouted, rushing up to Dark. "She ain't no whore and if you don't see that, you're a purblind idiot! You're worse than ever she is by far, cuddling up to them poor Jacks and pretending to be their mate, and then peaching on 'em!"

"You'll be quiet, brat, if you know what's good for you."

"Well, you don't, and that's for sure! Never have done, have you, you stupid addlepate!" yelled Gin, by now quite beside herself, tears spurting down her thin cheeks. "You can't see a good thing if it comes up and shakes you by the hand and puts gold in it!"

"Jane," Polly said sharply, seeing the white blaze of answering fury in Dark's face, "go downstairs this instant." And then, as the child seemed about to strike him, "*Jane! Go now!*"

With a strangled sob, Gin turned and ran out of the room. The thunder of her footsteps down the stairs indicated that there was no risk that she would be listening at the door, for a while at least.

"Insolent brat," said Dark harshly. His face was savage

with anger, and she did not dare glance at his eyes. "Well, whichever view you take, you do not look so delicious now, do you, Paradice? You have either betrayed the King, or the Pretender."

"Are you so fragrant yourself?" Polly demanded, so sorely hurt by the injustice of his accusations that she struck out in her turn. "You are very much more than you seem, are you not, Dark? You appear in Newgate under a different name, and there is only one conclusion to be put on that. Or are you taking money from *both* sides?"

Dark took a step towards her, his fists clenched so hard the knuckles were white. "If you were a man, I would call you out for that insult."

"But I am not a man, I am just a whore of no account, so you may take me or leave me as you please."

"Then I will leave you, and I will not be back. I should never have taken up with such a deceitful little strumpet."

"And good riddance to you, Dark – go on, get out, and take your jealousy and insults with you – I never want to see you again!"

"Have no fear, madam, for you will not meet me this side of hell."

The door slammed behind him so hard that the window rattled. She heard his steps descending, the front door banged, and then silence.

The fire crackled and the cat stretched before it, yawning heartlessly.

"Oh, dear God," Polly whispered, her hand to her mouth. "What have we done?"

CHAPTER NINETEEN

'Through winding Alleys to her Cobweb Room'

Samuel Jessop trod carefully down James Street to keep his appointment, his eyes on the way ahead. The raw cold seemed to leech all the life from his limbs, and although the street was short, the walk from Long Acre seemed interminable because of the ice underfoot and the numerous obstacles – heaps of frozen snow, lumps of cinder and piles of rubbish – which seemed to have been placed in his path specifically to trip up unwary pedestrians.

At last the broad space of the Piazza opened up before him, dotted with scavenging birds. Most of the ramshackle wooden stalls were vacant, though one or two market women, hardier or more desperate than the rest, huddled under blankets behind their scanty wares, too chilled and dispirited even to shout their usual raucous cries. He had to step into the road to pass a very stout elderly couple, proceeding extremely slowly and clinging to each other as if their lives depended on it. Fortunately the only wheeled traffic in sight was a solitary wagon parked further up King Street. He spotted the unmistakable sign of the Essex Serpent, its vast coils throttling the green painted landscape, and not far beyond it was the place he sought.

He recognised the large doorman, who bowed and said, in a strongly Welsh accent, "Welcome to the Paradise Coffee-House, Mr. Jessop. Madam is waiting for you upstairs, and Jane will conduct you to her."

A little maidservant, also curiously familiar, curtseyed and indicated that he should follow her. In the gloom of the hallway, thick with pipe smoke from the coffee rooms, he could not quite see the details of her face, but as they climbed the stairs, leaving the brisk buzz of masculine talk below them, he said, "I'm sure I remember you from somewhere. Were you part of Mistress Paradice's household in Flying Horse Court?"

The girl turned and grinned down at him. "Don't you know me, sir?" she said chirpily. "I'm Gin."

Sam stopped in utter astonishment. "*Gin?* Well, bless my soul. Yes, I can see it now. Who found that out?"

"That I'm a girl? Madam, of course. I owe everything to her," said Gin, with the simplicity of pure truth. "If it wasn't for her I'd likely be dead by now, or worse." She added politely, "Nice to see you again, Mr. Jessop. Are you well?"

"Well enough, considering the weather," said Sam, reluctant to satisfy her sharp-eyed curiosity any further. Obviously aware of his reticence, Gin uttered an audible sniff, and knocked on the nearest door at the top of the stairs. Before any reply could be made, she flung it open with a crash and said loudly, "Here's Mr Jessop to see you, madam, I showed him up like you asked me to."

Polly Paradice sat by the glowing fire that made the room so deliciously warm. She looked as elegant as he remembered her, small and exquisite in a sapphire blue gown, stroking the tabby cat on her lap. With a wonderful smile of welcome, she set the animal on the floor, rose to her feet and held out her hands. "Oh, Sam, how *happy* I am to see you! But what terrible weather it is! Are you quite frozen solid?"

"I am warmer already," Sam assured her, smiling. "And it is very good to see you again, Polly."

"Jane, bring us a pot of coffee, and some of those rolls if there are any left. Don't stand there gawping, girl, step out briskly!"

"Yes'm," said Gin, making a curtsey that better resembled a twitch than a bob, and fled in advance of a scolding.

Still holding his hands, Polly reached up on tiptoe and kissed his cold cheek. "Come sit by the fire and thaw yourself out. How long have you been in town? Did you have a terrible journey from Oxford? I heard that some coaches are taking weeks rather than days, the roads are so bad."

"I believe so," said Sam. Before his own fire, he would have turned his back and raised his coat to warm his nether regions, but he had no intention of behaving in such a vulgar way in the presence of Polly, however down-to-earth her manner. Instead, he held out his hands to the blaze, noticing that his breeches and stockings were beginning to steam. "Mine was two days on the road, whereas in summer you can leave at sunrise and be in London before dark."

"Poor Sam," Polly said sympathetically. "Well, you are here now, and you will be warm as toast very shortly, and Hannah's coffee is a marvellous tonic for the tired mind." She settled back in her chair again, smiling. "What a wonderful surprise this is! I had no idea you had come to London until your note arrived."

Sam was a perceptive soul, and he had already sensed some sadness underlying the warmth of her welcome. But he knew better than to pry: he had no doubt that Polly would confide in him sooner or later, if she wished: and if she did not, well, that was her affair.

The door opened and Gin entered, rather red in the face, bearing a large tray on which she had placed a steaming pewter pot of coffee, and two cups and saucers. She looked round anxiously, and Polly, immediately divining her need, pulled over a little round table which usually stood against the wall by the fireplace. "Here, Jane, put it on this. Were there no rolls left, then?"

"Oh, beg pardon, ma'am, I forgot," said Gin, with a

grimace of dismay. She set her burden down with evident relief. "Shall I pour for you?" she added, with a dubious glance at her mistress.

"Perhaps it's best if I do so," Polly said hastily: Gin was not yet fully accustomed to handling expensive porcelain, and there had been several breakages. "You may go down and fetch the rolls. And don't forget, they'll need plates to sit on, and knives and butter as well!"

When Gin had gone out again, Sam asked, "What happened in Bath, after I had taken Mary back to Oxford?"

Polly described, as best she could from what Dark had told her, the capture of the Jacobite conspirators and the arms they had gathered in and around the city. Sam listened intently, and interrupted as her tale reached its conclusion. "So, tell me if I have this aright – Sinclair was taken prisoner?"

"Indeed he was – but he escaped a few days later."

"So he is still at liberty? Then he may be anywhere, in this country or even in France – so God only knows where Mary might be!"

Polly paused in her pouring and stared at him in horrified surprise. "You cannot mean that she has run away *again?* But in your last letter, you said that she was happy, and that you had found a nice young man you hoped would marry her."

"I did," Sam said heavily. "But I was deceived."

"Is that why you have come to town, then? To look for Mary? When did she disappear?"

"Ten days ago," Sam said. He surveyed the dish of coffee sadly. "She had arranged to stay for a little while in the New Year with her friend Peggy Croft, who has recently married and moved to Wheatley. I didn't suspect a thing – Peggy was her dearest friend, and Mary said she wanted to tell her that she might soon be wed, they had so much to discuss – God help me, I never thought it was all a lie! She seemed so pleased to be seeing her friend again, they hadn't met since before she ran away in August. I put her on the coach myself, and never gave it another thought. But when I rode out there the following week to fetch her home, as planned, Peggy told me that she had never arrived, and instead had sent a note telling them that she was ill and could not come. For five days I had assumed she was in Wheatley. And I have no idea where she is, except that I am sure she has gone in search of Sinclair. So I came to town because the coaches for London pass through Wheatley, and perhaps she was planning to come here all along – so her supposed visit to Peggy would be a good ploy."

"So has Sinclair been in contact with her?" Polly asked in bewilderment. "Has she received any messages or letters recently?"

"Well, I thought she had not," Sam said despairingly. "But when I asked round all her friends in Oxford, one of them – Eliza Middleton, a silly little jade with nothing in her head except young men and romances and fashions – let slip that she had arranged with Mary to receive letters for her, and that one such had lately arrived. And soon afterwards, Mary asked to visit Peggy, to discuss the wedding."

"So Mary seemed to like the young man, then?" Polly felt considerable sympathy for Sam's plight, but also considerable exasperation at his innocence of feminine wiles, and his daughter's ruthless exploitation of it.

"Oh, yes, she professed herself very keen, he is a pleasant fellow, steady, good prospects, handsome – and above all, he knows of her liaison with Sinclair, it only seemed fair to tell him, and he was so enamoured of her that he was quite prepared to overlook the indiscretions in her past. Poor George," said Sam unhappily. "I have not told him any of this – I hoped that I might find her quickly, so that he would never know she had run away again. At present he thinks she is still in Wheatley with Peggy, kept there by the weather and a winter chill."

Privately, Polly thought that the sooner Mary's intended husband realised the extent of her transgressions, the better. Few men, however besotted, would be happy to find themselves shackled to a bride given to running off to her lover without a backward glance.

"I suppose that many fathers would be tempted to wash their hands of such a daughter entirely," Sam went on. "But I cannot. She is my own flesh and blood, my only child. I came to London to ask your help. I know that you have your own life to lead and that you have already done more for me than I can ever repay, but I did not know where else to turn. I am utterly at a loss, for I have no idea where Sinclair is."

Polly took a deep breath, for now was the time to confess. "Sam, he is a prisoner in Newgate."

He gave an exclamation of surprise. "In Newgate? Are you sure?"

As he was speaking, Gin returned with the rolls, golden brown and still slightly warm from the baker's, on a blue and white plate. She set it down beside the coffee pot and said brightly, "Course she's sure, Mr. Jessop sir, and so am I, cos we went to visit him before Christmas."

There was a significant pause. Polly said cautiously, fearing Sam's reaction, "Yes, as I was about to tell you. After he escaped from Bath, he must have gone north to join the rebels there, for he was taken with the other Jacobites at Preston and brought down to London for prison and trial."

"And after all he had done, you went to visit him?" The hurt bewilderment in Sam's voice was evident. "Please, I must know why? Why did you – "

Gin interrupted him. "Because he asked her to, and spun her a tale about needing comfort, and she wanted to tell him she wouldn't be at his beck and call ever again, and when we got there it was all lies what he'd said and he was living high and mighty as a prince."

"Jane! Kindly learn to guard your tongue and refrain from speaking out of turn," Polly said, more severely than she had intended. "Now go downstairs and tell Hannah that she is to find you some unpleasant task – perhaps the privy needs cleaning. I shall check on your progress later, and woe betide you if I am not satisfied."

"I beg your pardon, madam," said Gin, her face scarlet, and fled.

When she had gone, Sam said, "But I don't understand – Sinclair betrayed you. And still you helped him. Why?"

"Oh, Sam, I didn't help him," Polly said. "As Jane said, I intended to tell him that I wanted nothing more to do with him, and other home truths, and now I wish most fervently that I had ignored him, for I have fallen out with Dark over it, and I do not know how that can ever be mended." And to her own surprise and embarrassment, she burst into tears.

Sam was used to feminine distress: without fuss, he gave Polly a very large plain handkerchief, and waited in a patient silence until she had wiped her eyes, blown her nose and regained some portion of her usual composure. She sent him a rather watery smile. "I am so sorry, Sam. I had no intention of imposing my own private affairs on you. I have had no-one to talk to about it, but I thought that I would be strong enough to ignore my feelings. It seems I was wrong."

"There is no need to apologise, my dear."

"Thank you. Well, Dark discovered that I had visited Sinclair in Newgate, and he took it as a personal betrayal." She had already decided that she would not tell Sam, yet, that Dark had also been in Newgate, as a spy.

"I see." Sam was looking at her thoughtfully. "So I take it that you and Dark are lovers? It does not surprise me, I had a notion, when we were all in Bath, that the wind was blowing in that direction."

"You are right, of course," Polly said sadly.

"And do you love him?"

"I desired him, wanted him, enjoyed his company, yes, and now that he has left my life, I am desolate. When he was in the same room, it was as if nothing and no-one else mattered – he alone was clad in colours, and everything else was grey and drab. Strange, when he habitually wears black. So, is that love?"

"Some would think it so. For my part, I suspect that there are as many different kinds of love as there are people in the world. Your idea of it may not be the same as mine."

"And certainly not the same as Dark's," Polly said. "In any case, it hardly matters now, for our quarrel was so fierce that I do not think he will ever darken this door again." She thought of his picture, the conversation piece of herself and Hannah and Gin, now forever left unfinished, and resolutely strengthened her heart. Lovers came and went: it was in their nature, and hers, to be inconstant, to move from one to the next without a backward glance.

Given the savage, desperate ache which had burdened her ever since that final dispute, she was not convinced. But she knew that in time the pain would inevitably grow less, until it almost faded away. And meanwhile, there was more urgent business to attend to.

"But no more of me," she added, trying to make her expression bright and cheerful, despite the sleepless rings around her eyes, and the pallor of her cheeks. "What of Mary?

We must contrive a way to locate her."

"And if Sinclair is in Newgate, she will surely go to visit him." Sam became almost animated as the idea took hold. "So if we are to find her – "

"We must keep a watch on Newgate. Always assuming, of course, that he has failed to escape." Polly gasped suddenly as a very obvious thought struck her. "Of course! That must be why he summoned Mary. He asked me to help him, and as you can imagine, I refused point blank – his plan was so ridiculous that it could never have succeeded, he wanted me to give him some of my clothes so he could disguise himself as a woman." She looked apologetically at Sam. "So it may be all my fault – if I had given in and helped him, he would never have turned to Mary."

"Polly, my dear, you cannot possibly say that for certain! Who can guess at his reasons? A man like that will always act in the most venal and despicable manner, and you must not blame yourself. It is rather my responsibility, for being so lax and indulgent a father that Mary must think me a sad sack of a fellow and pathetically easy to deceive." He sighed heavily. "Be thankful that you are not a parent. There is not a minute of any day when I do not think of her, and worry about her, and never more so than now. Where is she? What is she doing? I fear I will not like the answer, and yet I am desperate to find her."

A little later, a chastened Gin trudged carefully up the stairs to her mistress's parlour, bearing another pot of coffee and some little apple tarts on a wooden tray. She paused outside the door, and wedged the tray between the wood and her scrawny waist. Then, with a deep breath, she knocked.

After a brief pause, Polly called "Enter!" and Gin, the tray still more or less securely wedged, though tilting alarmingly, turned the handle and pushed the door open with her foot, at the same time gripping her burden again with both hands.

Hannah had taught her this little manoeuvre, and she had almost mastered it now, but there were still some tricky moments when the tray was only supported by one hand. She had been made to practise with pewter, just in case.

She bobbed a curtsey and set her tray down on the table by Polly's chair. "Will that be all, ma'am?"

"I have something to say to you, so wait a moment." Polly was sitting comfortably by the fire with the cat Sly on her lap, and only the constant, rhythmic stroking of the sleek tabby fur gave a hint of any untoward emotion behind that calm and exquisite face.

Nonplussed, for she had assumed that she was in disgrace, Gin hesitated for a moment, and then said, "Yes, ma'am?"

"Mr. Jessop and I have a task for you."

Sam, sitting on the other side of the fire, smiled warmly at her. "Indeed that is so, Gin – I mean Jane."

"I prefers Gin, sir," said the little maid, with a spark of her usual impudence. "Jane don't sound like me, somehow."

Polly glanced at Sam, then turned back to the girl. "Gin was – *was* – a ragamuffin street urchin. Jane is a young serving maid who might one day amount to something if she works hard and does as she's told. I understand the difference, and I think you do too. Am I right?"

"Yes'm," said Gin, with an obedient duck of her head, but she was suppressing a grin.

"Now, as you're here, I have to tell you of what we wish you to do. You collect that Mr. Jessop's daughter has run away again?"

"Yes'm."

"It seems very likely that Mary has come to London to

see Sinclair, perhaps in answer to a summons from him," Polly said briskly. "Obviously it would be impossible to discover where she might be lodging, but we do have some inkling of where she could be seen, sooner or later."

"At Newgate Gaol," Gin said.

"Exactly so. Before long she must surely come there to visit Sinclair – perhaps to take him comfort, or to help him escape."

"So, you see, Gin, the simplest course of action is to wait for her outside the prison," said Sam.

"But she knows us," Polly went on. "One glimpse of her father, and she will turn tail and run, and we will never find her. And she will surely recognise me – after all, we met in Bath. The only person who would not be familiar to her – "

"Me, ain't it," said Gin eagerly. "You wants me to skulk around outside Newgate and watch for her, don't you? And follow her home?"

"Your quick wits do you great credit, Jane," said Polly approvingly, and Gin flushed with pleasure. "Yes, that is precisely what I was about to suggest. I doubt she paid you much attention when you were a boy – she will never recognise you now that you are a respectable maidservant, like so many others. You can slip unnoticed at her heels and see where she lives."

"There's such a thing as 'easier said than done'," Gin muttered, but she was pleased. "So, when do you want me to go there, ma'am? She could be there now! Shall I go this instant? We might miss her else. I can carry a basket like I was running an errand, and she'll never notice me!"

Sam looked very dubious. "But if she does suspect you, then we are done for – there will be no chance of tracking her down after that."

"But we have no alternative," Polly pointed out. "The streets are full of maids running errands, it is so commonplace I doubt your daughter will give her a second glance. And of course you know the streets very well, do you not, Jane?"

"Like the back of me hand," said the child smugly. "Trust me, ma'am, I can do it! When do I start?"

* * *

Gin had been loitering in the streets around the entrance to Newgate for several hours now, and although she was tough and used to the cold, her feet had grown numb and her hands, encased in an old pair of woollen mittens, had almost lost their feeling. To add to her woes, there had been no sign, amongst all the hurrying people passing, and sometimes entering, Newgate, of any young woman who resembled her quarry, and now it was late afternoon. "I reckon her Pa's mistaken," she muttered resentfully to herself, trying to rub some sensation back into her fingers. "She won't come now."

It was at moments like these that Gin fully appreciated the debt she owed to Mistress Paradice, who had rescued her from a life that made scrubbing floors and scouring pewter seem as sweet and easy as a dream. Earlier, her mistress had made sure that Gin was warmly wrapped against the cold, with an extra pair of stockings, two more petticoats than usual, and a woollen shift which made the girl grumble, complaining that it itched. "And it ain't lice, ma'am, I ain't got no more lice since Hannah started making me *wash*." She delivered the final word in tones of deepest contempt.

"I don't care, Jane, so long as it keeps you from catching your death of cold," Polly had told her, without sympathy. "And then who could keep watch for us? Now off you go, for if you delay much longer it will be dark before you reach Newgate."

Muttering, Gin had tramped off eastwards, into the heart of the city. She had taken notice of the people she passed in the streets, hoping that a lucky chance would deliver Mary Jessop to her on a plate, but without success. It was snowing yet again, and the flakes, spun through the air by a wickedly sharp wind, were blowing straight into her face, so she kept her head down and wished heartily that it was the end of the day and she was on her way home.

Because of the weather, the street outside Newgate was emptier than usual: most of the loiterers had decided to stay indoors, and everyone else was bustling along, eager to reach their destinations. She found an inconspicuous place to lurk, some yards from the prison gate, but from where she could keep watch. Eventually the snow stopped and the sun came out, but its rays were feeble and failed to warm her, although she stood full in their light. When hunger pangs began, she bought a hot pie from a baker over the way. It warmed her hands for a little, and filled her belly. A man propositioned her, offering a way of earning far more than a maidservant's paltry wages, and very pleasant polite gentlemen to do the business with her. Gin declined his suggestions in no uncertain terms, and her screams of abuse followed him down the street, to the amusement of other passers-by.

She turned back and saw Mary Jessop coming towards her.

There was no doubt of it. Gin had seen her clearly enough in Bath, and the memory was still vivid. The dark hair, blue eyes and heart-shaped face were the same, and so, unfortunately, was the sulky, wilful mouth. She was wearing a fine black velvet mantle, with the fur-lined hood thrown back to reveal her pale, beautiful features, and she was alone, although more than one man turned to watch her as she passed. Gin realised that she must be staring too, and hastily turned her face away.

She need not have feared: it was just as her mistress had predicted, and Mary Jessop's blank gaze swept right over her without a hint of recognition. To Gin's sharp eyes, she looked preoccupied and apprehensive, a frown of tension between her neatly plucked brows. She was carrying a basket under the mantle, covered with a cloth, and her hooped skirts almost brushed against Gin's drooping garments as she passed, so close the maid could have put out a hand to touch her. She walked right up to the prison gate, and after a brief conversation with the turnkey on duty, and an exchange of coin, she was admitted.

A vast wild energy swept over Gin, making her feet itch to dance with joy. The plan had worked. Mary Jessop was here. And now it was all up to her, to discover where she was lodging.

Eagerly she fastened her gaze upon the lowering gate, but the afternoon wore on, her legs were aching and her feet numb with cold, and no-one left the prison save for an elderly gentleman in a plum-coloured coat. Gin glanced up at the threatening sky with apprehension. By the look of the heavy clouds, it would shortly start to snow again, and she did not care to make her way home in a blizzard after nightfall. And yet she knew that Mary Jessop was still inside Newgate: she could not abandon her task, not when it was so agonisingly close to fulfilment.

"Why, it's Jane, ain't it?"

The woman's voice jerked her out of her anxious thoughts. Gin's startled gaze shot to the figure who had halted in front of her, and was looking her up and down with an all-too-familiar expression of languid amusement on her lightly painted face. "I declare, I never thought to see one of Poll's maids loitering hereabouts," said Jenny Garnet, raising one interrogative eyebrow. "Does she know that you're out alone in this weather?"

"Course she does, ma'am," said Gin. "I does what I'm told."

"And she told you to come here – of all places?" Jenny's tone was frankly incredulous. "When her lover is inside those very walls?"

"He ain't her lover no more," said Gin, annoyed. Why, oh why, had the wretched mort come along now? Why couldn't she have left well alone? And Jenny Garnet was incapable of keeping a secret: Mistress Paradice had once made a joke of it, saying that a single word in her friend's ear was better than pasting bills all over town.

"So she says." Jenny's voice conveyed considerable scepticism. "And why are you here, then, Jane? Part of some plot to help him escape?"

To Gin's absolute horror, she saw the door of the prison swing slowly open. Rooted to her small patch of cobbles, she prayed desperately that it would be another elderly gentleman in a plum coat, the King of France, even Old Nick himself - anyone, in fact, rather than Sam's wayward daughter.

Her prayer was not granted. Miss Jessop, hugging her cloak close around her, emerged blinking into the limited light of the winter afternoon, glanced around, and then made her way purposefully past them. Something had to be done, and done fast. "Begging your pardon, ma'am, but I got to go somewhere," Gin said, and without waiting for a response, dived up the street in frantic pursuit.

Unfortunately, black cloaks were very common on the streets of London, and Mary Jessop was not particularly tall. Gin fixed her eyes on one promising hooded head, glimpsed past a sedan chair, and only realised her mistake when the stout middle-aged matron turned down Seacoal Lane. She looked wildly round the crowded street, filled with people anxious to make their way home before darkness and snow fell together, and to her utter relief saw the real Mary Jessop almost immediately, gazing eagerly at the hats on display in the window of a milliner's shop. Gin loitered in a doorway, watching her from a safe distance, until Sam's daughter turned away and walked on up Snow Hill towards Holborn Bridge.

It was obvious that Miss Jessop was unfamiliar with the streets, for she kept looking about her, as if to fix her eye on significant landmarks. Gin allowed herself a contemptuous snort. The girl was an obvious country bumpkin, ripe for the plucking to those who could read the signs. At the very least, she would surely have her pocket picked sooner or later. Gin just hoped that it would happen at some other time. For now, she was longing for the warmth of the coffee-house and the chance to melt her toes by the kitchen hearth.

She had assumed that Mary would have taken lodgings close to Newgate, but unfortunately it soon became clear that this was not the case. Sometimes Gin had to break into a trot to keep up, but ensured that the other girl was still in view, despite the passing hackneys, wagons and sedans. At last, worried about losing her, she crossed the road in her turn and hurried on, her eyes straining through the gathering gloom, and praying that Miss Jessop would reach her destination before much longer.

But they came to the bustle and confusion of Fleet Street, where Gin nearly lost her quarry behind two stage coaches rumbling up from the country with mud and snow on their wheels. Luckily, she caught a glimpse of the familiar back crossing to the other side, and hurried after it. Please God, her weary feet cried, let this be over soon!

The area to the south side of Fleet Street around Bridewell was a part of London which Gin knew particularly well. With some trepidation, she kept close behind, for she had no intention of losing Mary at the last moment, after all this trouble and effort. It was fortunate that she did, for the turn came so suddenly that she almost missed the quick swish of the other girl's cloak, the paler flash of her skirts in the glow from a lantern just lit by a conscientious householder who was not too careful of the price of candles. With a muttered curse and a sinking heart, Gin followed reluctantly: for she knew the evil reputation of this narrow lane, too close to Alsatia to be respectable.

To her relief, Mary Jessop stopped only a few doors down, knocked, and was admitted after a brief pause. Gin waited only to fix the exact location in her mind, before beating a very hasty retreat. She had rather venture into the slums of St Giles than linger here a moment longer than was necessary.

Triumph gave her aching muscles new and joyous life. She ran back towards Fleet Street, dodging passers-by. Then it was not far to Temple Bar and the Strand, a dash through the Piazza, and she arrived panting but jubilant at the Paradise coffee-house. In her haste, she almost collided with a stout gentleman also entering the doorway, and it was only when he exclaimed, and put out a hand to steady her, that she realised that she had nearly run into Mr. Jessop himself.

"Why, Gin, my dear, what's the hurry?" he asked kindly. "Has something happened? Is someone pursuing you?"

"Oh, Mr. Jessop, sir!" Gin gasped, fighting for the breath to pass on her news. "I've found her! I followed her and I found where she lives!"

Hannah had lit the lamp outside the door: it showed her his face, suddenly ablaze with joy and relief. "Is that really so? Are you *sure* of it, Gin?"

"I seen her with my own eyes, sir, just now going into a house in Salisbury Court," Gin said. She paused to take in some much-needed air, and added, "That's just off Fleet Street, Mr. Jessop, near to Bridewell."

"Well, bless my soul, Gin, and you followed her all the way from Newgate?" At the girl's proud, happy nod, he took her arm and opened the door. "At the very least, you've earned a rest and a cup of chocolate to warm yourself, and Mistress Paradice must hear of this, it will greatly gladden her heart. I wonder, is she in the coffee house, or upstairs?"

But Hannah was presiding behind the bar, and at Sam's entrance she pointed upstairs, with a significant look. There were a few customers clustered round a young man reciting a flowery ode to his rapt audience. No-one noticed them, and Sam and Gin went out and climbed the stairs to the parlour.

Polly was indeed there, but she was not alone: for, draped languorously over the day bed, wearing her favourite crimson gown, was Jenny Garnet.

CHAPTER TWENTY

'Deluded Maids'

"Ah, Jane." Polly smiled at her. "Mrs. Garnet has been telling me that she saw you earlier, lurking outside Newgate, and that you ran off when she asked you to explain yourself. Surely she must be mistaken?"

In the few wild heartbeats since Sam had opened the door, Gin's mind had been working frantically. Jenny Garnet couldn't keep her mouth closed, not if she was offered a winning lottery ticket, and she was a Jack, well known for it. She obviously thought that Gin was part of some plot to help Sinclair escape, but nothing could be further from the truth. *The last thing Madam needs,* Gin thought grimly, *is that good-for-nothing Lazy Lawrence back on her doorstep, threatening and abusing her.* Her single meeting with Robbie had not made a favourable impression.

But that was by the by – for now, the most important matter was how to deflect Jenny Garnet, who was looking at Sam with great interest. And she must do it without revealing the real reason why she had been outside Newgate. But what to say instead?

Inspiration struck with blessed swiftness. Gin said brightly, "I was on my way to meet Mr. Jessop. Madam asked me to look out for him and show him the way back here, because he ain't never been to the Paradise before." She glanced up at Sam, praying that he would be quick enough to back her up. A look of bewilderment now would be disastrous.

"That is so," Sam said, smiling. "And very glad of her help I was too, for I am not familiar with this part of town."

"Are you not?" Jenny drawled, a slender hand spread

elegantly over her scarf-clad bosom, the better to display her collection of rings. "But pray present your friend, Poll – your latest beau, I collect?"

Oh my lord, thought Gin, alarmed, *Madam won't like that.* She glanced anxiously at Polly, but to her surprise her mistress was still smiling and calm. She said mildly, "Why, Jen, whatever makes you think such a thing? Mr. Jessop is an old friend come to London on business."

The formal introductions were made, courtesies were exchanged, and then Jenny rose, saying that she must go, or her chairmen would grow tired of waiting.

"Jane will escort you downstairs," said Polly, and with a sinking heart Gin did as she was told, though she knew what would happen.

She was right. Halfway down the stairs, Mrs. Garnet put a hand on her shoulder. "Come, child, you and Poll may think you can fool me, but I know better. You're all in it together, the pair of you and Mr. Jessop, whoever he may be." In the dim light of the candles in their sconces above their heads, her eyes gleamed avidly. "You're planning to spring Sinclair from prison, aren't you? Don't be mum, girl, you can tell me, I'm your friend."

Now, at least, Gin could be honest with a clear conscience. She said at once, "We ain't planning no such thing, ma'am, I can tell you that for certain. He asked Madam to help him get out and she said no. She don't want nothing more to do with him, Mrs. Garnet, because he wouldn't approve of what she's doing with the coffee-house and all."

"I can imagine he would not," said Jenny, sounding disappointed. "Well, I had best go before my chairmen demand another sixpence for their wait. I hope Mr. Jessop rewarded you well for braving such a cold day, Jane?"

"Oh, yes, ma'am," Gin said glibly. "He gave me a whole

shilling."

"Well, spend it wisely," Jenny told her, and went out to her chair, which, because of the limited space in the hallway, had had to wait outside in the snow. Gin saw it borne off towards Cooks Court near the Playhouse, where Mrs. Garnet lodged, and then went back up the stairs two at a time, to give her mistress and Mr. Jessop her news of Mary.

Polly and Sam made a most gratifying and attentive audience. Gin, gazing at their rapt expressions, felt for the first time the power that it was possible to wield simply by telling a story, whether true or fanciful. She embroidered the details – "A coach nearly got me crossing Fleet Street, knocked me in the gutter and a wagon would've done for me if I hadn't rolled out the way *just* in time!" – and kept the suspense running at a feverish height until her breathless, almost whispered description of the sinister alleys by Salisbury Court, with their ominous noises and lurking, creeping shadows.

"And she is there? My dear Mary is lodging *there*, in that den of robbers and murderers?" Sam said at last. He had turned quite pale, and his plump cheeks seemed to have sagged inward, hanging off the bones beneath. "We must rescue her at once!"

"I suspect that Gin is exaggerating a trifle," said Polly, with a shrewd glance at her discomfited maid. "Salisbury Court is not such a desperate location as she has made it sound."

"Thank the good Lord for that," Sam said, with a look of relief.

"However, Mary might not want to be rescued," Polly went on. "She has obviously come to London of her own free will, and I suspect that if we turn up on her doorstep tomorrow morning, eager to save her from Sinclair's clutches, she will laugh in our faces and tell us to go away."

"But that is a chance I must take," said Sam. "I have not gone through all this agony again, to falter at the final obstacle. And I think it is best if I go alone. She will not feel so intimidated if there is only one voice raised against her."

"You'll need me, though, won't you, sir," Gin pointed out. "You don't know where Salisbury Court is, nor the house neither, and if you ask people to point it out they'll make any number of excuses. I knows the door what she went in, and I can take you there." She glared belligerently at him, her lower lip stuck out. "Though of course I ain't forcing you, Mr Jessop. You can go alone and get set upon, if you really want, I ain't going to stop you."

"Yes, go you must," said Polly. "And I have promised to sing for my customers tomorrow morning, on pain of breaking many hearts if I do not, so I shall happily lend you Gin, should you wish to take advantage of her most generous offer. And Will Evans too, with a good stout cudgel, in case of mishap."

* * *

And so it came to pass that the following morning, bright and early before the clocks had struck nine, Sam presented himself at the Paradise coffee-house, partook of a quick warming cup (it was snowing again) and then set off for Fleet Street with Gin, well wrapped in her oversized cloak, hopping with excited self-importance at his side, and the burly Will, drab and mutely menacing, keeping a few discreet paces behind. By now, Sam was tolerably familiar with the main streets, and he made his way confidently across St. Paul's churchyard, down Henrietta Street, and turned left along Bedford Street, heading for the Strand. On the other side of Chandos Street, the thoroughfare narrowed, and Gin said suddenly, "That's where Dark lives, in Half Moon Street. That house there, with the blue door."

"Indeed," said Sam, looking at the place with interest. The windows were grimy with dust and soot, and the paint was peeling sadly. Gin glanced up at the attic windows, where Dark's studio was, but all the shutters were closed. She said sadly, "He and Madam had a terrible quarrel and now they ain't speaking."

"So I understand. Well, Gin, these things happen, and sometimes they cannot be put right, however much we may wish it otherwise."

"But you don't think that way, sir," said Gin, as they reached the junction with the Strand. "Or you wouldn't keep chasing after that silly mort of yours."

"That's different." Sam stood poised behind the posts, glancing to left and right, waiting for a gap in the traffic, which was as thick and urgent as if the city were not held tight in the fist of winter. "She is my daughter, and very young – too young to know what a terrible mistake she is making, and she will have the rest of her life in which to regret it most bitterly, if I do not succeed in saving her from herself. But Dark and Mrs. Paradice are fully adult, and know their own minds, and it is not our business to meddle in their private affairs." He smiled down at Gin. "Come, do not look so anxious."

"Can't help it, Mr. Jessop, not when you're trying to cross and there ain't no need yet. It's better to wait till we get near Temple Bar, there's always a crowd stuck on either side and we can dodge through the traffic."

With her guidance, they successfully negotiated the busy street further along, and walked eastwards. Gin's heart was hammering nervously, and her back felt sweaty, despite the chilly air. She had been so proud of her achievement in finding where Mary Jessop lived: it had been worth the long cold wait, and the blisters, and the aching feet that were still tingling now. But what if Sam's daughter proved to be well guarded by a gang of bully boys armed with clubs? Or, even worse, had realised that she had been followed, and disappeared again? So much could go wrong. And the most likely outcome, Miss Jessop telling her father to leave her alone and go away, in no uncertain terms, would be devastating to Sam. He loved his daughter dearly, and he was still unable to accept her rejection.

At last they came to Salisbury Court. The alley was lined with tall, skinny houses, each with a door giving directly onto the street. Here and there, fresh paint and clean windows showed where a respectable household lived, but most inhabitants seemed to have abandoned the struggle against grime and poverty. The sewer ran down the middle of the roadway, choked with ice and snow and anonymous lumps of filth, and even in this freezing weather the stench was considerable.

"That one there," Gin said, pointing at the house which Mary Jessop had entered. In daylight, it looked a little more prosperous than the dirty brickwork and broken windows on either side, and a sign, depicting a crudely-drawn pair of stays, swung from the frontage, just above head height.

Staymakers were notorious pimps and procurers. Gin, glancing up at Sam's expectant yet anxious face, wondered if he realised this, and hoped he did not. She said urgently, "Begging your pardon, sir, but I don't reckon I ought to go in with you. If she scarpers I'm the only one of us what can follow her without her knowing me."

"A very good idea, Gin," said Sam. "Will you wait there for me, on the corner with Fleet Street? And here's sixpence to buy yourself a hot pie while I'm gone."

"Thank you very much, Mr. Jessop, sir," said Gin, delighted. It might prove to be a long wait, for Mary would not have come so far, and risked so much, to surrender tamely at her father's first appearance on her doorstep. Such meekness and obedience was not at all in her character.

She watched as Sam, with Will Evans as his escort, walked up to the house and hammered on the door. After a pause, it opened. A brief discussion followed, money seemed to change hands, and then Sam vanished within, while Evans took up a position outside.

They had passed a pastry-cook's shop a few minutes ago, and the memory of that aroma still lingered somewhere in Gin's nostrils. She wished she could be a spider on the ceiling, to watch and listen when Sam encountered his runaway daughter again: but in the absence of magical powers, she would settle for a hot pie. Humming tunelessly, she retraced her steps to the cookshop, and hoped, but without much conviction, that Mr. Jessop would succeed in persuading Mary to come home.

* * *

Sam, who knew Mary better than anyone, did not have very much confidence in his powers of persuasion either, but he was here, and he must try his best. And the presence of Evans, solid and silent at his back, was enormously reassuring. At least he would not be robbed or beaten, even if he was about to be bitterly humiliated by his own daughter.

The door was opened by a young boy, more or less Gin's age, with a round, freckled face. He was quite well dressed, in a neat dark brown coat and breeches. In answer to Sam's query, he looked blank. "There ain't no Miss Jessop here, sir - are you sure this is the house you want?"

"I believe so," said Sam, his heart sinking. Could Gin have erred? Although she had been absolutely certain that this was the place, in the dim evening light she might easily have mistaken it for one of its neighbours. "Or ... perhaps she is going under another name. She is a young lady, a little taller than you, with dark brown hair and blue eyes, come to town about two weeks ago. Have you anyone lodging with you who fits that description?"

The boy had begun to look worried, his guileless face screwed up into a frown. "Me ma's out measuring," he said anxiously. "I should ask her before I let you in."

"You don't need to ask her anything, surely," said Sam, smiling now, for the boy's behaviour indicated clearly that this was indeed the right house. "You must know – either my daughter is lodging here, or she is not."

"Your daughter, sir? You are Mrs. Sinclair's father?"

"If that is what she is calling herself, yes, I am, and I have come to take her home to the man who hopes to marry her."

"But I think she's already married," the boy blurted. "Ma said she was married to a poor Jack in Newgate."

Sam closed his eyes briefly at the thought. Could it be true? Had she somehow found an unscrupulous parson? Was it really possible that she might be Sinclair's wife? He did not know enough about the law to be certain. He said, "Perhaps there has been some mistake. But whatever has happened, I wish to see her and speak with her. I mean her no harm, and I give you my word that I will make no attempt to force her to come away with me."

The boy's eyes went eloquently to Evans, standing squarely behind Sam with his thick arms folded round his cudgel. He said doubtfully, "Then what's *he* doing here, then, sir?"

"I was advised to bring him along to ensure my own safety," Sam said. "If it would make you happier, he can wait outside."

Inside the house, someone called. The boy glanced back over his shoulder and then turned again to Sam. "Me Da wants me. You can come in if *he* stays out."

"Thank you very much indeed," said Sam, smiling with relief. He fumbled in his pocket and drew out a shilling. "Here you are – some recompense for you. You're right to be cautious in these troubled times."

"Thank you, sir!" the child cried, taking the coin with a delighted grin. "Come in, come in, and I'll show you up to her room."

Sam's generosity had made the boy loquacious: as he climbed, he chattered about his Da, who had some creeping sickness that affected his legs, so he couldn't get out, but he still made the best pair of stays in town, and his Ma made lace as well as measuring the ladies, and there were plenty of fine ladies hereabouts, and he himself worked for his Da, learning the trade, and to make ends meet his Ma took in lodgers, respectable women like Mrs. Sinclair, though some of the neighbours told nasty tales and said she was running a leaping house. If Mrs. Sinclair really was not married to her Jack in Newgate, perhaps his Ma would ask her to leave – although she got on famously with Mrs. Sinclair, they would laugh together over a cup of tea.

As he talked, he skipped up the second flight of stairs, with Sam floundering breathlessly in his wake. It appeared, unfortunately, that Mary Jessop occupied a room in the very pinnacle of the building, for the final landing had a steeply pitched roof above. By the time he reached it, he was puffing like a leaky pair of bellows, and despite the cold, his face was running with sweat.

"It's this'n here, sir," said his guide, and rapped smartly at the first of the three doors. A woman's voice sounded within, and he opened it with a flourish worthy of a highly trained footman. "A gentleman to see you, Mrs. Sinclair."

"Oh!" cried Mary's voice, high with joyful excitement,

and over the boy's shoulder Sam saw her leap up from her chair, her face brilliant. "Is he here already? But I thought that it would be tomorrow!" Then, as Sam came forward and she recognised him, the look of delight changed in an instant to angry disappointment. "Father! What in heaven's name are you doing here?"

"So he really is your Da," said the boy, who was still lingering in the doorway, obviously consumed with curiosity. At once Mary rounded on him. "You noddle, Jack, why did you let him in? You were *told* not to tell anyone that I was here!"

"I'm sorry, Mrs. Sinclair, but he said he was your father and I thought it would be all right," said the boy. "And he gave me a whole shilling," he added, beaming.

"Well, you're a greedy little fool and I'll tell your mother! Now get out before I throw you out!"

The boy fled, slamming the door behind him. "Impertinent brat!" Mary said. She strode to the window, her skirts kicking up in a bad-tempered way, looked out, and then turned back to Sam. "I don't want you here, Father, go away."

Much though he loved his daughter, Sam looked at her frowning, peevish face and thought that if she did not take care, in a few years ill nature would remove most of her loveliness. He tried to harden his heart, and said, "I am here to ask you to come home with me. I miss you dreadfully."

"Really? I'm desolate. Now get out."

"No, not until we have talked. Mary, what do you think you're doing? Staying in this place, visiting Sinclair in Newgate – "

"How do you know that?" Mary demanded furiously. "You've been *spying* on me, haven't you?"

"But you are in contact with him, are you not?"

"And what if I am? Is it a crime, to visit my true love in

prison?"

"Perhaps not," Sam acknowledged. "But it is certainly a crime if he is a rebel taken in arms, and you plan to help him escape."

With all of her truculent wilfulness, she was still very young: she flushed right up to the roots of her rich brown hair, and said in a voice that was hardly convincing, "No, I'm not!"

"Oh, Mary," Sam cried, in mingled pity and exasperation. "Why do you not forget him and come home with me? George is waiting for you – "

"That boring lump of lard? Well, he can wait forever for all I care."

"He is very fond of you, Mary, and you made no objection when marriage was suggested – indeed, you seemed to welcome it. Why do that, if you truly think he is so uninteresting?"

"That was before – " The girl broke off, and Sam finished the sentence for her. "That was before Sinclair wrote to you, asking you for help. And he still has such a hold over you, you were willing to throw away everything for a second time, to go to him. What did he offer you? He has no money, no future – "

"He *has*!" Mary cried. "When he's free he'll take me to Paris and we'll be wed and he'll fight for the King of France!"

"Is that what you want? Is it really what you want, to live in a foreign land far from all who love you – "

"*He* loves me! And I love him!" Mary drew herself up proudly. "We will be together, and that is all that matters to us!"

Sam thought of that unscrupulous, manipulative man in Newgate, happy to encourage and exploit the girl's infatuation for his own selfish ends, and felt sick. How could he make her understand that her dream was just a hopeless delusion? Even if Sinclair allowed her to accompany him to France – assuming that he did succeed in escaping, of course – he would quickly tire of her, probably in weeks rather than months, and abandon her as soon as he met another young woman who took his fancy. It was all so dreadfully predictable, but he knew that she would dismiss his fears out of hand and go trustingly, eagerly forward to her fate.

He gazed at his beloved daughter in mute, helpless despair, and she laughed. "There's nothing you can do to persuade me to come with you, Father, so you can go. You're annoying me – go on, get out of my room!"

Sam knew it was useless to protest, but he could not resist one last try. "Mary, please, you're deluding yourself, you mean nothing to him."

"That's a lie," said Mary, and her face grew suddenly triumphant. "If I mean so little to Robbie, why am I expecting his child? You're the deluded noddle, Father, not me. Now go away and don't come back – I never want to see you ever again!"

"A *child*? No, no, you can't be carrying his child, you've only been here for two weeks, how could you possibly know for sure?"

"I tell you, I am. So there it is, Father. George won't want to wait for me now, will he, if it means he'll have another man's baby foisted on him."

Sam looked at her self-satisfied face and knew that it was hopeless, but still he persisted. "Mary, I beg you, come home with me now – don't throw away your prospects of a happy future for a worthless rogue! *Please*, poppet, if you will just come home we can forget all about this – "

"Well, I don't want to forget," Mary said. "He wants me and needs me and he has told me so, he has such great things planned, you have no idea, and you can go to hell for all I care, Father, so go away and leave me in peace."

It was the most difficult thing that Sam had ever done, to leave her there armoured in her pride and her delusion. But he could not go without giving her some straw to cling to, should Sinclair prove false.

"Dear child," he said, his hand on the latch, "if you ever have need of a friend, go to Mrs Paradice's coffee-house in King Street in Covent Garden, and she will do her utmost to help you."

"*Her*?" cried Mary indignantly. "I'd *die* rather than ask *her* for anything – and in any case I won't need to, will I?"

There was nothing more he could do. He stepped heavily down the four flights of stairs, and found Evans waiting outside with Gin, her mouth greasy with the remains of the pie. When she realised that he had come away without his daughter, her exasperation spilled over.

"You ain't telling me you're going to *leave* her here! You do *know* what they say about staymakers, don't you?" Gin leapt from one foot to the other in an extremity of agitation. "An' it's usually true! You've got to go back in there an' drag her out, it don't matter what she says, just do it!"

They regained the comparative safety of Fleet Street and paused for a moment, with passers-by skirting round them. Ignoring their curious glances, Sam said forcefully, "She says she's carrying his child."

Gin hooted with derision. "And you fell for that tale? Then you're a bigger tomdoodle even than you look, Mr. Jessop!"

"Of course I believe her," said Sam indignantly, conscious of Evans just behind him. "Why should I not?"

"Because she can't know she is yet, you macaroni! Ain't you got the sense you was born with, eh? She's saying what she knows will get you to go away. And what she don't know is that if she is, it'll get *him* to go away too, once she grows fat and her bubbies drop, he'll find some other mort to swive and forget all about her, I know he will because that's what happened to my mam when she fell for me, a fine sprig he was, son of a lord so she said, but you couldn't see his heels for dust when she told him I was on the way, and Sinclair'll be just the same. She was younger'n your mort an' all, but it didn't make no difference, that's what men do, one minute they says they loves you and the next you're thrown away like piss out a jordan. So if you wants to save her it ain't no good just talking to her and going off, she won't follow you, you have to *make* her."

"I can't do that." Sam began to walk briskly towards Temple Bar. "I have never forced her to do anything."

"Gawd give me strength!" Gin cried. "Then perhaps you oughter start now. Or do you *want* to see her dead like my mam was, from grief and drink and the pox?"

"Of course I do not – but I don't believe force is the answer, it will only make her hate me."

"Then what is?" Gin demanded. "Letting her go her own way to hell? You ain't got no more backbone than a worm, Mr. Jessop!"

"I think," said Sam, after a pungent pause spent negotiating a heap of rotting refuse, "that you have overstated your case somewhat, Gin, and I suggest you keep silence rather than let your tongue run away with you again."

She kept it, though it was a considerable struggle, all the way back along the Strand, but when they turned up Half Moon Street, she said urgently, "Mr. Jessop, sir, I've got an idea."

"Oh?" Sam's tone was designed to discourage wild schemes. He was still smarting from Gin's harsh words, and he felt uncomfortable, not to say humiliated, that the truth had been pointed out to him by a scrawny and disreputable servant girl.

"Shall I tell you, sir?" Without waiting for a response, Gin rattled on. "We're just coming up to Mr. Dark's house, sir, and I'm sure he'll help us. He ain't got no quarrel with *you*, Mr. Jessop."

Sam paused, ostensibly to let a chair go by. He hated to admit it, but once more the child was right. And despite his overwhelming concern for Mary's plight, he might have the chance, if occasion allowed, to do something to mend matters between the artist and Polly. A kindly soul, Sam hated to see his friends fall out.

"Very well, Gin," he said. "Which was the house? The one with the blue door?"

"Yes, sir, and don't mind Madame Rousselle, her bark's much worse than her bite, an' anyway she ain't no more a Frenchy than what I am."

Not without some trepidation, for this was the first time he had heard of Madame Rousselle and he had no idea of her function in Dark's establishment, Sam stepped up to the shabby blue door and knocked smartly on it. After due pause, it was opened by an extremely supercilious footman in a powdered wig and with gold froggings on his bright carnation coat. "Yes?" he enquired, looking down at Sam and his rather disreputable little party.

"We wish to see Mr. Dark," said Sam.

"I regret to say, sir, that Mr. Dark is not at home."

"Don't you come the high horse with me, Jacky Simpson!" Gin said scornfully. "You didn't used to give yourself such airs and graces when you kept the door at the Hole in the Wall, did you? Now tell us straight, is he home or not? It's urgent."

"Gawd love us!" said the footman, descending with

great rapidity from his superior pose. "You're Gin, ain't you? What are you doing all dressed up like a molly, eh, lad?"

"On account of how I ain't a lad, and never have been," Gin said. "Come on, Jacky, is he in or ain't he? We ain't got the time to pussyfoot around."

"He's upstairs in his studio," said Simpson, and opened the door with something resembling a smile. "So you ain't a lad? You made a better lad than maid, I reckon."

"Why, thank 'ee for your kind words, Jacky Simpson," said Gin, with withering sarcasm. "Next time I wants a compliment, I ain't going fishing near you. I knows the way, I'll take the gentleman up."

"What's that I hear?" A cracked, harsh voice echoed in the hall as they all entered. "Aha, I see you're in your true colours at last, brat. Who found that out, eh? Not a man, I'll be bound."

An extremely ancient woman tottered out in front of them, her slight weight supported on two stout sticks. She looked Sam up and down with a malicious interest that raised the hairs on the back of his neck. "And who's this wants to see Dark? You ain't come to have your likeness taken, that's for sure."

"I do not believe that I have had the pleasure of your acquaintance, ma'am," said Sam formally.

"No, you ain't. I'm Madame Marie Rousselle, sir, mistress of a king and the darling of the London stage in my youth, though you wouldn't think it to look at me now, would you? Eh, Mr. Jessop?"

"How do you know my name?" asked Sam, startled out of politeness.

"I ain't as senile as I look, I knows how many beans make five," said Madame Rousselle, cackling. "Go on, child, take him up and much good may it do you both – he's been like a bear with a sore head for days."

Sam climbed the dark stairs, following the indomitable Gin once more. At another time, the old harridan would have intrigued him, but now the chief feeling within his ample chest was one of acute apprehension. He knew, only too well, just how unpleasant Dark at his worst could be, and Madame's description had done nothing to allay his fears. This would undoubtedly turn out to be a waste of time.

For her part, Gin was equally nervous. She had peculiarly vivid and disagreeable memories of Dark in the days of their earliest acquaintance, after his lover had betrayed him. True, the circumstances now were rather different – Polly had not been seeing a string of other men without his knowledge while protesting her undying love for him, nor had she abused him with foul words and slandered him round the town – but Gin knew just how vulnerable he was, and the blackness of the moods that could overtake him when times were bad. She imagined a trembling, unshaven wreck, sodden with Geneva and brandy, and knocked on the door of his attic studio with extreme trepidation.

To her relief, the voice bidding her enter was, although abrupt and annoyed, clearly quite sober. Gin carefully opened the door and beheld her former mentor, in his shirtsleeves and wearing the silk turban, standing before a large canvas in the centre of the long room, a sheaf of brushes in one hand and a palette of bright colours in the other. The colourman's boy, whom he sometimes borrowed to assist him at busy times, was stirring something noxious over the fire, and looking decidedly green.

Gin knew the size and shape of that canvas. "Morning, Mr. Dark," she said brightly. "Have you finished painting me yet?"

"I have, but have you finished plaguing me?" Dark put

down his palette and brushes and walked out from behind the easel. “Good morning, Sam. I did not know you were back in town.”

Then his spies must have failed him, Gin thought, but for once, wisely, kept her mouth shut. She watched, hands decorously folded, as the two men exchanged bows and eyed each other rather warily, as if they both felt they had something to hide. Then Sam said, “I did not know I would be here myself until a few days ago.”

“Ah.” Dark turned to the colourman’s boy, who had stopped stirring and was looking at the newcomers with considerable curiosity. “Eli, have you finished what you were doing?”

“Yes, Mr. Dark.”

“Then you may go. Same time tomorrow, and don’t forget to bring the paints and canvas I ordered.”

“Yes, Mr. Dark.” With a last avid glance at Sam, the boy bowed obediently and went out. They listened as his footsteps clattered loudly down the stairs and out of earshot: only when there was silence in the room, save for the cooing of a pigeon on the chimney stack above them, did Dark say, “Do I collect that your ... daughter has disappeared again?”

Sam presumed that a word, perhaps ‘wretched’ or even ‘infernal’, had been intended to fill the pause in the question. He said hesitantly, “I very much regret to say that yes, she has.”

“Don’t tell me – let me guess. She has come to London to give comfort to Sinclair in Newgate.”

“Yes. He must have summoned her when Polly refused to help him.” Sam gave Dark a shrewd glance. “I understand that you and she have quarrelled over this.”

“Not precisely. Doubtless she has told you her side of the tale, suitably abbreviated. I have no intention of favouring you with mine, since it is none of your business."

"As you wish." Sam paused, wondering how best to proceed. Dark's manner, although not yet hostile, was markedly cool. He added, "Through the good work and keen eyes of Gin here, we have managed to track Mary down."

"But she refuses to desert her lover in his hour of need? And so, desperate for assistance, you have called on me," said Dark. "But what do you imagine I can do? If she has failed to yield to your persuasive powers as a father, she is unlikely to listen to me unless I employ some form of coercion – and my rack and thumbscrews are rusty from lack of use these days."

Sam began to think that this was all essentially futile. Dark was right: if Mary remained obdurate, anything short of force would be useless. And despite the child's urgings, he would not use any kind of violence on his daughter, for if he did, she would surely despise him forever. He shook his head sadly. "I am sorry to have troubled you, Dark – I knew this would be a waste of time."

Gin spoke up suddenly. "No, it ain't. What if she's planning to get him out of Newgate, eh? You must know something about that, you was in there too, spying on them!" She then put her hands over her mouth and a great rush of scarlet washed over her face.

"Dear Gin, when will you learn not to let your tongue run away with you?"

"I'm sorry, Mr. Dark, very sorry, I won't let it happen again!" Gin gulped, her wide eyes fixed on his stern face.

"You might not live long enough to have the opportunity."

"Wait," Sam said, his heart thudding. "You were in *Newgate*, Dark? As a prisoner?"

"No, he was informing on 'em," said Gin, who had

decided to be hanged for a sheep as well as for a lamb. "Madam and I saw him there when we was visiting Sinclair. That's why you fell out, ain't it? You thought she was going back to being his lover, and giving him help, an' so you got on your high horse and called her a whore, and of course she didn't like that one bit. Gawd love us," said Gin in exasperation, "ain't neither of you got the sense you was born with? You're both on the same side if you'd only look at it straight, an' you should know better than to trust anything that good-for-nothing Jack says. Anyway, that's all gone and passed, what are we going to do now? Because I reckon that Miss Jessop is planning to spring him out."

"Surely that would be very difficult," Sam said, since Dark seemed to be temporarily bereft of speech.

"Nah, course not, sir, happens all the time. He wanted Madam to bring him women's clothes and dress him up in them, and she couldn't help but laugh, and he was *furious*, but it'd make more sense if he slipped the turnkey a few guineas to turn a blind eye. Did your mort have money with her, Mr. Jessop?"

"My mort? You mean Mary? Very little, although she took some of her jewellery, including several valuable rings she had from her grandmother."

"The people she's lodging with will have told her where to fence them, for sure." Gin spoke with complete authority: she was, after all, an expert in the dubious practices of London's lower forms of life. "You'd best get Sinclair clapped in irons, then, Mr. Dark, because it don't look like he'll be in Newgate much longer. Then it'll be away over the sea to his Pretender, and Miss Jessop with him, and we'll never see either of 'em again."

"Before we continue," said Sam, looking at Dark as if he had crawled out from under a stone, "is what she says true? Were you in Newgate as an informer?"

"I was, for a short while. I did not discover very much. A London Jacobite called Thomas Wright was brought in, and he recognised me – we were schoolfellows."

"So you had to scarper quick before they knifed you in your bed," Gin muttered.

Sam shook his head in bewilderment. "Whose orders do you follow, Dark? Who controls you? Who do you report to?"

"He ain't going to tell you that," said Gin scornfully. "It'd be more than his life was worth."

"Dear God. And my sweet, innocent Mary is mixed up in all this."

"She ain't so sweet and innocent now, eh, sir?" Gin turned from Sam and fixed Dark with a beady eye. "So what are you going to do? Sit back and let 'em get on with it? Or have Sinclair put in irons and double the guard?"

Dark took a deep breath. He looked from Gin to Sam and back again, the harsh lines between nose and mouth particularly pronounced. Above their heads, the single cooing pigeon had been joined by another, providing a soft and subtle harmony. At last he said, "I need to have the word of you both that you will not talk of this to anyone else."

"Not even Mrs. Paradice?" asked Gin. "She knows what you've been up to as well as we do."

"If you must – but no further. Or you will find yourself in Bridewell, Gin, and no comfort from anyone." He held her gaze with his own until she flushed and looked down at the floor. "Yes, I will go to the Governor of Newgate and tell him what is afoot. From the information I gleaned when I was in there, it is not only Sinclair who plans to escape – they are hoping to flee *en masse*. Up until recently, many of them were enjoying prison life too much, but the seven lords taken in rebellion are impeached today, so that is bound to remind the prisoners that their own trials will probably follow. Yes, I think they may well be planning to escape very soon. In fact I hope to find that when I visit the Governor, he will have the matter already in hand."

"I very much hope so too," Sam said. He remembered what Mary had said in her fury, and added, "My daughter obviously knows something. She talked about the great things he had planned. Presumably she meant the escape."

"Perhaps – although I would put nothing past Sinclair. He is hot for the Pretender, and very eager to make his mark. Certainly leading his comrades out of Newgate, under the noses of the Governor and the turnkeys, would fit that bill – or he may have something else hidden up his sleeve. What are you doing, Gin?"

The girl, taking advantage of his attention being temporarily directed elsewhere, had darted round behind him, to the other side of the easel. She said triumphantly, "I thought so! You never put it aside like you said you had!"

For a moment Dark seemed nonplussed: then, with a return to his cool manner, he said, "I decided that it would be a waste of all that effort, if I did nothing more to it."

Gin was studying the picture. "It ain't half bad," she said at last, her head on one side and her eyes bright. "You've caught Madam to a tee – and that haughty look on Hannah's face. How did you finish it without any of us to sit for you, eh?"

"Don't be impertinent, brat. Fortunately, I have an excellent memory – although you may find that your counterfeit flatters you somewhat."

Intensely curious, Sam walked over to inspect the painting. He knew little about such things, but he was struck at once by the vivid likenesses set out on the flat canvas, looking so real that he was tempted to speak to them. Polly Paradice sat at the round table, lifting a blue and white dish of coffee to her lips: she was gazing out at the spectator, and her brilliant sapphire eyes sparkled with life and mischief. He had seen that expression so often, and could imagine only too well what she might be about to say. Sitting beside her, Hannah Rose was pouring another cup from a silver pot, her face stern with concentration. Behind them hovered Gin with a tray, her wayward brown hair escaping from her cap and her striped calico gown slightly too large for her. Dark's magic had captured one brief moment in the lives of these three people: captured it, so that it was recorded for all time. Sam had seen his swift sketches, but this was an entirely and breathtakingly different order of skill.

"Dear God," he said, his voice hushed in awe. "This is wonderful – I had no idea you were such a consummate artist. I'm sure Kneller could not do so well."

"Don't you dare mention Kneller in the same breath, you noddle," said Gin indignantly. "He's a two guinea dauber beside Mr. Dark."

"Your support for me is very touching," Dark said, and for the first time a smile deepened the lines around his mouth. "But alas, if I could command but a small fraction of the prices Sir Godfrey charges, I would be a very wealthy man. As indeed he is."

"You love her, don't you," said Gin suddenly. Her pointed, pimply chin swivelled belligerently in Dark's direction. "You couldn't paint her like that if you didn't. So why aren't you over there now, saying you're sorry and treating her right? If you'd asked me, I could've *told* you she didn't help Sinclair, nor climb into his bed neither, so whatever he said, he was lying. Take her the painting and tell her the truth."

"It's none of your business, is it?" said Dark, but there was warmth in his voice now. "I don't need you to tell me the rules of polite and courteous behaviour, Gin."

"Well, *someone* oughter."

"Someone who *knows* the rules of polite behaviour. If I were you, child, I would make myself scarce immediately, before I forget them."

Although no other words were spoken, they seemed to understand each other well enough, for Gin gave her unpractised duck of a curtsey, flashed an insolent joyful grin at the two men, and fled from the studio.

It was curious, Sam thought, how abruptly the air had lightened within the long bright room. He said, "She is an oddity, that child, but she has a good heart."

"And she means well, but that does not always mean that matters will end well."

"Did she speak the truth? About your feelings for Polly?"

Dark turned to look at the woman in the painting, the perfect counterfeit save that she did not live, or breathe, or provoke disturbing emotions. He said at last, his voice suddenly rough, "*'What is love? 'Tis not hereafter, Present mirth hath present laughter.'* I do not know, Sam. I only know that she is the most exasperating wilful pig-headed and exquisitely beautiful woman in all Christendom and beyond – and that she should not matter so much."

"But she does."

"Yes," Dark said softly. "Yes, she does. And I do not know how to put it right, for the last time we met, we both swore never to see each other again. And in any case, I have no idea of her true feelings for me. She is adept at hiding them behind mischief and laughter." He sighed, still staring at the portrait. "Sinclair boasted to me that they had shared a bed in Newgate, and to my everlasting shame, I believed him, and took her to task for it. If I had paused to think, instead of being blinded by jealousy, I would have realised that he was lying."

"You will find, were you to seek her out, that she deeply regrets your quarrel." Sam paused, and then added, "I will be your go-between if you like. Nothing would please me more than to see the pair of you reach an understanding."

"That is very kind of you, Sam. Gin is not the only one with a good heart." Dark smiled at him suddenly. "Now, if you will excuse me, I have much to do. Not only must I deliver two hundred skyrockets to Mr. Baker's warehouse in Lambeth, for the celebrations of Prince Frederick's birthday tomorrow, I must go to Newgate and do my best to persuade Governor Pitt that Sinclair is plotting escape, without telling him why I suspect it, or mentioning the part your daughter is probably playing. Is it at all possible, do you think? Or are we completely wasting our time?"

"Alas," Sam said, with an unhappy smile, "I fear only time will tell."

CHAPTER TWENTY-ONE

'Pent round with Perils'

Dark was of course acquainted with the Governor of Newgate, for it was by his leave that he had been placed inside the gaol as a pretended prisoner. Acquaintance, however, did not mean that he was friendly with the man: far from it, for he found him peculiarly repellent. Pitt was short, but excessively corpulent, and although he was not old, the skin of his face already bore the tell-tale puffiness, blotches and broken veins of one who is overly fond of the brandy bottle. Newgate rumour stated that he had paid between one and five thousand pounds (the amount varying wildly according to the speaker) for his privileged position, and he had been recouping his outlay ever since with a venal rapacity that was probably unmatched anywhere in London, or beyond. Newgate rumour had also informed Dark, more privily, that Pitt was suspected of being more than half a Jacobite, and certainly the prisoners in his care were allowed an extraordinary amount of licence, even by the gaol's normally lax standards. He listened to Dark's account of escape plans with barely concealed boredom, and his eyes kept straying to the squat green glass bottle on the side table, the contents of which he had failed to offer to his guest.

"You've said all this before," he complained, when Dark had finished. "They're all talk and no action, these Jacks, it's all of a piece with their fighting. Fill 'em with enough wine and they'll produce a string of wild notions to make your blood run cold, but will they carry 'em out? Not on your life!" He sat back, his hands clasped over his ample belly, and gave the other man a remarkably self-satisfied smirk.

"At least clap Sinclair in irons," said Dark, keeping grim hold on his temper. "He is one of the boldest, and he's managed to obtain help from outside. Also, it has come to my notice that he may be planning some particularly outrageous and daring exploit when he obtains his freedom."

"Most unlikely," Pitt said. "They've no more thought in their heads than how best to enjoy the largesse that has been showered on them by misguided sympathisers. That's my stratagem, Dark – make their lives so comfortable that they'll have no thought of escape."

"They will have, now that the seven lords are being impeached. The prospect of execution, however distant, tends to concentrate a man's mind wonderfully."

"Pah!" said Pitt. "Hogwash and flummery. I assure you, there is no danger – no danger whatsoever. I am a busy man and cannot spare the time to deal in wild stories and moonshine, so I'll bid you good day, sir."

Fortunately, the Governor's house was separate from the main part of the prison, with an entrance that gave directly onto the street outside, so Dark had no chance of encountering any of the men with whom he had briefly been incarcerated. He was certain that Thomas Wright had recognised him, even though they had merely glimpsed each other across the Press Yard. By now, every one of the Jacobite prisoners would know his real name, and the reason for his presence amongst them. He stood by the arched gate for a moment, deep in thought, and then set off at a brisk walk away from the prison.

* * *

At approximately the same time, Mary Jessop was making herself ready for her next visit to Newgate. She put the most important items at the bottom of her large straw basket, and on top of these she placed the more innocent things which her lover had requested: a fresh shirt, some soap and a store of pipes and tobacco. She made sure that the coins heavy in her pocket were out of reach of any frisker or kiddy-nipper, as Mrs. Maynard, her landlady, had advised. Then, nervously but full of hope, she made her way down the stairs with her shilling clutched tight in her hand, to hail a hackney in Fleet Street.

There were none to be had, however, so with her hood well over her face to shield her perfect complexion, she walked to St. Paul's. Really, she thought, she was doing remarkably well, considering that she had not been in London above two weeks. True, she had had a great deal of help from Sinclair, who had given her the name of a friendly family with whom she could lodge. The Maynards were not Papists, but they were passionately attached to the Jacobite cause, and although they lived in a poor part of town, they had welcomed her most warmly, and supplied her with enough money to make her life comfortable. She had felt lost and alone at first, but now she knew her way to Newgate as if she had been born here, she thought with satisfaction. A country bumpkin no longer!

She found a hackney in Ludgate Hill which took her there in comparative comfort, it having leather seats so new that the aroma of fresh tanned hide overpowered any other smells. And as she had done so often, paid over another shilling to the gatekeeper and entered the glowering walls of the prison where her lover was held. The grimness of her surroundings, the smell and the cold sweating walls, the lascivious looks and suggestive comments of the inmates did not affect her in the slightest: her heart was light and glad, for she went to meet Robbie Sinclair, and nothing else in her life mattered.

By now, his comrades knew her and one of them, a tall stout Londoner called Wright, who seemed now to be Robbie's particular friend, conducted her to him. It was bitterly cold outside, so the Press Yard itself was empty, but the fire in his chamber was burning brightly, heaped with expensive coals, and more in a full bucket by the hearth. There were three other men in the room, two playing cards on a bed, the third reading: at a significant look from Robbie, they grinned and left, one of them giving Mary a lingering leer on the way out. She did not notice it, for when Robbie was with her, he was the centre of her world.

But today, it seemed, she was not the centre of his. Instead of taking her in his arms and kissing her with his usual passion, he grabbed at her basket, saying in an urgent undertone, "Have ye got the suit of clothes I asked ye to bring? Where is it?"

"Yes, I've got it, and the wig," said Mary indignantly. She had taken particular care with her hair and her clothes, and she was wearing the lace he had given her in Bath, so long ago it seemed, but he had failed to notice. "Don't I even have a kiss?"

Sinclair ignored her: he tipped the contents of the basket out on the bed and seized on the light brown full-bottomed wig that she had secreted at the bottom, along with a shabby snuff-coloured coat and breeches. "Where did ye get these sorry rags? From some street seller?"

"They belong to Mr. Maynard," said Mary, her lower lip pushed out in a way that her father would have recognised with a sigh. "You said to find some plain ordinary clothes that wouldn't make the gatekeeper notice you, and I did."

"Well, I suppose they'll have to do, lassie, but they're no' what I'm used to." He held up the wig, draped over the point of one finger, and surveyed it with distaste. "There'll be lice a-plenty in there, I'll be bound."

"It won't matter if there are," Mary pointed out. "You only have to wear it until you're safe out of here."

Sinclair walked over to the fire and shook the wig vigorously over it, dislodging many stray hairs, dust, and sundry other things. He took off his own headpiece, a fashionable campaign wig, sleekly powdered, and replaced it with Mary's contribution. There was no mirror, so he peered at his reflection in the barred window, moving the wig this way and that till it was settled to his satisfaction. "How does that look?"

"Very unlike yourself," said Mary, after a sulky pause. "Is that not what you wanted?"

For the first time, Sinclair seemed to notice that his young mistress was not best pleased by her reception. He smiled warmly at her. "Of course it is, lassie – of course it is! Ye've done very well, all things considered."

Not greatly mollified, Mary gave him a petulant glance. "Aren't you going to kiss me?" she demanded, with the pretty pout he had said he liked so much.

Hastily, Sinclair took her in her arms for a smacking embrace. It was plain that she would have liked much more, but he quickly disentangled himself and began taking off his coat and breeches, a handsome suit of good blue velvet with a quantity of gold lace and buttons. In silence, she packed his discarded clothes in her basket, and then watched as he donned Mr. Maynard's despised garments, which were much too loose and rather short. They were also no longer in the height of fashion, if indeed they ever had been, and therefore went well with the full-bottomed wig, a style out of favour with young bloods like Sinclair.

"If you push something down the front of your shirt, you'll fill the breeches out," Mary said at last, as her lover gazed down in dismay at the folds of cloths hanging from his waist. "That will be an even better disguise."

Sinclair gave her an eloquent look, but did as she suggested, choosing the oldest and least plump of the bolsters on the beds, and pulling the brown coat across to cover the worst of the lumps. To Mary's partisan eye, it completed the transformation. "Oh, Robbie," she breathed, "it's perfect, the gatekeeper will never recognise you – you look exactly like a fat old shopkeeper!"

As her beloved glared at her from beneath the sagging curls of the wig, she realised belatedly that it might not have been the most tactful thing to say. "But of course a very *handsome* fat old shopkeeper," she added hastily.

If anything, the glower intensified. "Did ye remember the guineas?"

"Yes, I have them here," said Mary, scrabbling around in the folds of her skirt until she found the pocket slit. She dropped the purse into his outstretched hand. "Mrs. Maynard gave them to me without question, yet I thought they were poor."

"Jamie Stuart is not," said Robbie, his fingers clenched around the precious guineas. "This is his gold."

"I still don't understand." Mary stared at her lover in puzzlement. "Why do you need guineas when you're just going back to the Maynards' house?"

Sinclair cast his eyes heavenward. "The good Lord give me strength! To bribe the gatekeeper, of course, if he should try to detain me! What did ye think I'd do with them, throw them into the Press Yard?"

"Oh, Robbie," Mary cried, taking refuge, as she usually did, in tears. She could cry very prettily, or so she had been told, and this occasion was no exception: dewdrops trembled affectingly on her long dark lashes, her soft red mouth quivered, and she gazed at him in moist reproach. "You are so hard, so cruel ... "

Usually this ploy seemed to end Robbie's moments of anger: he would look uncomfortable, mumble an apology, and take her in his arms. Such episodes were part of the currency of their association, and she had learned to rely on such wiles to manipulate any circumstance to her advantage. But not today, it seemed: Robbie merely frowned at her in obvious irritation. "Oh, quit your foolish greetin', woman, we've no time for all this nonsense! Now wipe your eyes and get ye gone."

Taken aback by the failure of her stratagem, Mary gaped at him, the false tears drying unshed on her lashes. "What?"

"I said," Robbie repeated, thrusting his face very close to hers and giving each word a hissing, vehement emphasis, "dry – your – tears – and *go*! Did ye no' hear me the first time?"

"Yes," said Mary, still bewildered, "but why the hurry?"

"Ye'd be in a hurry if ye'd been locked up in this filthy dungeon for weeks," said Sinclair. "And there's a deal for me to do, once I'm free from here. People I must see, plans to make, vengeance to take." He thrust the purse into an inner pocket of the despised coat, and crossed to the bed in the corner, which Mary knew was not his. Swiftly he fumbled below the mattress, drew out another purse very similar, and a gold watch on a chain. As she watched, astonished and appalled, he checked each of the other beds, withdrawing rings, two more purses, a necklace, and a small folded packet of papers.

"Robbie!" Mary cried in horror, as all this followed the first purse into his pocket. "For heaven's sake, what are you doing?"

"Are you still there, woman? I told ye to go, didn't I?"

"But those things belong to your *friends*," said Mary faintly.

"All's fair in love and war, lassie, and will go to the good o' the Cause." Robbie turned and gave her a look that would have fried the marrow of anyone less devoted, or deluded.

"What's wrong, sweetheart? It's a small matter late to be squeamish. And if ye don't go now I swear I'll tie ye to those bars and leave you for my *friends*."

Mary swallowed. "Very well, Robbie, but what must I do?"

"Give me strength! Ye do what ye always do, woman, ye leave as if ye'd not a care in the world and give a smile to the gatekeeper on the way out. Then ye go back to Salisbury Court and wait for me at the Maynards' house, but don't go straight there, d'ye understand? Take a chair to Holborn and walk, or a hackney to Cheapside and then a chair. That way, if anybody wants to follow ye, it'll be hard for them. Understand? Now for the last time, woman, *go*."

She was so alarmed and upset by the look on his face that she turned and fled without even wishing him good luck. All the way back through the labyrinthine prison, her heart hammered like a hundred drums and her skin under her shift was slippery with sweat, despite the cold. If they discovered that she had helped him to escape, she would be locked up in here too, with those hellcats whose screeching abuse regularly assailed the ears of every visitor to Newgate, and many of those passing in the street outside. And she knew that she would almost rather die than suffer such a fate.

She encountered one of the turnkeys in the yard, and felt that her guilt must be emblazoned on her forehead, but to her surprise and relief he did not seem to notice her nervousness. The gatekeeper spoke to her with his usual sneering jocularity, but she was a familiar figure and he let her by without question. She scurried out into the street, her basket clutched in one hand and the other holding her hood against the cold, and heard the great door creak shut behind her. She was out, and free!

At that moment, with a rare flash of insight, she understood her lover's desperate need for liberty. But surely,

surely, the gatekeeper could not possibly let him by without question? He would be bound to notice that the man in the plain snuff-coloured coat trying to leave the prison had not passed him earlier that day. He would stop him, and call the other guards, and then Robbie would be put in irons and chained to the wall until his trial, with no chance of escape and no hope of reprieve. And then his great plan, of which he had frequently hinted in such grandiose terms, the glorious design which would reap him such rich rewards from his royal master, would all come to nothing.

She could not, she could *not*, just tamely return to Salisbury Court and wait for him. She had to see for herself that he had escaped. *It's best if I do,* Mary told herself. *After all, if he is caught – and please God he will not be, but if he is, then if I have gone back to the Maynards I'll know nothing about it except that he won't come home, and I won't be able to find out what's happened to him because if I return to Newgate, I'll be arrested too ...*

The very thought turned her blood to ice. She looked around for a place where she could loiter unnoticed, and chose a shop window, conveniently displaying a variety of lace fripperies and knickknacks. She had her back to the prison gate, but it was reflected in the glass, and she would soon spot any activity.

But there was none. The wind whistled round her, and icy draughts sneaked up inside her skirts. She blew on her hands to warm them, and tucked them inside the sleeves of her mantle. If she had known it would be so cold, she would have brought her squirrel-fur muff.

Then she remembered that her squirrel-fur muff had been left behind in Oxford, discarded with the rest of her previous comfortable life. For the first time in this adventure, a sudden longing for her cosy home and the warm love of her father swept over Mary Jessop, and she suppressed a sob. She could not, could *not* go back, for she had promised Robbie to be faithful and loyal to him and his Cause. Even though what he did in the Pretender's name sometimes disturbed her: as when, just now, he had stolen the precious possessions of his comrades in adversity, men with whom he professed the bond of brotherhood.

A movement in the glass drove the uncomfortable memory right out of her head. She turned and saw her lover, looking strange in his squalid disguise, emerge from the portal of Newgate Prison and walk purposefully away from it as if he had every right to do so. Mary's heart gave a huge, joyful leap. He had done it! He was free! And once he had carried out his grand plan, they could flee together to France, safe in the warmth of King James's approval and protection. Paris! She thought of the silks and jewels she would have, the life of a great lady at Court, feted for her beauty and wit ...

Then she saw that he was walking in the wrong direction, down Newgate Street. Puzzled, she stared after him for a moment, then decided that he must have an acquaintance in that area. Robbie's network of Jacobite friends and fellow-conspirators extended all over London and beyond, so it was hardly surprising. Or perhaps he was taking his own advice, and making it difficult for any spy to follow him. Whatever the truth of it, she was relieved, for he had told her to wait for him at the Maynards' house, and she must get back there first, or he would be angry with her for disobeying him.

Glad that she had waited, glad that he had not spotted her, she skipped lightly up Snow Hill until she found a chair for hire, and hummed a happy tune all the way back to Fleet Street. She bought some dried scented leaves and petals from the apothecary opposite the turning to Salisbury Court, and a bruised little nosegay of snowdrops from a street girl, to brighten up her room in welcome. She could have asked Mrs. Maynard some food, but she had already discovered that the cookshop round the corner produced better fare, and in any case her landlady proved to be absent, having gone out to measure up a client for a new pair of stays. So Mary tidied and folded her clothes, shook the creases out of Robbie's blue suit that she had brought away from Newgate and hung it up, then made the bed, though it was hard work plumping up the bulky feather mattress without a maid to help her. The fire had gone out, so she carried kindling and coals laboriously up the three flights of stairs, lit it after several attempts, and set her little black kettle over it to boil water for tea. By this time it was almost dusk, so she sent the boy off to get some mutton chops and wine to go with the bread she had bought earlier in the day, and then settled down with bright and eager anticipation, to wait for her lover.

It grew dark, and she lit the beeswax candles she had been saving for his return. The chamber was warm now, and she made a small pot of her precious tea. The chops, keeping hot under a cloth on a pewter plate by the hearth, sent their rich savoury aroma wafting past her nostrils, and her mouth watered: she was very hungry, not having eaten all day, but she was determined to leave them until Robbie came, for he would doubtless be hungrier still.

But he did not come. Outside in the darkness of the city, church clocks struck six, then seven, then eight. When she inspected the chops, she found that they had grown dry and shrivelled in a puddle of half-congealed fat. The bread was hard now, and the candles burnt down almost to stubs. She grew at once anxious, in case he had been captured after all, and angry. Why had he not come straight to Salisbury Court? Did he not know how dangerous it was for an escaped prisoner to be roaming round the city? Why could he not think of *her* for once, when she had gone to all this trouble for him? He would not have escaped without her, he owed his freedom to her, and this was how he repaid her – by behaving, once he was at liberty, as if she did not exist.

She put the last of the coal on the fire and lay down on the bed where she had hoped he would take her, from joy and gratitude at his escape. Despite the warmth, she was shivering, and drew the shabby quilt over herself. One by one, the candles went out, the clocks struck midnight, and he did not come.

There followed a wretched, sleepless night, for the thoughts and emotions churning round in her head made any rest impossible. And still Robbie did not appear, and that sly little worm of doubt fed on her anxiety, and whispered of betrayal.

CHAPTER TWENTY TWO

'Whither wilt thou fly?'

When dawn eventually came, Mary resolved to keep to her room, afraid that he would return while she was out. But the face in her tarnished little mirror was haggard with sleeplessness and worry, and her hair was matted and tangled where she had tossed and turned in bed. She tried to drag a comb through it, a painful and ultimately futile task. Only water would help her achieve the neat sleek head that Robbie had liked to stroke, and there was no more than a little stale puddle in the bottom of the ewer. Moreover, she needed more coals, and the chamber pot was beginning to smell, nastily.

With a sigh, Mary made her way slowly downstairs with the empty ewer hooked over one arm and the foul, brimming chamber pot carried carefully with both hands. Of course, she could just have done as all the other lodgers did, and hurled the contents out of her window into the festering heaps and slicks of similar ejections, all down Salisbury Court, but she had been brought up in a household with high standards of cleanliness, and in the better part of Oxford you emptied your pot into the privy, not into the street. Even now, she could not bring herself to foul her own doorstep.

The privy in the Maynards' house was a squalid, stinking shack only loosely attached to the rear wall. Every so often the night soil collector, universally known as Tom Turdman, would come round with his buckets and make some attempt to empty it, but he had not been for several days and the stench, despite the icy weather, was enough to make her eyes water. Holding her nose, Mary poured the contents of her pot down the hole, and rinsed it with a handful of ashy snow from the yard. Then she took her battered ewer over to the well and, setting her teeth, performed the laborious movements necessary for raising a few pints of water from the dubious depths. She put the cover back on and made her way back to the house, treading very carefully on the treacherous patches of steel-grey ice too hard to scrape away from the ancient cobbles beneath. She lifted a hand to the latch and then checked as a man's voice, dearly familiar, spoke just the other side of the door. "Aye, it was easy enough. With any luck, they didna find me gone till lock-up time. Though of course I havena returned to ask if they've missed me!"

Mrs. Maynard had a loud, hearty laugh which usually cheered Mary, but for some reason she did not feel like smiling now. "I should hope not," the landlady said, her voice slightly more distant than Sinclair's. "They'd have those fine legs of yours in irons, for sure."

"They'll have to catch me first," said Robbie, and the very timbre of his voice made Mary's knees quiver. "But they willna find me – I'd die rather than return to that hell-hole!" She could imagine him so clearly, standing there tall and straight and proud, his handsome face shining with passion, and almost she lifted the latch and went running into the kitchen to greet him. But she remembered the chamber-pot in her hand, and her unkempt hair, and the fact that she was wearing her oldest and shabbiest gown, and vanity stayed her hand.

"Besides," he added, in a more confidential tone, "as ye well know, dearest Peg, I've an important duty to discharge, and I'll no' let anything, or anyone, stand in the way of it. I've waited a long time for this chance to have my revenge on Hanover, and I'll be damned if I abandon it now."

A murmur from Mrs. Maynard made him laugh contemptuously. "Oh, I'm no' bothered about that silly whining little jade! Aye, she's been useful, I'm no' denying it, but now she's a terrible millstone round my neck, especially if her da's sniffing round after her again. You'd think he'd have given her up as a bad lot, long ago."

Something frozen clenched at Mary's stomach, colder and more deadly by far than the air around her. She listened as the man who had professed to love her continued. "No, I'm sick and tired of her whining round me. 'Oh, Robbie, pay me some attention! Oh, Robbie, will ye not give me a kiss? Oh, Robbie, why do ye look at me so grimly?'" His mimicry was cruelly accurate. "I tell you, Peg, any man would look grimly if he had to put up wi' her complaint and moan all day."

Mary clung desperately to the rough wood of the doorpost, as if it were a talisman to ward off evil. This, *this* was what Robbie truly thought of her. Shame and anguish washed her face scarlet, despite the cold.

"Aye, I'll grant ye she's a pretty lass," Robbie went on, in response to a mumbled comment from Mrs. Maynard. "So she'll have no trouble finding another when I'm gone. Or ye can introduce her to your – cousin, is it? The one who keeps a nunnery off Long Acre."

The landlady's laugh was even coarser than before. "Our minds have been travelling on much the same lines! I'd thought of that myself. She's ripe for the plucking – a few weeks at Nan's country place in Kensington will restore her virginity and give her some polish, then she'll be fit to come on the Town and earn us a pretty penny."

"Well, I'll let the pair o' ye have all the profits, Peg – ye can call it payment in kind, for services to the Cause," said Robbie, and his casual callousness struck Mary to the heart. Her legs had lost all strength, and she slid silently down the rough door to rest on the icy step, her cold cheek pressed against the splintery wood, and the tears pouring down her face.

"So where will you go now?" Mrs. Maynard was asking.

"Jack Templeman – d'ye ken him? He has a door ever open for those who hate Hanover and love King James and the Pope. And as he lives in the heart o' Westminster, he has contacts close to the court, so he knows what's afoot. But don't let any of this slip to the lassie, will ye? I dinna want her turning up on Jack's doorstep and ruining our plans. Ye can tell her I've been called away on the king's business if ye like. Then, after a week or two of your kindness, when she's low and in despair, ye can suggest that she goes to your cousin." He sniggered. "The poor wee lass might even be grateful to ye."

"A truly excellent idea – Nan will pay handsomely for a pretty chit like her. Now, Robbie dear, will you have one of these pasties before you go? They're hot and fresh."

"Aye, that I will, to eat as I walk in the good free air. And my grateful thanks to ye, for all you've done for me and for the Cause. There are not so many I can trust as I can trust ye, Peg. Even in amongst my comrades in Newgate, there was a traitor – claimed he was a London Jack when all the while he was spying on us." He laughed, and it was not a pleasant sound. "He fled once he knew we'd smoked him, and as well for him he did, the craven coward, or he'd have felt my dirk in his ribs. But I tell ye this, Peg, he may think he's safe now but he'll never escape me, for I'll have my revenge on Mr. Black, as he calls himself, aye, and on Hanover too. One thing's for sure, no-one will ever forget that boy's birthday!"

There was another indistinct murmur from Mrs. Maynard, and Robbie's loud, harsh laugh. "Ye werena so squeamish before, Peg! And it's too late for second thoughts. If they catch us, I'll hang and you'll burn, and your man and your boy will beg for their bread on the streets. So ye willna breathe a word to anyone, will ye, Peg? And in particular not to that silly glaikit little hussy I was fool enough to tempt into my bed."

"How can you think I would do such a thing?" Mrs.

Maynard demanded indignantly. "You know I would die rather than betray you, Robbie. It's just that I can't help feeling sorry for his wife and children."

"Ye needna. One bang and it's all over. He could catch a fever tomorrow and linger in pain for days, and I know which end I'd rather. Now where's that pasty, Peg? I'm in sore need of something to keep out the cold."

Their voices moved away, and presently Mary heard a door slam on the other side of the house. But she was shaking so violently, from cold and terror, that she could not move. If Robbie had found her, if he ever discovered that she had eavesdropped on that dreadful conversation, then she realised that he would probably kill her without compunction.

But if Robbie must not find her, neither must Mrs. Maynard, who was obviously a comrade, perhaps even a past lover, rather than the casual acquaintance Mary had blithely assumed. She had been oblivious to so much for so long, she had deceived herself and ignored the obvious, even when it was placed under her nose, and now she felt as if the solid ground had suddenly plummeted away from beneath her feet, leaving her trembling on the brink of a terrible abyss. Far from loving her, Robbie despised her. He had abandoned her without a thought to the tender mercies of Mrs. Maynard and her cousin. Even Mary, cocooned from reality for so long, knew exactly what they planned for her. And never, never had the cosy, stifling boredom of life with her parents seemed so wonderful and so attractive.

"Home," she whimpered, cowering on the icy step. "I want to go home."

But how could she? Pride forbade her, and even now she had a few rags of it left. How could she return to her father with her tail between her legs, and beg for the mercy he would have no hesitation in granting her? She could not bear to face his loving sympathy, knowing how she had hurt and disappointed him so many times, and knowing that she did not deserve such kindness. It would have been easier to deal with a vengeful father wielding a stick, for he would administer the punishment she knew she deserved.

But there was someone to whom she could turn. The woman called Poll Paradice would surely understand how Mary felt, even if her sympathy was in short supply. She offered the hope of a refuge both from Robbie's vengeance, if he ever realised that she knew too much, and from her father's pity and forgiveness. Yes, that was where she must go, and quickly, before Mrs. Maynard guessed that something was wrong, and the reason for it. Mary knew that she could not look that duplicitous bawd in the face without revealing that she no longer trusted her landlady.

The old, childish Mary, long ago before Sinclair had so disastrously entered her life, had been a thoughtless and impulsive creature of the moment, unaccustomed to planning and deceit. Her experiences over the past few months had taught her much and now, even in this extremity of fear, she was thinking ahead. If she could leave the house with her few most precious possessions, and without encountering Mrs. Maynard, she would be safe. There was no noise from the kitchen. Slowly, finding some strength in her cramped limbs, she got to her feet and emptied the ewer, whose contents were already crusted with delicate shards of ice, heedlessly onto the ground. Then, with numbed, cautious fingers, she lifted the latch.

The warm snug kitchen beyond was blessedly, wonderfully empty. With a prayer of thankfulness, Mary scurried through it and into the hall beyond. That was empty too, though she could hear Mrs. Maynard talking to her husband in the front room where he worked. In haste she ran up the stairs, still carrying the ewer and the chamber pot, because to abandon them in the yard would have aroused suspicion. Old Joe Willis, who lodged on the second floor, was slinking down, wrapped in scarf and hat, doubtless on his way to some squalid bawdy house. Usually, in a confined space, it was difficult to avoid him and his groping, filthy hands, but today she was moving too fast to be caught, and had put a flight of stairs between them before he had even finished suggesting what they might do together when he returned.

At the door of her garret room, she paused, breathing hard, suddenly afraid that Robbie might have come up here after all, but when she opened the door at last, the bleak little chamber was just as she had left it. It took only a few minutes to gather up her best silk gown, her pearl necklace, and the remainder of the hidden store of coins that Mrs. Maynard had given her to help Robbie. She wrapped her winter cloak around her, hiding the bulging bag beneath, and hurried from the room without a backward glance.

It was only when she was standing in Fleet Street, with people and traffic flowing around her and an old beggar man shouting at her for alms, that she realised with sudden panic that she could not remember where Mrs. Paradice lived.

Almost, then, she broke. But although Mary Jessop was a wilful, spoilt and self-centred brat, at this moment of *extremis* she did not lack courage. She fought the soaring, suffocating sense of nightmare, wiped the tears from her face, and took a long, calming breath. What had her father said? She had paid him little heed at the time, she had only wanted him gone so that she could continue in her pathetic delusion, and she did not like to think of the look on his face when at last she had forced him to bid her goodbye.

A moment's frantic searching of her memory, and she had the answer. "Dear child, if you ever have need of a friend, go to Polly Paradice's coffee-house in King Street."

Now that the prospect was imminent, she did not want to. On the occasion of their only meeting, Mary had found Mrs.

Paradice and her sparkling, effortless sophistication extremely intimidating, and she clearly remembered behaving with embarrassing rudeness. Mrs. Paradice would probably show her the door or, worse, refuse even to see her. And if that happened, Mary had nowhere else to go, save home to Oxford.

Her pearls would get her home. And even as the comforting thought leapt into her head, a ragged street boy cannoned into her, knocking her off balance, whisked the bag from her hands, and vanished into an alleyway on the other side of the street, taking with him everything she possessed of any value.

There was no point whatsoever in raising a hue and cry, and in any case she had just realised, rather belatedly, that she must not draw attention to herself. What if Robbie was still close by? Or if Mrs. Maynard came out of the house on some errand? Her only hope now lay in reaching the coffee-house as quickly and unobtrusively as possible, and throwing herself on the doubtful mercy of Mrs. Paradice.

With the tears cold on her cheeks, she pulled her hood over her head to make herself as inconspicuous as possible, and tried not to panic. Her father had mentioned King Street, but London was full of King Streets. Which one was it? She had a sudden dreadful vision of trudging round the city looking for each one, growing more and more exhausted until she collapsed in the street, or until the fate described so graphically for her by Mrs. Maynard became preferable to starvation and death.

Just as she was beginning to think she would never recall it, the answer suddenly popped into her head. Covent Garden - she was sure that her father had mentioned Covent Garden. She did not know if there was a King Street in that area, but it seemed possible. And it was not very far away, just along Fleet Street and off the Strand.

With a new sense of purpose, she wrapped her cloak

tightly around her and set off briskly through the crowds, praying more urgently than she had ever prayed before, that Poll Paradice would offer her sanctuary in her most desperate hour of need.

It took longer than she had expected to reach the Piazza. She did not want to draw attention to herself by stopping to ask directions, and in any case she felt extraordinarily vulnerable, so she kept her head down and walked confidently, as if she knew exactly where she was going. Even this brisk exercise, however, could not keep out the icy blast of the north wind, whistling across the Strand from every lane and alleyway on the north side of the street, and her fingers had long since lost all feeling. In a little while, the steely sky above her began to disgorge a light scattering of fat snowflakes that swirled around the hurrying people and skittered playfully over the frozen ground as if they were also too cold to stay still. Despite the weather, Southampton Street was still full of the most desperate whores and beggars, ragged and filthy, their blue skin covered in sores, stretching out foul, crooked hands or shouting obscene suggestions to potential customers. One ancient creature, huddled in a doorway, was being searched by two scrawny children, and Mary realised with horror that the beggar – man or woman, she could not tell – had frozen to death. It was a dreadfully potent reminder of what might lie in store for her if she did not find Mrs. Paradice, and she scurried past them, too cold even to shiver, intent now only on reaching the Piazza and locating the coffee-house – *if* it was there.

When she arrived at the broad heart of Covent Garden, the snow was falling more thickly and there were very few people about. She stood under the shelter of the arches, looking round frantically, with no idea what to do next. A man came up and offered her a shilling to go down an alley with him, but she shook him off and ran out into the snow-covered square to escape him. Fortunately he did not follow her, but turned away in search of more willing prey: unfortunately, in her haste to flee, she slipped on a patch of ice and fell heavily, jarring her hip so painfully that she cried out.

Just for a moment, she was tempted to lie here in the snow and let the cold take her as it had taken the old beggar, and she began to sob. No-one cared, no-one wanted her, Robbie hated her and she wished she were dead.

* * *

Gin's day had begun well. After breaking her fast with a thick slab of yesterday's bread, smeared generously with butter and topped with a wedge of tangy cheese, washed down with a weak but sugary cup of tea, she lit the coals laid ready in the two coffee rooms, put the cups on the counter ready for the first customers of the day – the Paradise would open at dawn – and then went upstairs to set the fire in her mistress's bedroom.

Polly was already up, and sitting in front of her mirror, while Hannah expertly arranged and pinned her hair. She smiled as Gin entered, lugging a bucket of coal in one hand and carrying a candle in the other. "Good morning, Jane!"

"Morning, madam, come to do your fire," said Gin, although this fact was obvious. She had been taught the art of laying a hearth by Hannah, and under the other maid's judgemental gaze, carefully arranged paper, kindling and coals in a pyramid, before lighting it from the candle. Fortunately, the dry wood caught at once, and soon the flames were blazing up merrily, bringing warmth to the chilly room. Sly the cat, who had been curled up tightly in the remaining warmth of the bed, decided that she would move to a more congenial spot, and was soon washing herself industriously on the rug before the hearth.

"I've made all ready downstairs, madam," Gin said, as

Hannah put a clean, lace-edged cap on Polly's dark hair, and pinned it carefully in place. "Fires lit, floors swept, cups all laid out, and Will is clearing the snow outside. Will that be all?" She was beginning to be more proficient in the language of servants, and thought she saw a look of approval from Hannah, her most exacting teacher.

"For the moment, yes, but I have an errand for you later," said Polly, rising to her feet. "Once the shop is opened for business, you may go down to the pastrycook's in the Strand with your basket, and fetch some cakes – I have a fancy for some gingerbread, and I believe Mr. Jessop may be joining us in a short while."

It was not only Sam Jessop who would be arriving at the coffee-house, but Gin was not going to tell Polly that. She nodded enthusiastically. "Yes'm."

"And if you perform your duties to my satisfaction today, you may find it to your advantage."

"Yes'm!" Gin hoped that the advantage would be at least a groat, if not sixpence. She fairly skipped back downstairs with the empty bucket, and busied herself with all the preparations necessary to get the Paradise ready for the first customers of the day. Things were looking up. Not only might she earn herself a little extra coin, but Dark was coming this morning, and she prayed that he and Madam would make it up and be friends again. Sometimes, she thought wisely, giving the mantelpiece in the main bar a thorough dusting, it took a few home truths to set people back in their right course.

It was mid-morning before the bustle in the coffee-house had eased, although there would be another rush around dinner-time, when many customers would come in with food from one of the local chop-houses or pie shops, to supplement their meal with coffee and a pipe in the warm. Polly went upstairs to do her accounts, leaving Hannah in charge, and Gin wrapped her warm cloak around her, secreted the money that her mistress had given her inside the pocket of her dress, and ventured out into the bitter cold of King Street.

The quickest way down to the Strand was across the Piazza. As Gin trotted along, clutching her basket with one mittened hand and avoiding patches of ice, the steely sky above her began to disgorge a light scattering of fat snowflakes that swirled around the hurrying people and skittered playfully over the frozen ground as if they were also too cold to stay still. The porch of Paul's church was crowded with homeless beggars, but Gin ignored them and hurried past, very conscious of her warm clothing and her full belly. Running an errand, even in such bitter cold, was perfectly tolerable if you had a blazing fire and a hot drink at the end of it.

As she crossed the Piazza, which was almost empty, she saw another woman coming towards her. There was something familiar about the cloaked figure, but just as Gin realised who it was, the woman slipped and fell heavily to the ground. She did not get up, but lay there, shoulders shaking, obviously overcome with misery. With a sudden feeling of exultation, Gin walked up to her. She surveyed her with some disdain, and then said caustically, "Ain't you Mr. Jessop's mort?"

The other girl raised her head. Gin added, "I should stop all that weeping an' wailing, there's plenty far worse off."

"Who are you?"

"I'm maid to Mrs. Paradice," said Gin, with considerable pride. "And I remembers you from Bath. Have you had second thoughts, then? Or has your fine Jack lover said goodbye? Here, have this," she added, and scrabbled in her sleeve. "Clean yourself up, you look a proper fright."

"Thank you," said Mary, without sarcasm. She took the proffered handkerchief, even though it was none too clean, and scrubbed the tears from her face. Then she struggled to her feet, ignoring Gin's outstretched hand. "Tell me, is Mrs. Paradice at home?"

"She is," said Gin, eyeing Mary dubiously. "But she's busy. You don't run a coffee-house by putting your feet up all day, you know."

"Perhaps she will see me, just for a moment," Mary said. "I – I need to talk to her."

"Oh, really." Gin looked up at her with narrowed eyes, not troubling to hide her contempt or her exasperation. "Gawd, you've led us all a pretty dance, Miss Jessop! I hope you've seen some sense at last, for your poor pa's sake, he's a good kind man and he don't deserve what you've done to him. If I was him, I'd kick you out and forget I ever had a daughter."

"And I wouldn't blame him," said Mary. "Thank you – I don't know your name."

"It's Gi – Jane."

"Thank you, Jane. Pray will you conduct me to Mrs. Paradice's coffee-house? I do not know precisely where it is."

"It's just over there, left hand side of King Street, past the Essex Serpent," said Gin, with a pert glance: she had never had a favourable opinion of Mary Jessop, and this encounter had not changed her mind. "I shall guide you there if you cannot find the way by yourself."

She escorted Mary to the door of the Paradise coffee-house. On this sombre wintry morning, the candles were lit inside, and a diffused golden glow filtered through the misted windows. The promise of warmth and safety was plainly so welcome that tears were beginning to fill Mary's eyes, and she wiped them away with her sleeve.

Gin opened the door, letting a blast of warm air, the rich aroma of fresh coffee, and a haze of tobacco smoke swell over them. "Go on," she said, as Mary hesitated in the hallway, obviously afraid to enter the noisy room on her left. "Up the stairs. Madam's doing her books."

"I – I don't know where to go," said Mary feebly. "I've never been here before."

"Gawd help us!" cried Gin, casting her eyes heavenwards. "All right, I'll show you. Follow me." She took the stairs at a run, while Mary, bruised from her fall, toiled laboriously in her footsteps. At the top, she knocked, flung open a door, stood to one side, and announced in raucous tones, "Here, madam, just look what the cat dragged in."

Polly had in fact finished her accounts, which showed a very encouraging profit, and was looking through some of the recent broadsheet ballads that she had bought, searching for something new and fresh to delight her customers. Risqué songs always went down well, or a comical dialogue in which she could take both parts. Or, depending on their mood, she could try a sentimental tune that everyone knew, so that they could sing along. Though sometimes, the words struck too close to home.

She hummed softly:

"'Why should we submit to folly,
Or why should I so silly be
To settle my love and my affections
Upon the man that loves not me?'"

My life's story, Polly thought wryly. *When will I ever learn? But they'll listen and love it and even weep a little, and never know how true it is, for I will not let them.*

The sound of heavy footsteps, running up the stairs, distracted her. It could only be Gin. She called out, "Come in!" at the expected knock, and waited, wondering what was afoot. A dispute over a bill, perhaps, or some other crisis – or none, for despite repeated instruction, Gin always galloped around the house as if there were some dire emergency.

"Look what the cat dragged in!" cried her maid triumphantly, flinging the door wide, and Polly, with astonishment, beheld the white, desperate face of Mary Jessop.

The girl was obviously at the stage where the least act of kindness would cause a complete collapse of control. Polly rose to her feet, calm and cool, and said, "This is a very pleasant surprise, Miss Jessop. Pray take a chair. Will you drink a dish of chocolate with me? Bring us a pot, Jane, as quick as may be."

Mary dropped her damp cloak on the floor, made her way over to the high-backed chair opposite Polly at the table, and sat down abruptly. At a significant glance from her mistress, Gin picked up the discarded garment and walked out of the room as demurely as her air of triumph would allow. When the door had shut behind her, Polly said, "It is still very cold outside, I collect? I saw that there was more snow falling."

At this trivial remark, Mary gave her a look of utter bewilderment, and said thinly, "Yes, there is, a little."

"Are you warm enough, Miss Jessop? If you are not, I can ask Jane to put more coals on the fire."

"Yes, I thank you," said Mary, and then, as if she could contain herself no longer, "Aren't you going to ask me what I'm doing here?"

"All in good time. Let you sink some of the chocolate, when it arrives, and a bite to eat perhaps, and then you will feel more the thing."

"He's left me," said Mary, her voice tottering on the edge of hysteria. "He's left me, abandoned me, I thought he loved me but he lied!"

"I take it you are referring to Robbie Sinclair? If so, he did the same to me," Polly told her.

"To *you*?" Mary gaped at her.

"Yes, I was also his mistress, before you, and he abandoned me without a backward glance when I no longer served his purpose, just as he has now abandoned you." Polly studied her. The girl did have some backbone, it seemed, and at least she had not immediately disintegrated into a soggy heap. "Well, you have learned the truth at last – Sinclair is a selfish, lying scoundrel whose loyalty is first and foremost to himself and then, a long way after, to his failed Cause. His women, Miss Jessop, count for nothing."

"He was going to *sell* me! To Mrs. Maynard's cousin's nunnery!"

"Dear God," said Polly, startled. "That's coming it a bit strong, even for Robbie. Did he tell you this himself?"

"I overheard them talking," Mary said, her voice swollen with indignation at the memory. "He said I was a terrible liability and he wanted rid of me."

Polly said cautiously, "When did this happen?"

"An hour or so ago."

"Then I take it he has escaped from prison?" She knew that she must inform Dark, but the very thought of being in his presence again made her spine shiver.

"I *helped* him!" Mary cried. "I took the clothes and the wig yesterday to Newgate yesterday, I *helped* him and he never even thanked me! Then I waited outside and I saw him come out wearing the suit I brought him, but he didn't turn the right way for home, so I thought he was going to see some of his friends, and I went back and got him some chops and wine to celebrate when he returned, but he didn't come, and I waited all night for him and he never appeared – and then I heard him and Mrs. Maynard talking in the kitchen. And he said some terrible things about – about me!"

"He always was an ungrateful wretch." Polly paused,

collecting her thoughts. Robbie was free to do mischief, which was just what Dark had been dreading. But at least Mary had had her eyes opened at last, albeit in a rather brutal fashion. She added, "So when exactly did he escape?"

"Late yesterday afternoon." Her lower lip jutted out peevishly. "But when he didn't come back, I thought he'd been captured again. I kept thinking of him in irons. And all the while I expect he was with some trollop!"

"I don't doubt it," said Polly dryly. "So how did you come to overhear him talking to Mrs. Maynard?"

"I had to empty the pot in the privy," Mary said, with a blush. "And when I was coming back to the kitchen door, I heard his voice, and I didn't want him to see me in my old gown with the pot, so I waited at the door. And he said such dreadful things about me, I *couldn't* go back in. After all I've done for him – I've been true as true, I've never even *looked* at another man, I did everything he asked of me, I helped him escape and then he casts me off like – like an old *shoe*! Oh, how could he have been so cruel!"

"Did they realise you were listening?"

The girl shook her head vehemently. "No, I'm sure they didn't. I waited until they'd gone from the kitchen, Robbie went out somewhere and Mrs. Maynard went to help her husband, he can't walk, and I ran upstairs and got my cloak and left as quickly as I could. Because Robbie's planning something, some revenge on a traitor, and I think he'd have killed me if he'd thought I knew anything."

"So what did you hear, concerning this plan he's hatching?"

"Oh, I don't know." Mary waved an impatient hand. "Something to do with someone's birthday, and a Mr. Black who was in Newgate but turned out to be a spy. I can't remember much of it."

A terrible sense of foreboding filled Polly. "Mr. Black? Are you sure that was the name?"

"I think so," Mary said distractedly. "And he mentioned someone called Templeman as well."

Polly's mind had begun to work feverishly. She did not recognise the name of Templeman, but she knew only too well who 'Mr. Black' was. It had never entered her head that Robbie might want belated revenge on the man who had spied on them in Newgate, still less that he would have the opportunity to do it. She had not seriously expected that he would really manage to escape, and, if he had, she had assumed that he would lose no time in fleeing to France, taking Mary Jessop with him.

But Mary Jessop was here, shocked and betrayed, and Sinclair was loose in London, and Dark was in danger. For it was plain that Robbie knew a great deal more about his activities than either he or she had realised. She must find her lover – her *former* lover – and warn him, as soon as possible.

And here was the means to do it, clumping up the stairs with the chocolate. As soon as Gin had put it down and poured it, Polly said, "Wait, Jane, I have another errand for you. Miss Jessop, your father has not yet given up hope of you changing your mind, and is still in town. Would you like to send any word to him?"

Mary stared at her suspiciously. At last she said, "I have behaved so badly, he may not listen."

"Of course he will," Polly said briskly. "Your father is a kind and forgiving man. I grant you he has a very great deal to forgive, but you are safe on that score. Why else would he stay in London, rather than go home to Oxford? He has always believed that you would see sense eventually, and now, happily, you have proved him right. He has been so worried about you, and I think the least you could do is to let him know that you are safe. You do not even have to see him if you do not wish it, but please, just reassure him that you are no longer in Sinclair's power."

"You make it sound as if I was Robbie's prisoner," Mary complained. "And why are you so concerned about my father, anyway? Are you his lover?"

Despite herself, Polly laughed. "His *lover*? No, Miss Jessop, it is perfectly possible to have high regard for a man without feeling the need to climb into his bed. Your father is a very good friend, and I wish only to see him happy – which will not come to pass until he has taken you back home with him."

For an instant, she could have sworn that a look of eagerness entered Mary's face, but then it was replaced by the angry, mulish expression she had worn for much of this conversation. She said sulkily, "I'm *not* going back. How can I go back? Everyone must be talking and gossiping about me."

"I doubt it. Your father has been very discreet. I think you will find that you have been stranded in Wheatley during the bad weather, and that no-one will realise what has actually happened. You can resume your old life, and this escapade with Sinclair will come in time to seem like a nightmare long since over."

"But what if I'm with child?"

"It seems unlikely to me. How many times have you lain with him since coming to town?"

A blushing but defiant Mary muttered, at last, that it had been no more than twice, for opportunity in Newgate was scarce, and expensive.

"When are your courses due? Good. And he never got you with child when you were with him before, did he? Well, *if* you do prove to be so, which I very much doubt, then we must plan accordingly, but if you are not, then no-one in Oxford save your father will be any the wiser. And perhaps the experience will have taught you some valuable lessons. Now, do you want me to send a message to him?"

"Do as you please, I don't care either way," Mary said sulkily, taking a large, ungenteel swig of chocolate. "And I don't like being lectured, either. You're not my mother, are you?"

Since there was no verbal answer she wished to make to this comment, Polly ignored it, suppressed the desire to slap the ungrateful little hussy, and turned to Gin, who was hovering with a look of eager expectancy. "You know where Mr. Jessop's inn is, don't you, in Holborn? It's called the Black Swan. Go there as quickly as possible and tell him what's happened. And then, if you can, find Mr. Dark. Go on, child, don't just stand there like a gawcum, *go*!"

As Gin hurried off downstairs, omitting to shut the door behind her, Polly turned again to Mary. "So, Robbie sent you a message to you in Oxford, asking for your help to escape from Newgate?"

The girl nodded. She had finished her chocolate, and there was a little colour now in her plump cheeks, but the expression of sulky defiance had gone. She looked very young, and frightened, but Polly remembered that the child's own foolishness had brought her to this pass, and for the moment hardened her heart. She went on. "He asked me for help too, but I refused, because I had realised that the only person who matters to Robbie Sinclair, is Robbie Sinclair."

"I thought he loved me!" Mary wailed, now quite beside herself with anguish. "He *said* he loved me, over and over again! But he doesn't care about me at all, he despises me!" And she burst into wild, hysterical sobs.

Polly had meant to remain detached, but discovered, to her dismay, that it was not possible to stand by while this confused, foolish child's heart was breaking. With an uncomfortable sensation of sympathy, she put her arms round Mary and patted her shoulders gently. "Oh, my dear, life is cruel, and men are cruel, and Sinclair more cruel than most. But you're safe from him now, and you will get over this sooner than you think."

"I can't bear it!" Mary sobbed, her tears soaking Polly's lace scarf. "I want to die!"

"No, you don't. What you want," said Polly, surprised by the depth of her anger against Robbie, "is revenge. And dying is not the means to obtain it. He wouldn't be sorry if you died – he would be glad, for then there would be one less witness to inform against him, should he be captured again."

There was a pause in the sobs. Mary raised her swollen, scarlet, tear-blubbered face and stared intently at Polly. "I hate him!" she said. "I want him to pay for what he's done to me!"

That's more like it, Polly thought. Aloud, she said, "Remember, you are not in the least to blame for all of this. The fault is entirely Sinclair's. He seduced you and enticed you away from your home with false promises. You were hardly more than a child – how were you to know any better? He has behaved abominably, and his plan to sell you to a nunnery was utterly despicable. All in all, he has treated you far worse than he treated me – for I was a woman of the world, and embarked on our affair with my eyes open. And yet he gulled me too, with his fine style and his charm – I did not see his arrogance and selfishness until too late."

"What a fool I've been!" said Mary angrily. "I hate him, he's a false and deceiving lover, and I wish he was dead!"

Polly had not thought that she would be in agreement. Yes, she had wanted vengeance too, she had wanted Sinclair to be forced to realise the suffering and harm he had done, but she had not wanted him to die: she had envisaged him escaping to France, leaving her life as completely as a bad dream, painful at the time but soon largely forgotten. But now, knowing that he planned some ghastly deed, that he wanted revenge on Dark, she had changed her mind. For if it came down to a choice between Robbie's life or Dark's, there would be no contest. She would plunge the knife herself into Sinclair's false heart, rather than see André Dark harmed in any way.

CHAPTER TWENTY THREE

'Now man with utmost Fortitude thy Soul'

Gin knew that Sam had arranged to meet Dark at his lodgings before they came on to the Paradise to surprise Polly, and so she did not even hesitate when she emerged from the coffee-house: rather than heading for Drury Lane and Holborn, she turned in the direction of Half Moon Street. She clutched her old shabby cloak around her, thankful that the snow seemed to be lessening now, and made her way carefully over the treacherous, icy cobbles. Not for anything did she wish to suffer the same humiliating fall as Mary Jessop.

As she walked down Bedford Street, she saw two men approaching. It was hard to be sure of their identity through the whirling snowflakes, but one was tall, lean and dressed in black, while the other's much shorter and bulkier form was clad in plain dark green. With a leap of joy, she hurried towards them. "Mr. Dark! Mr. Jessop!"

"Why, hello, Gin," said Sam, smiling at her, though his eyes were filled with sadness and he did not look as though he had slept much. "What are you doing out in this weather?"

"I got news for you, Mr. Jessop," she said breathlessly. "Your daughter's at King Street – Mrs Paradice sent me to find you both."

"Thank God!" Sam said, delight suddenly flooding his face. "Is she safe? Is she well?"

"Yes, sir, and right sorry for all she's done," said Gin, who thought a little embroidery of what Mary had actually said would not come amiss.

"Both of us?" said Dark quickly. "She sent for me as

well?"

"Yes, she didn't know you was coming to see her anyway, and she needs your help cos Sinclair's free, and she reckons he's planning something bad," Gin said in a hoarse whisper, although the street was empty.

Dark cursed viciously, using words that even Gin, in her former incarnation, would have hesitated to employ. "I knew it! I warned Pitt yesterday, and he was more interested in finishing his brandy bottle than in what I had to tell him. It wouldn't surprise me if he turned out to be in league with the Jacobites. Well, come on, child, stretch out those legs, this is not the time nor the weather to linger."

"It's all right for the both of you," Gin said resentfully, turning back the way she had just come. "You ain't got all them skirts flapping round your ankles, have you?"

By the time they reached the coffee-house, the snow had dwindled to a scattering of thick flakes, drifting lazily down from a pale sky, and far ahead of them, above the white-burdened rooftops and chimney pots, there was a thin bar of opalescent blue. Gin sniffed the icy air. "Thaw's coming," she said. "Feels softer, somehow."

"And about time too," said Sam. "This weather's fit for neither man nor beast." The news about Mary had wrought a splendid change in him, and he sprang up the stairs as lightly as a boy, while Dark and Gin followed far behind.

"Did she come of her own accord?" Dark asked, as they arrived at the half landing.

"Seems so – I found her in the Piazza. Properly sorry for herself, she was, cos she'd found out the truth about him – that he's a lying, cheating thatch-gallows." Gin gave an unsympathetic cackle. "Still, you can't tell some people, can you? They needs to be hit over the head with it afore they'll believe it."

This was not only aimed at Miss Jessop, but Dark ignored her and continued up the stairs. At the top, the door was open, and a touching scene of reconciliation met their gaze. Sam and his daughter were clinging to each other as if they never wished to let go, and both were weeping.

"Aah," said Gin fondly. "Just like the last scene at Drury Lane, innit."

"If I were you, brat," said Dark, in a voice she knew better than to disobey, "I would keep very, very quiet. Who knows what may hang on the next few minutes? And *I* will direct the proceedings."

"Yes, sir," said Gin meekly, though there was a spark of defiance in her eyes as she entered the room in his wake.

"That was very quick, Jane," said Polly, with a wary look at Dark. "And you found both of them!"

"They was coming along Bedford Street together, ma'am," said Gin, with a brief curtsey. "So I didn't have far to go."

"You did very well," Polly told her. "Now shut the door – you're the only one in the household who might be tempted to listen at it, so I'll have you in here to keep an eye on you. Stand in that corner and don't speak unless you're spoken to."

"Yes'm," said Gin, trying to give the impression that this time she would do exactly as she was told.

Polly, who had no faith whatsoever that she would, watched her maid take her place by the handsome walnut tallboy. She avoided looking at Dark, but even the thought of his eyes on her was enough to make her heart change its rhythm and her breath falter in her throat.

"Oh, Papa," Mary sobbed, her copious tears soaking the front of his coat. "Oh, how glad I am to see you! I'll never, ever run away again, I promise!"

"Good," said Dark. "I hope you've learned your lesson, Miss Jessop, because I for one am heartily sick of trailing round the country in your erratic wake."

Mary's head jerked up and she stared at him in surprise. "You're the man Robbie attacked in Bath! What are you doing here?"

"I would like to ask you some questions, Miss Jessop, concerning your former lover."

Polly privately thought that his tone might have been more conciliatory if he wanted the girl's co-operation. Plainly Sam was in agreement, for he frowned and said, "Can't it wait, Dark?"

"No, I'm afraid it cannot, for it may be a matter of life and death. Sinclair is apparently plotting some devilish act, and Miss Jessop is our only hope of find out what he is planning, and where and when he is going to do it."

Seeing the girl tremble, Polly felt it was time to intervene. "Mary," she said quickly. "Mary, listen to me. *Mary*!"

The girl raised her tear-blubbered face and wiped her nose on her sleeve like an ill-bred child. "Yes?"

"Mr. Dark means you no harm, Mary, he just wants you to try to remember what Sinclair said, about what he is plotting. If you help us to stop him, perhaps you will even receive a reward from King George." Dark opened his mouth, but she silenced him with a vehement gesture. "Tell us, Mary. Tell us what you overheard. And then you can go home and forget all about Sinclair and what he did to you."

"He called me a silly whining little jade," said Mary, her tears vanishing as her indignation was renewed.

There was a muffled snort from Gin in the corner. Polly hastily continued. "No, not that – tell us what you heard him say to Mrs. Maynard about – a birthday, was it not? And some talk of revenge?" She smiled encouragingly. "You have already made the hardest decision of all, Mary – the decision to leave him. And it *was* difficult, as I know only too well myself. His charm is very potent, but as you and I have discovered, it is false, for he is no more than a self-seeking, ruthless and utterly unprincipled rogue. He must be caught before he can do any more harm – and you, Mary, are the only one who can help."

The girl hesitated, and Polly smiled again. "Don't worry. You'll see, it will all come right in the end. Try to remember. You said that Robbie was planning revenge on someone."

"There was a man who spied on them in Newgate," said Mary slowly, her brow furrowed with effort. "I think his name was Black. Robbie said something about how he might think he was safe now, but he'd never escape – he'd have his revenge on him and on Hanover too."

"And what else? You mentioned another name – Templeman, was it?"

"Templeman?" said Dark sharply.

Mary flinched at the sound of his voice, and Polly glared at him. "What did he say about Mr. Templeman?" she asked patiently.

"He – he just said he had contacts close to the court, and that he knew everything. Robbie was going to see him." Mary glanced anxiously at Dark, who, in his obvious impatience, looked as if he would have liked to turn her upside down and shake her until all the answers rattled out.

"A notorious Jacobite called Jack Templeman lives in Westminster," he said. "Did Sinclair mention his first name?"

The girl gulped and nodded. "Yes, he called him Jack."

"Then at least we know where he might be now."

"There was something else you overheard," Polly prompted her gently. "Something about a birthday?"

She saw Dark stiffen. Mary frowned, oblivious. "Yes – he said, I remember now, he said, 'No-one will ever forget that boy's birthday!' And then he said something about, 'One bang and it'll all be over.' But I don't know what he meant."

"I do," said Dark grimly. "What day is it, Sam?"

"Why, it's Friday."

"And the date?"

"January – the twentieth, I believe."

"You are correct. And today is the ninth birthday of Prince Frederick, eldest son of the Prince of Wales." There was a brief, uneasy silence before his next words, spoken softly and full of sudden foreboding. "Which means, my friends, that whatever Sinclair is plotting, it is planned to take place today. Fortunately, the child is safe in Hanover, but his father and mother of course are here in London, at St. James's Palace. And I'm willing to bet that the Prince of Wales is Sinclair's target."

"Oh, my God," Sam whispered, appalled. "Surely he would not do cold-blooded murder?"

"To further his own ends, I think Robbie would do anything," Polly said. Her mouth was dry, and her hands were shaking. "Dark, tell us, what is most likely? And how in God's name can we stop him?"

"I know that the Prince was planning to visit the Frost Fair on the Thames at Westminster today. There is an ox being roast in honour of his son's birthday, and various other festivities – indeed, I am in charge of a display of skyrockets at dusk. And the Prince makes a virtue of his courage, his willingness to go about in public with no more than a few courtiers for his escort. All of Westminster knows of this, and so, surely, must Templeman." Dark swung round and addressed Gin, still standing in her corner. "Gin, do you know where the soldiers are camped, in Hyde Park?"

"Course I do. Sir."

"Well, I want you to find Captain Short of the Foot Guards." He crossed to the table, where Polly's account books were lying, drew one of the loose pieces of blank paper towards him and began to write on it, cursing under his breath as the pen, cut in an unfamiliar fashion, spluttered ink across the page. Swiftly he blew on it, sanded it and folded it into four. "Wax, Poll?"

Silently she handed him a stick, and he softened it in the flame of a taper lit from the fire, before sealing the letter. "Here you are, Gin. If Short is there, he will act on this. If he is not, do not give it to anyone else, do you understand? To *no-one else.* Now go, and as fast as you can!"

"Yes, sir!" Gin gasped, and ran from the room.

"What can I do?" Sam asked, his face pale. "Anything, Dark – I will do anything you ask."

"Then come with me, and let us find Robbie Sinclair before he has the chance to put his plan into action. We'll go first to Templeman's, he may still be there. Quickly, Jessop, there is not a moment to be lost!"

Polly and Mary were left standing alone in the room, staring at each other. The younger girl's face was still streaked with tears, and pale with fright. "Is that really what Robbie's going to do?" she said, her voice trembling. "Is he *really* going to try and kill the Prince?"

"I don't know. Who can guess what Robbie is planning, save for Robbie himself? But I wouldn't put it beyond him, would you?"

"Are we going to follow?"

Polly looked at her. Mary was obviously exhausted as well as terrified. If they went after Dark and Sam, she would be a serious liability. What if she had a last-minute change of heart and decided to warn Sinclair that his plot had been discovered? Polly said reassuringly, "No, I think we can leave that business to them. You are safe here now. Would you like to rest for a while? You look quite done up."

The girl needed little persuasion. She allowed herself to be led to the adjoining chamber, where Polly helped her to take off her outer garments and her stays, and then settled her down in the soft embrace of her own bed. "I'll send Hannah up with another dish of hot chocolate," she said softly. "And then I think the best thing for you would be a good long sleep."

Hannah, told of this addition to her duties, glanced at her mistress significantly. "Are you sure? She's been nothing but trouble, that one."

"Oh, I know that, none better. But I have to go out, Hannah, and I daren't take her with me. And if you add a drop or two of that soothing draught to the chocolate, she may well sleep till the evening."

"Very well," Hannah said reluctantly. "Dan can serve while I go upstairs. It ain't crowded, and I doubt business will pick up much until midday. Don't forget you've promised to sing tonight, madam!"

"Of course I haven't. Oh, Hannah, many thanks for this. You deserve an increase in your wages." She grinned suddenly. "Or perhaps a change in the name of this place? To 'The Rose', perhaps?"

And with her maid's chuckles sounding softly in her ears, she wrapped her winter mantle closely round her and ran out into King Street. With so much at stake, Dark would be in considerable danger, and she could not forget Robbie's vow of revenge. She had no idea what she could do to help, only a vague yet urgent sensation of imminent catastrophe.

A hackney carriage was disgorging its passenger in the Piazza. Polly hurried over and hailed the driver. "Take me to

Westminster, and as quick as ever you can – there'll be an extra shilling for you if you hurry!"

The elderly gentleman who had also hoped to hire the hackney stopped, disappointed, as she climbed inside. The driver shouted to his horse, cracked his whip, and the conveyance lurched forward over the rough icy cobbles. As it turned towards the Strand, the sun came out, bright and chilly over the frost-bound streets and roofs of the city: but Polly, sick with worry for Dark and Sam, could not dare to take it as an omen.

There was a busy tangle of coaches, carts, chairs and pedestrians in another King Street, the main thoroughfare through Westminster. As the hackney crawled forward, Polly realised with a renewed feeling of panic that she had no idea where Jack Templeman lived. His house probably lay in the maze of ancient, squalid dwellings around the Abbey, but that was no more than a guess. She did not care for the thought of wandering, even in broad daylight, down Thieving Lane or Long Ditch, haunts of robbers and night-walkers, still less for any knocking on doors. If he was concerned in murder and treason, Templeman would probably offer violence to any inconveniently curious stranger enquiring after him. Dark had the advantage that he knew his destination. As if in a nightmare, she was condemned to blundering blindly about, imperilling both herself and her friends with her ignorance.

All the way from the Piazza, she had scanned the pavements, looking for Sam and his companion, but although the hackney was proceeding slowly, so that she had time for a thorough search, she could not see them. Perhaps they had taken a short cut through the alleys or, more likely, they had walked so fast that they were still ahead of her. After all, settling Mary and finding the hackney had taken her some time, so the two men had had a good start.

She was beginning to wonder, anxiously, why she had

come. Even if she could locate Templeman's house, the business would all be done before she got there. Either Robbie would be in custody, to be returned to Newgate and kept in irons until his trial, or he was already away, intent on the grand coup that would simultaneously strike a terrible blow against Hanover and wreak vengeance on Dark. How could she, a woman unarmed save for her wits, hope to prevent him? And what, in God's name, was he planning to do? They only knew that something was set to happen today: anything further was pure guesswork.

The hackney finally came to a halt, to the accompaniment of grumbles and muttered curses from the driver. They were approaching the Abbey: perhaps this would be a good moment to alight. She put her head out of the window. "What's the delay?"

"Crowds up ahead, all cheering," said the man on the box. "The King, maybe – or the Prince of Wales more like, he's a sociable cove. It'll take a long time to get through, ma'am."

"Then I'll get out here," Polly told him. In a moment, having parted with the promised two shillings, and received grateful thanks, she was standing on the rutted icy ground of King Street, wondering what to do and where to go.

Well, if the crowds were cheering royalty, Robbie obviously had not yet had the chance to carry out his plan. On the other hand, Polly thought, avoiding a steaming heap of dung and making her way carefully past the stationary traffic, if royalty was abroad on this cold and menacing day, then it was vulnerable. She did not know what she could do, but that sense of impending doom kept her walking onwards, past the Abbey and into Old Palace Yard, where the crowds seemed to be thickest and the noise loudest. There she could see very little, because of the great press of people, but an elderly woman told her that it was the party from St. James's Palace, out to visit the Frost Fair that had been in full swing on the frozen Thames since the start of the icy weather. "I heard they was coming this morning," she confided, her soft plump face beaming with good will. "He's ever so brave, isn't he, the Prince? Walking about on the ice with just a few of his lords, and never a soldier in sight. You'd think with all them wicked Jacks still at large that they'd all be hiding in their palaces, but not a bit of it, there he is, bold as you please, carried down in a chair with the Duke of Marlborough, just like any ordinary gentleman."

But her last words fell on other ears, for Polly, gripped by a sudden impulse, had plunged deep into the crowd, heading not for the thickest press, where the lords of the court were still gathering, but for New Palace Yard and the frozen Thames.

The watermen, of course, had been put out of work by the weather, but some of the more enterprising had discovered that helping sightseers onto the ice provided a lucrative alternative. As Polly pushed her way through the throng to Westminster Stairs, they set up their hopeful cries. "Lead you on the river, ma'am!" "Only sixpence for the best guide!" "You're safe with me, ma'am, I won't let you stumble or fall!"

She looked keenly at them, knowing that she would need some kind of escort, though she still had no idea what she would do if she saw Robbie out there on the ice. Order the waterman to attack him? Shout, "Stop thief!" very loudly?

It was foolish beyond belief. She should never have come. She should have stayed at the coffee-house and sung her songs and pretended that she had never heard of André Dark or Robbie Sinclair or a possible plot to kill the Prince of Wales. But it was too late now. Committed, Polly chose the nearest waterman, a huge fellow who looked as if he would sink any boat he tried to row, and gave him sixpence. Holding his arm for support on the slippery ice, she stepped out onto the frozen Thames.

The great frost had gripped the river since well before Christmas, and the constant traffic of people, not to mention sledges, carts and even coaches, had worn numerous pathways through the jagged, lumpy ice, like deep tracks through a muddy field. Along the centre of the Thames stood an array of tents, stalls and booths, lavishly decorated with bunting and flags in honour of the royal visit. Like Gin, earlier in the day, Polly noticed the changed quality of the wind, and the fact that the sun, fitfully glittering on the ice, almost had a touch of warmth in it. The wintry weather seemed to have endured forever, but perhaps the end was in prospect at last.

If it had not been for the frantic anxiety which filled her mind, she might have enjoyed the spectacle. There was a huge and luxurious variety of goods for sale, cried up enthusiastically by the men and women on the stalls: gloves, glass, leather, lace, fine silks, even, she noticed with distant surprise, a goldsmith. In the middle they were roasting an ox, and many people were gathered round, men, women and children, raising mugs and cups of beer or wine to toast the occasion. Polly feverishly scanned the crowd, seeking Sinclair, but she recognised no-one amongst the throng.

Her escort was a taciturn man, a change from the normally loquacious watermen who were notoriously ready to air their contentious opinions to the passengers captive in their boats. He took her arm to help her negotiate the more difficult lumps of ice, but otherwise kept decorously a couple of paces behind her, for which she was grateful. She tried to appear interested in the displays on the stalls, sniffing a perfumed ball, examining gloves and buying some gingerbread or inspecting an array of rings, but all the while constantly watching for any sign of Robbie Sinclair. But there were hundreds of people here, queuing to have souvenir cards printed, huddled round the wine or coffee booths, holding out chilled hands to the blaze under the roasting ox. And distant cheering, growing closer, told her that the royal party had made their way down to the ice, eager to view the delights of the Fair before the approaching thaw.

She came to a stall selling pieces of magnificent lace, laid out in elaborate profusion on dark blue velvet to show them to best advantage. Polly paused, and picked up an exquisitely intricate piece of edging. The serving woman beamed at her. "The finest lace from the fair city of Bruges, madam, you won't find better in all of London town."

The woman's clothes were shabby, and she had grimy hands, but the lace was as purely white as new-fallen snow. "It's so lovely," Polly said with a smile. "How much is it?"

"For ye, my dear, the price might be too high," said a soft, menacing voice in her ear.

It was Robbie. She whipped round, but he instantly seized her arm in a vicious grasp and pulled her close to him. "And what are ye doing here?" he went on, smiling at her. She had never noticed before how tall he was, looming over her, and his teeth seemed very sharp, like some dreadful beast of prey.

Wild instinct told Polly that making a scene was her best method of defence. "Let *go* of me!" she shouted. Where was that damned waterman? With his muscles, he would surely be able to deal with Sinclair.

"I'm afraid your bear of an escort seems to have disappeared," Robbie said. "Amazing, is it not, what a coin or two can accomplish. And I really would advise ye to calm yourself, madam. Do ye mind that wee dirk I use to clean my nails? It's sharper now, and if I slide it between your ribs no-one will know what has happened till ye fall dead on the ground." Something stroked along her side, under the cloak, and she felt the stiff buckram lining of her bodice part under its pressure. "Understand, lassie? I don't want to kill ye, that would be a shocking waste, but if I have to I will, and no' think twice about it."

"I understand," Polly whispered. Her mouth felt as if it

was coated in ashes, and her threatened heart was hammering frantically within her ribs. She thought of that wicked little knife, and what it might do to her, and terror froze her limbs.

"But if ye do as I say, there'll be no problem. I'll do what I have to do, and be on my way, and ye'll be free of me forever." Sinclair kept hold of her arm so tightly that she seemed to have lost all feeling in her hand. Polly could not believe that no-one had noticed her plight: surely the lace-seller must have realised that something was amiss? But when she cautiously turned her head to look at the woman, she was giving Robbie a significant nod. They plainly knew each other, and she must be part of the plot too. And her wares were fine enough to tempt any lord – or prince ...

Polly bitterly regretted the impulse that had brought her here and put her life in deadly peril. What was the Prince of Wales to her? She had never even clapped eyes on him save at a great distance, walking with his entourage in St. James's Park or out on the river in one of the royal barges. What did it matter if he lived or died?

It mattered because she might be able to prevent it. She saw that with sudden clarity, as if a brilliant ray of sunlight had illuminated her path. Robbie obviously thought that she was completely cowed by his threats, and already his grip had relaxed a little: her hand was tingling with returning life. She said, in a small, tremulous voice, "Please, don't hurt me – I'll do whatever you want."

"There's a good lassie," Sinclair said. "I know ye'd see sense. Now stay close to me – very close – as close as a lover." She felt the knife caress her bodice, more lightly than before, but with no diminution of menace. "There's a fine selection of wares ye've chosen, Mrs. Templeman – fit for a Prince, I've nae doot."

"Indeed they are, sir," said the slatternly woman. "Not long to wait now, by the sound of it."

Still keeping close hold on her, Sinclair edged round the stall so that he was standing next to Mrs. Templeman, and looking towards the Westminster bank. Polly saw that the royal party was now on the ice, surrounded by cheering crowds. There were many finely dressed men in bright colours and gold lace, and several wore the blue sash of the Garter, but the small man in front, burdened by a wig too large for his spindly frame, must surely be George, Prince of Wales.

They came nearer, and nearer. The group seemed to be aiming for the further end of the double line of booths and stalls. She could feel Robbie's quick breaths: the wildness of his excitement was so transparent that she could not understand why none of the people passing by the stall had noticed it. But no-one gave them any attention: the crowd's collective gaze was fixed on the Prince, splendid and faintly ridiculous in that huge wig.

"Not long now," said Robbie, almost to himself. "Not long now. Are ye ready, Mrs. Templeman?"

"I'm ready," said the woman, but her face betrayed none of her accomplice's exultation. A sheen of sweat, incongruous in the cold air, gleamed on her broad pale forehead, and she was biting her lip. Polly's despairing gaze slid across the shifting crowd, seeking someone, anyone who might be able to help her, but there was no-one whom she knew. She could hear admiring snatches of conversation concerning the Prince's courage, and then a child's high, indignant voice. "*That's* the Prince of Wales? But it can't be, he looks just like a little ape in a wig too big for him!"

Beside her, Robbie sniggered. "Out o' the mouths of babes ... " he said gleefully. "How true, the innocent words of a child. Come closer, my puny, worthless wee man, and meet your doom."

Polly wondered how that doom was to be inflicted: surely not with the knife which he still held to her ribs? No, she would bet a large sum that a brace of pistols, ready primed and loaded, lay concealed beneath the boards and trestles of the stall. What a perfect, simple plan. She could envisage it all too clearly. The Prince would stop at the enticing display, and the obsequious Mrs. Templeman would show him her wares: then, while he was absorbed and his escort off guard, Robbie, hitherto unnoticed in the background, would grab the hidden pistols and fire. At such point-blank range, he could hardly miss. And then he would use the resultant terror and confusion to escape, while she and Mrs. Templeman would be left to face the wrath of the mob. Polly would have no chance to explain that she was not a willing accomplice. At best, she would be flung into Newgate, to await the hideous death meted out to female traitors. At worst, she would be beaten to death on the ice by furious Whigs ...

The full horror of what she faced broke over her in a wave of panic, and she looked wildly round, straight into the lean, sombre face of André Dark.

He was perhaps only ten yards away, and as their eyes met she saw the shock of recognition, the relief instantly replaced by horror as he realised the identity of her companion, and the danger she faced: and in that instant, she knew what he felt for her, and rejoiced.

And so she took a long deep breath, that might be her last, and shouted at the full strength of her lungs. "Dark! *Do* something! He's going to kill the Prince!"

As the words left her, Robbie cursed, and flung her aside so violently that she slipped and fell on the treacherous ice. Gasping, she saw him reach past her with a swift, furious movement, and snatch two heavy horse pistols from beneath the counter of the stall.

Everything seemed to erupt around her. Screaming, as those nearest realised what was happening: shouts further along the row of stalls, where the Prince had paused: and the deafening crash as Sinclair discharged the first pistol over her head. Desperate to stop him firing again, Polly flung her arms round his legs, and with a shouted oath he tried to beat her away with the pistol. A glancing, savage blow flung her backwards, her head reeling, and she saw him raise and aim the second gun straight at Dark, just the other side of the counter.

The screaming faltered. With a sob, Polly looked her last at her lover's living face: and Robbie pulled the trigger.

CHAPTER TWENTY FOUR

'Desp'rate Deeds and Mischiefs done'

Sinclair pulled the trigger: and there was a small, apologetic click as the weapon misfired. For an instant the two men stared at each other as if they could not believe that there had been no explosion, no bullet, no death: and then Robbie hurled the useless pistol at his enemy, turned and ran. As Polly, weak with the extremity of her relief, struggled to her knees, Dark vaulted the counter, sending cloth and lace sliding to the ice, and almost treading on her hand. He brushed past her as if she had not been there, and was gone in pursuit.

"Polly! Polly, my dear, are you all right?"

Thank God, it was Sam, dear, kind, reliable Sam, bending over her. She ignored the shouted questions and comments of other, less sympathetic bystanders, and said urgently, "Help me up, please, Sam!"

"Madam, you're bleeding," said another voice, and she saw a young, well-dressed man in a powdered wig looking down at her with lively concern. "Did that villain strike you?"

"Of course he did!" Polly snapped, losing patience with well-meaning sympathy. "Sam, I beg you, help me, he has a knife, he'll kill Dark if he has the chance, you saw what happened just now –"

"Madam," said Powdered Wig, speaking slowly and clearly as if to someone turned in her wits, "you are hurt, perhaps sorely. As a physician, I must insist on immediate rest. A darkened room, cupping perhaps half a pint, and the application of a few leeches should be of benefit to a disordered mind – "

"Oh, you and your leeches can go to hell!" Polly cried, and pulled herself up with the aid of Sam's stout and willing arm. "Where have they gone?"

As the physician stepped back, startled and offended, she followed Sam's pointing finger and saw two figures, one a few yards behind the other, running towards the further bank of the river. Behind them, other pursuers streamed out in a wide fan like the trailing edge of a cloak. There had not been so much traffic on that side of the Thames, which was mostly lined with wharves and timber yards, fields and rope walks, so the ice was still sharp and hummocked, difficult to negotiate. She saw Sinclair stumble and crash to the ground, and gasped, but before Dark could reach him, he had scrambled to his feet and was fleeing onwards, towards the land. Once amongst the maze of warehouses and stacks of logs and timber, he would surely soon lose the hunters – or find a place to ambush the chief of them.

"Come on, Sam!" Polly cried, impelled by a dreadful vision of Sinclair leaping out on his unsuspecting quarry, knife in hand, determined to kill.

But Sam was standing stricken, as if his feet had frozen to the ice, staring at the two men. He said, in a voice quite unlike his usual tones, "Whose warehouses are those?"

"What?" Polly cried in bewilderment. "Whose *warehouses*? How should I know? And anyway, what does it matter? Come *on*!" And she pulled impatiently at his sleeve.

"It matters," said Sam, with the memory of his cheerful conversation with Dark still horribly fresh in his mind, "because there is to be a firework display on the ice later, in honour of Prince Frederick's birthday. And the skyrockets, two hundred of them which Dark has made up ready, have been stored in Mr. Baker's timber warehouse in Lambeth. He told me so himself, just this morning."

There was a small, hideous silence. Polly felt suddenly sick at the thought of what might happen, and of what Sinclair might be desperate enough to do. Her hands crept to her mouth, and she whispered, "Oh, my God."

"Someone must warn those people," Sam said, suddenly as brisk as if he had been shaken. "But you must stay here – you *must*, Polly, do you understand me? At the best of times a timber warehouse is like a tinderbox, an inferno in waiting. If it is also filled with gunpowder ... well, you might not be safe even here." He looked round. "There are soldiers coming – perhaps they are the ones Gin went to find. Go and tell them that Mr. Baker's warehouse may be at risk, and the reason. They will know better than I, what effect any explosion might have. I'll try and persuade the hounds that pursuit is too dangerous."

"But what about Dark?"

"He knows the risks, my dear, none better," said Sam, and gave her a smile which failed to convince either of them that all would be well. "If anyone can stop Sinclair before he sets light to that warehouse, it will be Dark. Now for the love of God, go and tell those soldiers!"

As he hurried away, Polly turned frantically in the opposite direction. There was a great deal of activity along the lines of booths, tents and stalls. The royal party still seemed to be on the river, apparently oblivious to the commotion, although they must have realised by now that there had been some disturbance. The running soldiers, their coats blazing scarlet against the glistening silver ice and the duller clothes of the people, were hardly inconspicuous. One file made a protective ring around the Prince and his entourage, while the others, holding their muskets at the ready, marched briskly towards the far bank, an officer at their head with sword drawn.

Polly ran towards them, waving her hands and

shouting to attract the captain's attention. After a quick glance he ignored her, obviously assuming her to be a silly hysterical woman. It was only when she placed herself right in his path that he was forced to take notice. "Out of my way, madam, I am on the King's business, seeking a Jacobite who has attempted the life of the Prince of Wales."

"I know that!" Polly cried furiously. "I stopped him! And I know what he plans to do. One of those warehouses contains the fireworks they were going to set off tonight for the young Prince's birthday, and he's going to blow everything up if you don't do something!"

Now she had his full attention. "Do you know which building?"

"Only that it belongs to a Mr. Baker. It must be one of those over there, but I don't know which one."

"We'll find it, madam, never fear," said the officer. "And my thanks. This assassin – what does he look like?"

"He's a tall man in a blue coat and a brown wig. Dark's chasing him –"

"Dark, do you say? Trust him to be in at the death," the captain said with a smile. "Well, between us we'll soon have that Jack cornered, madam."

Wishing she shared his confidence, she stepped back out of their way. All around her, people were standing in groups, talking animatedly and inaccurately about what had just happened. The lace stall had been pillaged of its wares in the confusion, and there was no sign of Robbie's slatternly accomplice, who had presumably made herself scarce. Amidst the overturned boards and trestles, something lay half-hidden, and with considerable relief Polly recognised it as Sinclair's wicked little dagger, which he must have dropped as he picked up the pistols. At least she did not now have to worry about Robbie stabbing Dark in any struggle.

"Madam! Madam!" Gin's raucous voice echoed over the ice. "Oh, Madam, thank Gawd I've found you!" The child came running up, breathless and scarlet in the face. She must have fallen in her haste to deliver her message to the soldiers, for her apron was torn and filthy, and she had lost her cap. "Oh, Madam, what's happened, where's Dark? They're saying a mad Jack's tried to kill the Prince of Wales, but he can't have done because he's over there chatting away as if he ain't got a care in the world!"

"Sinclair ran across the river," Polly said, gesturing at the warehouses. She could see crowds of pursuers surging aimlessly amongst the stacked timbers and, closer at hand and just reaching the causeway, the red-coated soldiers, now moving at a cautious but purposeful trot. "And Dark went after him."

"So which one's got the skyrockets in, then?" demanded Gin. "That one they're all standing next to?"

"How do you know about the fireworks?"

"Oh, I knows everyfink," said Gin, not without a certain smugness. "Anyways, what Dark does with gunpowder ain't never been no secret. Well, we'd better go and stop 'em all being blown to Kingdom Come, hadn't we? Come on, ma'am, what you waiting for?"

What indeed. Her heart thudding madly within her slashed bodice, and the winter wind cold on her face, Polly turned and, with Gin at her side, hurried as fast as the ice and her shoes would allow, across the river towards the Surrey bank.

"So what happened, ma'am?" Gin asked, puffing: after all, she had been to Hyde Park and then down to Westminster, and even for a quick, agile child it was a long way to run. "*Did* Sinclair take a pot shot at the Prince?"

"No, oh no – he never came near the Prince at all." As

they struggled across the lumpy, frozen surface of the river, Polly gave her a succinct account of events at the lace-seller's booth.

"Gawd help us," was Gin's awed comment. "An' if that pistol hadn't misfired, Dark's brains would'er been splattered all over the ice."

"You don't have to labour the point," said Polly, who knew that the dreadful image of what might have happened would haunt her sleepless hours for a long time to come. "And it's not over yet. What are those soldiers doing?"

They had almost reached the Lambeth shore. The long incline, rising out of the waves of ice, was almost as treacherous underfoot as the river, and several people were sliding and falling around them. Supporting each other and moving with care, Polly and Gin negotiated the slippery slope, and arrived at last on the crusted mud of the timber yard. Perhaps thirty yards in front of them stood a huge warehouse, newly built like a country barn of tarred wood under a red tiled roof, and stacked all around it were the logs of deal and pine, oak and elm, and the more exotic mahogany and teak, shipped upriver in huge barges to lie here until required to satisfy London's insatiable need for building timber. Over to the left of the building was a saw-pit, surrounded by neat piles of snow-shrouded planks, and beyond lay a rough fence and more timber yards strung along the bank of the river, all constructed in a similar pattern to this.

Some of the soldiers were trying to herd the confused, reluctant gaggle of pursuers back towards the safety of the river, while others poked industriously into every nook or cranny, including some which had scarcely room for a mouse to hide. There was no sign of Sinclair, and Polly, frantically craning her neck, could not see Dark either: both men seemed to have vanished into the timber yards without trace. But there was Sam not ten yards away, bent over and gasping, his hands on his knees and his face crimson with unaccustomed exertion. At once she hurried over, Gin following.

"Polly! What are you doing here? I thought I told you to stay well clear of all this! Please, my dear, go back before something terrible happens."

"I have no intention of doing so," she said resolutely. "Do you know which warehouse contains the fireworks?"

"No, I don't, and no-one else seems to either. The soldiers are conducting a search. Polly, *please*, I beg you, leave now – it's for your own safety. And in any case, now the soldiers are here, Dark is in no danger."

"But he *is*!" Polly cried, almost weeping with vexation at his obtuseness. "Don't you see? Sinclair has staked everything on his plot to kill the Prince, and now that we have foiled him, what has he left to lose? He wants revenge, and if he's trapped, he'll have no scruples about taking it. Or about blowing everyone around him to bits."

"Which is why you must both go back *now*," said Sam. "And I'm sure the soldiers will find him before he can do any harm," he added, with what he obviously considered to be encouraging reassurance. For the first time in their friendship, Polly felt considerable irritation at his failure to understand, but resolved to conceal it, for he meant well. In fact, she thought in exasperation, those three words would probably be written on his tombstone.

"Don't you understand?" she said urgently. "Something terrible is going to happen, I know it is, I can feel it – and if I can only find Dark, I can warn him!"

"He already knows the danger," Sam pointed out, patting her arm. "And he will appear in a moment or two, depend on it. Polly, you are shivering, take my coat."

A shout went up from the crowd, and she pushed

forward to see. Two of the soldiers had emerged from the warehouse, dragging between then a rather battered figure, loudly protesting his innocence. "What's this, a madhouse? I don't know who you're looking for, but it ain't me!"

"So you says," cried one of his captors, "but what was you doing skulking around in there like a common napper, eh?"

"On account of how I *works* here, you stupid noodle!" shouted the unfortunate man.

"Then you can tell us which is Mr. Baker's warehouse," said the captain, striding forward.

"It's that one, innit," said the resentful prisoner, jabbing an indignant finger at the next yard downriver. "An' if it's that fancy cove in the blue coat and the fellow in black chasing him you're after, well, that's where they went!"

At that moment, a succession of muted cracks, like distant gunfire, came from the neighbouring warehouse. Instantly, every gaze swung leftwards, and a great gasp emerged as a broad smudge of grey smoke climbed with leisurely insolence into the milky sky.

"Oh, my God!" Sam cried. Someone screamed wildly, "Fire!" The rest of the crowd took up the cry, and at once the soldiers pushed forward, shouting at everyone to get back onto the river. But there were not enough of them, and the Londoners' instinct, fifty years after the great conflagration that had destroyed their city, was to run towards the blaze, not away from it. The redcoats were swept aside as scores of men and women, apparently unaware of the danger of explosion, surged forward to help extinguish the flames. And Polly, desperate to discover what was happening, ran with them.

* * *

Nothing in his largely disreputable life had prepared André Dark for the surge of emotions which overwhelmed him when he saw Polly by Sinclair's side. In the first instant, it was pure, naked jealousy: how *dared* she consort with that vicious rogue again, after all he had done to her? And then he saw the expression on her face, terror mingled with relief, and realised the truth.

The more rational part of his mind knew that it was vital that Sinclair was caught before he could hatch any more murderous plots, but something deeper and more primeval goaded him to greater efforts. He hated Sinclair for what he had done and tried to do to Polly, and he wanted him dead. If the soldiers that he had summoned arrived in time – and Captain Short was an old friend and comrade, who would know the moment he scanned his message that the situation must be serious – then Sinclair would not outlive the day.

By the time he reached the long causeway sliding up out of the Thames, he had fallen three times on the treacherous ice. Sinclair, however, must be more sure-footed, or more fortunate, for he had only come down once, and was further ahead than before. He reached the top of the ramp and paused, glancing back at Dark with a most extraordinary look of unholy, gleeful triumph on his face. Then he ran on, but not towards the bulk of the nearest warehouse, straight ahead of them amidst the piles of logs. He dodged round the first stack on the left, and with sudden horror, Dark realised where he was heading, and what he must know. Wright, in Newgate, must have told him all about his old schoolfellow, who dabbled with skyrockets and had a habit of storing gunpowder in bulk: and Jack Templeman would have added the information about this evening's display, thus presenting Sinclair with the perfect opportunity for revenge.

But he had locked the skyrockets safely away until the time came to set them out on the ice, in holes already drilled for them. Could Sinclair have discovered where they were hidden, broken into the storeroom and removed them, all within the space of his hours of freedom since escaping from Newgate? If he had acted alone, surely not. But he would have had plenty of eager accomplices.

Behind Dark, the mob was pouring over the ice, intoxicated with the joy of the chase and hallooing like country yokels after a fox. Now, though, it was not only their prey who was in mortal danger. With renewed urgency, he ran after his foe.

By the time he had climbed over the fence dividing the two yards, Sinclair had vanished. Dark looked around, although he already suspected where his quarry might have gone. Mr. Baker's warehouse was almost identical to its neighbour, but constructed on an altogether more generous scale, for he was one of the most prosperous timber merchants in London, with suppliers in Sweden, West Africa and Jamaica, as well as his own plantations and woods in Kent and the Forest of Dean. His wares lay around it in ordered piles, sawn and unsawn, although the inclement weather had halted most building work since before Christmas, and of course the timber could not be transported along the river while it was frozen. As a consequence, most of the workers had been laid off, and there was no-one in the yard save for a couple of men standing by a covered cart, staring in mild bewilderment at the warehouse. Following their pointing fingers, Dark ran over to the great doors, which were slightly ajar, and stepped cautiously inside.

It was as hushed and dim as a cathedral. The cold still air was filled with the fragrance of pine and the gentle tickle of dust. Around him in the gloom, planks lay stacked one above the other, awaiting their hour of usefulness. Dark stood very still and listened intently, while his eyes adjusted to the limited light. He heard the distant cries of the mob, still searching the wrong warehouse, and nearer, a soft scuttering from a fleeing rat or mouse. If Sinclair had indeed taken refuge inside here, he was keeping very quiet.

As silently as possible, Dark drew his sword. They had fought in Bath, and Dark had lost then, but he had seen, pursuing Sinclair across the ice, that his quarry was unarmed. Even so, he had no illusions about the likely outcome of this encounter, for the Scot had already given ample proof of his murderous intent. It would be a fight to the death.

The voices and shouts came nearer, reminding him that others were also in danger. He must find Sinclair quickly, before he could set off the fireworks. His senses, straining desperately for some clue, caught a tiny, harsh scraping sound on the very edge of silence. It was so familiar, in this unfamiliar location, that for a moment he could not place it. And then his nostrils detected an acrid tang in the air, and he knew.

Now that his eyes were accustomed to the darkness, he could see the faintest glow away to his right, not far off. With infinitesimal caution, he crept towards it, trying to control his breathing, trying to listen for any betraying sound. Sinclair was, as he knew only too well, a devious and subtle man, and must surely have planned an ambush –

The first rocket came screaming at him out of the darkness, trailing a prodigious cloud of glittering amber. Before he had realised what was happening, it had slammed into the wall of the warehouse, a few feet away from him, and exploded in a torrent of sparks, showering him with flecks of fire.

Acting purely on instinct, Dark dropped to the floor and crawled into the shelter of the nearest stack of wood. A couple of heartbeats later, a second rocket flashed past, and burst in almost the same place as its predecessor.

There was time for two thoughts: that if he did not stop Sinclair, the warehouse would surely catch fire, and set light to the rest of the fireworks: and that he must keep low and hidden, for the rockets came faster than any possible reaction to them, and if one hit him he was dead. The memory came back to him, at once sweet and bitter, of that evening at the Tower. He had told Polly that the sticks had to be planted in the ground, as it was too dangerous to hold them. But it was certainly possible: he had done it himself, showing off to an audience of young bloods. All you needed was a strong nerve, a steady hand, and very stout gloves. And Sinclair was desperate for vengeance at any price.

He raised his head cautiously and called. "Sinclair!"

The answer came not in the form of a single rocket, but several in rapid succession, right over his head. He would not make that mistake again. Very carefully, he moved so that he could see behind him. One had landed on a heap of rubbish by the doors, and set it alight. Soon the dry wood and sawdust would be burning fiercely, cutting off any chance of escape in that direction. But the warehouse had another exit, a smaller door at the side of the building. And whatever happened, he had no intention of letting Sinclair get away.

Trying not to make any sound which might betray his position, he wriggled like a snake towards the further end of the stack, and peered round it. The fire shed some light on the huge ramparts of timber, and above his head the rafters were flickering orange, while there was a strong smell of smoke. Sinclair must be lurking somewhere in the further reaches of the warehouse, close to the internal store room where the rockets had supposedly been secured, but the shadows there were deep and impenetrable. Dark still had his sword, though. Keeping watch on the area where he thought the Jacobite might be hiding, he threw it behind him, so it landed with a skittering thud roughly where he had been lying a moment before.

This time, he saw the rocket rise with a whoosh of sparks from a place just to the right of where he had marked. The flight spun wildly off course and crashed in a spray of burning embers, two stacks away. Almost before it had landed, Dark sprang to his feet and ran, keeping his head low, to the shelter of the next pile of planks. He crouched down, his hands crossed protectively over his bare head, for his wig had fallen off when he dropped to the floor, and listened intently.

No sound came from within the warehouse save his own breathing, which seemed dangerously loud despite his efforts to control it. He could hear shouts outside, and they were getting closer. If the mob arrived at the doors, he knew Sinclair would fire the rockets at them, and there would be carnage. If Polly, or Sam, were amongst the crowd ...

"Black! Dark, or whatever ye call yourself! D'ye hear me? I'll do a deal with ye!" Sinclair's voice was so loud that he must be only a few yards away from where Dark crouched. "They'll be here any moment. Ye wouldn't want innocent blood shed, now would ye, man? Be reasonable! Turn your head while I slip away, there's a ship waiting downriver that'll take me to France, and I'll never trouble ye again."

Dark knew better than to respond, and give away how close he was. Urgently, he searched his memory. Only a few days ago, he had come here with Mr. Baker, the owner, to inspect the place. It had seemed ideal – secure, well guarded, close to the river, and with an internal storage room intended for tools and equipment, where the finished skyrockets could be safely stored until needed. The foreman, carrying a lantern, had shown them round, but he had not paid much attention to the layout of the warehouse itself. He tried to remember exactly where the side door was, and how many rows of stacks. But although he strove to call up the details, his usual powers of observation seemed to have failed him entirely.

"I know you're still there, Dark!" The voice had acquired a definite note of mockery. "Come on, man, see sense! Ye wouldn't want to see Poll hurt, now would ye? Yes, I know all about ye and Poll – the gossip of the town, Wright told me. Dear Lord, she must be desperate to have taken up with scum like ye – no wonder she was so eager to come back to me in Newgate! But then she's hardly in her first flush, is she? Is that withering trollop the only woman willing to share your bed, eh?"

Despite the rage that boiled up inside him, Dark knew that Sinclair was trying to provoke him into revealing himself. It was a good ploy, but unnecessary. The Jacobite only had to wait until the smoke, drifting thickly past his nose and unwillingly drawn into his lungs with every breath, would force him to cough.

"Still no answer? Let's see if this'll flush ye out!"

Three rockets, one after the other, shot up to the rafters and burst above them. In the confines of the building, the noise was shockingly loud. Two of the sticks dropped to the floor just beside him, still burning, and the third a few feet to the rear. Dark had made two hundred: his adversary still had plenty of ammunition left.

"Where are ye, ye whoreson bastard?" Sinclair yelled angrily. "Come out and show yourself, or it'll be the worse for ye!"

Dark now had a very good idea of where his quarry was skulking: he must be about twenty feet distant as the rat ran, behind the timber stack two rows away from the one by which he himself was sheltering. That meant that he was probably quite close to the side door, and escape. Tendrils of smoke tickled his nose and the back of his throat, and he stifled a cough. He must act now, before the crowds arrived, before he lost the vital element of surprise. As the next rockets soared up towards the roof, he leapt to his feet and ran.

The brilliant light from the starburst illuminated the stacks of timber and showed him his path. He dived round the furthest pile and there, his mouth open, a skyrocket's stick in one hand and a glowing length of slow match in the other, stood his quarry, his eyes gleaming red in the hellish, flickering light. But before he could fall on Sinclair, the great doors of the warehouse were flung wide open by the mob, eager to douse the blaze, and the fire roared up to the rafters with a splendid new vigour.

Dark whirled round. He could see the people framed in the wide opening, lit with the glow of the flames against the brightness of the day outside. "Get back!" he roared, at the full pitch of his lungs, and at the same instant Sinclair set the match to the fuse of the rocket he was holding. It flew from his gloved hand, leaving a wild, twisting trail of silver sparks, and howled straight over the heads of the crowd into the comparative safety of the open air.

That worked far better than any shouted warning. Screaming, the pursuers turned and ran, falling over each other in their haste to escape. Sinclair snatched up another rocket from the pile at his feet, and aimed it full at Dark's chest. "Ye'll no' escape so easy, ye treacherous sneaking spy!" he cried. "I'll see ye dead if it's the last thing I do!"

That seemed very likely, for the flames were leaping up, fastening greedily upon the dry racks of seasoned timber that lay between the two men and the warehouse doors. In a few minutes there would be no stopping it, for the Thames was frozen and buckets of well water would be futile. He saw the glowing end of the match move inexorably towards the fuse of the skyrocket, not six feet from him. And because there was no alternative, Dark launched himself straight at his enemy.

The speed and power of his assault sent them both crashing against the rear wall of the warehouse. Dark felt the bulk of the rocket between them, and knew that if Sinclair had managed to light the fuse and it went off, both of them would be killed. His hands scrabbled for the narrow cylinder of pasteboard and gunpowder. The other man was gasping and cursing, trying to fend him off. With a furious strength he had not realised he possessed, Dark wrenched the rocket out of Sinclair's clutching fingers and hurled it away from them. He saw the bright glint of the fuse, and turned his face away just in time as the rocket exploded. Flaming embers sprayed in all directions. Sinclair screamed, and twisted convulsively. With enormous force, he thrust Dark off and staggered blindly away into the smoke, his hands to his burnt face. And then, crackling merrily, the rest of the rockets began to go off.

* * *

Polly had been running at the rear of the crowd making for the warehouse, hampered by her cloak and skirts and unable to move as fast as men in breeches. When the doors were hauled wide, she had a brief glimpse of the leaping flames and pouring smoke, and then something shot over her head with a screech, and exploded in a crackle of pallid sparks.

"Oh, my God!" Sam cried beside her, and dragged her out of the way as the people screamed and scattered. "No, no, stay back Polly, you can't do anything!"

"Dark's in there, you booby!" she shouted at him, as raucous as any fishwife. "Let me go! Let me *go*, will you?"

He had his arms tight around her, and though a small man, well into middle age, he was far more powerful than she was. She kicked and fought him, but he dragged her back as more rockets went off inside the warehouse, and by this time Gin was beside her, bawling frantically into her ear. "No, it ain't no good, you can't do nothing, for Gawd's sake ma'am, don't go getting yourself killed as well!"

As well. The words burned into her mind like a brand. Between them, they pulled her backwards, out of reach of the smoke and the flames and the deranged rockets that could still be heard, and occasionally seen in a flash of sparks, inside the warehouse. There was a small pile of logs near to the wharf, well away from any danger, and Sam pushed her firmly down onto it and sat beside her, still holding her, with Gin on the other side.

In a terrible silence, they watched the fire. Some men were trying to organise a chain of buckets from a nearby well to douse the flames, but it was a completely futile task, and their efforts ended abruptly when another rocket shot spinning from the inferno and burst on the ground near to the rescuers, inflicting serious burns on one of them. His colleagues carried him, blackened and groaning, to the comparative safety of the adjoining yard, while the people also moved back, stunned and appalled at the terrible speed with which the blaze had taken hold. The walls of the warehouse, thickly coated with pitch, burned marvellously well, and a huge boiling plume of smoke climbed up high towards the clouds, a beacon of ill omen that could probably be seen all over London and for many miles beyond.

Inevitably, as the fire grew, it threatened to ignite not only the timber stacked around it, but the other warehouses on either side. There were several smaller outbreaks not far from where they sat, and Polly watched in numb despair as shouting men stamped and beat with coats or cloaks. A body of soldiers came up at a run, carrying long hooks. She realised suddenly what they were about, and leapt to her feet with a cry of horror, but Sam pulled her down again and held her close. "Polly, my dear, they must do this, to stop the blaze spreading. There is nothing that can be done to help them now, they must both be dead."

So she stared dry eyed, disbelieving, as the soldiers

pulled at the flaming walls, dragging at the beams supporting the roof until with a sudden roar it fell on top of the inferno within. A vast, monstrous pall of black smoke rushed up and out over the yard: and in the midst of it, the last of Dark's skyrockets soared heavenwards in mocking celebration of the devastation beneath.

Polly could not have watched any more, even if she had wanted to: the smoke filled her lungs, covered her hair, her clothes, hot cinders burned her skin and stung her eyes. With a choking gasp, she bent her head, covered her face with her cloak and listened to the shouts and cries and noises all around her as the remains of Mr. Baker's fine warehouse collapsed into charcoal and ash. Beside her, she could feel Gin's small body shaking with silent sobs, and put her arm around her. Then there was a long, long interval, in which she tried to accept that Dark was dead, and that she would never see him again. As a result of his courage, the Prince was safe, but he and Sinclair had both had died in that dreadful pyre, with the rockets to mark their passing.

"The smoke is easing now," Sam said gently, at long last. "But you don't have to look if you don't want to."

Slowly, wearily, Polly put aside her hood, and sat upright. The cold air was full of ash, blown softly around them by a wind which promised warmer weather. In place of the warehouse was a huge heap of blackened tiles, charred wood and fat plumes of smoke still rising from within, fed on fires that had not been quenched by the fall of the roof. Groups of men and women stood around the ruined building, stunned and dazed by the speed and totality of the destruction. Ignoring Sam's detaining hand, she got to her feet and walked towards the remains of the warehouse. He had been right. Nothing and no-one could have survived that. With a sob of grief, Polly sank to her knees and buried her face in her hands. He was dead. She had never met anyone like him before, and she never would again. And though she had only known him for such a short time, those few days and weeks would surely colour the rest of her life.

A hand touched her shoulder. Sam, offering sympathy that she did not want, but could not turn away. She must get up, and walk, and talk, and deal with the mundane matters of life, for the sake of those who depended on her. Feeling as burdened with grief and cares as an old, old woman, she clambered painfully to her feet, and turned.

A figure much taller and leaner than Sam stood before her. A man clothed from head to foot in soot and ash, with hands and face raw and bleeding from several injuries and burns. He had eyes that were brown, but lightly flecked with green and amber: she had remarked on them before. And he was smiling at her.

For two heartbeats, maybe three, she could not believe what she saw. Then he said softly, "Polly, it's me," and she knew that at last she could trust the evidence of her own eyes.

"Dark?" Suddenly the tears were streaming down her face, she was weeping for his resurrection as she had not wept for his death. "Is it really you? I thought you were dead!"

"There was a rumour in the army that I was indestructible," Dark said. "Perhaps it's true."

Shaking, she put out a hand to touch him, for at that moment he was the dearest thing on earth to her. He felt solid enough, and his deep chuckle of amusement confirmed it. "I'm not a phantom, darling Poll, I promise you. No phantom I ever heard of would do this." And he put his arms around her and held her close, while she wept for joy and relief on his filthy chest.

"You certainly seem to have as many lives as my cat," said Polly at last, rather shakily. "And how glad I am of it."

"So am I." The old dry, teasing tone that she liked so well was back in his voice. "I am sorry that I left you on the ice, dear Paradice, but I could not wait, or I would have lost Sinclair. How is your head?"

"My head?" She had forgotten about it in the wild pursuit that had followed. "Oh, pray do not trouble yourself on that score, sir, it hardly hurts at all."

"But you are shivering." He took her torn, dirty cloak and wrapped it closer around her. "I have to tell you that he is dead. If nothing else, he had a great deal of courage."

"He should have put it to better use," Polly said bleakly. "It is hardly courageous to plot the cold-blooded murder of an unarmed Prince, or to try to blow up half of Lambeth in a grand gesture of revenge. I do not think that the Pretender will miss his services. He is better off without men like Robbie Sinclair."

There was an apologetic cough, and she looked round. The captain stood in front of them, a broad smile on his face. "How d'you fare, Dark, after all these years? Trust you to be in the thick of it, as usual." His eyes glanced appreciatively at her. "And pray present me to your charming companion – we have already met, but there was no opportunity for introductions."

Dark was smiling warmly in return. "Mistress Paradice, this is Captain Short, of His Majesty's Foot Guards, and an old comrade in arms."

"We fought together in Marlborough's wars," said Short, whose name seemed particularly apt, since he was not much taller than Polly, and comfortably rotund. "Well, Dark, this is a fine state of affairs – an escaped Jack, an assassin to boot, and half of Lambeth up in flames! I don't need to ask why *you* are here – he has a nose like a hound's for trouble, ma'am, and I could tell you some tales that would raise the hairs on your pretty head – but how does such a delightful young lady come to be concerned in such a sorry pickle?"

Polly gave her lover a wry, speaking glance, and he laughed. "How indeed! It's a long tale, and I suspect I only have the half of it. But she saved the Prince's life today, at some cost to herself."

"So I see – I do trust you are not seriously hurt, ma'am? I would not like to think of such enchanting beauty scarred for life."

There was a twinkle in his eyes as he said it, and Polly, usually acutely sensitive to insincere flattery, warmed to him at once. "I think not, sir – a minor scratch, no more. I shall be restored to my usual self in no time. And once I have changed my clothes and washed away the soot, I shall be almost presentable."

"You look extremely presentable to me now," Short said, grinning. "Well, I have much to do here, so I'll speak to you in more detail later, Dark – I'll need your information for my report. Rest assured, the part you both played in saving the Prince from such a dangerous rogue will not go unrecognised. In the meantime, alas, duty calls. Your humble servant, ma'am." He bowed, and turned away.

"There are many things I would like to ask you, concerning your role in all this, Paradice," Dark murmured in her ear. "But I think it best to let sleeping dogs lie."

"A sentiment with which I am entirely in agreement. If you ask me no questions," Polly said drily, "then I will fire none at you, for whereas there are five things I have not told you, there must be five hundred that you have not told me."

"Then am I to infer from those words that our acquaintance is to continue?"

Polly glanced up at him. "Once, I foolishly cast something away, and did not realise how greatly I valued it, until it was gone. Now it lies in my palm for the taking, and I have no intention of being so stupid again."

He was staring at her very intently. At last, he said, "Do you mean what I think you mean?"

"I trust so. We have suffered from a considerable number of misunderstandings and ridiculous disagreements, Dark – and just as much on my side as yours, before you snap my head off again – but on the whole we shall do very well together, do you not think so? You may paint in your garret all day, and fend off the attentions of that dreadful old hag downstairs, and then you can come to the Paradise and forget all your cares with a cup or two of coffee and a song."

"And afterwards?"

"Afterwards," Polly murmured, feeling her knees tremble with the force of her desire, "you may join me upstairs for a night-cap. If, of course, you are so inclined."

"My inclinations may tend that way, I confess." He bent forward. His lips were warm and dry, and tasted of wood ash and soot. "Paradice, you are the most annoying, provoking, delicious woman I have ever encountered, and I am not sure I shall ever have my fill of you, however hard I try."

"You may try as hard as you wish, sir, but you must promise to smile at least once an hour, and not sink into the dumps more than once a year. Or I shall have to work upon you night and day until your spirits are lightened."

"I can hardly wait."

"Excellent," Polly said, and smiled happily up at him. "Now, I command that you kiss me properly, no holds barred."

"I spoke the truth, did I not, when I said to you in Bath, that to attract a woman's interest, I should arrange to appear dead?" And he stopped her laughter with his mouth.

Gin's shriek of joy intruded uncouthly on their embrace.

"It's him, it's Dark! Look, Mr. Jessop, he's back from the dead!"

Polly wiped her eyes, leaving black smears all over her face, and turned to see her maid and Sam hurrying up. "Yes," she said, laughing and crying simultaneously. "I don't know how, but he's alive."

"I hardly know either," Dark said. He kept his arm tight round Polly, and she could feel his warmth seep through her clothes to her heart. "I thought I would die in there, along with Sinclair."

"I hope *he's* dead," said Gin callously. "Is he?"

"Oh, yes." Dark looked down at Polly, his face sombre. "He was blinded and burnt when one of the rockets exploded too close to him – I saw him staggering away, and then I lost him in the smoke. But I knew that I couldn't go after him, I had to escape, or die. I found the side door in time, thank God, and managed to get out, just before the roof came down."

Sam shook his head sadly. "I suppose his end was very terrible, but I think it was deserved. And of course Mary is now forever safe from him."

"We are all safer for his death," said Polly. She thought of how she had once loved him, and of how he had exploited, manipulated and betrayed that love, and then deliberately set the past behind her. It was over, and done, and could not now be changed. And how could she regret something that had never truly existed? Especially as his seduction of Mary Jessop had led to her meeting Dark. With sudden and overwhelming affection, she stood on tiptoe and kissed his battered, blackened cheek.

"Here, let's have none of that!" Gin shouted. "That's public indecency, that is, and didn't oughter be allowed in broad daylight. Anyway, you'll upset Mr. Jessop."

"On the contrary," said Sam, "I can think of no sight that

pleases me more. And may I say, Dark, how very glad I am to see you safe, if not exactly sound."

"An' so says all of us," Gin remarked. "Well, Sinclair's dead, and good riddance to him. Can we go home now? I'm froze to me very marrer."

Polly found Dark's hand, warm despite the chilly air, and her fingers wound amongst his. He looked down at her, and smiled. "An excellent idea. There is no reason why we should linger here any longer, and I for one would very much welcome a good strong cup of coffee to restore some life to me. I feel as if I have been ground up in a mill and spat out into a furnace."

"An' you look as if you have," Gin pointed out rudely. "If I was you, ma'am," she added, with a sly glance at Polly, "I'd say no to him getting into bed with you till you'd washed him all over."

"Another excellent idea," Polly said, and her hand squeezed her lover's, promising future delights. "Well, before darkness falls and we freeze to the ground, let us return to our Paradise."

"Which once I thought was lost to me forever," Dark said softly, as Gin and Sam moved off towards the river. "But now, darling Polly, you are truly my Paradice, regained."

They walked together out onto the Thames, their shadows behind them, long and blue across the ice. In front of them, the sun was sinking, glowing ruddy gold above the roofs of Westminster, and the western wind blew softly on their faces, promising a change in the weather at last, and the warmth of a new and hopeful spring.

HISTORICAL NOTE

The Jacobite Rebellion of 1715 is not so well known as that of 1745, but paradoxically it stood a much greater chance of success, and if its leaders had mobilised earlier, immediately after Queen Anne's death in 1714, popular support in much of England and Scotland might have swept James Stuart, the 'Old Pretender', to the throne. However, incompetence, cowardice and sheer bad luck combined to bring it to the ignominious end I have described.

Although a work of fiction, *A Parcel of Rogues* is firmly rooted in fact. Bath was indeed a hot-bed of Jacobite conspiracy, and the plotters (amongst whom was a Captain Sinclair, though nothing more is known about him than his name) were arrested with, it is presumed, the timely information provided by Ralph Allen, then the Postmaster of the city and later to be one of its greatest benefactors. Certainly the rise in his fortunes dates from this time, as does his friendship with General Wade, who secured Bath for King George. There is, however, no mention in the documents of a certain Mrs. Paradice, although that surname is not uncommon in Wiltshire and Somerset.

Life for the Jacobite prisoners in Newgate was, astonishingly, very much as I have described, and indeed, a few weeks after the end of the book, a group of them escaped *en masse* with little effort apparently made to stop them. Their leader, General Forster, also absconded: he got Governor Pitt drunk, stole his keys and just walked out, very much as Robbie Sinclair did.

The Thames did freeze over in 1715/16, and there was a Frost Fair on the ice from the end of November until February. The Prince of Wales (afterwards George II) visited the Fair on his son's birthday, for which a firework display was planned, but there is no record of any assassination attempt on him there (though there were others made later in his life).

In making *A Parcel of Rogues* the title for this book, I have taken a certain liberty, since the song of that name is the work of Robert Burns, who lived many years afterwards. However, he seems to have re-worked older, more traditional material, and the aptness of the title was too tempting to resist!

Finally, the quotations at the head of each chapter are taken from *Trivia: or the Art of Walking the Streets of London*, an entertaining poem written in 1716 by John Gay, later famous as the author of *The Beggar's Opera*.

Pamela Belle, June 2024

The cover illustration: 'Interior Scene with Figures', by Marcellus Laroon the Younger (1679-1772), in the Tate Gallery.

Look out for 'The Supposed Sister', the next adventure of Paradice and Dark, coming soon!

Acknowledgements

Many people over the years have helped me with my writing, and with this book - so many that I couldn't possibly mention them all. My thanks are due first to my family and friends, who have always believed in me and supported me, and also to my former agent, Vivienne Schuster, now enjoying her retirement, who guided my career from the beginning and took my side, even when the going got tough. I would also like to thank E M Swift-Hook and Sasha Garwood Lloyd, who read *A Parcel of Rogues* in its later incarnation, and made numerous comments and suggestions. Any egregious errors remaining are entirely down to me! I'm also very grateful to the members of the Facebook group, Historical Writers Forum, who have been lavish with information, help and encouragement. And I should mention my debt to the staff of the London Library, who have supplied me with many rare, vital and otherwise unobtainable works of reference, and also to my colleagues in the Wiltshire Library Service, who have kept me going through good times and bad, and who understand that I frequently need to take full advantage of my staff quota of 30 books borrowed!

Thank you all so much.

Pamela Belle
June, 2024

ABOUT THE AUTHOR

Pamela Belle

I've been telling stories since before I could even read or write, and began my first book, The Moon in the Water, at the age of thirteen. Amongst many other jobs, I've been a primary school teacher, a charity shop manager, and a library assistant. I live in Wiltshire with Phoebe, my young Burmese cat, and I have two lovely adult sons I'm very proud of. Writing, though, is my passion, and I'm currently working on a new instalment in the 'Paradice and Dark' series begun with 'A Parcel of Rogues', and to be continued with 'The Supposed Sister'.

BOOKS BY THIS AUTHOR

The Moon In The Water

My first novel - begun when I was about thirteen, and known in my family as The Epic.
The Heron Quartet, Book 1
In 1635, at the age of ten, Thomazine Heron is orphaned, and sent to live with her uncle, Sir Simon Heron, and his family. She is quickly accepted by her five cousins, especially Lucy, the only girl, and Francis, whose poetic, sensitive nature puts him at odds with his domineering father and his grimly conventional eldest brother, Simon. As the children grow up, Thomazine and Francis fall in love, despite the fact that she has been betrothed to another, more distant cousin as a child. Then civil war intervenes, and the Heron family must choose sides, while tragedy looms on the horizon ...

The Chains Of Fate

The Heron Quartet, Book 2
Believing that her beloved cousin Francis is dead, Thomazine, numb with grief, has married her cousin Dominic, a young man she dislikes and mistrusts. Then, astonishingly, she learns that she has been tricked, and that Francis is still alive, and in Scotland. She makes the heart-wrenching and momentous decision to leave her baby behind, and to set out in search of her lost love. But in the twists and turns of battle and siege, defeat and treachery, can she and Francis ever be reunited, and find happiness together despite the chains of fate?

Alathea

The Heron Quartet, Book 3
Alathea Heron, daughter of Thomazine and Francis, shows precocious talent as an artist. Her very first commission is to draw the boy she meets, by chance, on the hills above her home. Years later, a trained portrait painter at the beginning of her career, she encounters him again in London, and learns that the boy she knew as John Wilmot is actually the notorious Earl of Rochester. They are imediately attracted to each other, but can her desire to become a celebrated artist defeat her growing love for this wild, dangerous and supremely gifted young man, or will she give in to his advances, and risk destroying her talent for painting?

The Lodestar

The Heron Quartet, Book 4, but the first, chronologically.
Christie Heron, young, able and intensely ambitious, secures a good position in the household of Richard, Duke of Gloucester, younger brother of King Edward IV. The lodestar of his life is his beautiful sister Meg, about to enter into a prestigious marriage with Sir Robert Drakelon. Christie has serious doubts about the match, and promises Meg that if she is ever in trouble, he will come to her aid. Sure enough, Meg soon finds that her husband is a cruel and jealous man, but when she begs Christie for help, he ignores her plea because he feels the Duke's favour is more important. His betrayal devastates Meg, and she vows never to forgive him.
Years later, Christie has become the trusted friend and henchman of Gloucester, now Richard III, and is married to a wealthy heiress who loathes him. He is beginning to realise that his ruthless and selfish pursuit of his ambitions has come at a heavy price. Can he persuade his wife to love him? And can he ever be reconciled with Meg, who plots her own

vengeance?
Then Henry Tudor invades, and everything Christie has worked for is in danger.

Wintercombe

The Wintercombe Quartet, Book 1
Silence has been married for years to Sir George St Barbe, owner of Wintercombe in Somerset, a very much older widower with three children. She has learned to keep her emotions hidden, and to be a good and dutiful wife and mother, taking pleasure in her garden and in her children and stepchildren.
Then civil war breaks out, Sir George and his eldest son leave to fight for Parliament, and Silence is left in charge of Wintercombe. But war cannot be kept at bay for ever, and a garrison of Cavaliers, led by the cruel and debauched Colonel Ridgeley, invades the house, bringing chaos, desecration and danger. Her only ally seems to be Captain Hellier, who protects her and her children and household from the worst excesses of the soldiers, but is it just friendship he offers her, or something more? And when Wintercombe becomes a battleground, will he take her side, or Colonel Ridgeley's?

Herald Of Joy

The Wintercombe Quartet, Book 2
At Wintercombe, Sir George St Barbe is dying, mourned only by his eldest daughter, Rachael, who is desperate to fulfil her father's last wish and marry his friend's son, a young man who, her stepmother Silence can see, will only make her miserable. But Sir George's death also means that his young wife is free to reunite with the man she loves, Nick Hellier, a member of the garrison that nearly wrecked Wintercombe six years ago. But she has no idea where Nick is, how to reach him,

or even if he is still alive.

Nick, however, is very much alive, and now a member of the army which the new young king, Charles II, has gathered in his attempt to take back his throne. But Cromwell and his army catch up with them at Worcester, and in the aftermath of defeat, Nick finds himself on the run, hampered by the aristocratic and idiotic Mervyn Touchet, who bears a dangerous resemblance to the king. The only place that might offer them refuge is Wintercombe, but their arrival will run the risk of putting Silence and all her family in deadly danger.

A Falling Star

The Wintercombe Quartet, Book 3

Silence's nephew, Sir Alexander St Barbe, returns from dissolute exile in Holland to take up his inheritance at Wintercombe. His arrival appalls his cousin Charles, who had hopes of inheriting Wintercombe by default, but delights and intrigues one of his other cousins, Louise, who has been brought up in France and is far more sophisticated than most of the St Barbe family. Before long, to her grandmother Silence's alarm, Louise finds herself increasingly attracted to the dangerous Alex, enraging Charles, who had hoped to make her his wife.

Rising tensions are exacerbated by the rebellion of the Duke of Monmouth, who lands in Somerset in a doomed bid to take the throne. As the St Barbes choose sides, can they avoid the tragedy and retribution that must come in the aftermath of crushing defeat?

Treason's Gift

The Wintercombe Quartet, Book 4

Louise and Alex's lively and tempestuous marriage is shattered by the death of their baby son. A catastrophic betrayal causes Alex to seek exile in Holland once more, and his cousin Charles returns to Wintercombe, eager to take Alex's place and worm his way back into Louise's affections. But the king, James II, has alienated many powerful people: revolution is in the air, and Alex is at the heart of it. Will King James be overthrown? Can Charles be evicted from Wintercombe? Will Alex and Louise be reconciled, despite what he has done? And will his plain, bookish sister Phoebe accept the proposal of the courtier, Hugh Trevelyan, Alex's friend and the younger half-brother of Francis Heron?

The final volume of the Wintercombe quartet.

The Silver City

My foray into fantasy, set in a world I first dreamed up at the back of the class as a teenager. Much more interesting than 'office practice'!
The first book in the Silver City trilogy
Young members of the Tanathi tribe are on a hunting expedition in the hills when they stumble upon a huge army of Ska'i, savage nomads fuelled by dangerous magic, and learn that they plan to attack Zithirian, known as the Silver City. Halthris is sent by her brother to warn the people there, and encounters a decadent royal family tainted by madness, magic and hidden ambitions. Her tale is believed only by Prince Ansaryon, widely assumed to be a sinister and evil sorcerer. When the Ska'i attack, a terrible act of treachery leads to the fall of the city, and Ansaryon and Halthris are forced to flee. Together, they must seek help to free Zithirian and its remaining inhabitants of the murderous Ska'i and the evil witch D'thliss, who is aided by a mysterious small boy, Bron, who suffers under her spell and her command, and whose powers rival her own.

The Wolf Within

Book 2 in the Silver City trilogy.
Bron, son of the sorcerer king Ansaryon, grows up with the terrible knowledge of the extent of his own power, fuelled by the wolf-god who has taken up residence in his heart and mind. Fearing that his magic will endanger those he loves, he leaves Zithirian in search of some way of controlling the wolf within him. In the decadent city of Toktel'yi, centre of a cruel empire, he meets Mallaso, a former child slave who is a survivor of the empire's brutal invasion of her homeland, Penya. Together, they travel to the enchanted island of Jo'ami, seeking a way of banishing the wolf forever, but the sorcerers there know of a prophecy concerning Bron, and have their own agenda. And with the Silver City now in mortal danger from the Toktel'yan Emperor Ba'alekkt and his huge army, Bron must return to save Zithirian before invasion and brutal conquest destroy everything he once loved.

Blood Imperial

Book 3 of The Silver City Trilogy
Ba'alekkt is dead, and Zithirian is safe. But the Emperor left no direct heir, and his numerous relatives are free to employ any means, fair or foul, in pursuit of the wealth and power of the Onyx Throne. When the deadly dance is done, one sinister and devious man is left to become Emperor, and take Ba'alekkt's sister Djeneb as his bride. But his cruelty turns many against him, and there are other, hidden forces at work. Who is the Flamebearer, who enters dreams and spreads ideas of rebellion? And what part will Mallaso and her small daughter Kyu play, as the Toktel'yan empire stands on the brink of disintegration?

Printed in Great Britain
by Amazon

57876083R00280